Learning to Fly

Learning to Fly

MARY HOSTY

POOLBEG

This novel is entirely a work of fiction. The names, characters and incidents portrayed in it are the work of the author's imagination. Any resemblance to actual persons, living or dead, events or localities is entirely coincidental.

Published 2004
by Poolbeg Press Ltd
123 Grange Hill, Baldoyle
Dublin 13, Ireland
E-mail: poolbeg@poolbeg.com

1 3 5 7 9 10 8 6 4 2

A catalogue record for this book is available from the British Library.

ISBN 1-84223-140-5

Typeset by Magpie Designs in Goudy 10.5/14 pt
Printed by Litografia Roses, Spain

www.poolbeg.com

About the Author

Mary Hosty has published extensively in newspapers and magazines and in the field of education. Her first novel, *The Men in Her Life*, was published in 2003. She has taught English for several years. She lives in Dublin with one husband and two sons.

To Patrick J Hosty
1909 - 2003

Chapter 1

Clouded jade waves crested with white foam broke softly on the Nauset Beach shore. Sophie could just make out a ferry on its way to Nantucket, barely visible in the foggy grey early morning light. The deserted stretch of sand was quiet and peaceful, half shrouded in mist, the warm blustery Atlantic wind swishing through banks of reeds in the background. The surfers and holidaymakers had not yet arrived and the beach ahead was empty except for a solitary hawk hovering purposefully in the air and a lone figure in the distance, bending occasionally to gather shells or other beachcombing treasures.

Sophie walked briskly in a light blue tracksuit, the wind tugging at her long dark-blonde hair, blustering onto her sweet round face, the salt air of the marshes in her nostrils and on her tongue. At last, when she felt she could go no further, she turned for home and ambled back to Brody's Beach bar where she sat alone at a windswept table sipping coffee. It was the very best time of day and sitting here, beside the beach, in the pale morning Cape Cod light, with the lighthouse flickering comfortingly through the mist, she felt a small measure of calmness return to her life.

On the way back, she took a detour past the house that she and Daniel were to have lived in. She sat for a while admiring it regretfully. It was the nicest house in that quiet tree-lined road. Built in the early nineteenth century by a Cape Cod whaling captain as a retirement home, it was irregular in shape, made up of spacious old timbered rooms with shuttered windows. No-one had lived there for years and it needed plenty of work. For months she had looked forward to the day when they could move in and set about the task of restoring it. Now she felt distant from it.

She drove to Fleet Point and parked on the main street, calling in at the dry-cleaner's, Maddox Real Estate and the bank, and lastly at the bakery to buy fresh bread.

Maggie, an elderly neighbour, was there too buying some doughnuts.

"Don't tell on me, Sophie. I'm not supposed to, you know. It's the cholesterol, or the sugar. To be honest I'm not sure which. But I'd rather die of a doughnut than die of boredom."

Sophie smiled and tried to look cheerful.

"You don't look too perky," observed Maggie.

Hard to say the words. She'd been trying to frame them in her own head for days now. But how to let go, take what was left of her courage in her hands, turn around and take her life in an entirely different direction? How to leave it all behind – the man she had loved, a perfect lifestyle, a future home? Fleet Point – a trifle suffocating but so beautiful?

"I'm going home, Maggie. Home to Ireland. Alone."

Maggie glanced sharply at Sophie for a brief moment, paid the shop assistant with a selection of small coins and put the bag of doughnuts in her shopping bag, then turned to Sophie once more. Pale brown eyes scanned briefly and sympathetically across her face. "I'm sorry to hear that. I'll miss you, my dear," she said tactfully, taking Sophie's hand in hers for a moment, as sweet little old ladies do. "But you don't look too pleased about it."

"It's not as easy as I thought it would be. That's all. But it's for the best." Sophie fought the urge to cry as tears welled up in her clear blue eyes.

They walked out onto the street, warm spring sunshine making the little painted clapboard village look like something from a fairytale. Sophie walked Maggie to her car.

"What will you do there?" Maggie asked. "Do you have a job, a place to live? Friends?"

"There's a house in Dublin. My mother left it to me – my brother tells me it's in mint condition, with a ground-floor apartment ready to walk into – so at least I have a nice home to return to . . . then there's my grandmother, you'd love her, and Isobel my dearest closest friend – and lots of other old friends to catch up with."

Maggie smiled fondly at her. "Well, take care. You've

been a very kind neighbour to me and I will miss you very much."

Sophie found herself being hugged tightly in full view of the neighbourhood and she felt yet another wave of tears threaten to engulf her.

"Don't forget to write," said Maggie. "My son and daughter-in-law haven't started censoring my letters yet – but I guess that's just a matter of time. My son Bob thinks I should sit silently in a corner and be wheeled on for family occasions, smelling of lavender talcum powder and peppermint breath, reciting 'The Road Not Taken' by Robert Frost – like some kind of old wind-up doll. Think they're afraid I'm going to take up with some toy-boy and spend all their inheritance."

Sophie couldn't help smiling.

"Which I might just do," continued Maggie. "I liked sex. I miss it and there's plenty of life in me yet."

At home, the atmosphere was thick with animosity and suppressed rage. Daniel was sullen. Rejection made him arrogant towards her. The whole thing would never have happened in the first place if she'd been more understanding and encouraging about his work, he said. She ought to be more sensible. She was twenty-eight not eighteen. Did she not see how much money he was going to lose on the sale of the house? She was being irrational, foolish, selfish in fact.

Sophie steeled herself not to retaliate. In a strange way his hostility was helpful – because it proved that she was doing the right thing in leaving him. And though there were moments when out of sheer panic she might have reconsidered her decision to leave, she knew in her heart that there could be no turning back now. She was going to a place where life was simpler, calmer and easier, where she would try to put a new life together for herself. She was going home for good.

Chapter 2

Isobel Kearney glared at herself in the mirror, there being no-one else around at that precise moment to glare at. She was alone and explosively angry. It was the sort of anger that seemed capable of filling every nerve and vein from the tips of her toes to the lobes of her ears, the sort of anger that washed over her in suffocating waves. It knotted her stomach, hovered menacingly on her *Vogue*-style cheekbones, twisted her full mouth, narrowed her dark hazel eyes, furrowed her brow, flared the nostrils of her slender nose and blotched her smooth, creamy, carefully tended skin. She backed away from the mirror in horror.

"I look like Cruella De Ville with advanced *rigor mortis*!"

Which wasn't strictly true – because Cruella's hair would have been in much better coiffured shape than Isobel's mane of tousled deep chestnut. And at least if

Isobel had *rigor mortis*, it would have stopped her full sensuous lips from somehow imploding into a tight crevice of self-loathing.

It would have been a relief to cry but she was far too angry for that. For the past five years she'd invested all her emotions and energies in Phil Campion. She'd also been quite happy to finance his further education, which seemed to be taking an awfully long time. But it would be worth it when he got a proper job as a journalist here in Dublin, once he'd finished his Media Studies course.

She was deeply in love, and happy to help him. He'd had a hard life. His mother beat his father who was an alcoholic. His father sold the family home and drank the proceedings. Then his mother ran away with the roadie from a little-known punk band called The Black Leather Satanic Sex Muffins and was living in a tin hut in Wales. His sister was in jail for setting fire to her old school. His brother was a cleaning-fluids addict and living rough in a drain in New York. Phil himself suffered nightmares and panic attacks which sometimes prevented him from working, attacks which were brought on as a result of some terrible traumatic event in his childhood that he really couldn't ever bring himself to talk about.

Isobel's heart had melted in a flash when she first laid eyes on Phil Campion.

She was at a party in a friend's house and a thoroughly tanned car salesman from Limerick was doing his best to chat her up. But she wasn't that interested. She excused herself and because it was a balmy summer night she refilled her glass and sat out on the little decked patio at the rear of the house.

She was looking particularly well that night – long-legged and lean, her dark chestnut hair falling in luxurious waves about her slightly angular face and shoulders. She was wearing a halterneck top which showed off smooth, sculpted shoulders (and which didn't do too much to hide her full rounded breasts either), and a floaty chiffon skirt that fell away here and there to reveal the aforementioned long legs. Yes – Isobel was not a classic beauty but she could turn heads.

She didn't even notice him at first. He was sitting in a corner, leaning forward, elbows resting on his knees, clutching a bottle of beer in his hand and idly scuffing the grass beneath.

"Not much of a party," he said glumly at last.

"I just came out to get some air."

"Can I get you a refill?"

There was something exquisitely vulnerable about him, as if he'd never quite shaken off the shackles of boyhood. When he got up and came closer in the moonlight she discovered he was quite attractive – lean with short, black, wavy hair and slightly startled-looking blue eyes.

He went and brought back two bottles of beer and sat beside her on the bench.

"I'm Phil, by the way. Not much of a one for parties, I'm afraid. They seem so trivial somehow."

"How do you mean?"

He sighed and swigged from his bottle and stared into the distance with sizzling gloom. "There's too much suffering in the world – people in so much pain – what gives us the right?"

She'd gone out to the patio to find refuge from the tanned salesman and she'd found a deep and noble man, racked with guilt for the suffering of his fellow man.

"That is so true!" she said, there and then vowing that she would never attend another party again – well, not the frivolous ones anyway. He was absolutely right. It was wrong to take such careless pleasure in the world.

He sighed some more and ran a hand through his black hair.

"You see," he said passionately, "I know a great deal about pain, about suffering."

"Pain and suffering my arse!" Isobel said now as she whisked his photo from the Maplewood sideboard, tore it from its frame and ripped it into a hundred pieces. "I'll give you pain and suffering – you miserable, lying, cheating *shit*!"

Isobel didn't usually swear.

Work at the exclusive Athena Health and Leisure Club, ordinarily a source of stress, frustration and much responsibility, now offered respite from the waves of despair and anger which were threatening to engulf her. I have nothing else, she told herself, but at least I have work. She vowed to fling herself into it with a vengeance. She would work longer hours, commit herself even more deeply, apply for the promotion she'd been half-heartedly considering and wash Phil Campion right out of her hair for good this time.

Fired with a new sense of purpose, she set off to the Athena Club. Breezing through the lobby, she pasted on her most cheerful smile and stopped at reception to chat briefly with Zoë and Claire. When tall and impossibly beautiful Beatrice Heavenly wafted by on a cloud of money and high maintenance, the eyes of all three girls followed her with expressions of admiration and envy.

"But is she happy though?" said Zoe mischieviously.

"Probably!" retorted Isobel darkly before disappearing down the corridor to look over the squash courts.

The last thing she did before she sat at her desk was to check the towel room, as she did every morning. It was a source of particular pride to Isobel that clients in the Athena Club could always be guaranteed a plentiful supply of freshly laundered sumptuous towels. Len Crolly was forever grumbling about the cost but, in Isobel's eyes at least, the club would be just like any other sports centre without her attention to those important and luxurious little details.

A board meeting at ten o'clock meant she had little time to catch up on more mundane matters at the office until later in the day. But she closed the door of her office to tackle the rosters. Isobel was a fast and deadly accurate worker, never more so than when she was angry or out of love. By nine fifty-five, she had checked over the rosters from the team of department managers, signed and authorised several invoices for payment and made three appointments to show prospective corporate clients the facilities.

Then Laura, one of the accountants, appeared with

two mugs of frothy cappuccino.

"Thanks. Don't know what I'd do without you," Isobel said as chirpily as she could, and forced a tight smile. She was desperate to hide the aching gaping festering wound that had once been her heart.

"Don't mention it," Laura answered simply and picked up the small pile of signed invoices. "These ready?"

"All signed," Isobel said absently and returned to sorting the day's emails.

Laura sipped on her coffee, then pursed her lips, frowned and said hesitantly, "What's wrong? You don't look too great."

"Time of the month, that's all!" Isobel said a bit sharply.

"I get the feeling it's more than that," Laura probed gently. "If you need to talk – I'm here. And if it's something private – don't worry, I won't tell a soul."

"I know that," Isobel said, instantly regretting her earlier sharpness. Laura was one of the few people at work she knew she could trust completely. Her voice softened and a horrible lump formed in her throat. "And thanks. It's just a man problem. I'll get over it."

"Of course, you will." Laura smiled reassuringly once more and disappeared back into her own office next door.

Isobel's heart warmed slightly when she saw a brief email from Sophie. Since Sophie had gone to live in the States some years ago, Isobel had missed her terribly. Together they'd sat in the classroom of the little village primary school in Hollymaine, swinging their chubby little legs over the sides of tiny chairs, full of harmless mischief and pranks, then at secondary school in the Convent of Perpetual Caution, and later as young women about town.

Sophie seemed to be hinting that she would be home soon. Good! Very good, thought Isobel! Because she would sympathise with Isobel's tragic heartbreak story, would understand the true depth of Isobel's despair.

But no! Not good at all! Bad! Very Bad! Sophie was living with Daniel Fielding, the most perfectly wonderful man on the planet! Handsome! Ruggedly handsome! Intelligent! Successful! Witty! Charming! Born rich and destined to get even richer! Absolutely and completely nuts about Sophie! Isobel's heart plunged to new and cavernous depths of despair. She dwelled on these thoughts for a few minutes but at last with an effort that would have won an Olympic medal if it had been a sport, she forced thoughts of Phil's treachery out of her mind.

The very last thing she did before going upstairs to attend the board meeting was to place a new file on her desk, inside it an application form for promotion.

Glistening drops of water clung to the smooth tanned body and sun-bleached hair of Hendro Sayers as his tall muscular frame emerged like a Roman gladiator from the Athena swimming-pool. He had just completed two hours in the gym followed by an easy fifty lengths in the pool. Now he sank into the simmering spa bath, immersing himself in steaming hot bubbles, head reclining against the rim.

Eyes half shut, he surveyed the scene before him.

No one grabbed his attention until Beatrice Heavenly glided by, her long, slender legs as usual drawing the attention of every man in the place. Gloriously above and beyond such banal human interactions as smiles or nods or even eye contact, Beatrice whisked up her luxurious towel and disappeared quickly into the changing rooms. Hendro contemplated the celestial beauty of Beatrice for a few moments and then, emptying his mind completely, rested in the hot tub for fifteen minutes. Then he quickly plunged into the ice-cold pool, before showering and dressing.

He slid into his soft-top BMW and drove the two miles to a charming mews he'd recently bought in Raglan Lane. It was a big mews, stretching some two thousand feet over two open-plan floors and he'd spent quite a lot of money having it converted from a family home with nursery to a stylish bachelor pad.

His days fell into a regular routine. In the morning he did twenty minutes of stretches at home before keeping an appointment with the physiotherapist. This week a sciatic nerve was giving him trouble. Then there followed a gruelling two hours on the pitch with the rest of the rugby team as coach Gary Burton put them through their paces, after that a rigorous team run, then hot baths and ice-tubs, followed by rest at midday and power weights in the afternoon. He spent an hour most afternoons catching up on calls and emails to his family and friends back in Melbourne. Then if the weather held or the days were bright, Hendro often went sailing or played a game of golf or tennis with friends in the evenings.

But he quite liked to end his days with the most deliciously athletic and invigorating sport of all – the sport which set all his nerves tingling, which shot through him like a million sweet little electric shocks: spontaneous, uncomplicated sex.

Hendro's life was unconsciously governed by two simple and unshakeable rules, by which he lived contentedly and prospered well:

My body is a temple.

It is my duty to offer the sanctuary of this temple to as many needy women as possible.

There were, of course, several ground rules – discretion being top of the list. A gentleman never boasted of his exploits. A good lover made each woman he touched feel like a goddess. No comparing. No criticising. No demands. No false smarmy compliments. No cruel promises to call. Edible gifts only! If Hendro had been poor he would have made the perfect gigolo.

Chapter 3

Sophie had forgotten one thing amidst the suffocating emotional turmoil of disentangling her life from Daniel's and the complete annihilation of her confidence – staggering as she was beneath the endless paperwork and tiresome phone calls to banks, insurance companies, estate agent's and health-care plans – laden down with the mammoth task of sorting, discarding, packing and shipping her things back home. Standing now in the departure lounge of Logan Airport, clutching her boarding card, a bottle of Youth Dew perfume for her grandmother and a bottle of Southern Comfort for Isobel, Sophie remembered with a rapidly growing knot of anxiety that she didn't like flying – not even slightly.

She found herself breaking out in a cold clammy sweat.

She reached for the Marlboro Lights to calm herself until she remembered that all stateside airports were no-smoking zones now. The sooner she got away from the land of the smoke-free and back to Ireland where she could occasionally indulge her little weakness in peace the better. She edged her way through the throng of passengers and stood in line behind several other trembling addicted wretches at the pharmacy counter to buy a set of nicotine patches and nicotine chewing-gum. With half an hour to go before the flight, the patches and gum having little or no effect on her nervous state, she went to the bar and fortified herself with a very large gin and tonic.

On board at last and only slightly calmed by the gin and the nicotine patches, Sophie observed the other passengers intently. Several hundred people on the plane meant that statistically at least one of them had to be a threat of some kind. She spotted a man looking around him shiftily. Then he leaned down to tie his shoelace and nobody paid any attention. Perhaps she should bring it to the attention of one of the hostesses. Further along the aisle there was an extremely red-haired man who looked like he was about to explode. Red-haired people were notoriously quick-tempered and she felt sure that if a survey were done about air-rage incidents they would find most of them were caused by red-headed people. She tried to bury her head in a novel but found she couldn't concentrate.

They were cruising smoothly now at high altitude and, for a while, fortified with a glass of wine and the airline lunch, Sophie was able to convince herself that she was just sitting at home in the armchair. But still she couldn't concentrate on the book. She tried desperately to force the events of the past couple of months from her mind but it was like some old tape that kept rewinding in her head of its own accord. While the other passengers pushed their seats back and fell into various states and positions of rest, she sat wide awake and tried desperately to remember what kind of person she had been before her personality, her desires, her hopes and dreams had become tangled up with those of another human being. The end of the relationship, however necessary, left her now with a strange and vague emptiness, as though she were almost a non-person. So used to being one half of the couple "Sophie and Daniel", she had completely forgotten how to be just simply Sophie. Also in the back of her mind was a nagging fear that perhaps there wasn't much to Sophie Flanagan anyway. Well – she was about to find out.

When she'd emailed Cian letting him know that she was coming home for good, she was only mildly surprised when he replied that he was off on yet another last and absolutely final back-packing tour of South America. He would be gone for months if not years, and so the apartment on Raglan Road was hers for the foreseeable future. The apartment, he reassured her, was in fine condition. She would be genuinely impressed by its tasteful and elegant decor and surprised but pleased at how well he and his mates had maintained it over the past two years. It was something at least. Sophie was in such a fragile state that about the only thing keeping her going as she winged across the Atlantic, speeding away from the old life and hurtling towards the new, was the knowledge that there was a nice home ready and waiting for her.

Sophie had hardly seen the house since her mother's death. Even during her mother's lifetime she hadn't seen much of it, since they lived in rather less luxurious circumstances in a much smaller house in Rathmines. The house on Raglan Road was what her mother called "my income and capital investment". Her mother, never trained for anything much, had supported the family by buying the house cheap in the early '80s when times were tough, giving it a lick of paint and renting it out room by room. Now the mortgage was paid off, the basement had been rented out to a retired lady, and the top floor to some company or other. But the ground floor, with grand steps leading up to it and its decked balcony overlooking the lush back garden, was always kept vacant for Sophie and Cian.

Sophie paid the taxi-driver now and hoisted her bags up the slightly crumbling stone steps of Number 21. She stood on the threshold for a moment in the afternoon sunshine and took in her surroundings: the road lined with mature trees, their leaves the bright fresh green of early May, and the old houses with their distinctive oatmeal and straw-coloured brickwork, pretty gleaming fanlights and sashed windows, most of them lavishly restored since she had been here last, their gardens now sumptuously landscaped. She tried to ignore the fine selection of weeds breaking through her own gravelled driveway and let herself through the front door into the gloomy cavernous hall. She had never felt more alone in her life. She switched on the light and looked apprehensively around her.

It was a grand old hall all right. Three doors led off it, one to the left into her new apartment home, one to the right which led to the stairs, and one at the end, leading perhaps to a lobby and the garden. But what had Cian said – tasteful and elegant decor? She almost reached for the sunglasses when she saw the bright Day-Glo yellow walls, the beautiful mouldings on the ceiling and above the rail painted by way of contrast in a muddy purple, all complemented by a screaming red cartwheel-patterned Axminister carpet. If it had been in good condition she wouldn't have minded so much but the carpet was lifting and curling up at the edges and frayed in the middle, and not even the garish pattern could disguise several sinister-looking stains and a truly awful smell. What on earth was it? A magnificent arched window to the front of the house ran almost from floor to ceiling and the decorator had excelled himself here. A pair of heavy tangerine curtains with a blue rose pattern hung or rather stood framing the window. They fell in faded pleats, stiffened with years of dust and grime. And what furniture in the grand and elegantly tasteful hall? One table – cheaply veneered mock-Victorian bargain-basement, circa 1987, with legs on the verge of collapse.

Still, it was only a hall and Cian, being a lad, mightn't have paid much attention to the hall. It was most likely the apartment he intended to describe as tasteful and elegant. She put a key in the door-lock and turned it, hoping for the best.

It didn't take long for any lingering flutter of hope to evaporate.

"Oh Cian – how could you!" was as much as she could manage when she looked around her.

In one corner stood a carefully constructed, perilously stacked pyramid of empty beer cans from around the world, in another a simpler more freestyle mound of cans coated in a light frosting of dust. Walls of algae green were decorated here and there with posters of semi-nude actresses and models.

She set the bags down and roamed gingerly through each room, barely noticing the high ceilings, the tall windows, the timbered floors, the grand dimensions, seeing instead several years of single male occupancy – a battered old sofa scarcely visible beneath a pile of newspapers and magazines, a grand marble fireplace blackened and now home to an eclectic collection of beer-mats and discarded old eighties CDs. The kitchen, situated at the base of a short flight of steps to the back of the house, was large and might have had potential but it smelt of years of lingering fry-ups and almost everything was coated in grease. A lovely range was dulled and grimy from lack of use. A big old dresser housed chipped and stained crockery and china, several take-out menus, piles of junk mail, near-empty tins of paint used for touching up parts of the house and a fine selection of antique garden fertilisers and sprays.

The one redeeming feature as far as she could see was that the kitchen opened onto a large expanse of decking, which housed sturdy wooden garden furniture and was quite well lit. Though even out here there was evidence of Cian's glamorous bachelor lifestyle: a stack of empty wine bottles, an array of discarded, mud-encrusted football boots, and some sinister little clumps – which might have been sports socks. She decided not to investigate and swept them all into a large plastic bag she found under the sink.

She'd vowed to give herself a few days to readjust to her new situation before contacting anyone but now she realised her resolution wouldn't hold. She picked up the phone and dialled Isobel's number and her spirits lifted at the sound of the familiar voice.

"When are you coming home?" Isobel asked almost at once.

"I'm here," Sophie said. "Back in Dublin – just for a while . . ." Her voice trailed away.

"That's brilliant," said Isobel after a slight pause and Sophie could hear the surprise in her voice. "I knew you were due a visit – but I just didn't think it would be this soon."

"Yeah, well . . . here I am." She tried to make her voice sound breezy and easy – but failed completely.

"What's wrong? You sound miserable."

"It's just jet-lag. I'm fine. Fancy coming over for a Chinese and a bottle of wine – like old times?" She could almost hear the desperation in her own voice and hated it. When Isobel didn't answer instantly she started to backtrack quickly. "Oh, but you and Phil have probably got plans for the evening – I wasn't thinking. Typical me – rolling into town and expecting you to drop everything. I'm here for a few weeks anyway – plenty of time to catch up." She fought back a sudden childish urge to cry.

"Wong's or The Jade Dragon?" said Isobel briskly.

Back in the kitchen, Sophie rummaged in a cupboard, found a near-empty box of tea bags, made tea without milk, kicked off her shoes, and sat outside on the deck smoking a cigarette – her first since leaving Fleet Point now that Ireland seemed to be turning into a no-smoking zone as well. She felt horribly displaced, misplaced, lost, and suddenly deeply, dreadfully alone. But there was no point in sitting around feeling sorry for herself. She was here and she'd have to make the most of it.

She drank back the last of the black tea as she surveyed the garden. Steps led down to a raggedy patio from the deck. The grass was overgrown but along the borders were pretty though unpruned shrubs, and towards the end of the garden some very grand trees. At least it showed some potential and if she could get hold of a good gardener, it wouldn't be too difficult to smarten it up. She saw that someone was using the bottom of her garden for storing a sailing dinghy – presumably the person who had just bought the mews, which was half hidden by an old brick wall and the trees at the end of the garden. Cian had told her about the sale but, typically, had made no mention of the dinghy. She hoped the mews-dwellers wouldn't be too put out when she asked for it to be moved.

While she waited for Isobel, she set about cleaning the bedroom. She took down the yellowed net curtains and put them to boil in some bleach she found under the sink. She unhooked the faded green curtains and dumped them in the bin. Then she washed down the woodwork with warm soapy water and mopped the floor. Even though she was jet-lagged and exhausted, Sophie knew that it was best to keep herself occupied. So she kept going, clearing out the big old wardrobe and a mahogany chest of drawers and lining them with the scented tissue paper she'd used to pack some of her more delicate items of clothes. She made up the bed with cotton sheets she'd brought from Fleet Point, and a new pillow and Foxford blanket she'd found still in their wrapping in the wardrobe. An attached note read: *"Thought these might come in handy. Cian. PS The mattress is new as well."* It was typical of him to leave the place in a mess and to know she'd get through it all and forgive him if she only had a clean and comfortable bed to sleep in.

At last she stood back and surveyed her work. The net curtains had come out quite well and had dried quickly in the light May breeze. The window was open and the room filled with fresh air and the scent of clean laundry, bleach and polish. She had just started unpacking her things and storing them in the newly cleared wardrobe when Isobel arrived.

Chapter 4

The passengers queuing for the ErinAir flight EA 193 from London Stansted waited patiently in the departure lounge. Boarding passes in hand, they shuffled forward slowly as stewardesses checked them through. They were a mixed bag of travellers, a sleepy bunch of city lads returning from a tour of Old Trafford, decked out in red and black club jerseys and scarves, an extended family group of grandparents, parents and squealing infants travelling to a wedding anniversary party in Dingle, and scattered here and there individuals on little voyages of their own.

From the back of the queue, Paul Brehony surveyed these various groups, towering over the group of lads immediately in front of him, an expression of keen interest on his face. He was not broodingly, smoulderingly handsome but yet he stood out from the crowd with tousled dark hair, deep-set eyes and a nose that had been rearranged by accident during a hurling match some years ago.

As a child, growing up in the Dublin suburb of Glennstown, Paul remembered money being so tight that when his uncle in Kilburn died, the family had been forced to borrow the cost of one return flight from the Credit Union, just so that his father could attend the funeral. There was no question of the entire family travelling. As for happy occasions like weddings, anniversaries and birthdays – a card was sent along with a well-wrapped box of Kimberley biscuits or, if they were "flush", a small piece of Belleek china. Every second year for their holidays, the Brehony family took the boat to Holyhead and the train to Llandudno, where they would spend a week all cramped into a tiny, leaky caravan.

As a child, Paul felt himself very isolated from the rest of the world and longed for day trips to Anfield or even Glasgow to see Celtic play at home. But his dad would pat him affectionately on the head and say "Dream on, son. Ireland is an island nation – and you have to learn to live with it – just like the rest of us."

From her position at the check-in desk, the air hostess was able to pick Paul out quite easily.

"Good evening, Mr Brehony." She smiled brightly at him, watchful in case anything might be amiss which would earn his disapproval.

"Evening," he said with a fleeting smile. He waved a boarding pass briefly before her and made his way to the relative calm of the executive lounge.

He was returning home from a lengthy and very draining meeting in London to discuss the latest financial figures. Things had been rather shaky in the airline business lately and in the past few weeks a number of gloomy rumours about Paul's company had appeared in the newspapers: hints of hostile takeovers, jittery shareholders and unhappy directors. Most of the stories were nonsense, of course.

He folded his lean frame into the deep leather seat, retrieved his laptop from its slim leather briefcase and read through a list of emails. He responded to the more urgent ones, then down at the very bottom he spied a note from Henry Gilhooley.

"Gilhooley, you pest," Paul said under his breath, chuckling briefly with childish delight.

Paul,

I hope you will forgive this highly presumptuous intrusion upon your valuable time. Consequently I will be brief. As you know, we are shortly reaching the close of the academic year here in Glennstown Secondary School, and with it the sad – but essentially heartening – passing out of our sixth-year boys, as they step hesitantly onto the treacherous, yet ultimately exhilarating, treadmill of life. You have been, are still indeed, a magnificent source of inspiration to the boys, dare I say, a beacon of hope to those whom life has cast into the turbulent waters of misfortune.

It therefore behoves me, as principal, to cordially invite you, Paul, as one of our most esteemed past pupils to address our humble graduation ceremony on the last day of the month. I realise, of course, that the exigencies of time management are not easily calibrated for a man in your position. However, if you could find a short window of opportunity, your presence here would provide the icing on the rich tapestry of the evening.

Sincere Regards
Your old friend
Henry Gilhooley

Paul reread the letter and chuckled again. He keyed in a hasty reply. *Henry – will check my diary and get back to you. Regards, Paul.*

Paul had been up since five thirty. He was tired now and he leaned his head back, stretched out his legs and closed his eyes.

His mind drifted back inevitably to his days as a teacher in Glennstown Secondary School. He hadn't strayed far in his brief teaching career, attending the school first as a student, then almost straight there from college as a teacher of English and Business Studies. Looking back on it now, more than twelve years later, it really did seem like someone else's life in some strange and foreign country . . .

"While I'm here, I might throw a party and invite the neighbours, what do you think?" Sophie said to Isobel, idly watching the wisps of tobacco smoke curling up into the cool night air.

They were sitting out on the deck, the rickety plastic table littered with takeaway boxes, and it felt like they'd never been away from one another. They'd simply taken up where they left off a few years earlier and they sat back now, full and relaxed in each other's company, more than happy to speculate about the neighbours. Anything was better than talking about their love lives.

Besides Sophie itched to know about her new neighbours anyway. Daniel used to scold her about it, telling her how provincial it was to show excessive interest in one's neighbours.

"But I am provincial," she always replied. "And people are always fascinating. It's not a sin to be interested in people, is it?"

Now she dismissed the thought of Daniel with a shake of the head.

"Sounds like a good plan. Who else lives in the house?" asked Isobel. "Do you know any of them?"

"Downstairs is Clementine Barragry, a slightly dotty retired costume designer, according to Cian. Some company rents the place upstairs. Next door is owned by a couple who spend most of their time abroad. And the mews has just been bought by someone with a dinghy – as you can see. That's all I can tell you for now."

She showed Sophie Cian's email. In spite of the awful state of the flat, he'd done his best to help her settle back in. He'd even given her the name of Nick Lynch, a friend who landscaped gardens for a living and who, to quote Cian exactly, was "*dead sound . . . an all-round good sort . . . has great contacts . . . I'd trust him with my life. . . I'll leave his card at the flat just in case you need help sorting the garden out . . .*"

She had shoved the card in the back of a drawer, amused at her brother's high recommendation.

"The last time I checked, Cian's interpretation of 'dead sound' was someone who could get after hours into the best bars in town," said Isobel, pouring another glass of wine.

"My thought exactly."

They chatted away about Cian for a while and then Isobel steeled herself to ask belatedly, "How's Daniel?"

"Great. Terribly busy as usual." Which was, strictly speaking, the truth. "How's Phil?"

"Brilliant. We've never been happier." Isobel looked at her watch. "Oh, look at the time – must go, early start." She drained her wineglass and stood up. "Glad you're home, Sophie – even if it's only for a few weeks."

Sophie wasn't a natural born liar. She wasn't even sure why she lied but she felt shabby about being less than honest with Isobel. When they hugged goodnight on the steps, she almost blurted out the truth – but didn't.

She showered beneath a tepid drizzle of water, brushed her teeth, and didn't bother to floss, climbed into the large old bed, which was surprisingly comfortable despite being a little bit too high off the ground, slid down between the cool sheets and drifted off into a deep, exhausted sleep.

The plane had reached cruising altitude. Paul undid his safety belt, put his seat back into the sleep position and let his mind drift back to the past again . . .

"It might look like a simple poem about a fish – but it's also about the spirit of human endurance . . ."

Paul read from the poem, his deep, rich voice resonating around the grim stuffy classroom. Some of the students were deeply transfixed, others deeply bored, still others deeply asleep.

"Is it on the course?" asked Colin Deeley, who had enough brains to run the Space Programme single-handed.

"No," replied Paul in even tones. "It's not. But it's a fine poem and there's no law that says we have to limit our study to what's on the course."

"Why would we study something which isn't on the course?" enquired the brainiest boy on the planet.

Paul suppressed a sigh of mild irritation. He was tired, hung-over, and his confidence had taken a denting. Or rather Martina Clancy had given it a bit of a dent – well, more of a head-on, full-impact collision really – that had left his confidence crashed, bashed, crumpled, folded, buckled, bolloxed and fit only for the scrapyard.

He smiled patiently at Colin Deeley.

"Anything which broadens the mind or forces us to think beyond the narrow confines of our own lives is valuable in educational terms."

"Sir?" said Colin, the prospect of victory clearly visible of his smooth young face. "If you follow that argument to its logical conclusion, then smoking cannabis forces us to think beyond the narrow confines of our own lives – and –"

Paul had walked right into it. He didn't ordinarily make that kind of stupid mistake.

"Colin, I think you know that's not what I meant. Now if we can continue –"

"Sir! Technically, I could sue you for this. I mean, supposing I don't do well in my Leaving Certificate exams, supposing I don't do as well as I'd hoped in English for instance, theoretically I could sue you for failing to apply class time effectively to the requirements of the course."

Paul opened his mouth to say something. It would probably have contained several swearwords and have got him barred from ever teaching anywhere again. It was coming and he couldn't control it. The words filled his mouth. How could he stop himself from calling Colin Deeley a cocky little –

But just at that moment, from a large unmoving and unwieldy mass of matter slumped over a desk at the back of the class, came the clearly audible and classically constructed sentence:

"Shut the fuck up, Deeley. You're only a wanker."

"Yeah, Deeley!" came a chorus of belated support.

"Carry on, sir," said Michael Plunkett, stirring briefly from his slumped position. "And read us the rest of that grand poem."

Afterwards, deeply grateful as he was to Michael Plunkett for saving the day, Paul wondered fleetingly if Colin Deeley could sue him. Though right at that precise moment, he wasn't all that bothered. What he really wanted to do was to slink away and lick his post-Martina-Clancy wounds in the peace and quiet of his own comfort zone – the bar of the Mardi Gras pub, five minutes from his own front door.

But he couldn't because the principal of Glennstown Secondary School had summoned him to the office. Paul wondered what it would be this time – probably a form not filled in, a report not filed or a lengthy teaching plan not submitted. Arriving at Henry Gilhooley's door now, he knocked and braced himself.

Across a wide expanse of carpeted floor, sitting at his desk and munching heartily on a multi-layered club sandwich, sat portly Henry. The walls of his office were bedecked with framed quotations of the great writers, little *bon mots* to inspire the students, photographs of Henry with famous people. He wore a very large pin-stripe suit and a Hawaiian patterned shirt beneath.

"Paul! Come in! Sit yourself down. Pull up a chair. I'm just watching a little bird out there on the lawn – such exquisite poetry in the creatures of the air, don't you think?"

Paul sat uneasily, cautiously waiting, the palms of his hands a little sweaty, the hairs on the back of his neck prickling. You never knew where Henry Gilhooley's poetic thoughts would bring him but it would most probably lead to yet another veiled criticism of Paul's abject failings as a teacher. He would thrash around making vague threats about teachers who'd ended up with unfortunate timetables, round it all off with a few more quotations, metaphors, similes – and one of his awful little jokes. Paul, a straight-talking, clear-thinking practical bloke, found that five minutes in the company of Henry Gilhooley was the stress equivalent of a whole day of classes with 3F.

But, this lunch-time, Henry was unusually brief and Paul was fleetingly grateful for small mercies.

Henry chose to talk on the theme of animals. There were, of course, some very meaningful references to the dogs of war which were quickly followed by the cat with nine lives that somehow in mid-sentence transformed into a wise old owl. Then Henry slid quickly from the owl to the badger, from the badger to the otter and at last from the otter to the fish. Then he stopped abruptly, took a large bite of his club sandwich and munched diligently as he fixed his twinkling green eyes on Paul, who was momentarily at a loss. His normally uncluttered brain struggled manfully to find something which might in any way apply to him.

Henry chewed deliberately and repeated himself. "The fish, Paul! The fish!"

Then Paul remembered. Colin Deeley!

"We must be vigilant against any situations which might be open to litigation. Deeley is a bright young man. What if he did sue us? Could you stand up in a court of law and defend a fish that wasn't on the course? I couldn't. What if he sued us for loss of earnings in future years? Loss of career opportunities? It's all about duty of care, Paul. That fish wasn't on the course and Deeley is quite within his legal and constitutional rights not to have to grapple with the fish – if you catch me?"

He chuckled at his little joke, and then packed the last of the sandwich into his mouth. Paul shifted uneasily in his chair as Henry chewed and swallowed before resuming.

"The boy's mother was on. She wants my complete assurance that this type of thing won't happen again."

"No, Henry, I can guarantee you it won't happen again," Paul said steadily after a brief pause.

"That's the spirit. Marvellous! A splendid outcome!" Henry beamed.

He had located a neatly cling-wrapped slice of rich chocolate cake from the roomy lunch box which his wife packed for him each morning, and his podgy hands were now busy peeling the filmy paper away from the moist, dark pleasure within.

Paul stood up.

"It won't happen again because I quit. I became a teacher because I valued education. I thought I could make a difference. But turns out it's not about young people learning at all but about you and me filling in forms and covering our asses. That's not teaching, so I resign, Henry."

He was surprised at how calm he sounded.

Half a fistful of moist dark chocolate pleasure crumbled in Henry's hand and scattered messily onto his fine royal-blue carpet.

"Damnation! But my dear fellow – there's no need to take such extreme action –"

"Believe me. It's better this way."

He fought back all the things he'd promised himself that he would one day tell Henry Gilhooley. Now he realised it would be completely pointless. A waste of energy! It would be pissing against the wind – or in this case pissing against the windbag.

Chapter 5

Sophie led the builder through the flat and watched his face fall further and further as he progressed through the rooms. The kitchen and bathroom were the worst, with leaky plumbing, and fittings which had come loose. The toilet bowl was cracked. Ugly brass pipes clung to the mildewed walls, ready to fall away at any moment. Cian had done a patch-up job refastening one of the pipes to the wall with duct tape. The bathroom window had been smashed in and someone had painstakingly stuck all the pieces of glass together onto a large sheet of sticky contact paper and tacked it crudely onto the window frame. In the kitchen, big lumps of plaster had come away from the walls and ceiling and the cheap canary-wood fitted cupboards had been crudely attached to batons which in turn had been hammered mercilessly into the walls.

"It's going to be a big job," the builder said at last when he'd got over the initial shock. "No sense in lying to you and no sense in cutting corners, which is what the previous occupant clearly did."

Sophie's heart sank. Somehow she'd imagined simply getting the decorators in over the weekend and having the whole place in pristine condition in a matter of days. If Cian wasn't on the other side of the world in the other hemisphere, she would happily have wrung his neck.

"Oh dear," she said looking at him pleadingly.

"But you can still do the structural work – wiring, plastering, windows and all that. I know some good salvage places. We can even get that old range back to its former glory. I'd love to get my hands on this place. It really would be a labour of love. And I'd keep the costs down – I promise."

His name was Joe and he had a pleasant, honest-enough-looking face but all the same she eyed him doubtfully.

"Maybe I should just wait. I don't really know if I can afford to do anything to the place right now."

Now was his cue to say "Fair enough, love" and scarper quicker than you could say monkey-wrench. But he didn't.

"Are things that bad?"

She heaved a sigh. Only that morning a curt email had arrived from Daniel, informing her that, on his solicitor's advice, she would not be entitled to anything on the sale of the house in Fleet Point – not even her ten-thousand dollar deposit, since technically everything was in Daniel's name.

"You know what? Right now – I'd rather a nice little

two-up two-down somewhere than this headache."

"No – we can't have that. I'm not having that!" Joe smiled warmly at her. "This is a grand place. We'll do it up and we'll do it right. It will be a challenge."

Sophie was slowly getting used to the idea of life without Daniel and readjusting to her new, if less than fabulous, home and now she longed to see her grandmother Tess. She quite relished the prospect of a train journey, had fond memories of cosy, carefree journeys on the rickety old Hollymaine train, hours of restful time with nothing to do but read and watch the scenery roll by. But when she dialled the talking timetable she was annoyed to discover that trains didn't run to Hollymaine any more.

For a brief moment she considered renting a car and driving the tortuous four-hour journey to the west. But it had been a long time since she'd driven on Irish roads and she was quite anxious about it. So on the spur of the moment, she took her courage in her hands and booked a return flight to Knock. If she could manage to cross the Atlantic without cracking up, surely the flight from Dublin to Knock would only be a hop, skip and a jump – a piece of cake in fact. She would simply close her eyes and pretend she was sitting at home in her favourite armchair.

Sophie was up early the following morning. She washed as best she could under the ribbon of tepid water which drizzled from the plastic shower-hose, then dressed in a pair of jeans, a crisp white cotton shirt and flat pumps. She pulled her dark blonde hair into an untidy pony-tail, and slung a canvas rucksack over her shoulder. Then she set off for the airport.

When she was young, getting to Hollymaine had involved a long journey in the afore-mentioned rickety train and then a hair-raising drive along some very twisty back roads. Invariably squabbling broke out on the back seat as Sophie and Cian fought over anything that came into their heads and frequent stops as one or the other of them succumbed to car sickness. But she loved going to her grandmother's. It was a house without rules, at least none that she could detect. The more her mother tried to enforce city-style rules and so-called civilised behaviour, the more Tess undermined them. Now, even at the ripe old age of twenty-eight, the prospect of going to Hollymaine still filled Sophie with a childlike sense of excitement and anticipation, a feeling that the cares and pressures of life would somehow fall away and she would return to that lost carefree state of innocence.

She arrived at the airport early. It was a big mistake. She sat near the boarding gate, trying to remain calm, but an ominous knot of terror threatened to erupt in her tummy. Waiting for the short internal flight to be called, she tried to read the newspaper but couldn't concentrate. Not even a global nuclear crisis would have held her attention. She tried to concentrate on observing preparations for the flight. A pretty blonde hostess was checking through her passenger list. A pilot with an attaché case made his way briskly through the small cluster of people. Then a tall flight steward arrived, exchanged some words with the blonde hostess who smiled warmly at him and then followed the pilot onto the plane. The steward checked his watch and then took his place at the check-in desk. His mobile rang a couple of times and he spoke into it briefly and quickly. Sophie was becoming quite caught up in the non-drama of it all – the unremarkable minutiae of other people's working lives. Then she made her fatal mistake.

The blonde hostess had re-entered the picture very briefly. From what Sophie could see, the sole purpose of the blonde's return was to smile even more warmly at the steward, who didn't seem that interested. She became bored with the hostess and her steward and it was at that point that she made the mistake of looking out the window, and exposing her already tattered nerves to the full horror of what lay ahead. At first she could see nothing but when she looked down – way way down – beneath the window, a flimsy twenty-seater plane which looked like one of Cian's little Airfix planes of old, with wings that might well blow off, trembled on the tarmac like an abandoned puppy. She instantly regretted not taking the Valium. But there might still be time for a stiff gin and tonic. No sense in inflicting her own terror on the rest of the passengers. Terror had a nasty habit of spreading. It might even affect the pilot and that could lead to catastrophic results. There was no sign of the steward calling the flight so she darted quickly to the bar and ordered a gin and tonic.

"No! Wait! Make that a double," she said, casting another look in the direction of the flimsy little plane, shuddering helplessly in the blustering wind and waiting valiantly on the tarmac. She was sure one of the wings looked lopsided and briefly considered pointing out the matter to the steward. She rummaged in her purse for the correct change, then realising that her hands were shaking far too much to handle coins, handed over a note.

"Keep the change."

"Thank you, miss."

She raised the glass to her mouth with a trembling hand. The barman probably thought she was an alcoholic. Sophie didn't care. In the matter of flying, she was totally irrational, shamelessly weak and utterly without principles of any kind. If sleeping with the pilot could guarantee save arrival to her destination, she would do it gratefully.

"Dutch courage?" said a low voice from beside her at the bar.

She turned and came face to face with the steward.

He smiled encouragingly. "It's only a short flight and quite safe –"

"I'm perfectly all right!" she said, cutting him short, then instantly regretted her bad manners. "Sorry – I don't mean to be rude, but I'm not a good flyer and it makes me forget all the normal rules of polite social engagement."

"There's really no need for you to feel –"

"Cheers!" She cut him short, raised the glass defiantly and tossed the clear sharp liquid back. It naturally went straight to her head.

"Look, no offence," she went on, "but if the company you work for insists on stuffing its customers into little sewing machines like that thing out there on the runway then it has to concept the acciquences."

She detected the merest tic at the corner of his mouth. She didn't care. She'd far rather be slightly tipsy and make a fool of herself in front of a stranger than be forced to sit soberly through even five minutes in a treacherous death-trap like the one on the runway.

"Flying is statistically the safest means of –"

"Lies! Damn lies! And statistics!" she retorted, and then tried to soften the barbed tone in her voice with a wry smile. "Besides! If God had meant us to fly – then why did he invent gin and tonic?" She smiled at him again, slightly crookedly.

He looked confused. She wasn't surprised. It was one of the games she and Isobel used to play at school. It was mostly to annoy a certain very earnest teacher in the Convent of Perpetual Caution who insisted on girls training their minds to logical thought and away from the superficial fripperies of the modern age. The fun was in starting out with a wise old saying and finishing it off with something completely silly. Like: *If money is the root of all evil – then why was La Perla underwear invented?* Or: *If music be the food of love – why is it oysters that make you horny?* Or in moments of bleak rejection: *If pots and pans were ifs and ands – then where would we boil our ex's bunnies?*

"Excuse me, I have to go and call the flight."

She felt vaguely unsteady, her head slightly clouded now.

"It will be fine," he added. "Trust me."

She wanted to retrieve some dignity from the

situation, make some wonderfully witty and sharp reply, but found that the combined effects of pre-flight panic and a double gin had done nothing to sharpen her wits. She made her way in a haze which was not quite strong enough to dull her panic, down the terminus stairs, across the tarmac and up tiny steps into the little plane. She seated herself near the aisle, pulled out the emergency procedures leaflet, felt herself turn green and promptly stuffed it back into its place. It was horrendous how the other passengers seemed to have no sense of the terrible dangers ahead. Maybe they were all on Prozac.

A man next to her casually opened up his briefcase and began making notes for what looked like a board meeting. A lady in the seat across the aisle was busily applying make-up. Two old dears at the front were comparing photos of their grandchildren. The hostess took them through the safety procedures about oxygen masks and life-jackets and how to blow your whistle in the water to catch the attention of any passing trawlers.

Sophie felt like screaming at her: "Do you think we're complete fools!"

"It's such a wonderful service," said the man with the notes. "Saves hours in traffic."

Well, it would. When you're dead – there are no traffic jams.

"Do you often fly this route?" he asked.

"No. First time."

And last! And, oh God! Worse and worse! She could actually see the pilot! The array of dials! The front bloody window! How could she close her eyes now and convince herself that she was simply sitting at home in an armchair? She felt the blood drain from her face.

The plane taxied along the runway and took off bravely into the skies. Sophie clenched her fists, closed her eyes and said long-forgotten prayers.

Some ten minutes into the flight, she felt a light tap on her shoulder.

"All right?"

It was the steward.

"Fine thanks!" she said through gritted teeth.

He disappeared, probably to play a game of charades with the pilot, or how about blind man's buff? It was just the sort of mad cavalier thing that these people would get up to. Her mind brimmed with such ghastly scenarios.

But at last, to her great surprise, they landed. Safely! On the runway! Completely intact! The dodgy-looking wing hadn't even fallen off.

She was even more surprised to find the steward beside her as she made her way through the little airport terminal to pick up a hired car.

"It wasn't so bad now, was it?"

She nodded, a sense of rationality and common sense restored to her now.

"I enjoyed it actually," she said, managing a cool smile, noticing only now a head of glistening dark hair and a pair of deep brown eyes, that smiled warmly but gave nothing away.

"Have a pleasant stay in the west," he said and ambled off into the crowd.

Chapter 6

It took her some time to get used to the gear-stick. To begin with she chugged along, shifting jerkily from first to second, from second to third, revving hell out of the engine as she tried to hit forty in third, then finally remembering she ought to be in fourth gear. At last she found her coordination and soon she was motoring along the windy roads at a sensible forty.

The tractors drove her to distraction. Farmers pulled out regally in front of her, and chugged along at minus ten miles an hour. She was determined to be patient and philosophical about it to begin with, but when she encountered the fourth tractor, her patience began to wear thin. Each time, she was forced to follow the farmer for a mile or so until he swung in a grand and slow and majestically executed arc into a narrow gateway. At last she realised that there was nothing for it but to chug along slowly and enjoy the view.

She'd forgotten how beautiful it was. On either side of

her were rolling fields and lichened stone walls, with herds of sheep and cattle grazing contentedly. Every so often she came to a vast tract of bogland, dotted here and there with splashes of magenta and delicate pink bee-orchids, banks of black bog rush, purple moor grass and delicate quaking grass. The names of wild flowers that Tess had taught her in childhood came back to her as she drove along. Puffs of creamy white yarrow swayed in a gentle evening breeze. And everywhere she looked was colour – dove-white blotches of cotton grass, lush green hedges, soft clouds of yellow broom and purple heather, banks of moist black cutaway bog, smoky violet-grey mountains in the distance.

At last the road twisted beneath an old granite railway bridge and emerged on the far side to rise over a slight incline. Then it curved around to the right and there, on the brow of a low hill facing westwards, against a back-drop of green valley and meandering river and distant purple mountains, was the little village of Hollymaine.

Sophie's heart filled up with pleasure at the mere sight of it. Memories of happy innocent times flooded her mind.

It was the same but different.

A single broad main street flanked by two rows of neat well-maintained houses, some painted a restrained white with black windows and doors, others in bright blues and greens, her favourites a little terrace of two-storey cot-tages near the old Methodist kirk which were painted in an old-fashioned rose-wash, and brimming with hanging baskets and window boxes. The two lines of elegant lime trees were in full leaf, grown tall and sturdy now – Sophie had a vague memory of them being planted when she was a very young child. All the old shops were still there – Brehony's Grocery and Confectioner painted as always in startling orange and mauve, Garrivan's Select Bar and Lounge in sporting red and green, Miss Violet Barr's Magical Bookstore – a ladylike peach colour with soft lilac on the doors and window frames. But Sophie also noticed new shops – a video store, an internet café, an Italian restaurant called Leonardo's, an art gallery.

At the end of the street Sophie noticed the biggest change. Once there had stood a very old and rickety garage, built in the ruins of a mill, with round-faced, red-painted petrol pumps from the Ice Age. The garage had also incorporated a used-furniture store, a small garden centre, a hairdresser's, a beauty salon and a place for dipping sheep. Now it had been completely demolished and replaced by a shiningly brilliant, brightly painted, blue and yellow plastic and steel Scandinavian forecourt miniplaza with sleek new pumps, selling everything from spicy potato wedges to champagne. She felt oddly nostalgic for the old place.

She drove through the main street, guiltily racing past Kenny and Maeve Grennan's house, and out into the countryside once more, a short distance of a mile or so, before turning into the narrow country lane which led to Tess's house.

"I'm sorry, Sophie – truly I am. I wish you'd told me. I would have gone out there and given that Daniel a piece of my mind."

"I didn't want to worry you. And besides it's just a broken heart – nothing terminal." Sophie smiled bravely but telling her grandmother the whole tale of her break-up with Daniel was bringing it all into sharp focus – how confused and useless and abandoned she felt suddenly.

"Well, he's a fool to throw away a treasure like you. If I was him I would have been on the first plane back to Dublin after you."

Sophie's eyes brimmed with tears, touched by the fierceness of her grandmother's protective love, and she fought back the memories of what had almost been the perfect happy-ever-after story . . .

Sophie twirled the near-empty wineglass between her fingers as Lloyd Brewster observed her across the heavily laden table with hungry, mid-life-crisis admiration, in between long bursts of his travel and hunting memoirs.

"Hunting fish on horseback in the Amazon Basin was a high point in my life," he said with a smooth New England drawl.

She tried to fix her eyes on him. Forcing herself to be interested, she rested her chin on a finger and said enthusiastically: "It sounds amazing. Tell me all about it."

Lloyd took up his grisly tale eagerly.

"We were down in Rio for the carnival and then Johnny my brother got this notion that we should go to The Basin for some serious hunting . . ."

Daniel had been hijacked by Faye Brewster in the kitchen, and from snatches of conversation which wafted down the hall, it was clear that Faye was having a right good flirt with Daniel. Lloyd was Daniel's boss and Faye, his wife, was one of the leading social lights in Fleet Point.

Daniel and Sophie would soon be setting up home – in prosperous, pretty white-painted-clapboard, rickety-veranda, rolling-green-lawn, happy-ever-after couple-dom. It was certainly a dream about to come true for Sophie and not something she could have hoped for on her relatively modest bank salary. But she'd met Daniel, who'd fallen in love with her. Though he was the first to admit that she "had nice blue eyes, but wasn't exactly Cameron Diaz," he had grown to love her "homely charm" that reminded him of his "old Irish motherland". He was a smooth-skinned and youthful thirty-eight, on the brink of being made a partner in Brewster Architectural Solutions and Sophie knew only too well the importance of making a good impression that night, which was why she was now on her best, most elegant, most dignified, butter-wouldn't-melt-in-her-mouth behaviour.

The effort was killing her.

She'd dressed in a demure lilac shift dress, which was supposed to complement her deep blue eyes. It had a simple round collar and sleeves to the elbow. She'd spent ages trying to sweep her hair back into a classy chignon roll as Daniel had suggested. But despite applying industrial-strength hair lacquer and a clatter of clips, as always it tumbled down about her face, making her look as if she'd been caught in a particularly bad hurricane. It wouldn't have mattered so much if she had one of those magnificently high-cheek boned faces that could be framed by even the wildest of hairstyles. But Daniel was right. Sophie was more homely than heavenly.

Now he stuck his handsome, close-cropped head through the door, gave her the conspiratorial look which said that he was flirting manfully but very reluctantly for his country in the kitchen with Faye. She smiled fleetingly back at him then rolled her eyes discreetly heavenwards. Her patience was rapidly running out. A sudden craving for a cigarette had assumed monster-like proportions, making her stomach knot uncomfortably.

"Won't be long, you guys!" called Faye. "We're just working on the coffee."

Working on Daniel more like, thought Sophie. Faye Brewster got her kicks from flirting with other women's men, and most particularly if they were younger. She was full of seductive, knowing Mrs-Robinson-type looks and carried herself with an air of sexual superiority, as if to say she was, at fifty-two, by far the sexiest woman on the planet – if not in the entire universe.

The night was balmy with a warm breeze. The contradictory longings for a lungful of vile tobacco smoke and some sharp, fresh seaside air became unbearable.

"I'm terribly sorry. Would you excuse me?" she said at last, interrupting Lloyd.

She smiled sweetly at him and slid her hand into the chic black jet-beaded purse that rested on the table at her elbow. Then she swiftly produced a sealed and addressed envelope.

"I've just remembered. I forgot to post this birthday card to my little brother Cian."

Faye appeared at the kitchen door, dragging herself away from a pinned and wriggling Daniel.

"Lloyd will be only too happy to mail it for you in the morning," she trilled.

"No!" Sophie said a little too quickly. "Thanks. But I need to be sure he gets the card on time. You know how they are. Still a baby really!" She smiled fondly as she thought of him.

"Why don't I come with you?" offered Lloyd, an eager glint in his eyes.

"Thanks – but I'll be fine. Back in five minutes," she said.

Before he could protest, she whisked up her bag and swiftly disappeared out the front door.

She skipped quickly down the long and winding garden path and past the tall hornbeam hedge which obscured the house from view. Lurking behind the hedge, she fumbled in her purse, pulling out cigarette and lighter, then lit up and inhaled deeply. The sensation made her dizzy, the taste horrible in her mouth. Though she sometimes carried an emergency pack, she hadn't smoked in ages, had given up completely when she'd lived in Boston. There she'd had great friends and some wonderful cousins and an easy, uncomplicated social life that meant she'd never felt the urge to smoke at all. But here in Fleet Point it represented her private rebellion against the forces of relentless brightness and cholesterol-free cheerfulness – otherwise known as Faye Brewster.

She was pleased that the carefully stage-managed birthday-card ruse had worked well and it wasn't entirely a lie. She always did make a point of remembering Cian's birthday and technically, yes, he was her "little brother". However, he was twenty-four years old and would probably spend the evening of his birthday trawling around the bars and clubs of Dublin with his wide circle of mates, in search of craic and women. He wouldn't even notice if his older sister hadn't remembered his birthday.

Reaching the end of the cigarette she was faced with the usual dilemma – where to put the extinguished butt. Once, without thinking, she had stubbed it out on the ground in Queenstown, where it was possible to get every form of kinky sex known to man and beast, several forms of illegal drugs and a wide selection of firearms – quite readily. On that occasion, she'd been practically lynched on the spot by an angry baying mob of sadomasochistic, cocaine-snorting, pistol-toting, sheep-fancying, wife-swapping devil-worshippers. At least for all she knew, they might have been!

She dropped the extinguished butt in a trash can and hurried back to the Brewsters where Lloyd was still making great sport of dangling the partnership carrot under Daniel's nose. But he was a man well used to dangling and by the end of the evening, Daniel was no closer to knowing his fate.

Sophie must have yawned about twenty times as they drove the short distance home to their rented house, in Daniel's sleek, carefully restored 1957 turquoise-blue Chevrolet Bel Air. She glanced sideways at him and took a deep breath, knowing that he wouldn't approve of what she was about to say.

"It's none of my business I know," she tried to edge towards it gently, "and, of course, it's only my opinion, but I wish you didn't work for that man any more."

There, she'd said it and now she'd have to face the consequences.

A tense fuming silence hung in the enclosed space of the car as he negotiated a bend in the road with measured care, wearing an expression of weary patience. The sensible thing to do now was simply to apologise and squeeze his hand and the nasty little squall that threatened to erupt would most likely have blown over by the time they reached home.

"And I'm not sure you should go into partnership with him," she found herself continuing. "Why don't you take up that offer of a job in Boston? Bound to bring loads of exciting opportunities. We could sell the house here and buy a nice loft overlooking Boston Harbour. All our real friends live in Boston. Apart from the Brewsters, we hardly know anyone in Fleet Point."

What demon was driving her on?

He braked softly and turned left into the narrow lane that led to the house. Then he swung through the gateway and parked the car in a perfect straight line on the gravelled driveway. He gave a world-weary sigh before removed the keys from the ignition.

God, she'd been mad to say anything. She really ought to be grateful. Now he was bound to be angry. Her whole body tensed with anxiety.

"We'd only lose money on the house if we sold it now," he said deliberately. "I stand to lose more money than you – bigger investment, remember?" He spoke as if measuring the pauses between his words.

He was referring to the fact that whereas Sophie was paying a small percentage into the mortgage, he would be carrying the larger financial burden. Though she had pushed hard to buy a smaller place which they could pay off fifty-fifty as equal partners, he wouldn't hear of it. They would own everything equally anyway he'd said and besides he'd grown up in a big house on the outskirts of Dublin and he could never get used to living in a place that was cramped and pokey.

"I only mean that you are talented and I'm sure lots of other companies would be eager to employ you," she said, backtracking quickly.

"You've always had that unfortunate tendency to overreact to situations and that's why I'm not going to let this develop into some silly argument," he said, idly running a finger over the sleek black and chrome dashboard.

He got out of the car and walked purposefully across the gravel to let himself through the front door. He tossed the car keys into a ceramic bowl on the hall table. Then he ambled into the lounge and poured two brandies. Sophie flopped down on the expansive leather sofa and kicked off her shoes. She slung her feet up onto the sofa but Daniel shot her a disapproving look and she rearranged herself more demurely. He was particularly proud of the sofa and regarded it, along with his other highly prized period pieces, as a sacred object – to be adored and worshipped. His mobile buzzed with a message which he glanced at briefly before handing her the brandy.

"Just a reminder about a meeting tomorrow – damn nuisance!" he explained. "Think I'll go to bed."

"Daniel, we need to talk this out. It's important." She struggled to sound reasonable and matter-of-fact and failed miserably.

Dear God! Had Faye Brewster put something in her coffee? It was as if she'd suddenly lost complete control of her tongue. And what was she thinking of, questioning Daniel, who was handsome, charming, wealthy and the envy of all her friends, especially Isobel who was deeply in love with the completely unworthy Phil Campion? Even Granny O'Meara could find nothing wrong with Daniel. Even her mother would have been quite pleased with Daniel.

Sophie had been just into her second year of studying Commerce when her mother Rose was diagnosed with incurable cancer. Rose, quickly abandoned by Sophie's human-rights activist father, for a blonder, prettier human-rights activette, had long ago ditched her liberal outlook along with her poncho and desert boots and joined the vanguard of the seriously conservative, the ranks of the pathologically unadventurous.

"Don't go looking for adventure, Sophie darling. Look where it got me. Adventure and all forms of excitement are very dangerous. Get a Commerce degree, and a job that pays good money so that you can travel the world in a totally undangerous sort of way. And don't think too much about life. It isn't healthy. Keep well away from anyone who claims to be an 'ist' of any kind. Marry a hard-working, steady, high-earning family man. Engineers are always a reliable sort."

Anxious not to add to her mother's last months of agony, Sophie had promised to forswear adventure and embrace the warm security of a good job in the bank. She achieved it all remarkably quickly. At twenty-four, she was earning tidy sums of money with generous Christmas bonuses, had a fine apartment in the Dublin Docklands and a dull but high-earning civil-engineer boyfriend. She had fulfilled most of her mother's dreams. At twenty-five came a respectable promotion to Boston and a hasty farewell to the dull boyfriend. At twenty-six without even trying, she found Daniel, Dublin-born, talented, handsome, rich, ten years her senior.

Now she barely recognised the person she had become. Worse still, she wasn't sure she even liked the new Sophie Flanagan. She longed for home and straight-talking Isobel and Granny O'Meara and a sofa she could put her feet up on without feeling like a social misfit.

She looked across at him now, the cold smile frozen on his face.

"I"m sorry," she said. "I spoke out of turn. And you're right, of course."

He ignored her apology. "I've had enough of this." He drained his glass. "You don't know how lucky you are." He disappeared briefly into the kitchen with his empty glass, and returning continued, "Just answer me one question. Which would you really prefer? The wonderful new home I've bought for us and a life here in Fleet Point or some crummy little house in Boston on a third of the income? Next you'll be announcing you want to go back to Ireland. Is that what this is all about?"

He smiled coldly at her.

She didn't dare reply, didn't dare reveal that she longed to escape from The Land of the Smoke-Free and The Home of the Brave as fast as her less than shapely legs would carry her – with Daniel, of course. She couldn't do it without him.

"Because I'm never going back to Ireland," he continued, a cold smile hovering on his lips. "Never! Dublin is no place for an architect with vision."

Now, sitting in the comfort zone of Tess O'Meara's kitchen she realised that there had been a deeper chasm at the heart of their relationship than just his grubby treatment of her. He loved leather sofas, Bauhaus, Frank Lloyd Wright, 1950s Chevvies, post-modern perpendicular, glass and filtered light, steel colonnades, brick and reinforced concrete. What he didn't love was Sophie.

"You're certainly breaking the family trend. I was married at twenty-one – you were born when your mother was only twenty."

"Yes," said Sophie hugging her grandmother warmly. "Which is why I have the youngest, most beautiful, most glamorous granny in the country. But don't hold your breath for me to get married. I think I'll give men a wide berth for a while."

Tess had made apple-sponge for her granddaughter's

homecoming. The bright homely kitchen was warm with the smell of it. There had earlier been a procession of home-baked bread, home-baked ham, salads from the garden and even some highly prized wild salmon courtesy of Robert Franklin, who lived alone in Firthland House a few miles from the village. It was a massive, dilapidated pile that he'd inherited from his German father and Irish mother.

Simply baked in the oven with a dash of lemon, some butter and herbs from the garden, the salmon was finer than the most expensive and exquisitely prepared food in Manhattan. Sophie could feel her jeans tightening, wondered should she slip into the bedroom and put on her navy track suit, the one with the nicely expanding waistline, the only other item of clothing that she'd brought with her for the overnight trip.

"Your grandfather did that on me one time," Tess said quietly as they stacked plates in the dishwasher.

"He did?"

Sophie was shocked. Tess had always given the impression that her late husband had been a paragon of virtue and devotion. In family photos Thomas O'Meara smiled at the camera with brash confidence, his arm always affectionately around his wife's slender waist. Tess took down one such photo now and ran her fingers over it.

"Look at him. As if butter wouldn't melt in his mouth! The dirty old ram!" She looked at him fondly.

"That's an awful thing to say."

"What? Well, he was. No sense in denying it. But he was powerfully sexual. Ecstasy in bed! God, I sometimes still get the collywobbles when I think of him."

Sophie blushed.

"Now why are you blushing? I was trying out the Kama Sutra with your grandfather before your mother was even born. Anyway, that's not the point. The point is no matter what the forces of decency, righteousness and respectability say, it is not always necessary or even wise to leave a man simply because he has taken short leave of absence from the marital bed."

"It wasn't just because he was unfaithful. The whole thing wasn't right. Anyway it's different. You were married to the same man for over forty years. He may have been overcome with hormones once or twice – but all in all he loved you and he made sure you were well provided for ... well respected. And you were the steady rock – always faithful to him."

Tess smiled fondly at her granddaughter. "Do you want to know the secret of my long and deeply happy marriage to your grandfather? What kept the spark, the romance alive – until the very last moment?"

Yes! Yes, she did want to know. All around her, friends were darting from one stab at everlasting love to the next, reaching for it, never grasping it, and then lunging onwards into the next relationship, convinced that it too would be the perfect one. Perhaps she'd done the same with Daniel, allowed herself to be swept along on an initial tide of lust and rose-tinted optimism, only to scurry away at the first sign of a challenge. How had Tess stayed so happy through forty years of marriage – remained so vibrant, stayed so beautiful, sustained such optimism, held herself so connected to everything that was going on in the world?

"Well, tell me, Gran – of course I want to know!"

"I had a lover!"

Sophie gaped at her grandmother. "I'm sorry, Gran . . . ? I don't understand."

"Well, my dear – you can't be that naïve."

"You mean you . . ."

"Had a lover? Yes, I did. Of course, I did." She said it like a person might say they liked to play a bit of golf or go horse-racing. Then she was silent.

But that was adultery. And adultery just didn't happen in perfect places like Hollymaine. Adultery was for the seedy rich of London or Manhattan. No – Gran was just joking. She'd always had a wicked sense of humour – loved winding people up, delighted in shocking them.

But as the silence lengthened Sophie turned pale. Tess wasn't joking. She felt suddenly uncertain about qualities she'd always admired and loved in her grandmother – her steadfastness, her loyalty, her wisdom, her pure unselfish love for her family.

"Oh, now don't look so shocked. It doesn't suit you. He was a lover in the sense that he loved me, truly and with deep passion. And I loved him back – throughout my married life – while continuing to absolutely adore your grandfather, of course. But we didn't sneak off to Bundoran in his black Ford Anglia for dirty weekends, with a Foxford rug, a flask of tea, ham and mustard sandwiches, and currant cake – if that's what you're thinking. Though we did have one or two very pleasant picnics in

Leenane. I remember one time I baked some particularly nice onion tartlets – from a recipe I'd found in the parish newsletter of all places. The newsletter had recommended using margarine – and any pastry chef worth their salt knows that the only true pastry for tartlets and quiches must be made with pure butter . . . so I substituted butter for the margarine . . . I also caramelised the onions and ..."

Sophie struggled to remain expressionless. Her grandmother, whom she adored, admired, aspired to be like, was an adulteress! A wicked lady! Maybe she was just making it up? In the early stages of senile dementia?

"Did you . . . I mean . . . did he, this man, whoever he was . . ."

She couldn't keep the shock from her voice. Tess laid her hand lightly on Sophie's.

"Haven't you learned yet, child? Didn't I tell you years ago – not to ask a question if you think you mightn't like the answer?"

"So that's a yes! You did! I can't believe it of you!"

Tess said nothing for a moment but when she spoke there was a surprising and pointed coolness in her voice.

"What gives you the right to ask me such a personal question anyway? Because I'm your grandmother – is that it? Because being my offspring you think that gives you some sort of divine right to know every last detail about my private life? How would you feel if I lobbed the same question at you?"

The afternoon was going horribly wrong. She loved Tess more than anyone else in the world, had come home to be near her, and now though they hadn't seen one another for over a year, they were arguing – on the point of fighting. Sophie looked up into Tess's clear blue eyes – beautiful, brilliant and sparkling still, her skin smooth and clear, fine lines barely noticeable. She saw the beginnings of a tear starting to form, saw years of happy memories and also lost love, saw also affection for herself and somewhere too – the merest glint of a challenge.

"I didn't mean to pry – but you did raise the subject," she said lamely.

"That's true. Perhaps some day I'll tell you the story."

"Will you even tell me his name?" asked Sophie, trying to make amends now.

"Edmond."

"It's a nice name."

"He was a nice man," Tess said, then set about clearing dishes.

Sophie went for a walk along by the winding river and when she returned to the rambling old whitewashed cottage, she deftly steered the conversation into bland uncontroversial waters – news of relatives, the new pottery shop in the restored old Methodist kirk, the young parish priest from Brazil, Cian and when he might actually grow up and settle down, a new roof and other repairs to Tess's house. They did not mention Tess's adultery again and neither did they mention Sophie's father. He was rarely if ever mentioned.

A pleasant quietness had settled over them but suddenly Tess stood up, straightened her pale pink silk blouse, pulled a comb and lipstick from a drawer, rapidly ran the comb through her golden-blonde hair and skillfully applied a nice dusky shade of lipstick without the aid of a mirror.

"What is it?" asked Sophie, bemused.

"*Shhhh*! They're coming. I'll pretend to read the paper."

"Who?" Sophie looked out the front window. "There's no-one there, Gran. You're imagining things."

But Tess was no longer listening. She'd grabbed the daily paper and was reading the international news section intently. Sophie knew from seeing Isobel's grandfather that this was how Alzheimer's began. Everything would be going along as normal then the person would suddenly do something totally and utterly irrational. Perhaps it would be best to humour her.

"Who's coming, Gran?"

Tess didn't answer and seemed to be engrossed in the paper.

Moments later Sophie was quite surprised to hear a car sweep in through the gates and come to a halt on the gravel driveway.

"See! What did I tell you?"

Sophie peeked through the window and saw her mother's cousin, Kenny Grennan, holding the door of a smart blue Range Rover open for his wife Maeve who was dressed in a light cotton T-shirt and studded hip-skimming jeans. She stepped down as gracefully as if she was on her way to the Horse Show Ball in a sequinned Versace gown and diamante-encrusted mules.

Sophie turned to her grandmother. "But I didn't hear a thing. How did you know?"

Not senile at all! Not even close. And then again why would she be? For Christ's sake, if she lived in the States, she'd be still dating, going to nightclubs and travelling the world.

"I can hear that tank of theirs a mile off. I know the sound of it. And Kenny never was a great driver. He always does that funny choking thing with the gear-stick when he takes the hill over by O'Malleys."

There were hugs all round and then Maeve rummaged in her green straw basket brought back from a holiday in the West Indies and produced a freshly made brown cake. She placed it in the centre of the table.

"We thought you'd like to have something nice for the tea."

"That's very kind of you, Maeve," said Tess.

Kenny scraped a chair noisily across the beautifully polished flagstones, clasped his hands around Tess's, and smiled warmly at her. "Well, how are you?" he asked in a loud and hearty tone.

"Fine, thank you, Kenny – and nothing close to deaf yet."

"You look grand. Doesn't she look grand, Maeve? I bet you led the lads a merry dance when you were young. Now don't tell me otherwise, Tess O'Meara. And you still have a twinkle in your eye – fair play to you!" He patted her hand affectionately and examined the newspaper beside her. "Good woman – you're reading the paper. No flies on you!" He whisked the paper up, turning to the international-news page. "Well, that's a terrible state of affairs out there in the Middle East. Can't make head nor tail of it myself. Who's this the president of Israel is at all?" He pursed his thin lips pensively.

Sophie hardly knew the answer to Kenny's question herself. No, actually she didn't know it. Affairs in the Middle East had always been a hopeless muddle to her. Her only excuse was that the majority of people of the Middle East probably hadn't a clue who the Irish President was either.

"Tea anyone?" said Tess graciously, completely ignoring Kenny's question.

"Thank the Lord for that," Tess said when they'd gone.

"They mean well. You know they do!"

"You really think so? Day in, day out, they come patronising me, talking to me as if I'm daft, offering to help me do things which I'm perfectly capable of doing myself, insinuating all the time that I'm getting vague and forgetful. And by the way the president of Israel is Ariel Sharon."

"Tess, why didn't you say?"

"Because I like winding him up – that's why. He thinks I'm fooled by his relentless good humour and simpering concern, but I'm not. Robert says that Kenny's only after one thing."

"What?" asked Sophie, a little surprised that Robert Franklin was on so intimate a footing with her grandmother that he could make such a comment.

"This farm. This land. Because it's on the edge of the

village it's worth a lot now. I've been approached by three developers, all wanting to buy. But it's my home – where all my happiest memories are. Why would I leave all that behind? And besides . . ." She stopped, her clear blue eyes suddenly awash with tears.

"Besides what?"

"Nothing! They're wearing me down, Sophie. I don't think I can cope any more." A clean lace-trimmed hankie emerged suddenly from a pocket and Tess was dabbing at tears which coursed down her cheeks. "I'm sorry to burden you with this. It shouldn't be your worry."

"Of course, it's my worry. You're my grandmother and I love you dearly. But why don't you take a holiday? Go somewhere you've always wanted to go. Surely you have the money?"

There was the briefest of pauses before Tess said quickly, "The thing is, who could I go with?"

"There must be lots of people. What about Bridie? Or Phil? What about all your friends in the golf club? What about that cousin in Limerick you get on so well with?"

"I don't know . . . it's like I've suddenly lost the courage to do new things."

Not even thirty, Sophie could barely envisage a situation where she wouldn't have the courage to do new things. Her greatest problem at the moment was selecting which of all the new things she really wanted to do. In some ways she felt swamped by all the freedom, the knowledge that she could travel anywhere, see who she wanted, wear what she wanted, be who she wanted. Negotiating the limitless choices of the modern world required great skill and judgement – and now that she thought of it – quite a lot of courage.

"Oh nonsense! That's just nonsense, Gran. You're the most courageous woman I know."

Tess laughed – a short laugh, tinged with regret. "Well, at my age, living alone, you don't get much practice at trying anything much new. You get out of the habit of it somehow. I don't know how I'd cope if I didn't have Robert to turn to . . ." She stood up abruptly and went to fill a saucer of milk for Jacqueline the cat.

Sophie felt a definite sense of unease at this second mention of Robert. Was Tess perhaps becoming too fond of him? Though that could be natural enough: thirty-eight years old, he was probably a substitute for the son she'd never had.

Tess placed the saucer of milk outside the back door and then filled another dish with scraps of ham and potatoes and the leftovers of the salmon and shouted out across the orchard to the rear of the house. "Steve ... Stevie?"

A large dog – half Labrador, half something else altogether, golden in colour – bounded insanely down the orchard path and flung himself at her feet, then looked up at her with utter adoration. She patted his flat head and rubbed him gently behind the ears and he muzzled against her affectionately. Then she set the bowl of food down in front of him and he ate happily.

Tess insisted on driving Sophie into the village and dragging her around the various shops to show off her grandchild home from America. They had a light lunch in Garrivan's Select Bar and Lounge, popped into Brehony's for a chat about Katie Brehony's up-and-coming wedding, then ducked quickly past Kenny and Maeve's and drove home, relaxed and happy.

Sophie's flight wasn't until late that evening – so she had ample time to sit at the table and help her grandmother sort through her papers, a task Tess had been putting off for quite some time.

Sophie could see that plenty of things needed to be thrown out: old receipts and letters, correspondence with the bank going back years, phone and electricity bills which had long since been paid, newspaper cuttings, old racing and golf cards, all stored in a selection of Jacobs biscuit boxes in a large oak dresser in the dining-room.

"You really do need to throw a lot of this stuff out, Gran."

"But what? Every time I go to throw something out – I suddenly think of a reason why I should keep it."

"All these old bills and receipts could go for starters."

"But that's my proof of payment!" Tess held the bills firmly in her hand.

Sophie straightened up and faced her grandmother squarely across the table. She was well aware that a little power struggle was quietly raging. Her grandmother was a fiercely independent woman, not inclined to be told what to do by anyone. At the same time, she knew that Tess's best chance of maintaining her independence was to prove herself to be well and truly in control of her own destiny. So Sophie found herself in a slightly contradictory role. She would have to bully her grandmother a bit so that no-one else would try to bully her.

"They have to go. Hand them over." She was surprised at how bossy she sounded all of a sudden.

Their eyes locked for a few moments across the table, and then Tess relented. Sophie tore the bills in little pieces and tossed them into a large black refuse sack – for burning later. They worked for almost an hour, sorting through papers and stopping to have occasional wrangles. By the end of an hour and half a dozen biscuit boxes, Sophie was pleased to note that the black bag was half full. It was a clear sign of progress. There was only one more box to go and Tess slid it across the table quite pointedly.

Inside there was one large brown envelope marked in thick black letters: *Elizabeth O'Meara – Last Will and Testament*. Tess pointedly took it in her hand.

If it wasn't for the rather timely arrival of Robert Franklin, Sophie might have found herself in a most awkward situation.

Chapter 7

In the normal course of events, Isobel Kearney did not take much notice of the spectacular assortment of handsome men who passed with alarming frequency through the doors of the Athena Health and Fitness Club. To begin with, she was far too busy. And besides, for the past three years Isobel had eyes only for Phil Campion, the champion of suffering people the world over, the Patron Saint of Self-pity, founder of the International Federation of Lying Cheating Slimeballs. Now that he was removed from her life, Isobel doubted if she could ever again look at a man without feeling a serious psychotic incident coming on – *ever*. The days were passing. She was still doing her job, still getting up, still going to bed, still eating and breathing. But life would never be the same. Phil had seen to that.

Of course, he hadn't been in touch and he wouldn't be in touch until some deeply pressing need overcame him, like the loan of a hundred euro for "essential reading material for the course". God, how much money had she donated over the years to the "essential reading" fund? Money for weekend-away courses in video production, money for entertaining some of the millions of prospective clients he was going to have just as soon as he qualified. Phil was going to be the Corporate Video King of Dublin. He had loads of contacts, knew the marketing and PR people in most of the big multinational companies in Dublin. Was a close personal friend of the managing director of Outsell Software Manufacturing! Knew important people in Hollywood! In his dreams anyway!

Isobel forced herself to run through these salient facts about Phil every morning as she showered before leaving for work. Just as her grandmother would recite a bit of the Litany to the Virgin Mary as a form of mantra for settling her troubled mind, Isobel had a litany of her own. It was an essential part of her recovery plan – to remind herself every day, in every way, how awful he was, how dreadful his treachery. Otherwise, Isobel knew only too well what would happen – a brief but measured tango with common sense and realism would be chucked aside quickly in favour of a giddy, abandoned samba back into the arms of the utterly unworthy Phil.

Now she bustled about at work in a state of pathological efficiency. She met with the people who had been hired to redesign the over-flowing carpark, where once or twice in recent months fist-fights had threatened to erupt because of lack of parking space. Before she took a short morning break, she sat in on a maintenance meeting with the rackets manager and the pool manager. The tennis-court roofs needed ongoing maintenance to anticipate and prevent leaks. Levels of chlorine in the pool had to be carefully monitored. So although it didn't sound like a very important meeting, Isobel knew it was essential to get both matters sorted if she was to avoid having to shut down the courts or close off the pool. Both courses of action would be very damaging for the image of the club and inconvenient for members. Isobel was utterly ruthless in ensuring that the members of the Athena Club were well looked after. Under her management, things ran smoothly and members exercised and relaxed and tended to their bodies in an atmosphere of tranquillity and quiet efficiency. People came to work on time and took pride in their work – whether it was Jim who stacked the towels in the laundry room or Francesca the masseuse, or Antonio the cook. The courts were always open and in top order. The pool and steam-rooms were scrupulously clean. She'd even ensured that the shower-rooms were updated to include individual hair-dryers, lounge areas, and a TV and play area for children in the family changing-room. She'd overseen the design and decoration of a luxuriously quiet room with a coffee machine and soothing music for ladies who liked an atmosphere of serene calmness.

After the maintenance meeting, she showed a group of German diplomats around and was pleased when they signed up on a corporate membership. The embassies were especially lucrative customers and it was a measure of how impressive the club facilities were.

Her complete lack of awareness of the vast array of beautiful men in her workplace was, her friend Amy the occupational psychologist explained, the equivalent of being a child working in a sweet shop – handling all those sweets day after day, watching the nice ones disappear quickly off the shelves, seeing exciting new ones coming in, suppressing the occasional temptation to sneak one on the quiet when no-one was looking, observing the deep sensual pleasure the sweets brought to the lives of others. And so, Amy explained, Isobel had become "*desensitised*" to men and was failing to respond to them in a psychologically healthy, mentally dynamic sort of a way.

"You mean I don't drool when I see pop stars on the weight-machines and sports heroes diving into the pool?"

"Yes. It's not healthy."

"But I love Phil," Isobel used to say.

If she hadn't noticed before, she noticed these wondrous creations even less now in her new state of post-relationship depression. This morning in the gym the rows of magnificence on the treadmills had included Blood, the dark-haired, satanically good-looking lead singer from Californian heavy metal band The Savage Foxes, dashing Harry Dever the international tennis player with the floppy blond hair, the boyishly scrumptious Ireland out-half, endlessly pursued (and happily engaged) Conor O'Grady, and Hendro Sayers the tall sandy-haired Australian rugby player with smouldering green eyes. Isobel passed by all these top-drawer specimens of manhood with sublime and absolute indifference, did not stop to notice their broad muscular shoulders, did not linger for even one second on their bullet-hard, sweat-glistening thighs, remained utterly unconscious of their languid animal grace as they jogged manfully on the spot to an even higher plane of fitness and aerobic nirvana.

Besides she had other things on her mind. Colman Brady, the General Manager, had announced his intention of taking up a position as director of a new Ultra Exclusive Health Club in Kent. His job would become vacant in a matter of weeks and if anyone was qualified and experienced enough for the post it was Isobel. She'd been in the Athena for six years now, working her way up from junior secretary to Assistant General Manager. She knew every aspect of running the place, was on good friendly terms with most of the staff and many of the clientele. Often if a client had a problem, it was Isobel they approached – not Colman, who though very efficient and professional, was frequently unavailable and occasionally unapproachable.

Still she knew that if she wanted to succeed Colman, she would have to prepare her application well. Although she would be quite a popular choice with the clients and staff there were one or two people on the board whose toes she'd trod on over the years and they might try to block her appointment. But in her new post-relationship traumatic-stress-disorder phase, Isobel was not in the mood to be blocked by anyone.

Colman had invited her to lunch, to discuss her application for the post. They sat now in The Bayfield, a charming little old pub situated along the banks of the canal. It was slightly off the beaten track and they could talk in peace there. She knew that Colman would have a major say in who was appointed in his place and knew that he had much information and advice to impart to her.

They sat in a little panelled wooden alcove, huddled over plates of pasta and wild mushrooms, while Colman outlined the requirements of the job as he saw them.

"There will be big challenges for whoever takes over," he said. "The five acres of adjacent scrubland have to be developed into a new kind of sports amenity. And the planners are insisting that there be landscaped gardens as well. So it's going to be very exciting and I only wish I could stay to oversee it."

Isobel's face fell. "I wish you didn't have to go and besides I don't know the first thing about design or landscaping or gardening or plants."

"Then you'd better find out fast – that is, if you seriously want the job."

She braced herself. She could do it. She would do it. But perhaps Colman didn't think she was up to the task. She held her breath as he took a long swallow of his pint of Guinness.

Then he looked at her and said, "As far as I'm concerned, you've definitely got what it takes, Isobel."

She eyed him doubtfully. Perhaps he was only saying it to be nice.

"I really mean it," he said.

"Thanks. But I don't know about that."

"Don't knock yourself. There are plenty of other people who will be only too delighted to do that for you anyway. I'm surprised you're not more confident."

Isobel smiled weakly. She felt far from confident. Her confidence, in fact, lay in shredded, mangled, chewed-up tatters on the floor of her horribly empty life. If it wasn't for work, she didn't know how she'd cope. For three years she'd made Phil the centre of her life, to the exclusion of her family, who disliked him, of her friends who loathed, detested and despised him. Now she was all alone, isolated by her own stupidity – and it was nothing less than she deserved. The ending of a close relationship would be enough in itself to bring on a bout of depression and a sense of failure. But it was all the other stuff she'd found out about Phil that left her feeling stupid, foolish, idiotic, blind, ugly, fat, unwanted, unloved, unlovable. A big lump began to form in her throat, hot, stinging tears brimmed up helplessly in her eyes.

Then a hankie appeared and she began to sob uncontrollably and dab at her eyes.

"Have a good cry. No-one will see us here."

She sobbed and sobbed, shuddered and trembled, heaved and sighed, clenched her fists and wrung her hands. It was just as well it was only Colman. Just as well no-one could see her.

"Want to talk about it?"

She shook her wobbling head.

"Sure?"

This time her head wobbled so violently that she couldn't even get it to shake. It felt like she had some terrible neurological disease, wobbling and trembling from head to toe.

When at last the shuddering subsided, he smiled reassuringly at her. "Don't worry. I'm used to it. The wife will cry at the drop of a hat."

"Thanks."

She knew her face was a balloon of swollen, blotched, puffiness, that the layers of make-up she had applied so liberally this morning were now streaking down her face in strands of tan powder and navy-blue mascara, making her look like a tattered bistro awning.

"I must look a fright," she said but Colman shook his head and told her she looked grand.

As a matter of fact though, she did look a complete fright.

Hendro at least thought so, as he passed by the little booth and lingered just long enough to establish that it was the rather attractive girl with the mane of chestnut hair from the leisure centre who was awash with tears and clearly in a state of great distress. It was a great pity, he felt, to see her fine face crumpled into such a frightful grimace, sad to see an attractive young woman involved with a middle-aged man. And perhaps it might be timely to offer her the warm sanctuary of his generous arms.

Chapter 8

Paul Brehony's rise from failed teacher to managing director of a tidy little empire was one of the success stories of the decade, a tale frequently retold in the papers, a turn-of-the-century rags-to-riches fable which made him at times the darling hero of the nation, at others a ruthless villain who would cheerfully sell his own mother if the situation demanded it. The fact that his mother had passed away some years ago didn't alter that view. Stories of generous gifts to needy friends and acquaintances were set against the certain fact that he'd betrayed and swindled Dermot Stenson, his best friend who now lived virtually penniless in South America. Even Paul's looks encouraged media speculation. He was lean, tall and dark-haired, with deep almost black eyes, a nose that had been broken once during a hurling football match and never quite set properly, a smile which came less frequently and more guardedly than before, a rugged face – grown inscrutable and remote with the experience of success – a far cry from the fresh-faced teacher who'd struggled to impart his love of literature and his admiration of sound business practices to his students.

The day he'd walked out of Henry Gilhooley's office, having flung his resignation on the principal's desk, Paul was a man of few assets. He had not the slightest idea where he would go or even how he might make a living. A few mornings sprawled over the *Situations Vacant* page added to his despair. He could work at book-keeping and accounts – but the small number of meagre positions available paid even less than teaching. By the early nineties, the *Situations Vacant* page had shrunk to a column. Many of his contemporaries had drifted away to find work abroad. Others took jobs completely unsuited to their qualifications. Pat McNeill had a PhD in Economics and was selling educational text books. It was a very common story. Those who were very lucky found stable, permanent and pensionable jobs and clung there gratefully, displaying the sort of smug relief usually only seen on the faces of people who have managed to avoid terrible disasters – tidal waves, tornados, dodgy share investments, mullets, line-dancing.

What had he done? Throwing away his teaching career in a fit of temper? He was twenty-three. His only asset was a twelve-year-old yellow Renault 4, which had moss growing on the rubber window surrounds and which had the funny gear-stick up on the dashboard that stuck and jammed at the most awkward times.

But despite his dad's pleading to withdraw his resignation, Paul knew that he could never set foot in a classroom again. He'd had one burning ambition since a little boy, a silly craze really, like wanting to drive a tank or steer a ship – he wanted to learn how to fly, to take the controls of a little plane and steer it upwards into the skies. And when his grandmother left her four grandchildren a thousand pounds each to spend as they wanted, Paul knew exactly what he would do with his share. At least it would help keep his spirits up until he got the right job.

His Renault 4 to riches story began towards the end of the flying course when he invited his old schoolfriend Dermot Stenson to fly with him. It was to be his last flight. Still struggling to find a job that would challenge him, he had sublimated his energies into flying, quickly developing a reputation on the little airfield as a top-class pilot. That small sense of achievement kept him from sinking into depression and boosted his confidence.

Dermot, his best friend, had famously walked out of school at the age of fourteen, declaring to his teachers that he was far too stupid for school and promptly gone off to the States to make a tidy little fortune for himself in the bar trade. Back home in Ireland, Dermot applied his streetwise skill and hard nose to buying up old dilapidated bars and repackaging them for a younger more affluent clientele. Now in his late twenties, and earning several times more than all his old teachers put together, Dermot laughed quite good-naturedly about his friend's sudden departure from school. He'd offered to help Paul out, recognised in his friend the very qualities which went to make a successful businessman, and even offered him accountancy work, looking after the books for the several bars and restaurants in his possession. Paul was grateful but had no great interest in number-crunching. To show his gratitude, in the only way that he could afford, he took Dermot flying.

They soared up into the sky, wheeling out over the vastly spreading suburbs, flying over Paul's home, then banked and curved out over Dermot's brand new mansion in Rathmichael before turning for home. Back at base Dermot was full of excitement, booking himself in for lessons, and enquiring about buying a little plane for his own personal use.

"Come to think of it," he grinned boyishly as they tucked into two very welcome pints, "I think I'll buy an airline."

"Yes – and I'll buy up Dublin Airport."

"I'm serious."

Paul laughed. Dermot had always been full of hare-brained schemes, many of which never saw the light of day. "What do you know about airlines? And maybe you didn't notice, but there haven't been all that many airlines listed in the *For Sale* sections of the newspapers. They're not exactly all that thick on the ground."

"How much do you think it would cost? It's bound to be a growth area. We're a fucking island nation. The one thing we're always going to need is ways to get in and out of the place."

"My father used to say the opposite: that we're an

island nation but we have to learn to live with the fact and stay put!"

Dermot was undeterred. He'd made a nice few million taking mad business risks and impetuous leaps in the dark. "I've a million or two in the bank." He said it as if it was a couple of cans of beer he had in the fridge. "Put that with whatever the bank would cough up – bingo! We could call it DermotAir. Bound to be a winner."

Paul tried to enter in the spirit of the conversation. But lately he'd found himself sinking far too easily into a state of depressed torpor. His sense of failure was heightened by Dermot's success, Dermot whose teacher had told him rather unnecessarily that he was stuck permanently with a reading age of eight, whose grasp of English literature stopped resolutely at the nursery rhymes he read with jolly abandon to his small children. Yet Paul, whose bookshelves groaned with the weight of classical and modern literature, whose grasp and mastery of the English language was second to none, whose teachers said he would go far in whatever walk of life he chose, was penniless and jobless.

He hadn't the energy to think through this latest hare-brained scheme with Dermot. Life was slipping away from him. The way things were going, he'd end up sitting on a bar stool in the Mardi Gras becoming the thing he most despised – the self-pitying, hard-done-by alcoholic, who might have made it good if only some other bunch of bastards hadn't ruined it for him.

A few days later, he was called to an interview in Letterkenny, County Donegal. The position sounded mildly interesting – manager of a small office-supplies company. Donegal was a long way away but at least it would be a start. And perhaps the change would do him good.

He dressed in his best suit, quickly decided that the Renault 4 wasn't at all up to the long journey and got a bus into town to the main station where he waited two hours for the bus to Letterkenny. The journey was horrendous. Born and reared in Dublin, Paul had no idea that travelling around the country could be such a dreadful ordeal. And, of course, no trains ran to Donegal.

So he sat into the stuffy, steamed-up bus, hoping that he would just fall asleep and wake up in Letterkenny. But sleep didn't come. First there was a continuous traffic-jam. Then the bus had to navigate roads that twisted and wound like deranged snakes through the picturesque, hilly countryside.

Queasy and numbed from the seven-hour safari across the interior of his native land, he was not at his best when he arrived to be interviewed by Cal McLoughlin, the owner of the little company.

"Have ye any experience in a business environment?"

"Not as such. But I do have accountancy in my degree. I've taught business studies for three years."

He'd tried to freshen up in the cramped toilets, splashing cold water on his face, washing his hands with the dribble of soap he coaxed from the dispenser. But his head throbbed and his stomach rumbled and the receptionist hadn't offered him as much as a glass of water to recover from the journey.

"He who can does – he who can't teaches," Cal said, smiling glassily at him. "This is the real world we're talking about here – not some little school mini-company. I employed an ex-teacher before and he was hopeless. What makes you any different?"

"I'm sharp. I'm keen to learn. I'm a good team player. I've good business sense."

Paul felt vaguely like a prostitute.

"That's all very well, but I supply to the whole country with envelopes and staples and paper-clips. I need someone I can put my trust in."

"Check out my references. You'll find I'm trustworthy."

"Why did you leave teaching?"

Paul foolishly hadn't anticipated that question. And he quickly realised it was a trap. Whatever he said would probably reflect badly on him. He hesitated, faltered.

"I had a disagreement with the principal." He knew it made him sound troublesome. But at least he was honest and up front.

"A disagreement? Don't like the sound of that. What was it about?"

"It was about a student."

He was on the point of launching into a full explanation of the student's threat to sue him for teaching a poem that wasn't on the course, when he realised that a man like Cal McLoughlin would not, could not even begin to understand the deep frustration that Paul had felt, that had driven him to hand in his resignation and walk away from a job he had once loved.

"I'm sorry I can't tell you any more than that," he

continued. "It's a private school issue."

He watched his interviewer turn a greenish shade of purple and quickly realised his mistake, knew that he would have to explain – if he wasn't to be branded a trouble-maker – or worse. In his own mind the whole incident had receded to a tiny irksome memory somewhere in the back of his head and it was frustrating now to have to recall it. He could hear the resentment in his voice as he explained about the student who'd threatened legal action over a poem, the principal who had sided with the student. And he was right about Cal McLoughlin. He stopped listening almost as soon as he heard the words "legal action". He thanked Paul for his time and scurried off to oversee his paper-clip empire.

Paul walked away, full of blind rage, his sense of rejection and failure growing with every step. At last he came to a cosy little bar that served food. He sat up at the bar, ordered a roast-beef dinner and a pint of Guinness and glared sullenly into the space between him and the rows of bottles. The barmaid was pretty and friendly with a lovely lilting Donegal accent. At another time he might have chatted her up. She had shiny flaxen blonde hair and warm blue eyes and a happy, uncomplicated smile and she did her best to raise his spirits. At last she coaxed it out of him that he'd been for an interview and that it hadn't gone well. When he told her that Cal McLaughlin had interviewed him, she threw her head back and laughed and patted his hand lightly.

"You don't need to mind about Cal. He's only a wee prick. Even his mother avoids him."

Paul smiled weakly.

"True as God! Now have some more of that roast beef. Do you good."

On the interminable journey back to the capital city, he dozed and read snatches of the local newspaper he'd found lying on the seat next to him. It was a cultural education for him, full of stories about farming issues and agricultural competitions, amateur dramatic societies, tidy town competitions, local GAA clashes, beauty contests and business and tourism initiatives, births, deaths, marriages. The letters page held his attention for a while since many of the letters seemed particularly close to his heart at that precise moment, complaining as they did about the appalling state of the roads, the lack of a train service and the complete inadequacy of the bus service to and from the capital, not to mention other parts of the country.

On the bottom of the business page was a small square advertisement and it brought an involuntary smile to Paul's face. Had it been in the era of mobile phones, he would have sent his friend Dermot Stenson a funny text message, or called to wind him up. As it was, Paul had at least another four hours imprisoned in the rickety bus, four hours of bumps and jolts, four hours of squealing babies, squabbling children and gossipy old women and four hours of Country music on the radio, before he reached Busarus. He tried to sleep but couldn't help overhearing the conversation between two young student nurses seated behind him, deeply indignant that they had been summoned home to a family gathering and now because the bus was late as usual they were going to miss the best night's craic ever in McGowran's in Phibsboro. And even if he could have ignored them, there was absolutely no ignoring the frail little lady in the elegant check wool suit, who sat down right beside him, insisted on sharing a packet of Milky Mints with him, read the *Irish Times* from cover to cover, then midway through the journey produced her hankie and began to sob quietly into it. Paul had no option but to ask in the end. She was in great distress. It turned out that her only sister was very ill in a Dublin hospital, not expected to last the night. They'd fallen out over something small, never made it up and now, because the bus was running late, she wouldn't have the chance.

In hindsight they turned out to be the most important four hours of Paul Brehony's life to date.

It was almost one o'clock when Paul pressed the electronic buzzer on the elaborate wrought-iron gateway into Dermot Stenson's large mock-Tudor house. Sally, Dermot's wife, came sleepily to the intercom.

"It's me – Paul."

"Paul! It's the middle of the night. Is something wrong?"

"I've got to talk to Dermot."

"He's asleep. Can't it wait till morning? Have you been drinking?"

"It won't take long."

Sally yawned loudly, grumbled and pressed the buzzer to open the gates.

Minutes later, she was back in bed while Paul brewed up coffee in the large kitchen. Dermot slouched over the long antique pine table and tried to rub the sleep from his face.

"You're fucking mad, Brehony. Do you know that? Easy known you don't have kids. The baby will have us up at six in the morning. Did you think of that before you came over here in the middle of the night?"

"Sorry. I'll make it up to you."

He set the pot of strong coffee down on the table, filled two mugs and slid the little advertisement from the local newspaper across the table. Dermot gazed sleepily at the slip of paper.

"Is this why you got me out of my bed in the middle of the night?"

Paul read patiently:

"Going concern: Small local airline for sale. Four profitable routes at present. Splendid business opportunity, great scope for expansion. Applications in writing to Errigal Air at Donegal Regional Development. Finance available for suitable buyers."

"Splendid business opportunity my arse! That's not an airline. That's a taxi service for little old island ladies who come to the mainland to get their hair done and see their grandchildren. They probably take sheep as passengers. Come to think of it – the pilot is probably a sheep – or a cattle. Can you have one cattle?"

Paul would not be put off. "I can raise a small amount of money. I know a bit about flying and I know a bit about business. But you're a risk-taker. You could put up serious cash. And the bank will do the rest."

Dermot sat back and laughed at his friend's outrageousness, the sheer neck of turfing a man out of his bed in the middle of the night with such a daft idea. He was a risk-taker – not an idiot.

"It's not a runner, Paul. Neither of us knows enough about it. And ask yourself – if it's such a splendid going concern, why are they selling it off? Besides – we're Dubs. What would we be doing buying a few rustbucket planes in the back of beyond?"

Paul fiddled with his coffee mug. He knew now that this was what he wanted to do. Everything in his life to date seemed to point in this direction – his awareness even as a child of what it meant to be an island nation, his frustration with outdated modes of transport, his own deepening love of flying. A clear pattern was emerging, a sharp and vivid realisation at last of what he wanted to do with the rest of his life. It had evolved slowly over years and then finally over that four hours on the return bus journey to Dublin, seeing the tiredness and discomfort of the other passengers, feeling the knots of impatience in his own stomach as the bus inched forward through miles of snarled-up traffic. How wonderful it would be to soar above it all! Yet he didn't have the confidence to push the matter any further with Dermot.

"Is that your final word?"

He felt nasty stabs of emotions that he'd never experienced before – envy, spite, resentment, bitterness.

"Don't go all resentful on me. It just doesn't sound very practical."

"Fair enough." He stood up, grabbed the slip of paper, tore it in two and flung it in the wastepaper bin. "I'm sorry I took up your time. I'll see myself out."

The following day, he took up his position at the bar of the Mardi Gras, with some of the other hard-luck stories in the neighbourhood. He even had a reason now to join in their litany of failure, their Greek chorus of righteous indignation at the cruelty of the rest of mankind. His best friend in the entire world had abandoned him.

He slipped surprisingly easily into the role of hard-drinking layabout, often passing out over the bar in the late afternoon, his fine dark head coming to rest blearily on his beer-sodden sleeves. Sometimes his father would steer him homewards, with a heavy heart, and try to coax food into him, helpless to do anything else.

Though successful, Dermot Stenson was not the sharpest tool in the box – as he'd happily admit himself. The night Paul confronted him with the staggering plan of buying an airline in Donegal, Dermot had gone to bed, cross at having being woken, worried by his friend's odd behaviour. In the morning, tired and grumpy from the events of the night, he went to empty the bins. It was his job and if he didn't do it Sally was well capable of withdrawing diplomatic relations in the bedroom – for days on end. Tipping the wastepaper basket into the large refuse bin in his garden shed, Dermot's eyes came to rest on the torn advertisement. Without even thinking, he tucked it into his jogpants pocket and went about his chores, his spirits improving slightly as the morning wore on.

A few months after that, at around five o'clock one cold darkening evening, Paul Brehony felt himself shaken from his cosy beer-sodden oblivion at the counter of the Mardi Gras, by a firm pair of hands, lifted by the collar of his black T-shirt, and forcibly dragged into the carpark where he was bundled into a car and abducted to some place where he was stripped violently and shoved brutally under a bitterly cold shower. There was no question of escape. In the first place he was really too drunk, so drunk that he could neither speak, nor move. In the second place, each time he tried to lurch from the shower, a pair of hands shoved him backwards roughly.

A disembodied voice said: "You stay there until you're sober – you fucking wanker! You stay there until you promise that you'll never drink alcohol again."

Clearly in the hands of some psychopath who had an unfair and unreasonable prejudice against harmless alcoholics who minded their own business, Paul knew he had to play along, long enough to escape, long enough to get back to the bar and top up his oblivion tank. It was quite a posh shower. It even had a tiled seat in it, where he positioned himself very reluctantly as the icy cold water cascaded over him and waves of deeply unwelcome sobriety threatened to engulf him. At last the water stopped and a hand appeared with a large bath towel on the end of it.

"Out!"

He wrapped the towel around himself, held his head which was now drumming in acute pain, and stepping gingerly from the shower came face to face with Dermot Stenson, his ex-best friend. He knew he wasn't in great shape just now – but he had to take a swipe at the smug bastard. He stretched his arm out to deliver a stinging, fatal blow.

"You miserable, treacherous, smug ..." he slurred, then promptly collapsed on the floor.

Much later, he was sitting on Sally's midnight-blue silk fleur-de-lis sofa wearing borrowed jeans and T-shirt, and sheepishly sipped hot tea. Dermot was facing him across a low coffee table, a bundle of papers and documents spread out in front of him.

"Are you sober yet?"

He nodded. Sally had given him some painkillers, but his head was still drumming and hurt horribly.

"And is there anything else you'd like to say to me? Any other fucking crap you want to get off your chest?" Dermot had never looked so belligerent, so menacing.

Paul shook his head. He was miserable, deeply ashamed, all his anger spent. In his heart of hearts, he knew it wasn't Dermot's fault. He also knew that his confidence was at an all-time low, and that little slights and rejections seemed to have more effect on him than normal. Now he looked across the table as bravely as he could, hoping to withstand the force of his friend's legendary temper.

"Good. Now running a small airline is something I know fuck all about. So I need someone to run it for me."

Paul wasn't sure he was hearing right.

"Someone I can trust completely, who's got a bit of

business sense and an interest in planes and flying. Above all someone with – what's this you used to call it at school – vision! Someone with vision! Well, what do you say?"

"I'm not sure I understand."

"And I'm supposed to be the thick one!"

"You bought it! You bought Errigal Airlines!"

"Biggest fucking mistake of my life! But if it loses money, I can write it off against tax. It's not going to make huge money, mind. I've done the figures, talked to the accountants. But hell – it's nice to say I own an airline. You won't be earning much more than you did in teaching but do a good job on running it for me and I'll make you a major shareholder. Which of course will be worth fuck all – but it will sound good at some of our neighbours' poncy dinner parties and sure maybe it will help you pull a few birds anyway. Christ knows but you could do with a bit of help there."

Dermot was right about only two of those statements. It did sound great at dinner parties and most women were dead impressed.

Chapter 9

Sophie's drinks party was in full swing by the time Isobel arrived. Earlier in the week, Sophie had dropped invitations round to some of the other neighbours in the road, and to Clementine downstairs who was thrilled to be invited. Sophie had also called several times to the apartment upstairs but it appeared not to be occupied. She invited the people in the mews and toyed with also sending a polite little request to remove their dinghy but decided in the end to tackle the matter face to face over a friendly glass of wine. Joe had sent his kid brother round to mow the lawn and so even though the borders and plants were still an unruly mess at least the grass was neat and offered plenty of space for entertaining in the warm sunshine. She bought a few crates of cheap sparkling wine and cooked a mountain of cocktail sausages in the grimy battered oven which she'd spent an entire afternoon scouring clean.

Sophie thought Isobel looked drawn and slightly gaunt which didn't sit well on her fine-boned features. Isobel thought Sophie looked sad and pasty and slightly lost.

"You look fabulous," they told one another and tucked into a glass of sparkling wine on the deck before joining the others.

"So how's Daniel getting on without you?" asked Isobel.

"Daniel? He's just wonderful thanks. We've been emailing every day. He sends his love."

She wasn't sure why she continued with the lie at that point, probably because she couldn't face hearing about the gorgeously sexy though deeply unsavoury Phil Campion who Isobel loved so much and was busy throwing away her life's store of happiness on.

"Still madly in love with him?"

"Absolutely! Who wouldn't be?"

"So how come you're home without him?"

"Oh – you know, he's so busy. Hasn't a moment. He's in partnership now – with an incredibly top-drawer architecture firm – half of New England would give their eye teeth to get in there … so stylish, awesomely fashionable. And anyway he's that busy, so here I am, catching up with old friends, getting some work done on this house, and able to spend some time with Gran. How's Phil?"

Isobel's face made every attempt to fall but she held it up valiantly. Scalding tears threatened to burst forth in a tidal wave. But she fought them with all her might, forcing a smile that she hoped would suggest her easy contentment and deepening love for Phil. She was delighted, of course, with her friend's continuing good fortune on the deliriously happy-relationship front, but it only served to highlight her own dismal foolishness over Phil Campion. She took a hefty gulp of bubbly, sucked in her breath and summoned up the contented wistful smile once more. It wasn't easy.

"Oh, he's just great. He's setting up in business for himself – and, of course, we're ecstatically happy as ever. He's settled down, Sophie – mellowed so much. Very different from the old laid-back Phil you knew. In fact he's working all the hours God gives now – that's why he can't be here today. I think we've really found everlasting love and happiness at last."

Sophie's heart sank, remembering of old her friend's tendency to go on and on about whoever happened to be the current love of her life, and especially for the past three years since she'd met the despicable Phil. Sophie was desperate to get away from the subject of boyfriends and everlasting love.

"I'm having the builders in to do some structural work. But . . ." She was about to say that now she couldn't afford to do anything much else since Daniel had effectively done her out of most of her money but she stopped herself in time.

"But what?" asked Isobel.

"But it may take a while and . . . I might commute for a while."

It was a complete lie but like all good lies, not completely beyond the bounds of possibility.

"What about your job?"

"I got bored. I'm looking for a new challenge."

"What will you do?"

"Maybe I'll just temp for a while or go back to college."

"You're not serious?" Isobel scoffed.

The idea of Sophie, whose whole life since meeting Daniel had become a hymn to good taste and refinement, returning to a life of eating batterburgers and chips in the student canteen and campaigning for cheaper beer and an end to globalisation was scarcely imaginable. Isobel would rather die. She valued her little apartment in the Docklands far too much. She loved her red Mazda Sport (even if it was seven years old), could not live without holidays in far-flung places, certainly couldn't survive without dining out regularly in her favourite restaurant on the banks of the canal, would surely wilt and expire without her Donna Karan suits, fade to nothing if she didn't have sexy, clinging Diane Von Furstenberg dresses, and DKNY tops and jeans. Isobel was a genius with managing her money, in spite of Phil Campion's permanent drain on her resources. Now that he was gone, she told herself that she would have even more money to play around with. She might even take her mother on holidays, if her mother ever spoke to her again. They had fallen out rather badly about Phil. But going back to college, as far as Isobel was concerned, that was a step in entirely the wrong direction.

Ruth McRory and Emer Doyle, both friends from Sophie's first job in the bank, arrived with two pleasant-looking men in tow. Being both sweet and pretty and very sociable, in no time at all they had created a wonderful happy buzz about the garden. They were delighted that Sophie was home, tactfully didn't mention Daniel, admired the house, and took Clementine Barragry under their wing. They filled up her glass and fetched little plates of finger-food for her. Watching them flutter about bringing their particular brand of simple warmth and unconscious good manners to the company, Sophie realised how happy she was to be home amongst true friends. More people arrived and before long a group of thirty or so mingled easily in the garden. Tess had come to stay for a night or two, personally driven from Hollymaine by Robert Franklin who had gone off to stay with his cousin and do some archaeological research in the museum. Sophie admired her grandmother now as she sat beneath the shade of an old tree chatting to Joe. She looked more like a woman of fifty, with clear skin and bright perceptive eyes. Beyond the tree, Sophie's eye was drawn to the dinghy, and she felt vaguely annoyed at the sight of it cluttering up her garden. She hated the idea of getting sucked into some silly little turf war and she hoped the owner would respond to a polite and friendly request. But as yet there was no sign of the mews-dwellers.

Clementine Barragry scurried across the lawn in her floating organdie floral dress and lavender kitten-heel shoes, wafted up to Sophie's side and took her gently by the elbow, inspecting her with pale violet eyes.

"I must say it really is very kind of you to invite me to your little gathering, my dear. I get so few invitations anywhere these days. In fact I can't remember the last time I was at a party. Most days it's just me and Tiger. Have you met the new tenant upstairs yet? I wonder is it a man or a woman? Still at least they're not noisy like the last lot. What a charming blouse!" She spoke formally, with an old-fashioned genteel accent – somewhere between Dublin, Oxford and Paris, like someone from an Agatha Christie novel.

"Tiger?"

"Yes! Tiger after Tiger Woods. Oh, don't worry, she's a very well-behaved cat. She's great company and, of course, she thinks she's the real owner of this house. Patrols it night and day – when she's not sleeping or looking for tickles. By the way – don't let yourself be bullied into feeding her. She's very good at crying as if she hasn't been fed for days. And if she likes you, I'm afraid she's rather likely to bring you a mouse, in which case you will have to thank her and accept the mouse gratefully before disposing of it discreetly."

Sophie shuddered.

"I mean appear to accept the mouse. I'll come and deal with it if you like. Will you be staying in the apartment for long?"

"I'm not sure. I need to stay and get some work done on the house. But the place has been badly neglected I'm afraid and I'm going to have to get the builders in."

A look of anxiety flitted across Clementine's face and Sophie instantly realised she'd been tactless.

"I'm sorry. I should have mentioned it to you first. But it really has to be done. There's no way round it."

Clementine nodded anxiously and turned away.

"There's that naughty cat chasing a bird. Won't you excuse me, dear?" she said and scurried down to the bottom of the garden.

"I know that guy. I wonder what he's doing here," said Isobel pointing discreetly to the tall, sandy-haired vision of divine handsomeness that had appeared carrying what looked like a crate of bottles and accompanied by a slightly less tall but equally handsome male companion.

Sophie turned with mild curiosity. She was not often struck dumb by the beauty of men but at that moment she found her jaw dropping slightly and a familiar fluttery feeling somewhere beneath her stomach. Hendro Sayers had that unsettling effect on women.

"Sophie Flanagan, you're drooling! Shame on you – a practically married woman! I hope it's not some nasty little habit you picked up stateside," said Isobel with mock disgust. "Whatever would Daniel say?"

Sophie tore her eyes away from the gorgeous sight before her. Isobel was right. She was practically drooling. Perhaps it was the heat of the day. Perhaps it was the fact that she was a hungry, sexual creature and felt a sudden longing to feel the hard-muscled nakedness of a man next to her skin, a man who would truly satisfy her, a man who could wring waves of shuddering orgasms from her, someone who could cause the pit of her stomach to lurch, bring her to a state of warm, liquid arousal – by a mere few seconds of eye contact. Alas for Daniel, he'd never had that effect on her.

Hendro was jaded from the intense physical demands of his training schedule and quite looking forward to a genteel garden party with the little old lady from the big house. He'd glimpsed her several times over the garden wall. He had a particular fondness for little old ladies that stemmed from his absolute adoration of his own grandmother. While his father was busy trading in exotic fruits and his mother was frantically scrambling up the Melbourne social ladder, he'd been left in the care of his awesome grandmother – Maureen Campbell. She was his closest friend, his confidante, his true guiding light in matters social, philosophical and romantic – the woman who loved him most in the world but took no shit from him either.

He looked about the garden in search of Miss Sophie Flanagan. He knew he could charm and befriend her. Old ladies, indeed ladies of almost every sort, took instantly to Hendro. Besides he needed the space at the bottom of her garden for his dinghy. He recognised a slender-framed little lady with rigidly coiffed pale-gold hair who was scampering down the path after a cat. That must be her. He deposited the crate and his companion in the kitchen and bounded forth, catching up with the old lady in a matter of seconds.

"Miss Flanagan? Delighted to meet you. I'm Hendro Sayers. I live in the mews."

He extended his hand, smiling brilliantly at her.

"*Shoo! Shoo!* How do you do, Mr Hendro. I'm just chasing this cat away from the border."

"So nice of you to invite me to your garden party!"

"Tiger – *shoo* – *shoo!* Not the delphiniums! I'm sorry, what did you say?"

"It's a wonderful party. Thanks for inviting me. I hope you don't mind – I brought a friend."

Clementine Barragry's pale violet eyes looked up with some confusion into his tanned and handsome face, and in spite of the fact that she was happily and most contentedly in the autumn of her days, she couldn't stop her eyelashes from fluttering involuntarily. She was glad now that she'd taken the time to frame them with the merest hint of lilac eye-shadow.

"I think I'll have another glass of champagne," she said and linked her frail arm through his, allowing him to lead her back to a little garden seat beside a willow-tree.

"And who are you again, Mr –? You must excuse me not remembering but I'm old and dotty, of course."

"Hendro. I live in the mews just behind you. And you don't seem dotty to me and certainly not old."

"Oh nonsense!" She smiled with childlike delight. "Thank you."

He grabbed a glass of champagne from a passing waiter and gave it to her.

"Don't you drink?" she asked, her little nose wrinkling up from the bubbles.

"No! I'm a professional rugby player. Interferes with my game and tomorrow is our first big training session of the season. Coach Burton can tell just by looking at you if you've been drinking."

"A rugby player! How very exciting! You're Australian, aren't you? Do you play for the Wannabees?"

He smiled and dipped his head ruefully. "No, ma'am, I don't play for the Wallabies. Sadly I'm not good enough."

Hendro was delighted at how his meeting with Sophie Flanagan was going. He could win her confidence, charm her, reassure her that he was the sort of neighbour she could definitely call on if she were ever in trouble. He might even offer to mow the lawn for her. Then he would explain as gently as he could that there simply wasn't enough space in his glass-fountained, cobble-docked courtyard garden to store even a small sailing dinghy. She was a sweet old thing and he was sure she'd understand.

"I spent some time in Australia in my youth – a million years ago," said his companion. "Yes, I worked as a costume assistant in the theatre. I used to earn two pounds a week and that was good money in those days. I had a nice boyfriend. He worked as a teller in a bank and – oh, there's Sophie. Sophie dear, come here for a moment!"

Hendro followed the direction of her eyes in some confusion and saw a girl with straight blonde hair and nice blue eyes, dressed in a simple white cotton blouse, dark linen trousers and mules. He turned to the old lady.

"You're not Sophie Flanagan?"

"Whatever gave you that idea? I'm Miss Clementine Barragry. This is Sophie coming towards us." She leaned forward and whispered conspiratorially in his ear. "What do you think? Not bad, is she?"

He ducked his head in amused embarrassment. This old lady reminded him more and more of his grandmother, whose sole occupation at the moment seemed to be to find her grandson a true love match.

"Sophie Flanagan." She held out her hand and he gripped it firmly in his. She hadn't the faintest idea who he was, what he was doing here at her party, why he had brought a crate of bottles. She felt sure that she would have remembered inviting such a magnificent-looking person to her house. Again she felt a hot liquid bolt of pure lust at the pit of her stomach as she looked into his green eyes.

"Hendro Sayers. It's very nice to meet you."

He smiled warmly, a faint hint of sexual appreciation in his eyes. Sophie found it pleasantly unsettling.

"You needn't have bothered with those. We have lots of champagne."

"No, you have lots of sparkling wine! I brought some quite decent champagne. I hope you like it."

He smiled easily and she became even more dizzily aware of his tremendous presence standing so close to her, his large and muscled frame, the hard curve of his thighs beneath the fabric of his trousers, the broad and overwhelming sweep of his shoulders. She was sure that her pupils were dilating and she blinked and looked away momentarily to hide the hungry sluttishness that was threatening to break forth. It had been a very long time since a man had affected her in this way. In fact with Daniel she'd learned to do without really satisfying sex altogether, had pushed thoughts of it from her mind, and fallen into line with his architect's minimalist "less is more" attitude to sex. Except that it wasn't more – it was definitely less. Now released from the constraints of the relationship, she realised that a world of sexual possibility might also open up for her. But not just yet! It was far too soon. And who did Hendro Sayers think he was anyway with his cheeky comment about the cheap champagne?

Hendro was about to explain that he lived in the mews but just at that moment some other guests arrived and Sophie went to greet them.

Hendro caught sight of Isobel hovering disinterestedly on the edge of a conversation, excused himself to Clementine and strode across to Isobel.

But unlike Sophie, Isobel wasn't the slightest bit unsettled by Hendro's stunning presence, since she was well used to it and had seen it in many poses and in several different stages of undress and sweat-glistening muscle.

"I've seen you at the Athena Club? You're the Assistant Manager, aren't you?"

"Yes," she said, not feeling inclined to say any more.

"You're looking very nice," he continued hopefully.

Isobel tried to smile and thank him but all she could manage was a tight grimace.

"No, really!" he added, flashing her a smile that would have made most women tremble and capsize like wobbly jelly.

But he could pay her every compliment under the sun, and Isobel wasn't about to be impressed. She'd seen him many times strutting his stuff for the endless stream of admiring career women and impossibly glamorous young mothers, and single bright young things, who strained and lifted, pushed, pulled and jogged with such dainty elegance on the treadmills, and who quite often followed Hendro with hungry longing in their eyes. Apart from arctically cool Beatrice Heavenly of course – who did not do *hungry* or *longing* in any shape or form. As for Isobel, Hendro definitely wasn't her type. Phil had been her type: vulnerable, deeply intelligent, complex, a dark and dazzling presence. The tears welled up inside when she thought of him. She swallowed and forced them back, trying to distract herself by making conversation with Hendro. All female eyes were enviously on them as he chatted away easily to her about the health club, her work, how she liked to spend her spare time, where she liked to go on holidays, if she'd eaten in the new penthouse restaurant overlooking the docklands – easy, fluid conversation. It would have been plain rude not to talk back.

By the fourth glass of champagne, they were giggling and laughing, sitting on the wooden deck, now very much the focus of envious glances.

"So how come you know Sophie?" she asked him.

"I don't. Never clapped eyes on her until today."

"Then how –?"

He indicated the mews. "I live there. I got an invitation through the door a few days ago. To be quite honest, I thought it was from some little old dear. But your friend is definitely not an old dear."

"Do you fancy her?"

Hendro grinned sheepishly. It was hard to explain his simple outlook on life, that he fancied most good-looking women, that looking around he would gladly spend the night with any one of about five women at the party. Right now though, the person he most fancied spending the night with was the person he'd spent the most time talking to – Isobel.

"She seems OK."

But as he said it, his eyes lingered for a split second on Isobel's face, and in spite of her pure devotion to the memory of the emotionally deceased Phil Campion, she blushed slightly.

Later Isobel stood in the grand, crumbling doorway saying her goodbyes to the tall Australian.

"Well, I suppose I'll see you in the Athena." He bent and planted a light but lingering kiss on her cheek.

"Who knows?" she responded coolly.

As he disappeared down the steps Sophie joined her.

"Who is that guy? I never found out. And why was he kissing you? What would Phil say?"

"I know him from the gym. He lives in the mews. You invited him apparently."

"Damn!" Sophie said, remembering the dinghy. She darted down the steps and called after him. "Excuse me! Sorry to trouble you but could I have a brief word?"

He turned and waved cheerfully in the deepening darkness.

"Thanks for a great party. Goodnight," he said and disappeared down the lane.

"Damn! Damn!" she said feeling quite unaccountably piqued.

Chapter 10

A few days later, when Hendro passed by Isobel in her office, he looked in and winked at her. She seemed much more cheerful. He wondered briefly why she'd been so upset that day in the Bayfield and if she was romantically involved with her lunch companion of that day. She interested him vaguely. The mere fact that she didn't want to leap wantonly into his arms was intriguing in itself. But then he quickly dismissed all thought of her and ambled off in the direction of the gym for a session of extremely heavy power weights.

Isobel shut her door and worked through a pile of invoices that Laura had left on her desk, and queried one or two, before approving the rest for payment. Then she turned her mind to the job application. Colman was right. It was important to project herself as someone with good management skills but also someone with vision and workable ideas. She needed to come up with a sound and innovative plan for the five acres that would be in keeping with the sports centre. She drew out a map of the site and studied it intently – but to no great effect. It was pointless sitting at her desk and staring at a map of a chunk of land. She needed to find an expert, someone with ideas, who knew what could and couldn't be done.

Two days later, armed with several outline plans and a vastly increased knowledge of gardens and landscaping gleaned from Gavin Lacy, a friend of her father's, she met once more with Colman Brady in the Bayfield. This time there were no tears. Colman sat back in frank admiration as Isobel outlined her scheme for the five acres.

"First off – I really think that sports people aren't all that bothered about gardens. They're not going to reach a higher plane of fitness by strolling through a Japanese maple grove."

"Very true. So what's your plan?"

"It's simple. We build a running track around the perimeter of the site, surround it with trees and in the large expanse in the middle we create several different oases of calm. The city planners can't knock it because we're keeping it a green area and the members get another sports facility."

"It's simple and utterly brilliant! But how will people be able to cross the track without interfering with the runners?"

"We can build a little Japanese-style bridge. Or we can go for a more modern steel structure. Then in the main central expanse we could lay out a rose garden, a herb garden (with a health theme), perhaps a grove of young oaks and beeches with little paths and wooden seats, maybe a putting green. We might even find enough space to include a small play and picnic area for families. I'm having it all done out in computerised artist impression slides. It will look quite smart as my presentation."

"I'm beginning to wish I wasn't leaving now. I said you had what it takes. This will amaze them and they are going to give you the job. I will insist on it."

"I'm trying not to get my hopes up too much – but I feel up for it now – able to cope with the pressures and the responsibilities."

"That's my girl. The other candidates won't stand a chance."

There were only three other candidates for the job of General Manager of the Athena Club: Brian Hanlon who was the ambitious but relatively inexperienced sales and marketing manager, someone called Grace French who was a very serious community-health officer from County Kildare, and Len Crolly, the company accountant.

Of these, she knew she could rule out Crolly. For starters he didn't even look as if he belonged in a Health and Fitness club. He was girlishly slender with longish thin mousy hair and pale brown eyes, unhealthily pale skin and a tiny rather unpleasant little spike of very black beard on his chin that looked like it had been dabbed on badly by a drunk with a paintbrush. He was soft-spoken and much given to small enigmatic smiles and saddish wary looks. Most of all, he was unpopular and Isobel had heard more than once that he had a tendency to stand closer than necessary to some of the younger girls on the staff when he was talking to them.

"Especially not Crolly," she said confidently to Colman.

"He's a slippery customer – so watch him all the same."

Back at her desk, she put the finishing touches to the application, slid everything into a large brown envelope and placed it in the bottom drawer. She would post it in the morning.

Now less than three days away from her interview, Isobel was consumed with her enthusiasm for the job. Colman groomed her with tough questions. Sophie, whose experience in banking was invaluable, advised her on body language, tone of voice, choice of expression, what to wear.

They spent an afternoon in BT agonising between a very smart but ridiculously expensive fine woollen suit in deep petrol blue, and a very professional navy blue skirt and jacket from Paul Costello. She opted for the latter, bought low-heeled black court shoes, and some ivory silk and lace Lejaby underwear which she said would enhance her confidence no end. Then she treated herself to a manicure and a pedicure.

The evening before, she swam thirty lengths of the pool, ate a light supper of grilled sole and carrot puree, washed down with a glass of organic grape juice. Then she set up her laptop at the kitchen table, rehearsed her talk through the slide presentation, re-read through the long list of questions which Colman and Sophie had helped her prepare and rehearsed her answers to them. There were a few phone calls wishing her luck. Colman and Sophie, of course, then her mother, who told her to go easy on the lipstick, reminded her about posture and sitting up properly and making sure she had a spare pair of tights in her handbag.

She smiled contentedly to herself, smoothed a rich creamy mint-scented pack onto her face and lay back on her bed, feeling more positive and confident than she'd felt in a long time. Even when she was with Phil, she was constantly doubting herself: did he still love her, was she still attractive to him, would he notice the orange-peel cellulite on her thighs, could she manage another few days without a bikini wax? Now forced to do without him, she realised that he was part of the reason she had grown to doubt herself so much. Isobel knew she was not the most beautiful woman on the planet, and could live quite happily with the fact. She could see from her mother's face and figure that she would not be one of those women to emerge at the end of their thirties in a state of high classic beauty. But it wasn't until she'd met Phil Campion that she'd begun to find those truths about herself so hard to live with. Perhaps it was the way he constantly looked other women over with frank admiration while his eyes had begun to slide over her with barely disguised contempt. She wondered where he was now – who he was with. But she forced the memory of him and his pathetic deceit out of her mind. Thinking about Phil Campion wouldn't get her the job.

She removed the mask from her face, dabbed some light toner on her skin and slid into a warm sudsy bath.

Waiting outside the boardroom to be interviewed, Isobel felt surprisingly calm and focussed on the task in hand. She simply knew that she was going to go into that room and knock them speechless with her suitability for the job. Laura passed by, lingering to fix a straying lock of Isobel's hair, offering warm words of encouragement and a sisterly hug. Then Crolly emerged from his interview wearing one of his wary enigmatic smiles and wished her luck, before quickly disappearing down the corridor.

The interview began well. The board of three men and two women seemed mightily impressed with her work record, her cool efficiency, her excellent relations with staff, her success as a manager, thoughts on the expansion of the centre, ideas on how to enhance facilities for their clients, some well-thought-out strategies on salaries and bonuses.

Beginning hesitantly, she moved quickly into her stride, confidently cutting a swathe through the barrage of questions they threw out to test her. She was familiar with the financial reports, up to scratch on projections and targets for the coming years, aware of weak spots such as greater need for dedicated family areas and a more stringent emergency plan. By the time the first half hour was up, Isobel was thoroughly enjoying herself.

"How would you describe your relationship with the staff?"

"Mutual respect. I respect them and they respect me. I don't work at cultivating popularity but I tend naturally to get on well with most people. My job is to provide structures and environments that allow people to do their job well and happily. I'm primarily a facilitator – someone whose chief responsibility is to empower people to achieve their fullest potential." Yes, of course it was all a load of management babble – but in essence it was true. At any rate they seemed to like her answer.

All that remained now was the presentation – her crowning glory. Her dad's friend Gavin had done a fine job on the graphics, animating them in sharp bright colour to show how the running track and gardens would look through the changing seasons, including alternative and interchanging options – so that the whole thing looked very exciting and professional.

"I took the liberty of consulting a landscape architect," she began.

"Very enterprising."

"At my own expense, of course."

They smiled approvingly at her, sat up eagerly in their seats. The first slide came up – it was a simple mission statement. They nodded encouragingly, clearly impressed, not even bothering to conceal their approval. Now came an overall aerial view of what the site would look like – it looked stunning, a red-surfaced all-weather running track, and the different areas of the garden. She talked through it bubbling with enthusiasm, anticipating some of their reservations and offering alternative suggestions – such as the little walled garden of contemplation, a cycle track and the perfectly pretty little putting green. So carried away was she with the sheer brilliance of her performance that it took a while to notice that two of the men were quietly engrossed in their notes. Perhaps they'd seen enough. Perhaps she was talking too much. It was coming up to the last slide anyway. She finished up quickly and rounded off her comments with a neat sound bite:

"That's my plan – plain and simple – a garden to sport in."

Over an early evening supper with Sophie, Isobel was bursting with optimism and plans. Sophie tried to enter into the conversation with enthusiasm but was more inclined to caution than her friend.

"Isobel – I'm sure it's all going to work out fine – but don't you think it would be best to wait until …"

"Until what? It's like I'm really coming into my own – a woman in my own right. After all who needs –" She stopped suddenly, remembering that Sophie still didn't know about Phil. "Who needs second best?" she added weakly. "Um . . . what about you? Still thinking about going back to college?"

"Yes – I think so."

"You're mad. Half the banks in the country would be only delighted to snap you up and offer you good money. College life is very unglamorous, and broadening your educational horizons isn't all it's cracked up to be. Besides – what's Daniel going to think?"

"Oh, he's very encouraging about the entire thing,"

Sophie said dismissively.

At home that evening, Isobel gave herself up to thoughts of what she planned to do when she got the job. Her salary was about to double. It would mean that she could rent a larger apartment, perhaps even a nice little town house in somewhere pleasant like Rathgar. She would certainly have to seriously consider changing her old Mazda sports for something new and in keeping with her more senior position. There would be the option of a company car – but that mightn't be tax efficient. Her holidays were coming up in a few weeks and she hadn't yet booked anything since the original plan had been to go away with Phil to Turkey for three weeks. Now there was only herself to think of and on double the salary she could consider places she'd never been able to afford before. South America looked interesting. There was a very exclusive little enclave in the Bahamas which she longed to visit. Now, for the first time, travelling to truly glamorous and exotic places seemed like a real possibility.

The absence of Phil was becoming bearable – almost pleasant. It had been three weeks now since she'd thrown him out on the street and pelted a refuse-sack full of clothes after him. A few days ago, she'd felt able to scour the apartment of any last remaining vestiges of him – his shaving foam, his toothbrush, his Marillion CDs, a photo of him lying on the beach in Spain, a cigarette lighter with a cannabis-leaf logo on it.

Now she'd reclaimed the apartment completely. It was solely hers once more. The smell of stale cigarette smoke no longer lingered in the little living-room on her tapestried cushions, on the curtains, or in the compact kitchenette. Instead bowls of Jo Malone potpourri added a boudoir-like aura of tranquillity. She even allowed herself a fond gentle thought about Phil. Now free of him, she could afford such thoughts. If he walked through the door at that moment, she would be perfectly calm, able to resist his advances, ready to forgive his treachery. Ready to move on in fact!

The following morning she showered briskly, lightly made up with skin-toned lipstick, a pale foundation to smooth her complexion and the merest hint of shadow on her eyelids. Then she dressed in a sober black suit, and drove to work at seven thirty.

Phil Campion? Who's he? she said to herself smiling as she swung through the gates of the Athena Club at seven fifty-five, the sound of the Stereophonics thumping loudly in her car urging her to have a nice day. By eight o'clock she was sitting at her desk. No one could doubt Isobel Kearney's commitment to her job.

Chapter 11

In the evening, Sophie found an old bike in the garden shed and cycled in to the Docklands to see Isobel. She had decided to do without a car for the time being. No, the truth was she wouldn't be able to afford a car – in fact, right now, if this rickety old bicycle got a bad puncture, she'd be hard pushed to come up with the cash to repair it. She'd passed the college entry interview easily enough but the registrar had outlined the cost of being a mature student for a year and Sophie had been stunned by the amounts of money involved. The fees were astronomical and she was forced to settle for a short foundation course of a few months instead. Then it would be back on the work treadmill. Until then though she would have to survive on very little, which would be a challenge but she reminded herself that she'd been brought up by a mother who would have given Ebenezer Scrooge quite a run for his money.

Her own childhood, though not exactly poverty-stricken, was stark – minimalist before the term was fashionable. For a long time they had lived in Hollymaine with her grandmother. That was how she'd met Isobel in the first place and they had bonded instantly over a shared addiction to lemon bonbons which Isobel had to supply because Sophie was never allowed money for sweets. Then her mother announced that she'd bought a house in Dublin and they would live there. It was a solid house, always sparkling clean and neat and tidy – but it lacked many of the little homely touches that would have cost money. There were few ornaments and when her friends' mothers were busy redecorating their houses every few years, passing from woodchip and cork tiles, through chintz and lace and Austrian blinds, to the early stages of the stencilling and rag-rolling revolution, Sophie was forced to endure the embarrassment of old seventies brown furniture and very clean but threadbare carpets. Grocery items which her friends took almost entirely for granted like chocolate Swiss rolls, tomato ketchup, frozen pizzas, tubs of ice cream and Wagon Wheels were rarely seen in the Flanagan household. Small wonder that her mother was eventually able to buy a second home, the house in Raglan Road, which they could never afford to live in. Sophie wasn't bitter about it. Happiness and contentment after all didn't come in a pot of Farrow & Ball paint or with Egyptian cotton sheets.

Yes, cycling round the city on the rickety old bike would keep her fit and also help to get her bearings once more. The place had changed a lot, old roads closed off, new roads, new districts, and shabby old districts now chic and gentrified.

It was a pleasant evening, the sun setting in a golden arc behind the cheerful little Ha'penny Bridge as she secured her bike and pressed the buzzer to Isobel's apartment. There was no response and she tried again.

"Isobel – are you there? It's me – Sophie!"

At last she heard the intercom switch on and the sound of breathing but nothing else. She was about to turn and leave when Isobel's voice crackled weakly over the intercom.

"Sophie, is that you?" She sounded horribly desolate.

"Yes – what's wrong?" called Sophie in alarm. "Press the buzzer and let me in!"

By nine o'clock that morning, Isobel had cleared all the correspondence from her "pending" tray. It was hard to concentrate on her work, but she soldiered on valiantly.

She hoped they would break the news of her appointment before lunch. They would most probably take her aside and let her know unofficially, give her time to get used to the idea, before making the more formal public announcement. She wondered if her photo would appear in the recent appointments column of the business pages of the newspapers. *Miss Isobel Kearney has been appointed General Manager of the Athena Health and Fitness Club.* Her mother would probably buy up all the copies of the paper to be found in Hollymaine and show them to all her friends. She would enlarge the little newspaper cutting so that it took up an entire A4 page. Then she would take it to the printers and have it laminated and framed and hung in the hall. Isobel's mother did those daft kinds of things.

The excitement of it all unsettled her stomach and at lunchtime she merely nibbled on the tuna and salad wrap she'd ordered from the deli bar. Back in the office, she paid a visit to Colman's office down the corridor. He wasn't there. She was disappointed because he'd been the one person on the staff who'd understood her completely, who'd helped her so selflessly. And she wanted to thank him for all that.

Hendro dropped by, his sandy hair ruffled, skin glistening with sweat, his tall muscular frame eliciting the usual Mexican wave of longing looks as he passed by the girls at reception and the little cluster of women who were queuing up for Pilates classes. He stood for a moment at Isobel's door.

"Hi."

"Hendro! Shouldn't you be weighing in or something?"

"Just wanted to see how you are. I'm not stopping. Scrum Coach has us working on step-ins and strikes for the afternoon."

Isobel was bursting with good will and excitement, tingling with anticipation for the announcement of her promotion, and so in spite of the fact that she hadn't a clue what he was talking about she smiled warmly back at him.

He half-winked and disappeared down the corridor,

leaving her in mid-blush, feeling mightily pleased with herself. There was no sign of Colman – funnily enough, no sign of anyone. Even Len Crolly seemed to have gone into hiding, no doubt licking his wounds. She shut the door of her office and began working on the next month's staff rosters, reasoning that it was probably best if she just went about work in her normal, professional manner. Bad news travels fast – good news takes a little longer – she knew that for sure. She worked an hour past her normal finishing time and still there was no word. The evening shift came on – and still nothing. She gathered up her bag and her jacket, ran a brush through her gleaming chestnut hair and resigned herself to not hearing anything until the following morning.

Outside in the carpark, she was mildly taken aback to see Colman talking to Len Crolly, leaning up against his car, arms folded, squinting into the evening sun. He looked his easy, permanently good-humoured self. She smiled and waved over at him. Then she noticed Len Crolly. He didn't look the slightest bit like he was licking his wounds – licking his lips was more like it. He fiddled with his little spike of a beard, grinning quite happily as he chatted away to Colman. She froze, her stomach lurching and diving, her mouth drying up like she was in some silly nightmare. Colman waved back at her and she realised she was just being paranoid. It was perfectly natural for Colman to talk to Len Crolly in the carpark. After all, they were men of roughly the same age. She knew they both played golf and both had children the same age. Of course they would have lots to talk about.

And besides, Colman was just the sort of good-natured guy who would feel he had to talk Len through his disappointment personally.

She sat into the car, dismissed all thoughts of the two of them and headed for home. She'd showered, watched the news and drunk a cup of tea followed by a glass of wine when the phone rang. It was Colman.

"I was wondering when you'd call," she said. "Listen, I just want to thank you for all your help. I mean I really couldn't have done it without you. You've been a true friend . . ."

She was in such a state of excitement now that she found it impossible to stop talking. At last she came to the end of a litany of thanks and compliments.

"Isobel, will you listen?" He sounded sharp, not at all like his normal easy self.

"Sorry. I'm just babbling on. It's the excitement."

"The thing is – and there's no easy way of saying this – you didn't get the job."

She froze, her stomach capsizing, a horrible fishy, metallic taste in her mouth. She should never have had tuna. It just didn't agree with her.

Then she realised that Colman was probably winding her up and she laughed.

"Very funny, Colman! You almost had me."

"It's the truth. Len Crolly is the new manager. I'm sorry. I wanted to tell you earlier but, well, there were a lot of things to finalise before we could cut a deal with him. I'm sorry, I really am."

She felt like she'd been hit by a train – flattened and

pulverised with shock. It couldn't be. Len Crolly was useless. Colman had as much as told her the job was hers. Her presentation plan for the garden was unique. Len Crolly could never have come up with anything to equal it.

Staying calm in a crisis was a highly overrated virtue in Isobel's opinion. She had never understood what useful purpose it served. Now fury raged through her so powerfully that she thought she might be sick. She couldn't even find the words to frame her rage, her hurt, her disappointment. How long had Colman known without telling her? Had it all been decided before the interviews anyway? What had she done wrong? And why Len Crolly of all people? Len Crolly whose mission statement at last year's Annual General Meeting had been the riveting: "The secret to continuing success of the Athena Club is to achieve a higher state of financial solvency and …" Well, she couldn't even remember the rest. Len Crolly, who sat woodenly at office parties like a surly toad frozen in aspic jelly? It just didn't make sense.

"Isobel, are you still there? I know you're disappointed but it's not the end of the world. Len just had the edge. I know that he wants to talk to you about perhaps a more senior role in the company. I think he mentioned the title of Assistant Deputy Senior Manager."

He said it as though he was offering her the presidency of the United States.

"But what about my presentation? The plans for the garden – my grasp of human resource management, plans and financial strategies? He couldn't have done a better job! He just couldn't!"

"You're upset now. Tell you what – why don't we meet for coffee tomorrow? I'm really sorry, Isobel. Truly I am. I honestly thought you had it in the bag."

She hung up, poured herself another glass of wine, sloshed it back like water and quickly returned to the fridge for a refill. Her stomach was in bad shape, the shock of the news sending it into churning swirls of anxiety and despair. By the time Sophie arrived, she was quite drunk.

"Have you eaten anything? You look a bit seasick."

Sophie now busied herself with the coffee machine, wondering if she should pour the remaining half bottle of wine down the sink. Isobel had never been a wild drinker and it was surprising and a bit distressing now to see that she was truly drunk, falling down, incoherent, lurching to the fridge to top up her glass and then slumping on the sofa like an old wino. Sophie found some eggs and whisked up a plain omelette, tossing it into some hot butter on the pan and watching as the eggs set golden and mouth-watering. She slid it out onto a plate, garnished it with a couple of lonely cherry tomatoes she'd found lurking behind the pro-biotic drinks and set it down on the little coffee table in front of Isobel.

"Come on. Eat something," she coaxed gently.

Isobel eyed the omelette with mild curiosity. It didn't offer the warm sense of numbing oblivion which came guaranteed with a few glasses of wine. Her deepest hope at that moment was that she would pass out quickly and for a very very long time, that she would not have to confront ever again the mean, nasty, self-serving, sly, devious, conniving bunch of people known as the human race. Besides she'd started drinking on an empty stomach and now the mere thought of food made her nauseous. But Sophie was insistent. She propped Isobel up with some of her favourite tapestry cushions, cut up the omelette and placed the fork and knife in her hand.

"Can't."

"You need to eat. Just a few mouthfuls. And then a mug of coffee."

"Don't want to."

"Here." Sophie held up a sliver of egg on a fork and like an obedient child Isobel took the offering.

"There now. That's not so bad."

"Nnnnrrgggh. Sluvly. Thanks, Sophie," said Isobel as she leaned forward and obligingly took a second bite. This time though, the smell of the buttery egg was too much. She stumbled to her feet and crashed clumsily into the bathroom where she was promptly sick into the sink.

When at last she was cleaned up and relatively sober and tucked up in bed, Sophie broached the subject of Phil.

"Would you like me to call Phil?"

"No, thanks."

"Don't you think he should be here? It's better not to be on your own."

"No, really. He's down the country – doing a wedding video. He won't be back for a few days."

Isobel longed to tell the truth about Phil, but it would be the final humiliation – passed over for promotion – passed over for love. Her life was meaningless, empty and hopeless. She might as well be dead. She'd probably get the sack from the Athena Club as soon as they noticed her first wrinkle, and then she'd end her days promoting incontinence products in supermarkets and having a long and deeply unsatisfying relationship with some miserable old fat and bald married man who'd take her to the pub once a week for a drink and then demand halitosis sex with her. In the space of three weeks all her hopes and dreams for the future had shattered. How could she tell that to Sophie who had Mister Perfect, who had a beautiful home of her own, who was heading back to college – just for a little time out – and who could go on to pick and choose from almost any career she wanted.

"Would you like me to stay?"

"No. Thanks. I'm fine. Really."

"I think I should stay."

"I don't want you to!" she said sharply and instantly regretted it, adding by way of apology, "No offence, Sophie, but I just want to be alone."

"OK. But remember, I'm just a text message away if you need me. Get some sleep. It's their loss but it's not the end of the world, Isobel. Plenty more jobs in the sea."

Isobel smiled weakly, grateful to Sophie but wishing she'd leave and stop spewing out silly platitudes just to make her feel better.

"I'll call you tomorrow," said Sophie, letting herself out the front door.

She cycled back along the river, up past Trinity College, along Nassau Street, past the Shelbourne Hotel and

Merrion Square, then along the magnificent leafy roads of Ballsbridge until she came to Raglan Road. The evening with Isobel had left her feeling tired and drained. She made a cup of tea and sat out on the deck fretting about her friend and hoping she would feel better after a good night's sleep.

She picked up a book to read but couldn't concentrate and was startled to discover as she sat in the fading evening light that she was suddenly filled with a reckless hunger for sex. Sex with Daniel had been a measured and predictable dimension of their lives together. Daniel was the sort who stuck rigidly (or as rigidly as he could!) to a schedule – Wednesdays and Saturdays without fail, with every first Sunday of the month thrown in for good measure. Trying to deviate from this timetable was like trying to reschedule Christmas. She had never longed hungrily for him, never burned up with sizzling tremors of sexual desire at the thought of him. Yet now, alone and independent, she longed hotly for the feel of a man's hard rippling flesh, to smell his musky scented skin, to fold her legs about him, to feel him slide hard and hungry into her, his moist lips on her breasts, warm breath on her neck. Unexpected hot waves of longing rippled through her.

She stubbed out her cigarette abruptly and decided on a cool shower. Sex was a complication she definitely didn't need just now, and besides where would she get it? But just as she turned to go inside, a movement at the bottom of the garden caught her eye. It was him – the man from the mews, throwing a bag of rubbish into his wheelie bin. She could see the outline of his tall muscular figure clearly in the evening light, could observe his easy, languid walk as he turned back to the house.

"Right, Mister Muscles! No time like the present!"

Surely there was nothing like a good neighbourly territorial dispute to sublimate sexual frustration.

She pulled on an old navy fleece and a pair of battered white trainers and walked purposefully down the lane towards the mews. The door opened almost immediately and Hendro stood there in white T-shirt, pale blue shorts and a cheeky smile. She tried to avoid noticing his long tanned and muscular forearms and shins with the glistening sheen of bleached man-hair. He was barefooted, with patches of sweat on a T-shirt which did nothing to conceal the hard, perfectly honed body beneath.

Sophie swallowed, remembering the reckless hunger that had swept through her just a short time earlier.

"Miss Sophie Flanagan! It's very nice to see you again. Come in!"

Sophie's hand rushed to her throat in some primeval gesture that she couldn't control.

"No, thanks," she blurted out finally, wrestling with the hot spasm of lust that was bolting through her. "I just wanted a quick word about your dinghy."

She tried to sound cool and business-like, the sort of woman who would not be side-tracked by any frissons of a flirtatious nature, which she wasn't normally. In fact it had been a long time since Sophie had flirted with anyone, or even wanted to. It was a horrifyingly primitive means of communication in her view and definitely not to be encouraged in the workplace. But now released from the world of work and steady relationship, she found herself floundering a bit.

She looked at him now, steadily holding eye contact, making him aware in no uncertain terms that she meant business and nothing else.

"All the same – you might as well come in. The night is cool and I can't have you catching a chill."

He sounded so gallant, looked so innocently warm and friendly. If she didn't step inside, he might take her for some kind of weirdo. If she did step inside, she stood a better chance of appealing to his good nature.

"OK. Thanks."

She followed him through to a very stylish stainless-steel, maple and granite kitchen.

"Glass of wine? A beer? Water?"

"Nothing for me."

He poured himself a glass of still mineral water.

"Well, perhaps a small glass of water?" she said.

"Live dangerously!" he said, grinning at her mockingly.

"You're a fine one to talk," she said, rising instantly to the bait, "since you're only drinking water yourself."

"It's all part of my training programme. I'm only allowed a certain number of alcohol units a week. Besides, something tells me I need to keep my wits about me for this conversation. Tell you what though, my patio garden is heated. We can sit there and sort this matter out in no time."

Sophie was reluctant to pass beyond the kitchen. One could always keep order and discipline on a conversation or situation if it was taking place in a kitchen. Heated floodlit patios in the moonlight were another matter entirely. But still, she was curious to see what his garden was like. From the deck of her own house, all she could see was a high old cut-stone wall, clad in some unusual climbers, and occasionally a glimmer of light cutting through the foliage in the darkness.

She could barely contain her admiration when she stepped out into the perfectly lovely space. It was like a secret garden, immaculately planned, designed, executed, so that exotic plants, paving and stone and glass sculptures joined together to create the effect of both intimacy and space. In one corner stood a fountain with cool water rippling musically over smooth rounded pebbles.

"Nice, isn't it?" he said pulling up an African teak garden chair for her.

"It's just beautiful."

The walls were painted that deep dazzling blue that she'd noticed on many houses in Morocco, when she'd holidayed there once, and the blue coupled with the glass created the cool spacious feel. The lighting, the heat, the lush but neatly pruned clematis, rose, vine and jasmine on a pergola, exotic-looking palms and fern trees, the warm brick underfoot, the sounds of water rippling in the fountain, Miles Davis playing softly in the background – all combined to make the garden as intimate as any cosy little den.

"Cheers!" said Hendro, holding his glass up. He leaned his head back and boldly surveyed her from head to toe, like a connoisseur appraising a painting. He nodded approvingly.

He'd wrong-footed her. She should have seized the initiative and launched straight into business. Instead she had briefly frozen beneath his gaze. It wasn't like her to be side-tracked so easily. Time to get a grip!

She placed her glass on the African teak table and sat forward in her chair.

"I was hoping we could talk about the dinghy," she began hesitantly.

"Great!" he smiled broadly at her.

"What I mean is that we need to sort this business about your dinghy out."

"We do?"

"Yes! We do!"

"How do you mean exactly?"

"I mean it can't go on like this."

"No, I don't suppose it can."

"You will have to do something."

"I will?"

"Yes! You will have to take matters in hand."

"I'd be delighted to."

Floundering in the dark with an Australian rugby player – over the simple matter of a dinghy – nothing else. What was going on?

She stood and zipped up her jacket as though she was heading off on a bombing mission or into outer space.

"Mr Sayers, please –"

"Hendro."

She cleared her throat. "Hendro . . . please remove your thing from my garden. I don't want to be an awkward neighbour – but you simply have no right to use my garden as an extension of your own."

"Oh right! Now I see what you mean. I'll look into it first thing tomorrow," he said quite casually.

"Thanks." She felt vaguely dissatisfied at the way the conversation had gone and sensed that Hendro was not the sort to get over-excited about much in life.

She turned to leave and couldn't resist a proud little glance at the rear of her own house. Even in darkness, its solid Edwardian grandeur looked impressive. It was a fine place. Worth looking after, worth making sacrifices for.

"That's a nice house you've got there," Hendro said as if reading her thoughts. He'd stood up behind her and though she could feel the feather-light sensation of his breath near her skin, she wasn't really paying attention to him. There was something about the house that bothered her. Miss Clementine Barragry's light was on and Sophie could see Clementine setting down a saucer of milk for the cat. She'd left the deck floodlighting on and from Hendro's garden it looked almost warm and inviting. No, it was the apartment above – the one with the mysterious tenant that no-one had ever seen. The light was on and inside, though the blinds were drawn, Sophie could clearly make out the outline of a shadow moving around.

"Excuse me, I really must dash," she said.

By the time she reached the crumbling steps she was completely out of breath. But her curiosity propelled her forward and without even thinking she charged up the stairs, pressed the bell and rapped on the door for good measure. She listened but there was no sound. She pressed the bell once more and peeped through the keyhole – but could see no sign of anyone. Might she have imagined it? In any case it was really none of her business and she began to feel a bit foolish. She was glad of one thing though. The little incident had put all thought of Hendro's magnificent body right out of her mind.

Chapter 12

Hot buttered toast with lashings of strong tea was generally Isobel's simple but effective cure for hangovers. And this morning she had to contend with failure, treachery and despair into the bargain. Somehow she forced herself from the bed, edged her way into the little shower cubicle and set about washing some of the nausea and pain away. But the peach-scented shampoo made her want to throw up. Suddenly it didn't smell like peaches at all – it smelt of vomit. She tried a jojoba-scented one instead. It was worse. At last, sickened by almost every single one of her extensive and expensive range of shampoos – everything from tea tree to prickly pear to custard fruit, she sheepishly rummaged in the back of her bathroom cabinet and pulled out the economy size bottle of Clinic shampoo that Regina Kearney still insisted on buying for her daughter. Remarkably it didn't have the same nauseating smell as the rest and she lathered it through her hair before rinsing it out. Then she reached for Clarins Body Wash – her favourite – crisp-scented, light creamy foam and mild to the skin, but its perfume brought further waves of nausea. In desperation she shampooed herself all over with Clinic. At least she would smell clean and feel fresh. Of course, she would have to hide the half empty bottle from her mother who would shoot right off the maternal gloatometer with this latest evidence that her daughter was getting sense at last. It would be right up there with "You see – there's really nothing so tasty as plain old-fashioned roast beef", "You can't go far wrong with a pair of Bally courts" and "Girls should always play hard to get". Not a shred of truth in any of her mother's grand canon of old-fashioned sayings and observations on the meaning and fabric of life – nonetheless they stuck there, subtly watermarked into Isobel's subconscious.

She wrapped a cotton towel around her head and another about her body while she padded about the tiny kitchenette making toast and brewing tea. At least she could indulge in a little comfort-eating to lift her spirits. While the bread was toasting, she leafed leadenly through the morning post – bills, circulars, a final reminder from the landlord about the renewal of her lease and a card from Cousin Julie who was trekking around New Zealand and having the time of her life by all accounts. She dumped the little pile of mail into a corner of the sofa and retrieved the toast. Then with comfort in mind she spread a generous helping of butter on the toast and lifted it hungrily to her mouth. It was only then that she noticed the smell – the awful smell of butter. Isobel had always been a butter girl. When most of her friends, her mother even, had switched to low-fat, low-cholesterol spreads high in polyunsaturates, Isobel had stuck loyally to butter. How could you make a proper omelette without butter? What did you put on grilled fish or baked potatoes? Butter! How could you make any of the following without butter? Lemon butter? Garlic butter? Herb butter? Butter sauce? Butterscotch sauce? Banoffi pie? Nothing else could match the taste. Until now! Suddenly her stomach began to churn at the mere smell of it and her mouth filled up with a vile taste.

In the end she forced down half a cup of tea, vowed never to drink wine on an empty stomach again, struggled into her workday suit and drove miserably to work. Driving through the gates of the Athena Club, her already queasy stomach lurched and plunged in embarrassment and shame. She felt a fierce sense of failure and rejection. The journey from the little Mazda sports to her office required the summoning up of the few last remaining scraps of her confidence and self-esteem. Somehow she got herself through the main entrance, and along the corridor to her office without anyone noticing. Once inside, she pulled the door shut and sank into her chair. She didn't know what she might do, was still numb with shock from Len Crolly's appointment. But she'd have to give the matter some thought. She drew out a page and began to list her options. She could stay and take the job of Assistant Deputy Senior Manager. That would mean swallowing her pride and working very closely with Crolly, biting her lip when he stole her best ideas and presented them as his own, holding her tongue when he got it completely wrong. She would have to be contented with a measly salary increase that might, if managed properly, just about pay for an upgrade on her mobile phone.

Or she could leave the Athena, hand in her notice and look for work elsewhere. But where could she go? What sort of job should she look for? She'd been with the Athena for the crucial early years of her working life, had planned to stay there until she'd made it to a senior management position. At which point she would find it much easier to get a good job with another company. Besides Isobel was not a risktaker by nature, not at all like Sophie who all her life had made imaginative leaps in the dark and always seemed to land on her feet. Isobel liked security, continuity, routine. She liked to be able to plan ahead. Isobel didn't like surprises.

Colman met her in the restaurant, sat her down beside the windows overlooking the terrace.

She sipped water.

"How are you?" he asked with gentle solicitousness.

"How do you think I am?"

"I understand your disappointment."

"Do you?"

"Yes, of course. The wife had a very similar experience only last year. She'd hoped for a promotion and was let down."

"I'm not really interested in your wife just now, Colman."

"Isobel, I know this is hard but there's no need to be offensive."

"Isn't there? Isn't there?" She stood up, almost shouting now, not caring that half the clients in the restaurant were looking at her.

"You were supposed to be my friend! You encouraged me to apply for the post! Convinced me I'd get it!"

"Yes, and I thought you had a good chance."

"But you sat on the interview board and appointed Len Crolly all the same. Why? Why did you do that?"

"He was better on the day."

Her whole body trembled with rage and nausea – a hideous combination. She was keenly aware that she was making a complete fool of herself in public, in front of the lissom ladies who stretch and lunch, putting them right off their rocket salads. But she seemed to have lost complete control of her emotions.

"So much for loyalty, Colman!" she said hotly, close to tears.

She was unaware that just at the moment when the words hissed from her mouth, Hendro Sayers happened to be passing by on his way to the steam-room. He didn't like what he saw at all and somehow he sweated a little more than usual that afternoon in the steam-room.

Hendro wasn't the only person to have taken note of her outburst. Late in the afternoon, there was a knock on her office door. It was Len Crolly – looking like an anorexic Jesus Christ in an oversized Louis Copeland suit.

"Isobel? A word?"

She indicated a chair that he might sit on.

"I thought this might be less formal if I came to your office."

He eased himself down into the chair with the air of a

patronising frog. And there was also something monkish about him, a certain measured superiority in his movements and facial expression.

"I understand Colman has told you about my appointment."

She nodded and there was a brief silence as he clasped his hands and waited for her to congratulate him. She couldn't.

"Right then! I heard about your 'conversation' in inverted commas with Colman in the restaurant today."

"What of it?"

"Yes and we need to talk this thing through. It's simply not in anyone's interests to have that sort of thing going on, particularly when clients might overhear. It's my responsibility as leader of this company to – to...."

He paused. Silence filled up the room like a cloud of noxious fumes. But she had no intention of making it easy for him.

He smiled wanly and continued. "To show leadership – wisdom – to captain a happy little ship – oversee a contented crew. If any member of that crew is dissatisfied – then that's my responsibility."

Christ, he must have devoured at least ten management bibles. She wondered acidly what other little gems of managerial wisdom he might like to share with her. His pale brown eyes looked directly at her now – steady, earnest, appealing, sensing her pain but willing to extend the limp hand of friendship. Fearless leadership he'd probably call it. She wondered how he'd passed the personality test – he didn't have a personality.

"I have quite a lot of overtime sheets to work through," she said. "I'm sure you won't want me to fall behind in my work."

"Indeed. No hard feelings then?"

"Hard feelings?" She managed a tight grimace of a smile.

"Grand! Feel free to come and see me about any concerns you might have."

Then he glided out. He hadn't even mentioned the measly promotion that Colman had insisted was coming to her, hers by right.

She worked through the overtime forms, bad-tempered and irritable. There was another knock on the door. This time it was Hendro. He was showered and clean-shaven, now dressed in a cream polo shirt and jeans.

She glowered and glared, not even slightly in the mood for light banter or conversation.

"What do you want?"

"Is everything all right? Only I saw you earlier and you looked very upset."

"Why don't you mind your own business?"

Hendro smiled his easy, confident smile – the one that routinely induced a Mexican wave of female admiration.

"Fair enough if that's what you want. It's just that we seemed to hit it off the other day at Sophie's party. It's only neighbourly concern on my part."

Isobel stood up and began rummaging purposefully through a filing cabinet. "I don't mean to be rude – but I have a mountain of work to do."

"See you then. Take care," he said easily and left.

Chapter 13

Sophie had insisted that Isobel come to dinner. When she arrived at the house in Raglan Road, Sophie was putting the finishing touches to a simple meal of roast chicken breast, peppers and red onions served with a lightly dressed salad. She poured two glasses of chilled cheap and cheerful white Bordeaux and took them out to the deck with Isobel.

Isobel sipped her wine, glowering into the middle distance, reflecting on the base treachery of her fellow man. In an effort to keep the atmosphere light and cheerful, Sophie tried to steer the conversation into the relatively safe waters of food and house decoration.

"There's a company in London that specialises in doing up Edwardian houses – not Georgian, not Victorian, not Art Deco – just Edwardian."

"Really."

"Yes. Isn't it amazing? Not that I can afford it or anything but it seems they guarantee to find all original fittings and details – will even send over a team of craftsmen who work exclusively on Edwardian houses."

"That's nice."

"Stylistically the Edwardians were way ahead of the Victorians – with some surprisingly modern touches ..." She'd taken a few books from the library on the subject and after spending the morning scouring the kitchen, she had spent the afternoon browsing through them.

Alas, Isobel was less than riveted by this wonderful new store of architectural knowledge. She slouched glumly, barely picking at her food.

"Don't you like the food?"

"It's fine. I'm just not hungry."

Sophie produced raspberries and crème fraîche but Isobel shook her head vehemently. The mere thought of cream, which was, of course, a very close relation of butter, sent her insides into another nauseous swirl.

Isobel told her about the scene in the restaurant with Colman, the visit from Len Crolly and Colman's mention of the promotion which she would most certainly merit.

"I don't know what to do . . ." She buried her head miserably in her hands.

"What do you want to do?"

"I want to ritually disembowel Len Crolly with a rusty carving knife. And then I want to empty a bucket of slop over Colman Brady's head."

She was sorry she'd mentioned the word slop. She was still suffering the after-effects of all the wine the night before and it nauseated her just to say the word.

"It's a big disappointment and you wouldn't be human if you weren't upset," said Sophie. "But you've got to be professional about this. In business, you have to be able to shake off your disappointments and move on. Gracious in defeat and all that ..."

"It's not just a little disappointment. I was the best person for the job. That's not vanity or sour grapes. I know I could have done great things. I can't bear it – I can't even understand it. It doesn't add up."

"Meaning?"

"Meaning – someone shafted me. It's the only explanation."

"You're being a bit paranoid, aren't you? After all, someone had to be appointed, someone had to be disappointed. If you had got the job, how do you think it would feel if Len Crolly said you cheated him out of it?"

"Frankly, my dear, I don't give a damn. I don't know how I'm going to face them tomorrow and every other day."

"What about this promotion that Colman mentioned?"

Isobel shrugged. She knew it wasn't a promotion. It was just the consolation prize – the proof positive that she was a failure and that she couldn't even face being a failure and had to be humoured like some whingy little child who'd come last in an egg and spoon race.

"I think you should check it out, first thing tomorrow. Don't wait. Make an appointment to see Crolly, be honest about your disappointment, express your guarded support for him in his new job and mention your own promotion."

Sophie made it all sound simple. Her dispassionate analysis of the situation made things seem less dreadful. Could it be that simple?

"Honestly, Sophie – I just feel such a failure." She felt hot scalding tears brimming up and tried to force them back but couldn't. Next thing she knew she was sobbing her heart out and Sophie was hugging her – and saying "there there" and "have a good cry – it's the best thing".

"You're worse than my mother," Isobel said, half-laughing through the tears.

"What about Phil?" Sophie asked. "Have you told him yet?"

The question brought on a new bout of sobbing and Isobel wailed loudly. It was really about time she came clean about Phil.

"Sophie – about Phil … we … he –"

"*Sshh!*" Sophie hissed suddenly. "Be quiet!"

"But I want to tell you –"

"Stop! Immediately! Don't make a sound."

Isobel was temporarily distracted from her own woes by the odd sight of her old friend tiptoeing over the wooden decking, ear turned upwards towards the ceiling. Then suddenly Sophie dashed into the bedroom, pulled on a pair of trainers and went galloping up the stairs. She reappeared after a few minutes looking confused and perplexed.

"That time when I told you to be quiet – did you hear anything?"

"Anything?"

"Upstairs, I mean. Footsteps? I heard footsteps."

"So?"

"So I've been here for weeks and I haven't met or even laid eyes on the person who lives on the floor above. Don't you think that's strange? And once or twice there's been a light or the sound of footsteps and when I go to check it out – there's no-one there."

"Perhaps it's haunted!" said Isobel scornfully. The story of a phantom lodger upstairs in no way matched her own epic tale of human betrayal and despair and shattered dreams.

"I've spent the whole evening listening to your problems," said Sophie huffily, "and that's all you can say?"

"But it's hardly in the same league. I mean – I've been the victim of a great miscarriage of justice and you're just fretting about a reclusive neighbour and getting your windows replaced. There's no comparison!"

"I'm just curious, that's all," Sophie said coolly and began clearing away the dishes. Isobel made a few half-hearted offers of help but really she just wanted to go home and wallow in peace.

"I'd better go. Thanks for dinner."

"You didn't eat much. Tell you what – why don't you and Phil come round to lunch this Sunday?"

"But I – but we – but he –"

"I won't take no for an answer. I know that Phil and I haven't always seen eye to eye – but he's the love of your life – and so he can't be all bad. This time I'll try and cook something a bit nicer."

Isobel swallowed. She'd been about to tell Sophie about Phil when the business with the flat upstairs started. And now was the moment to tell the whole truth. Then Sophie would understand that the real cause of her despair wasn't just failing to get the job of manager. She'd lost the love of her life, the man to whom she'd given her heart, her soul and her Gold Visa card. And now nothing – but nothing – would ever be the same again.

"Thanks – I'll tell him."

After Isobel had gone, Sophie slumped into the big old battered sofa and leafed through the newspapers. The business with the apartment above had spooked her slightly. Sophie had always been prone to an over-active imagination and now she found herself watching out for sounds and vibrations, imagining all sorts of horror scenarios. The night was dark, no moon, with a light drizzle of rain falling, all of which added to her sense of unease.

The rain was getting heavier now, rattling against the window panes and increasing the feeling of isolation. She turned on the radio for company and, to keep busy, she set about clearing out the big old kitchen dresser. Joe said it was an early Victorian rustic piece. It was still covered in layers of blue paint, had completely missed out on the dipping and stripping craze of the nineties. The cupboards at the base were crammed full of old newspapers, chipped crockery, an ancient iron with old-fashioned woven flex, some strange utensils – a boiled-egg slicer still in its original box, and an old seventies fondue set also still in its box. She found a big cardboard box and threw everything into it, setting it down in the hall to be disposed of with the rubbish in the morning. Then she started on the two drawers – one full of booklets and manuals dating back to the fifties, the other containing nothing but a few badly tarnished pieces of cutlery and a wooden box. Inside the box were several sets of labelled keys – to the outhouses, to the side gate and to the little wooden door at the very back of the garden. Three newish sets of keys were numbered very clearly for the three apartments in the house, left there to be used in case of emergency – like if there was a burst pipe or an electrical fault. She felt vaguely uneasy about having them. They were none of her business and should be stored with the letting agency. In the morning, she would put them in an envelope and post them off. No sense at all in hanging on to them.

The rain at the back door seemed to be getting worse, louder at least, so loud that it sounded almost like harsh scraping.

Scraping?

She opened the door, looked out, got a blast of rain in the face, saw nothing and closed the door once more. When she resumed her place at the table, Tiger the cat was sitting elegantly on a chair and gazing at her intently.

"Oh, my God, cat, you gave me a fright!"

Why was she talking to a cat? She hated cats.

"*Miaow!*"

Tiger lowered herself daintily from the chair and ambled across the kitchen floor, sliding her sleek furry body against Sophie's legs, purring noisily.

"*Shoo!* Go away."

Sophie stood up, anxious to escape. She opened the door and indicated to the cat that it was time to leave. Tiger stared at her incredulously, bemused by her daft human antics, then strolled over to the fridge and positioned herself very pointedly at the door, refusing to budge until milk was produced. When the saucer was empty she rubbed herself against Sophie's legs once more, purring loudly as if to say "Now you're getting the idea!"

"Now will you go?" Sophie said, throwing open the back door once more.

The cat glanced out briefly into the darkness, took a cursory feline rain-check, then turned on her heel and rambled off to find the most comfortable chair in the house. What could Sophie do short of picking the creature up and risking a severe scratching? It looked like she had a companion for the night after all.

She woke suddenly to pitch darkness and sat bold upright in bed. It was past midnight. There was a noise of some sort. She was sure of it – some soft noise that she couldn't quite identify.

"Damn cat!"

But when she slipped out of the bed, she found the cat curled up, fast asleep in a warm corner of the vast old bed, head propped regally on a pillow. The cheek! But as she cursed the cat, Sophie realised something else. If the cat hadn't made the noise – someone or something else must have done.

All the telltale signs of terror now filled her – uncontrollable trembling, cold sweats, hair bristling at the back of her head. Noise in the house in the deep, dark middle of the night – empty apartment overhead! There was only one rational answer – a giant, man-eating, homicidal, slime-coated, weirdo, psychotic, mutant zombie creature from outer space! Oh God! It all made sense now! The reason why her mother had got the house so cheaply in the eighties! The way she'd never met the occupant of the apartment above! The strange lights and noises!

Tiger opened one accusing eye, repositioned herself for greater comfort and promptly went back to sleep. Little noises seemed to be coming from all directions now. What if this hatchet-wielding zombie weirdo slaughtered her? Who would notice? It wasn't as if she'd be expected in work the next day? She might lie there for days before being found. And then what if the cat got hungry?

She was being absurd. She knew it. Next thing she'd be checking under the bed and behind the curtains like she did as a little girl. She'd have to get a grip.

"You're a fat lot of use!" she said scornfully to the cat, who twitched an ear to indicate that she had no intention of getting involved in any middle-of-the-night disturbances.

Sophie went into the kitchen, and made a cup of tea. The everyday ritual of making, pouring and drinking the tea brought her back to her senses. She smiled at her own foolishness, rinsed her cup in the sink, dried it carefully and returned it to its place on the dresser.

Then she remembered the keys in the drawer.

Minutes later, tiptoeing up the stairs, she told herself that she wasn't doing anything wrong – not snooping, not spying really – just putting her mind at rest. Why else were the keys put there? After all there had to be someone in the house who had access to all the rooms. It was only common sense. Supposing Clementine got too ill to get out of bed? Supposing the unknown occupant got accidentally locked out? Sophie needed those keys. It was her responsibility to have those keys. And it was her responsibility now to ensure the safety of all the present occupants of the house – namely herself.

But, hovering outside the door of the apartment, it struck her that it might be more sensible to wait till morning. Mindful of all those horror movies where the heroine feels insanely compelled to go investigating in the dead of night, Sophie decided to bide her time. In just a few short hours it would be daylight. She could wait till then.

A couple of hours later daylight finally came. She hadn't slept a wink and, with her mind still brimming with horror scenarios, she hesitated outside the door of the apartment once more. She listened for sounds and heard nothing. Tiger had joined her – more in a spirit of mild curiosity than female solidarity – and sat patiently at her feet, waiting for the next stage of this strange human behaviour. Besides there was always the chance, however remote, that it might involve another saucer of warm milk.

Sophie turned the key in the door. She was sorry now that she hadn't armed herself with a weapon of some sort – an umbrella or a mop would have done well enough – even a can of deodorant might be effective. The door opened easily into a large oak-panelled lobby that was almost in complete darkness.

At first glance it didn't exactly seem like the lair of a seriously deranged mass murderer from outer space – no vile-looking implements of torture, no blood on the carpet, no spine-chilling still-smouldering cigar, and no terrifying shadowy corners. Early morning light spilled in through the large sashed windows and it all looked very – ordinary. She inspected the substantial bookshelves on either side of the fireplace first. Bookshelves were always a good indicator of personality. But she was mildly surprised to note that none of the following titles were to be found on the shelves:

Serial-killing for Dummies; Teach Yourself Mass Murder; The Seven Habits of Highly Effective Axe Murderers; Chicken Soup for the Living Dead! Instead the shelves groaned with a selection of history, politics, an array of biographies – Nelson Mandela, Bill Gates, Yuri Gagarin, Alf Ramsey, Paudie O'Shea and Roy Keane. Two shelves were given over entirely to sport – lots of golf, some horses, Gaelic, soccer and fishing. She pulled one or two books down, examined them for a name or a date – but they held no clues. Except, of course, the obvious one – the occupant of this apartment was most definitely a man. If the books hadn't told her, the rest of the room spelt it out in no uncertain terms. It was furnished in a heavy masculine way – generous black leather sofas complementing solid Victorian sideboards and tables, some prints on the wall of horses and golfers and ships, no curtains – just heavy blinds, no cushions, no bowls of potpourri, and no scented candles. A few magazines rested in an untidy pile on a coffee table, and a daily newspaper. She examined the date. Yesterday's!

She suppressed a shiver and continued to explore. In the main bedroom was a large bed, not slept in, more book shelves, a shower room tiled with black and white marble, and a small dressing-room. She couldn't resist checking the clothes. They were bound to offer some clue but he was a man of few clothes apparently. Two fine woollen suits – Italian – hung on the rail, freshly dry-cleaned, and a number of heavy woollen sweaters and corduroy trousers showed a preference for casual if slightly old-fashioned clothes. But there were no clues about his identity, no credit-card receipts, no monogrammed ties, no driver's licence. It was as if his clothes had been bought and arranged simply to make it look like someone was living there – almost like a film set.

She sat down into one of the deep sofas and was joined by Tiger. Sophie was tired, drained from the midnight terror. It was early morning and she was confused and perplexed and now that she'd wasted so much time inspecting the apartment, she was beginning to feel foolish and ashamed. Tiger nuzzled up against her. Without thinking she began rubbing the cat's cheek and was rewarded with loud purring, the sound of which was oddly soothing and which quite rapidly sent her into a deep, exhausted sleep.

She woke an hour later. On the floor was an empty milk saucer. Over her legs was a warm Foxford rug.

"Hello?" she called out.

There was no reply.

She could think of only two possible explanations – either the occupant had come and found her asleep on his sofa, which thought filled her with shame, embarrassment and fear – or Tiger was a very clever cat!

Chapter 14

The sun hovered over the purple-grey curves and dips of distant mountains, casting a warm orange glow on the village of Hollymaine.

"I'm bursting for the loo," Isobel told Sophie as soon as they'd parked the car. She jumped out and dashed into a nearby bar before Sophie could reply.

It had been a long hot drive, tiresome as always to be driving westward with the sun hitting her square in the eyes at every turn, but worth it in the end. For the past few days Isobel's body had been an aching tangle of bitterness and despair, her heart a mangled knot of emptiness – if there could possibly be such a thing as a mangled knot of emptiness? It made no sense – but that was how Isobel felt in her heart – a mangled knot of emptiness. It had taken all Sophie's powers of persuasion to talk her into going home for the weekend. Even driving westward she couldn't resist carping about the place.

"I couldn't live here. I've so left it behind. I can't imagine ever spending longer than a night in Hollymaine again." Once or twice on the journey, she'd crabbily insisted on stopping at a pub, making an urgent dash inside and then emerging some minutes later looking vaguely chirpier.

But almost as soon as her red Mazda sports car negotiated the little hump-backed bridge and swung round to the broad tree-lined street, Isobel had felt her heart unknotting. The treachery of Len Crolly – so violently felt in recent days – now seemed remote and unimportant. The heartbreak of Phil Campion became almost bearable. For a brief moment she practically even entertained that other great lie of her mother's: "Plenty more fish in the sea, Isobel pet."

Minutes later, Isobel reappeared and they decided on an ice cream in Nora Brehony's store.

Nora welcomed the girls home, while whipping up the Beluga caviar of the ice-cream world – Brehony's deliciously creamy and disgustingly large and fattening ninety-nines. Exotic ice creams in tubs that brought to mind all sorts of steamy nine-and-a-half-week-type scenarios were all very well in their place. But Nora's large, creamy, unpretentious ninety-nines were in a pleasure zone all of their own. She piled them high in soft erotic coils, and then pressed hard rippling Chocolate Flakes in, as she dispensed the less damaging snippets of local gossip.

"I see Maeve and Kenny are building an extension.

Oak floors, stained-glass panels, a glass bath – if you don't mind."

"Didn't know you could get such a thing," said Isobel as she sank her lips gratefully into the cold ice cream.

"What do you make of it, Sophie?"

"Good for Maeve," she said through a mouth full of ice cream and little shards of Flake.

"Glass bath – I ask you? Anyway – to more important things. Katie and Ronan have set the day. And I expect you girls to be there."

Katie was Nora's youngest daughter – full-figured, long-lashed big green eyes, with one dazzling smile that could melt a man's heart at fifty paces and another withering smile that could freeze his marrow and curdle his blood for all eternity. Ronan was a local farmer who ran a thriving little insurance business on the side. They'd been in love forever.

Isobel and Sophie drove to Tess's in silence, envious of love's young dream, baffled that Katie who'd never left the parish of Hollymaine should come so easily to happy-ever-afterdom. In a sense it wasn't fair.

Tess was in the garden when they arrived, digging over a small vacant patch of soil in a sunny border, where she intended to plant summer bulbs.

"Why don't you get Kenny to do that for you?" Sophie said.

"He might get dirt on his Calvin Kleins. Anyway, I like to be busy. And I've always kept a nice house and I don't plan to stop now." She leaned on the garden fork, flushed and breathless from exertion. "But I'm finished for today.

Come on inside. I've a lovely juicy rhubarb-tart, just ready from the oven."

Isobel was glad because she'd just spotted a worm wriggling in the newly turned earth and it was having quite a horrible effect on her. Or perhaps it was the large ice cream. Either way, her stomach was churning. Her mouth filled up with saliva. In the kitchen, the usually irresistible smell of Tess's home baking sent her reeling to the armchair with nausea.

"Are you all right? You're very pale," Tess said, eyeing her closely.

"I'm fine!" Isobel struggled to compose herself. "Too much cold ice cream on a warm stomach – that's all."

"Here, this might help," said Tess, offering her a glass of cool water.

"I was always a poor traveller. Don't you remember, Sophie, how my dad always had those funny strips hanging from the back of the car to stop me being sick all over his velour upholstery?"

She took a few sips from the glass hoping it would settle the waves of nausea that were threatening to engulf her. But it was no good. Somehow, she hauled herself from the chair, dashed into the little cloakroom off the hall and slammed the door just in time. Sophie listened in acute embarrassment to sounds of projectile vomiting, gasps and muffled swearing. She blushed and shifted uncomfortably, watching an array of expressions flash across her grandmother's face.

"I'm sorry, Gran. It must have been the ice cream. Don't worry, I'll clean up," she said apologetically. She had begun to feel a growing sense of unease about Isobel.

Tess waved her hand dismissively and made a pot of tea. "Just as well it didn't happen in Kenny and Maeve's house. They'd probably insist on having the whole place redecorated. It's a new religion with them. The house is like some kind of cathedral and anyone who visits has to put in at least an hour of worship at the shrine of interior decorating. Ridiculous!"

"I heard about the glass bath."

"Kenny saw it in a magazine and had to have it – mainly because no-one else in the parish has one."

Sounds of flushing came from the cloakroom, then running water. Isobel emerged, grey and drawn. She did get as far as bringing a bucket and mop to the door but a fresh wave of nausea overcame her and Sophie was forced to wade in and clean up as Isobel side-stepped the old rocking-chair which might induce further nausea and lowered herself gingerly into a sturdy chair by the range.

"You owe me big-time for this, Isobel Kearney," Sophie called out from the bathroom.

"I am really, really sorry, Mrs O'Meara. I am so deeply, truly, awfully sorry. I don't know how it could have happened."

"You'd better go and lie down. You don't look much better."

"Thanks," said Isobel before quickly scooping up her handbag and slinking off to the guest room at the top of the stairs.

While Sophie wiped and mopped and flush-brush-flushed, bleached and disinfected, blasted air freshener about and threw the window wide open, Tess sat at the table sorting through a collection of summer bulbs. When Sophie returned she looked up and eyed her granddaughter over the rim of her bifocals.

"You two must think I came down in the last shower. A sweet old lady who can't see past these little spectacles on the end of her nose."

"What do you mean, Gran?"

"I mean – it's perfectly clear what's wrong with Isobel Kearney so don't insult my intelligence."

Sophie had to think for a moment, unsure at first what her grandmother was implying. But then it came to her – why she had begun to feel uneasy about Isobel. Dear God – why hadn't she thought of it? It seemed so obvious now that Gran – sweet, wise, perceptive Gran – had mentioned it. And all the signs were there – only she'd been too stupid to notice them or realise their significance. The nausea, the ghastly complexion, the dreadful vomiting, the bouts of trembling, the weight loss, the excessive anxiety and depression over not getting the promotion, the sudden stops at bars on the journey westwards, the drunkenness, the generally erratic behaviour. There was only one possible explanation.

Isobel was an alcoholic – a secret alcoholic – clearly in the worst stages of it.

"I never thought ..." she said, realisation dawning.

"Well, you must be blind – that's all I can say."

"What can we do? She needs help. Urgently! I know a great doctor in Dublin. But I feel awful – like I should have known, should have recognised her cries for help.

What kind of friend am I?"

"There wasn't much you could have done to prevent it."

"I could have tried. Kept in touch, written, emailed, called. But maybe it's not too late."

"Too late?"

"To do something. This is the twenty-first century. It's not a big deal for a woman any more to –"

"Don't you think that's a decision that only Isobel can make?"

"I suppose so," said Sophie dubiously and would have teased the matter out further with her grandmother, but just at that moment Kenny and Maeve's Range Rover swept regally across the gravelled driveway and parked with presidential grandeur right in front of the kitchen window.

Maeve stepped down from the gleaming black vehicle, dressed on this occasion in a magnificently dazzling combination of tight paisley Moschino top, cropped slightly to reveal the merest hint of a smooth rounded and studded belly, low Prada boots under hip-slinging jeans and a Barbour hacking jacket. Her shoulder-length highlighted hair, cut recently and straightened to a standard of haute fashion that would put the fashionista of Milan or Paris to shame, gleamed and shimmered in the bright Mayo sunlight. Her full pink mouth glistened provocatively beneath layers of Shiseido lipstick. Pretty little blue eyes smouldered behind an elaborate frame of sparkling blue and green shades.

Sophie, who'd absent-mindedly lashed on a bit of lip

gloss on the long drive westwards, looked pale and dowdy in comparison, her jeans and loose T-shirt no match for Maeve's mega-fashionable fabulousness.

"And how do you think the bould Tess is looking? She's a game old woman, fair play to her. She'd put us all to shame with her energy."

Kenny babbled on as if Sophie's grandmother wasn't present at all and being always soft-spoken there was no way that Tess could shout him down even if she'd wanted to. All she could do, all anyone could do was to wait until the long stream of flaccid nonsense fizzled out – as it did eventually.

"Tea, anyone?" asked Tess.

"She's a very interesting woman, your grandmother." Kenny spoke in a slightly accusing tone to Sophie. "Full of stories about the old times – aren't you, Tess? – fair play to you!"

He caught Tess's hands between his and squeezed them affectionately.

Tess caught Sophie's eye as if to say 'This is the irritating crap that I have to put up with on a daily basis'. As if on cue, Maeve produced the remains of a fine joint of beef and half an apple-tart.

"I know you love a bit of beef, Tess. And I think one never bothers to cook beef when one is on one's own."

"No, I don't suppose one does," said Tess.

"I've got a lovely hat you can wear for Katie's wedding. I'll bring it next time and here is that coat I was telling you about. I'm sure it will look lovely on you."

Maeve held out a newly dry-cleaned black cashmere

coat, still in its cellophane wrapping. "All the way from Paris, Tess."

She pulled the wrapping away and held up the coat for the rest of the company to admire. It was undoubtedly a fine coat.

"I still love it – but it's just the teeniest bit too mature-looking for me."

"You'd look wonderful in anything." Kenny beamed at her and squeezed her hand affectionately.

Maeve smiled stiffly at him and unbuttoned the coat before draping it across Tess's shoulders.

"Now!" she said triumphantly. "You look like Lauren Bacall in that coat!"

"She's much older than me!" Tess said crossly and pulled a face.

"Then – like – like – Liz Taylor, Joan Collins, the Queen?" Maeve quickly exhausted her knowledge of glamorous women over the age of sixty.

Kenny intervened to smooth things over. "More like Julia Roberts, you are, Tess. Amn't I right, Sophie? Julia Roberts or that Cindy Crawford."

"Don't be ridiculous, Kenny!" Maeve snapped.

It was clear that Maeve meant well in spite of her tactlessness. And perhaps Tess was being the slightest bit oversensitive. It was a lovely coat. And all the women that Maeve mentioned were glamorous in their own way. As for Kenny – well, he might be just plain thick. And there was no law against being thick. Being thick didn't necessarily mean you were a bad person, did it?

"We'll be off," Kenny said now. "I'm sure you two

ladies have plenty to talk about. Get Tess talking about the old times – she can remember the fifties like it was yesterday – a national archive in her own right – fair play to her!"

Tess fumed quietly.

"And don't forget to tell Sophie about your little up-and-coming change of address," said Kenny with what was meant to be a mysterious smile.

Sophie looked at her grandmother in surprise.

"There's no need to tell her – because it won't be happening, Kenny," Tess said with pointed coolness.

"What won't be happening?" asked Sophie, now in some confusion.

"She needs to get some major work done on the house – the roof, plumbing – all that," said Kenny as if Tess wasn't there. "So she's going to move in with us for a while – and who knows, she might even stay. What's the sense in her living alone when she could have us for company?"

There was an uncomfortable silence while Maeve grinned foolishly at Tess and Kenny fumbled in his pocket for the car keys.

"Maybe you'll have a man with you the next time you're down, Sophie," he said then, squeezing her shoulders, a slight bit too affectionately.

"You see what I mean?" said Tess when they'd left.

Sophie thought it best to say nothing.

"Kenny has about as much tact as a herd of stampeding elephants."

"I'm sure they mean well."

"You think so?"

"Of course," said Sophie, trying hard not to catch her grandmother's eye, but failing miserably. Within moments they were laughing helplessly.

At last, when the giggles had subsided, Sophie said more seriously: "At least they're not mean to you, Gran. And it's always good to have someone you can call at a moment's notice."

Tess nodded but didn't reply.

"What's all this about you moving in with them?"

"It's nonsense. I'm going to rent a house while I get this place fixed up. Wild horses wouldn't drag me to Kenny and Maeve's place. I'd rather live in a tent."

"But if it's only for a few weeks – I don't see why you wouldn't –"

"It's out of the question," said Tess stubbornly.

"Then why don't you come to Dublin for a while? The break might do you good. We could shop and walk and you could help me out with choosing stuff for the house. Please say yes, Gran."

"Maybe in a few weeks," Tess said vaguely.

"Why not this week? There's a great new play on at the theatre, or that new George Clooney movie."

"Not just now," Tess said, oddly tetchy. "It doesn't really suit just now."

Sophie felt mildly puzzled but knew not to push the matter. Her grandmother had always been an intensely private person.

Chapter 15

In the morning, Isobel seemed much better. But Sophie's worst fears were realised when, checking for tell-tale signs of secret drinking, she found a whole bottle of brandy in Isobel's weekend case. Then, passing by Isobel's empty room, coming back from the bathroom, she couldn't resist having another quick rummage through the case which was thrown open messily on the bed. The brandy was gone. But she could hardly confront Isobel. She would probably deny it anyway. Sophie only knew one thing about alcoholism – that admitting the problem was half the battle. Perhaps she would bring it up casually in conversation on the journey back to Dublin. She might begin by telling Isobel how important their friendship was, how they were like sisters, how they should always feel they could confide absolutely anything to one another.

While they were having breakfast, Robert Franklin

arrived and while Tess rustled up an extra plate for him, Isobel mumbled quietly to Sophie: "He could still give Johnny Depp a run for his money!"

This morning he'd been for a long walk with the dogs and brought Tess a bunch of roses from the gardens of his strange estate.

"Does he still have the same weird living arrangements?" Isobel whispered.

"Yes, as far as I know."

He kissed Sophie lightly on the cheek and she marvelled as ever at his smooth tanned skin, his clear dark-brown eyes and how he always smelt of apples and fresh linen – definitely not bad going for a single man who lived alone.

"So – home on a flying visit?" he said, smiling easily at her.

"Something like that."

"Maybe you and Isobel will come and have dinner with me next time you visit Tess?"

Sophie and Isobel exchanged looks. As teenagers, they'd had the most enormous joint crush on Robert Franklin. They'd dreamed of being invited to spend an evening with him. Even now the idea put a warm sparkle in their eyes. And, of course, they were plain curious. The only person who'd ever set foot in Robert's place was Tess – a woman renowned for her discretion.

"We'd love to. Have you finished your book yet?"

Robert was compiling a book about pre-historic monuments of the West of Ireland. He'd been working on it ever since anyone could remember. He ran a lean, tanned hand through his thick chestnut hair and smiled modestly.

"I'm afraid to finish it."

"What do you mean?"

"Well, as soon as it's finished and bound and published, all the bona fide academics will be out in force to hack it to shreds."

"So?"

"And besides I'll have nothing to do with my time."

"Write another book."

His mouth curled up in a rueful smile. "You think it's that simple?"

"Of course. Just do it. We'll read it and we won't hack it to shreds. So there!" said Sophie, smiling warmly at him.

As Isobel still seemed a little off-colour, Sophie gathered up their things and loaded them into the boot of the car. At last everything including some of Tess's brown bread and scones was packed into the tiny boot.

"Need a hand with anything?" It was Robert.

"All done, thanks," she said, slamming the lid of the boot shut.

"It's nice to see you," he said, hands shoved into his jeans pockets.

"Thanks, and you too."

There was a moment's awkwardness as he lingered – like there was something else he wanted to say.

"I'm very fond of Tess," he said then.

"Yes, I know. I'm glad. She's very fond of you too."

He seemed surprised, very surprised, almost relieved.

"Are you? Glad, I mean? Because she means the world to me and I would never hurt her. Only I thought . . . you might have heard . . . and people say the stupidest things . . . the tale gets longer with the telling . . . you know how it is in small communities. So you don't mind?"

Sophie stared at him for a moment, trying to divine what he might be hinting at. She blanched, then blushed at the first thought that occurred to her. Her grandmother had only recently admitted to having had some kind of lover in years gone by. And now for a brief moment she wondered if there could possibly be something between Robert and Tess. But that was an absolutely ridiculous idea and instantly she lowered her head, embarrassed and a little amused by her over-active imagination. As if Robert would have any interest in her grandmother!

"Mind? What's to mind?" she said now quickly. "Eh – we really should be off." She hollered into the house, "Come on, Isobel – we're going! Hurry up!"

With Robert standing lazily by her side, Tess smiled placidly and wished them a pleasant trip back to Dublin.

"Bye, Gran – you take care of yourself and come and visit soon," Sophie said, hugging Tess tightly, and feeling very protective of her suddenly.

"Don't worry," said Tess. "I have good neighbours and Robert comes every day." She pressed fifty euro into Sophie's hand "to buy a little treat", despite doomed attempts at steely resistance. "And about Isobel ..."

"Don't worry, Gran – I'll make her get help."

"I was only going to say – tell her the best thing is to

stay away from anything except Jacobs Cream Crackers and plain spring water for a while."

It was strange advice to give to an alcoholic.

Isobel laughed heartily when she heard about Robert and Tess and what Sophie had fleetingly thought about them.

"You always had an over-active imagination. I mean that business with the upstairs apartment the other night, and then your ridiculous fear of flying. You invariably let things get completely out of proportion to the facts. As if Tess or Robert would have even the slightest romantic interest in one another!"

"No, of course not. But stranger things have happened."

"You're not seriously suggesting that your grandmother, a woman on the verge of seventy, who looks fantastic – but not that fantastic – is having rumpy-pumpy with hunky Robert?"

"No, of course not, but it does happen.. Look at all those film stars and their toy boys? The thing is – he might take advantage of her. He's penniless, you know. Maybe he's a closet gigolo."

Isobel had grown quiet, and Sophie wondered if she was straining at the leash to have her first drink of the day. She remembered the bottle of brandy in the weekend case and vowed to tackle Isobel about it later. They drove along in companionable silence for a while but they'd been on the road barely an hour when Isobel pulled up outside a run-down old pub and announced that she needed a toilet. Urgently!

"I'll come with you," said Sophie quickly.

"It's OK. I'll remember to flush and wash my hands."

"I need to go anyway."

Isobel dashed through the door of the bar, clattered across the wooden floor and flung herself into a dingy cubicle that proclaimed itself to be a toilet and just about managed to reach the sink before throwing up. Hot on her heels, Sophie flung open the door – expecting to find her sucking urgently from the neck of a brandy bottle.

"Oh God! I don't know what's wrong with me. I thought it was the wine the other night. Then I thought it was the cold ice cream yesterday – but I was really careful today and I just had scrambled egg on toast for breakfast."

At the mention of the word egg, she turned green again.

At last, when there was nothing left, Sophie decided she could contain herself no longer.

"Isobel, I can't stand by and watch you do this to yourself! I'm going to make you get help. I'm going to sit down with Phil and we are going to get you through this thing – whatever it takes. We're your friends. We love you."

Isobel was staring at her vacantly. "What thing?"

"This thing! This alcohol thing! Isobel, there's no sense in denying it to me. I know you too well."

"What on earth are you talking about? I haven't had a drink since that night in your house and that's almost a week ago."

"You see!" said Sophie triumphantly. "You've even been counting the days."

"Yes – seven days! That's hardly Priory Clinic time – is it?"

"Denial! You're in denial. And what about that bottle of brandy you got through last night? Oh yes, Isobel – I found it – I know I shouldn't have been snooping but I care about you and it's for your own good."

Isobel continued to stare at her blankly.

"Oh, what's the use?" Sophie went on. "I can't help you until you admit the truth to yourself. So I guess I'll just go on being your friend and hoping you take that first painful step to recovery. By the way for what it's worth, and God knows what she'd know about being an alcoholic, but Tess says that . . . well, her exact words were: stay away from anything except Jacobs Cream Crackers and plain spring water for a while."

Isobel, in the middle of splashing cold water on her face, froze. If it was possible for her to turn a greyer shade of grey and still maintain a strong green tinge, she did.

At last she found her voice. "Run that by me again, would you . . .?"

"What?"

"What Tess said? Just repeat it to me . . . word for word."

Sophie went back over Tess's advice.

"Now I do need a drink!" Isobel croaked.

"But you mustn't. You can't. You're an alcoholic. You're driving!"

"A brandy and port now! At the bar! You can drive! And I'm not an alcoholic, Sophie!" She tore out of the ladies' and made her way to the dingy counter.

Sophie could see there was little point in arguing. She sipped virtuously on coffee and puffed rather less virtuously on a cigarette and cast disapproving looks at Isobel as she raised the glass to her mouth with a trembling hand and drank in silence. It was truly pathetic to watch. Only when the glass was empty could Isobel speak.

"My mother told me that she lived on cream crackers and soda water for the first three months she was expecting me," she said dully.

Yes, that was another aspect of alcoholism – disordered thoughts, disjointed conversation! Paranoid delusions!

But all the same, a little shiver of something like fear shot down Sophie's spine. Briefly, she considered persisting with her alcoholic theory. In many respects it was by far the more manageable sort of catastrophe – Isobel could own her alcoholism, admit herself into the clinic, deal with her addiction and emerge as a great survivor, even sell her story to the newspapers. But this new unspoken possibility brought terror on a previously unimaginable scale – babies.

"Do you remember that lovely old Irish proverb?" said Isobel as she emerged from the toilet a second time.

"What?"

"One door never shuts – but another ten slam and knock the complete crap out of you? And by the way – that bottle of brandy you found in my bag?"

"Yes," croaked Sophie.

"It was a present for Tess. I gave it to her this morning before you got up."

Much, much later, when they'd arrived back in Dublin, when they were sitting in Sophie's kitchen and Isobel was sipping water very apprehensively, the full truth about Phil came out.

"But why didn't you tell me?"

"Because you are so happy ever after with Frank Lloyd Wright – the perfect man – I just couldn't face it."

Sophie laughed at the irony of it. Then it was time to come clean about Daniel. And it was strange but once she'd told Isobel, her decision to leave Daniel didn't seem so bad. They stared at each other for a moment then hugged and comforted one other, shed oceans of wretched tears and heaved mountains of anguished sighs. At last the storm of emotion passed.

"So we're both currently manless," Sophie said in a spirit of solidarity and hoping it would lessen Isobel's pain.

"Yeah, but you're not pregnant whereas I might be. You can pick yourself up and start a new life that has nothing to do with Daniel. You can go back to college, do a dazzlingly interesting course and carve out a whole new career for yourself. Me – I might be stuck with the memory of Phil Campion for the rest of my days – whether I like it or not. It was bad enough that he scrounged off me for the past several years – what if I have a bit of him with me forever? I couldn't bear it." She buried her head in her hands. "Oh God, I feel so awful!"

Sophie picked her words carefully. "Even if you are pregnant – you don't have to have it."

"How do you mean?"

"I mean you can get rid of it. You're not very pregnant – only very slightly. I mean you're only a few days late – and Tess may still be wrong. You're probably not pregnant at all."

"When was the last time Tess was wrong about something?"

Sophie racked her brains, rummaged frantically through the mists of time to remember a moment when her grandmother hadn't been proven right on just about every major aspect of life. "She lost a bit of money on those Vodaphone shares a while back."

"Not the same."

"She predicted hems would fall last autumn."

"This is not a time for flippancy."

"There's only one way you're going to find out for sure. I bought it for you on the way. It's in the bathroom cabinet. All you have to do is go in there, pee onto a strip of paper and wait for the thin blue line."

Isobel jumped up and made a bee-line for the bathroom. She closed and locked the door and Sophie waited for the dreadful news, trying to think herself into her friend's shoes – the awful spectre of an unwanted pregnancy – the terrifying thought that she might be carrying the child of someone as awful as Phil Campion, the alarming prospect of being stuck with a little piece of Phil Campion for the rest of her natural life.

Babies had not yet become a feature of their lives. None of their close friends had any, except for Mary O'Connor who was happily married and on her third child. Mary had arrived into this world with a label attached that read: *Absolutely and Completely Suited to Motherhood*. And she was. Sophie and Isobel regarded her with pity and a vague sense of envious disquiet. She was doormat, mobile milk-dispensing machine, all-day taxi service – her brain impaired from lack of sleep and the constant answering of a barrage of such deep philosophical questions as "Why are crows black? Where do frogs sleep? Can fish talk to one another? Do cars have feelings?" She smelt of congealed potato-mash and play-dough. Her favourite book was *Doctor Xargle's book of Earthlets*. She was in a Residents' Association.

The bathroom door opened and Isobel emerged.

"Well?"

"I can't do it."

"You have to."

"I can't do it and you can't make me do it."

"I can."

"How? You can't make me pee if I don't want to."

"It's better to know."

"It's better to not know. As long as I don't know for sure, I can just pretend I have a tummy-bug. I can go on pretending I have a tummy-bug for months on end."

"That's plain silly."

Isobel shrugged, picked up her keys and went home. She would not entertain the prospect of pregnancy for one moment longer. It didn't bear thinking about. And of course, Tess was wrong. It was merely a tummy-bug – nothing else.

Chapter 16

Almost a week had passed and Isobel still hadn't plucked up the courage to do the pregnancy test. The slender blue box sat on her dressing-table at home, mocking her cruelly. Her fate, her entire future, the size of her waistline, her body-fat ratio, the shape of her breasts even – lay in that little blue box. Strange that an insignificant little scrap of plastic could hold such power over human destiny. She covered it up with her best turquoise silk La Perla knickers and stuck it in the back of the knicker drawer. But it radiated its disturbing power at her all the same.

Mealtimes had shrunk to cream crackers and mineral water. Even that was a battle. She'd take the crackers from the box, place them defiantly on a plate, and chant and hum to herself, sipping water and willing herself to get the cracker to her mouth and into her stomach without retching. She discovered that if she ate one cracker and remained quite still for an hour afterwards the urge to throw up would eventually pass. The worst thing of all was the vile metallic taste in her mouth – as if she'd swallowed a bar of rusty iron. The only consolation was that such a vile taste couldn't possibly have anything to do with being pregnant.

In the space of three weeks she lost half a stone. She also lost all her energy, the sparkle in her warm hazel eyes, the colour in her cheeks, the shine in her chestnut-brown hair, the plump fresh pinkness of her lips and her usually athletic posture.

"I look like I'm dying," she told Isobel over the phone.

"Did you do the test?"

"What for? I can't be pregnant. It's not possible. I'm losing weight not gaining it. Maybe I am dying. Perhaps I should see a doctor. What if I die? I'm just not ready to die. It wouldn't be fair."

"You're not dying."

"How would you know?"

There was no-one at work she could talk to. Colman was away on one last business trip. Laura was up to her eyes in quarterly reports. To rub salt into her wounds, Len Crolly had called a compulsory meeting in the afternoon, no doubt to dazzle staff with his stunning plans for the five-acre site. She had to attend. And listen! And approve! And clap! And congratulate him! It was what losers did after all.

On the off-chance that her poor health was caused by bad diet and lack of exercise, she decided to use the gym during lunch-break. At least it was better than sitting in the restaurant where the smell of food was liable to send her scrambling for the lady's rest room.

Carina, one of the health instructors, set her up on the treadmill and suggested that since she was young and fit a good jogging pace for thirty minutes would be an ideal start. The treadmill started, slowly at first. Isobel's feet quickly found a rhythm, moving from stroll, through brisk walk to jog. But after only a few minutes her stomach began to roll and tumble like a ship tossing about on a stormy sea. Then the room seemed to shift, slightly at first, then began spinning rapidly.

"Oh God, I'm going to be sick," she wailed and careered off the treadmill like a drunken octopus.

She might have banged her head and suffered a nasty concussion, if it hadn't been for Hendro who just at that moment happened to be passing on his way to the weights room. Quick as a flash his massive arms gathered her up and whisked her away to a quiet rest area.

"You look awful."

"Thrmpks," she mumbled thickly.

"I mean you don't look well at all. Are you sick?"

"Sick? No. Yes. I think I'm dying. Something terminal. You shouldn't come close. It might be catching."

"I'd better get you home. You should see a doctor."

"No!" She sat up and made a valiant effort to look as if there was nothing wrong at all. "I have an important meeting."

No way was she going to give Crolly the chance to badmouth her for not turning up. Besides, cringingly awful as it was, she had to lick up to him, at least until she got the measly promotion that Colman had mentioned.

Hendro disappeared and quickly returned with a damp flannel and a glass of water. He sponged her face over and encouraged her to take little sips of water – not big gulps.

"Any better?"

"Yes. Thanks."

The little sips worked.

"I'm OK now. Thanks again."

She stood up carefully, straightened her hair and walked back gingerly to her office.

The boardroom was set up for all senior members of staff when Isobel arrived. Charlie from Marketing and Pete from Customer Care were there before her, using the time to dash off a few emails on their laptops. Crolly buzzed about self-importantly like a magician about to perform some breathtaking piece of wizardry. His laptop was primed and ready, a flashy computer-generated image of an athlete zapping across the screen to grab the audience's attention. And as if poor Laura didn't have enough work on her plate, Crolly had enlisted her help for the meeting. Now she dashed about placing folders and handouts in each person's place, setting down a tray with water and glasses, murmuring solemnly to Len about minutes and matters arising.

Isobel wished he'd just get on with it. It would probably bore the pants off everyone anyway. Crolly was about as interesting to listen to as static on a bad radio – and ten times more irritating. When the room was full and there were no more last-minute jobs for Laura, Crolly drew in his breath, fiddled with his polyester tie, did a little shimmy in his oversized Louis Copeland suit, cast a twinkling look about at his audience and began.

"Thanks all for coming – especially Isobel – these haven't been easy weeks for you, I know."

Wanker!

"Now I know you all have busy afternoon schedules, so this will be a quickie. The five acres – as we'll call it for now – has been . . ."

He droned on, his audience lost to him by the second minute. Charlie was texting his girlfriend. Pete was drafting a letter to members about the new aromatherapy and massage clinic. Chloe from Sydney was tugging at a nail that had snagged badly. At last the long-winded preamble came to an end.

"Laura, the lights!"

Laura leapt into action.

With the room in darkness, the athlete zapped briefly across the screen, to be quickly replaced by dazzling graphics and some very stirring rock music – "We are the Champions" – "I want to Break Free" – "A Hero Can Save Us" type of thing.

Suddenly the room was buzzing as pictures, photos and colourful plans flashing across the screen. Crolly was quiet – letting the dazzling display of images speak for themselves. And damn but they were good! Isobel hated to say it but they were brilliant. Sickeningly brilliant. So brilliant were they that it was a while before the awful truth registered. She froze.

"Cheap, lousy, thieving bastard!" she mumbled under her breath.

Crolly put the presentation on hold and smiled sympathetically at her.

"Was there something you wanted to share with us, Isobel?"

She opened her mouth to speak – but found she was incapable of uttering even one word, not a syllable.

She felt a fresh bout of nausea, intensified by the realisation that Crolly had stolen her plans for the five acres. Somehow she stumbled from her seat and mumbled something about just having remembered to send an important email to head office. On her way out, she caught the tail-end of a half-pitying, half-triumphant smile from Crolly.

Back in her office, trembling with rage and nausea, she couldn't stop herself and penned an email to Crolly, demanding to know how he'd got hold of her plans, when they had been under constant lock and key in her office. She hesitated for a moment, strongly tempted to send copies to Colman and head office as well. But she quickly abandoned the idea. Then she remembered how she'd seen Colman talking to Crolly in the carpark the day of the interview and everything made sense suddenly. She hastily typed another separate note to Colman telling him exactly what she thought of his treachery.

Sophie was horrified that she'd been so impetuous.

"You shouldn't have sent him that email. What good will it do getting his back up like that? No-one in authority likes to be challenged – no matter how thick-skinned they may appear to be. Crolly will never forgive you."

"But what he did was wrong – he stole my idea. And besides what can he do?"

"Just watch it, Isobel. I thought you'd have more sense. And as for sending Colman that email – you can't be sure it was him."

"Don't be so thick! Who else could it be?"

"I don't know. Colman seems too nice – that's all. Who else has access to your files?"

"Laura, of course – but she just wouldn't do a thing like that. She's loyal, dependable. We've always watched out for each other. I even pushed for her last promotion – against Crolly's wishes, as it happens. And there's no-one else. Hendro has been in a few times. But what reason would he have? I'm not sure he even knows who Len Crolly is." She mulled it over in her head and finally concluded: "No! It was Colman. It wouldn't make sense for anyone else to betray me like that."

When Isobel finally left, Sophie bathed and got ready for bed, swathed in a towelling dressing-gown. She half-heartedly watched an old movie on TV but was drifting off when the doorbell rang. Briefly she toyed with not answering it. Then she realised it might be Clementine and didn't want to leave her standing out in the cold.

She padded to the front door, barefooted and in a languid pre-sleep trance.

It was Hendro, in a flimsy T-shirt and jog pants, all smouldering green eyes and bearing a bottle of champagne. He grinned apologetically at her. "May I come in?"

"I was just on my way to bed."

"Some other time maybe?"

She nodded.

"It's just that I wanted to discuss the dinghy situation with you."

"There's nothing to discuss."

"I might have a solution which would suit us both."

Curiosity killed the cat and all that. Besides she was quite enjoying the shape of his chest which was clearly visible through the flimsy cotton material. What the heck! He wouldn't stay long. She'd hear what he had to say and send him packing. They would not drink champagne and get all cosy and mellow on the sofa.

She led him into the kitchen and he rummaged rudely through cupboards until he found two glasses.

"Please – I don't want a drink."

"Well, I do. This is my weekly allowance," he said, popping the cork and letting the frothy liquid spill over into the glasses. "Cheers!" He held out the glass to her.

She did not like the fact that he was standing so close. It meant that she could feel his breath, smell his musky man smell. She drew back, tightened her dressing-gown and sat primly at the kitchen table while taking a tiny sip of champagne.

"So what's this proposition?" she asked, determined to keep things firmly on a business footing. She fought with all her might the thought that it had been long months since she'd had the feel of a man inside her.

She blinked and gulped and drew her dressing-gown tighter and sat up even straighter.

"Proposition? Oh yes."

His eyes held hers for a fraction of a second and the

feeling made her burn up inside. She lowered her eyes, desperate to hide the hunger in them, tried to control her breathing as warm waves of pure desire engulfed her. Until she'd met Daniel, there had been one or two unremarkable boyfriends – neither of them skilled lovers. And Daniel hadn't inspired her to great erotic thoughts either. Daniel's interpretation of the word erotic was for her to go on top and tweak his nipples as he panted like a messenger bearing urgent news – *I'm coming, I'm coming! I've come!*

As he topped up her glass, Hendro's hand brushed lightly against hers. It might have been an accident. But somehow she doubted it. The touch burned, shot through her. If she didn't get her hands on him soon she'd just explode like a hot liquid volcano. It was an entirely new sensation – to be instantly overcome with pure blinding lust for a man – but the sensation was so overwhelming it had to be fed, satisfied. In a moment she would be on him, cupping her breasts for his mouth to explore, feeding him the sweet wetness of her from the tips of her fingers. God, what was happening? She had turned into a nymphomaniac. It was the only possible answer. Surely it couldn't be a normal state of affairs to be so overcome with lust for a man she barely knew?

As if sensing her confusion, he smiled engagingly at her. It was the cute little boy 'I'm bad but I can't help it' sort of smile.

"You're pretty." It was hardly original and she gave him her best 'I know exactly what you're up to smile'.

"No – I mean it – you are. You've got lovely blue eyes

– honest – but with a hint of mystique – that's nice . . . and as for this cute little turned up nose . . ." he brushed her face lightly with his thumb.

"Thank you," was all she could think to say now. No-one had ever told Sophie Flanagan she was pretty before – except for Gran and she didn't count. She didn't see herself as pretty and Daniel with his sharp artistic eye for objects of beauty had constantly felt obliged to remind her of her shortcomings in the prettiness department. In his eyes she was like a battered old table discovered at the back of some salvage merchants – plain and solid and serviceable – but essentially flawed and graceless.

And, of course, Hendro was probably only flattering her in the old, time-honoured way – with a view to getting into her knickers.

"Maybe I should go." He didn't move.

"Maybe."

He stood up. She stood up. He towered above her, bent to plant a kiss on her cheek. His lips moistened her skin. Then he brushed against the lobe of her ear and whispered so that she could barely hear:

"I'm very sorry for saying this but I would really like to fuck you right now."

His warm breath was on her neck. His hand brushed against her shoulder. She could have easily drawn back then, whacked him in the face – How dare you! and all that kind of thing – but she didn't. It was as if she was paralysed with longing and though she didn't offer herself yet, she stood unmoving as his hand found and unfastened the belt of her dressing-gown and slid over the soft curve of her hips then buttocks. Her face tilted up to him and they kissed, light grazings at first, then hungrily as her tongue flickered along his lips and he crushed her mouth like he would eat it.

"Do you want to stop?" he mumbled between kisses.

Oh, what the hell! She'd never ever had a one-night stand in her life. Men like Hendro didn't often turn up unexpectedly late at night. A one-night stand would mark the definite end of her relationship with Daniel.

"No! Don't stop!" she murmured softly to him.

She grabbed his hand and slid it between her legs and gasped as she realised how wet and ready for him she was. In the bedroom, stripped of his clothes the mere sight of him naked was almost enough to bring her to orgasm. They lay on the bed and he leant over her, his hard muscular body pressed against her. With his tongue and his lips he teased and taunted her, flickering over her nipples, working down to plant tantalising little puckers on her belly-button, sliding his fingers into her, hovering over her until she had to beg him to kiss her and pull his face onto her as he tipped at her lightly with his tongue and his lips, took her into his mouth like gently crushed berries and his face was drenched with the sweet salty taste of her. Then he was covering her, his heavy body pressing down on her, sliding into her, so that it felt like he might burst her open. She couldn't hold herself a moment longer. He thrust into her, massive steel bolts of power and she rose to him, her whole body parting to take him in deeply. Then shudders, trembling and gasping as she came, sucking and pulling him deeper into her until barely seconds later his taut body relaxed in waves of sweat-drenched shudders.

She fell back sated! She'd never been so sated in her life! She'd never even known it was possible to be so sated in her entire life! God, she felt cheated – to have got to almost thirty years of age and not to have known!

Head cupped in the crook of his shoulder, she stared up at the ceiling, absently stroking his chest.

"I don't know what to say," she murmured finally.

"Why say anything? You OK?"

"Yes! Oh yes!"

"You're happy and I'm happy – so what's left to say?"

"Nothing, I suppose."

"We can date if you like," he said, running a finger lightly through her hair.

"No, I don't think so."

"Sure?"

"Absolutely!"

"I date lots of people. But I'd be very happy to date you. Just to get that straight – pretty Sophie"

"Look, I don't want to date you – OK? I don't even want you to stay the night. And I am most definitely not interested in your love life. I do not want your mobile number. I will not be on the phone tomorrow with needy little hints about us meeting up again. I am not going to boil your bunny. Though I may take a sledge-hammer to your dinghy – but that's another matter. I'm not ready for a relationship. I don't want a relationship – and you are magnificent in bed – but you're really not my type. What just happened – was bloody terrific – but it means nothing . . ."

"It means we had a damn good fuck surely? And the world is full of people who have never had a damn good fuck."

There was no denying the truth of that statement. Unplanned, unexpected, unbelievably invigorating! She felt like doing cartwheels, like running a marathon, like dancing the samba across Europe. She felt like writing a book, composing a symphony. She felt like the most beautiful woman in the world.

Hendro dressed, and she admired his unconscious animal grace. It was a pity – but now she needed to address the matter of the dinghy. He'd read her thoughts.

"About the dinghy ..."

"You needn't think that because we just – well, that it gives you any right to leave your dinghy in my garden. Because it doesn't. I want it out of there."

"Of course. But don't you want to hear my proposition?"

"All right."

"I'm offering you fifty-per-cent ownership in my dinghy – as a gift – a gesture of neighbourliness – that way it's just as much your property as mine and you would be able to keep it in your garden."

What an operator!

"I don't want a dinghy. I don't, as it happens, even like sailing. Just get it out of my garden."

Hendro sighed. It was so tedious when people didn't do what he wanted. But he wasn't going to argue with her. He liked her. She was fun, straight, and what a sex-kitten in bed! Whoever got the chance to offer Sophie Flanagan undying love and devotion would be a very lucky man.

"By the way, I saw your friend Isobel today. She was in a bad way."

"Isobel. Yes, she's – well, she's not in good health."

"I hope she gets well soon. I should send her flowers or something."

"I wouldn't if I were you. And if you've got designs on her – well, don't waste your time. Right now if George Clooney were to offer his undying love – she'd probably impale him on a rusty nail."

He sat down beside her on the bed and planted a warm affectionate kiss on her lips. Then he took a small white envelope and slid it across the pillow. "Just a party invitation," he said as she raised a quizzical eyebrow.

"You're a cool woman, Sophie Flanagan. I like that. Tough but cool. Let's not let a dinghy get in the way of a budding friendship."

She was smitten – not with Hendro as a possible partner – but with Hendro as a man – a man friend. Tess had often reminded Sophie that men make wonderfully honourable friends – not great at keeping in touch perhaps – but loyal, faithful, uncomplicated – it was only when they became lovers that the betrayals and complications began.

"Just sort it out, Hendro. And don't come round here with any more bottles of champagne until you do."

"Yes sir, ma'am," he said winking at her with irritating good humour before he casually let himself out the back door and ambled home through the garden.

Sophie showered and slid back into bed, feeling wonderfully happy with herself. It was the first time since her return home that she felt even able to think about letting her life with Daniel go for good. Every night since leaving him, she'd found that the empty bed at the end of the day was the hardest loneliest time of all. Every night as she tried to sleep, the painful memories of the happy-ever-after dream she'd lost or thrown away flooded back to haunt her. She tossed and turned, racked with doubts and regrets about having made the decision to come home. She'd tried sleeping in the middle, even dug out an old teddybear from Tess's to hold onto at night. She hid it under the bed any time Isobel called round. Often times, she couldn't sleep and watched TV into the early hours. Tonight though, for the first time, she was able to think about Daniel with a new sense of detachment . . .

They'd been invited to spend the weekend with the Brewsters in their lakeside retreat in Maine. Sophie and Daniel arrived late on Friday evening to the pretty clapboard house, clutching a box of Faye's preferred handmade cholesterol-free chocolates and another box of Lloyd's favourite hand-rolled Cuban cigars. Daniel had suggested the chocolates and cigars and Sophie had spent ages trawling the shops for them.

Faye showed them to a comfortably sized bedroom facing onto woodland, all blue-painted furniture and patchwork quilts and drapes.

"It's a nice quiet room." said Faye with one of her knowing looks. "We're miles down the end of the corridor and won't hear a thing."

"Thank you," said Daniel, smiling warmly at her.

"I know what young love is like. Bet you can't keep your hands off him, Sophie. Can't say I blame you. What a handsome guy!"

Faye leered disconcertingly at him but Sophie forced herself not to notice and smiled sweetly. In spite of her own reservations about the Brewsters, she was quite happy to smile sweetly all weekend if it helped Daniel with his career. And she did smile, almost non-stop, through all the meals, the shopping trips with Faye, the leers of Lloyd, she kept it up – until Sunday afternoon to be precise.

Somehow on the Saturday, Sophie escaped to the lake shore and walked alone for almost an hour. Lloyd had gone fishing with an old friend and Faye had enlisted Daniel's help in bringing home a nice little Shaker table she'd found in the village antiques shop. Sophie sat at the end of a wooden jetty and dangled her feet in the water, even puffed defiantly on a Marlboro Light. The awful reality of life with the Brewsters filled her head. She and Daniel would fill the contradictory roles of surrogate children and lust objects. But Daniel couldn't see anything wrong with the situation and she wondered how he could be so blindingly naive? A wave of dangerous thoughts flooded her head. What am I doing here with these people? What do I really want from life? Do I really love Daniel? Is he by any chance a big thick eejit?

Gulp! What a ridiculous question! Of course she really loved Daniel. And he really loved her, in spite of the fact that she wasn't exactly Cameron Diaz. And that in fact answered all the other dangerous questions because he was what she really wanted from life and that was why she was here with these people. She stood up, seized with a new sense of purpose. She would get through this weekend, be nice to the Brewsters and learn to like them for his sake. Eventually he'd want to come home to Ireland. Surely he wouldn't want to stay in Fleet Point forever?

That evening there were other guests, the Lowells, a happy warm-hearted couple from nearby who were celebrating their thirtieth wedding anniversary, and the Brewsters' daughter Francesca, a pretty, feisty woman who laughed at her mother's silly vanities, and teased her father mercilessly about his age. She and Sophie had lots in common, and the night passed pleasantly enough.

Next morning, the household gathered around the long kitchen table for waffles and maple syrup and several helpings of coffee. Daniel was being very attentive to Faye who was more than happy with the attention. She was in particularly chirpy, flirtatious humour and looked quite fetching in a pair of fawn pedal-pushers and a loose denim shirt, her fair hair tumbling onto her shoulders for that just-out-of-bed Faye Dunaway 'I'm a totally irresistible sex goddess' look. Sophie was forced to admit that for a woman of fifty-two, Faye was holding her shape pretty well.

Faye, on the other hand, had no problem admitting it.

"I have the figure of a thirty-year-old woman," she said, running her hands along well-honed thighs which looked like they spent hours doing strange things with the weights machine at the local gym.

Despite being almost half her age, Sophie felt clumsy and ugly and gauche beside her. But that didn't deter Lloyd who seemed to be hovering in the background every time she turned round. At last, she escaped him and went back to the lakeshore once more where she spent a long time idly throwing pebbles in the water and watching the ripples. She checked the time on her watch. It would soon be time to leave and Daniel would be getting anxious. She walked briskly back to the house, hopeful that there might be good news about the partnership. There was no sign of anyone and she made her way upstairs to the bedroom and set about gathering up their things. It occurred to her that Daniel might have been summoned to Lloyd's office for the big announcement. Perhaps he was in there right now – learning his fate. She tried to concentrate on the packing but couldn't seem to get things in the right order. Downstairs once more she poured herself a glass of water and ambled out to the boatyard, lost in thought.

But she wasn't lost there for long. The door of the boathouse opened and Daniel emerged looking quite dishevelled and sheepish, followed by Faye Brewster looking like she'd just had the shag of her life. Of course appearances can be very deceptive and Sophie was perfectly prepared to give them the benefit of the doubt. They might have been wrestling with an outboard motor. Possibly they were chopping logs or putting petrol in the lawnmower. She lingered for a few moments behind a tree to watch them. Faye pulled Daniel's head towards hers and planted a slimy kiss on his lips. This, of course, was Daniel's cue to push her away disgustedly and stoutly declare his undying, unswerving, unflinching, unassailable love for Sophie! So Sophie was at first mildly surprised, amused even for a moment and then genuinely gobsmacked to see Daniel, a disgusting leer twisting his face, pull Faye's perfectly honed body tight against his and kiss her very passionately all over, neck and everything, for what seemed like ages, in an easy comfortable manner – like they were well used to each other.

It was at that moment the determined smile that Sophie had fixed to her face with such steadfast loyalty, two days earlier, came completely unstuck. Beneath it were layers of conflicting emotion – disbelief! fury! jealous rage! disgust! But a lady never shows her true feelings in public, especially not where a man is concerned – at least that's what the nuns in The Convent of Perpetual Caution, Hollymaine, County Mayo had always advised. Sophie followed their advice to the letter.

She summoned from somewhere deep within an expression of serene indifference and retreated quietly to the bedroom where she began packing carefully and methodically. She folded her silk blouse neatly between sheets of crisp sky-blue tissue paper, carefully slipped shoe-horns into her black sling-backs, folded Daniel's fine poplin shirts and his navy cashmere sweater – the one she'd bought him in Bergdorf Goodman's for his birthday. In the en-suite bathroom, she calmly gathered up his aftershave – the horrible sweet-scented one she didn't like but he insisted on wearing anyway – his electric toothbrush, razor, nailbrush, comb, deodorant.

At last he appeared through the door, flushed, smiling – happy. He opened his mouth to speak.

"I've just finished packing. Are we ready to leave?" There was enough ice in her voice to avert all future threats of global warming and probably freeze over a big corner of hell as well.

"Great. You're a treasure." He sidled up beside her and slid his hands around her waist. Then he planted an affectionate kiss on the nape of her neck. "Guess what?"

She closed the lid of the suitcase and pulled the zips shut.

"Are we right then?" she said, completely ignoring his question.

"Sophie – listen, I know it's been a drag for you this weekend, and I know I've been a bit tetchy – but I want you to know – you've been amazing."

She indicated to him that he should take up the suitcase and sailed past him, down the stairs and into the hall, where Lloyd and Faye stood waiting to wave them off.

"Bye, Lloyd and Faye. Thank you so much for a lovely time." She forced an impeccably serene smile, desperate to escape them, to get home and be alone with her aching sense of failure and rejection.

"Well done!" said Lloyd shaking her hand and planting a wet kiss on her cheek.

"It's been lovely having you. Such a darling girl!" added Faye, with a tinge of envy that could only be reassured by running freshly manicured hands over her own sleek hips.

Daniel followed with the suitcase.

"I'll drive," Sophie clipped, sliding into the driver's seat.

"Sure – but don't you want to know –"

"Know what?"

"I've done it! We've done it! I'm a partner – Brewster Fielding Architectural Solutions!"

"That's wonderful."

"You don't sound too happy. Am I missing something?"

"It really is great news. You must be so excited," she said and even managed a twitch at the corner of her mouth, which in subdued lighting might easily have passed for a fleeting smile.

"Of course, I'm excited!" said Daniel, floundering somewhat.

"It must be such a relief."

"Yes." He was trying to sustain his gleeful excitement but she could see he was finding it difficult.

"I expect there will be paperwork, legal stuff to settle up," she threw in blandly.

"I haven't even thought about that. We have to do something to celebrate. Today! Tonight! What about Rita Quinn's? Nowhere else will do."

Rita Quinn's was the best, most expensive seafood restaurant in Fleet Point, and it was a long-held dream that they would have dinner there, some night when they had something really big to celebrate. Now Sophie felt horribly empty, sad, like a part of life was slipping away from her, like nothing much mattered any more, least of all Rita Quinn's Seafood Restaurant. She would have to say something.

"Daniel, I saw you . . . at the boathouse with Faye . . . how long has it been going on?"

Her eyes filled with choking, scalding tears. She struggled to hold them back. Daniel shifted uneasily in the passenger seat, his face clouded with confusion.

"It's not what you think. I can explain."

"You can?"

"Yes, of course I can! Look, nothing happened. She's just lonely. I was consoling her – that's all."

She longed to believe him, even did force herself to believe him for a few days. But the discovery of hotel receipts in his dressing-table drawer, and the sound of him on the phone late at night when he thought she was asleep – left little room for doubt . . .

Sophie stretched and curled up in the bed contentedly now, her entire body awash with a delicious peaceful warmth and ease. It was as if in some way that she didn't fully understand, Hendro had cured her of Daniel.

Chapter 17

Under the new Crolly regime, things at the Athena Health and Fitness Club were becoming decidedly unpleasant – at least for Isobel. Struggling as she was to find a semblance of something even vaguely rewarding about her work now, she'd almost thrown up across her increasingly dishevelled desk when Crolly crept into her office that morning and handed her the next month's roster as if it was the Fourth Secret of Fatima, the Dead Sea Scrolls and the plans for the Lost City of Atlantis all rolled into one.

"Isobel – I know you're up to your eyes ..." he glanced sympathetically at the mountain range of papers on her desk, "but when you get a moment I'd value your opinion on the new roster set-up. I've spent quite a lot of time on it. Anyway, see what you think."

Then he'd smiled his saintly, enigmatic smile and glided out on a cloud of slick smugness. She picked up the sheet. Colman used to draw a few lines with a ruler, and write out the rosters with a thick black marker. This new roster was a thing of great beauty in its own right, a work of spreadsheet magic, a piece of Microsoft wizardry. Cleverly balancing his fonts and varying his type sizes, using framing boxes and shading in new and thrilling ways, Crolly had created a form so thoroughly produced that it would no doubt end up in The Ground-breaking Forms and Documents section of the National Museum.

She scanned down through the list of names. Aside from the painstakingly detailed formatting and one or two "humorous" clipart cartoons, it was hardly a piece of rocket science. It was no different in fact from Colman's handwritten and ruled roster.

She allowed herself a smug harumph and was about to pin it to the notice board when a name jumped out at her from the column marked *Late Evening – 20.00 to Midnight* . . .

It had to be a mistake. Everyone else listed on the late evening shift was from the ranks, or new, or had partners on similar shifts. It had always been an unwritten management rule. Senior long-standing members of the Athena workforce were never asked to do the late shift – except in a dire emergency and never without being consulted first.

But there was her name – in Times New Roman, Bold, 12 point, Italic – down for the late shift three Fridays in succession. It was as bald and cynical a piece of spitefulness as she'd ever come across.

She marched down the corridor, past the ladies' Pilates

group, past the aqua-aerobics group, glanced enviously at Beatrice Heavenly, pushed her way through the entire front row of Hendro's team-mates who also gazed with hopeless longing at the divine Beatrice – until she reached Crolly's new office. She didn't bother to knock.

He sat at his desk, speaking quietly into a phone, stroking his minute dab of a goatee beard – all business.

"We need to talk about this roster," she said, struggling desperately to remain calm.

"Take a seat. I'll be with you in one moment," he said, a smile of vague pity hovering about his thin, bloodless lips.

He made a big show of writing down figures, a bigger show of listening intently to the person on the other end of the line, then an even bigger show of explaining to that person that something had come up which he was unfortunately compelled to deal with on the spot. He replaced the receiver and swivelled round to face her.

She held up the fabulously formatted document and said evenly: "It is not your place to assign work duties to senior members of staff."

He made a steeple of his fingers and smiled regretfully at her across the desk.

"I take it you're not happy?"

"Happy? *Happy?*" She could feel any last remaining reserves of cool professionalism and sensible detachment slipping away rapidly.

"I've been asked to make cutbacks – economies if you like. We all have to pull together and make sacrifices – for the greater good. I'd do the late shift myself only it wouldn't be fitting for a person in my position."

Nausea swelled up from the pit of her stomach. She opened her mouth to speak but all that came out was a thin little croak. Crolly went on, speaking over his finger-steeple.

"There is an alternative, of course. But I don't think we want to go down that route at this moment in time. Tell you what? I'll leave it with you. Have a think about it. As I say, I value your feedback."

He got up and held the door open with a sickeningly unctuous smile as Isobel left the room, humiliated and utterly defeated.

Outside she bumped into Colman.

"I got your email but I think you've got the wrong end of the stick," he said facing her down.

"Have I? I don't think so."

"If you think I had anything to do with Crolly getting hold of your plans –"

"Spare me your explanations, Colman. You're worse than Crolly. At least he's never pretended to be my friend – how could you?"

If she'd expected Colman to blush, come clean, do the decent thing and own up – he didn't. He looked steadily into her eyes – no trace of shame or shiftiness or even sly malice.

"Do you honestly think I would do such a thing?" he said, then turned on his heel and walked off.

Chapter 18

The wedding of Katie Brehony was to be a grand affair: ceremony in Ballintubber Abbey, reception in Ashford Castle, honeymoon in the Maldives, a cut-stone granite mansion on the shores of Lough Mask just ready to move into. Standards of elegance, along with heels, would be staggeringly high and a girl's self-esteem might be seriously damaged by turning up in just any old chain-store outfit. So in an effort to calm and cheer the increasingly desperate Isobel, Sophie went shopping with her for a wedding outfit. She was keenly aware that many firm and steadfast friendships come to a sudden and violent end in the ladies' changing rooms of fashion stores. The question *"But what do you think of it really?"* was undoubtedly the poisoned chalice of sisterhood. Sophie tried on and quickly bought a flimsy silk dress in raspberry pink. It was a ferocious price and she would have to live on lettuce leaves and toast but she economised by not buying hat or shoes.

"I'm not that keen on it – but it will do," she said, playing down her own shopping success.

Two hours later an increasingly hysterical Isobel had tried on about fifteen outfits and pronounced all of them awful.

"I'm just too fat. Look!" she said catching hold of a good two fingers of new fat which seemed to have appeared quite suddenly around her midriff.

"I think the bit of weight suits you."

"Don't patronise me."

"I mean it. You were never meant to be scrawny thin – not with those great breasts of yours – and besides, it makes your head look too big."

"Oh, so now my head is too big for the rest of me!"

"You know that's not what I meant."

Isobel struggled into a clinging deep-green jersey silk Prada dress. A few weeks ago it might have looked stunning on her – but now it merely emphasised the fact that she was rapidly gaining weight.

"I look like a whale – no waist. And a pot belly! I've never had a pot belly – not even before my period. It must be a tumour. That's what it is."

The shop assistant was definitely earning her money – dashing about in a state of harassed helpfulness, bringing more and more suits and dresses to the changing-room. At last she returned with an elegant black Jill Sander shift dress.

"This one looks especially good on the expectant

mums," she said encouragingly, at which point Isobel said something rude, pulled on her loose combats and T-shirt and departed abruptly, leaving Sophie behind to make grovelling apologies.

Back in Raglan Road, Isobel was grumpy and morose.

"I don't want to go to the wedding. I hardly know Katie Brehony. Anyway who wants to look at all that frothy veiled petal-strewn romance and dewy-eyed happiness? Fifty per cent of marriages end on the rocks. And the other fifty ought to. It's a total hypocrisy. And I can't go alone."

"You won't be alone – I'll be with you."

"You don't count! I mean going with you will be like going with myself . . . I mean I won't have Phil. Oh God!" She broke down sobbing. "I'll never get another man!"

"Of course, you will. Plenty more fish –"

"Don't! I'm nearly thirty. My career is on the rocks. I'm swelling up from some dreadful illness. Maybe it's dropsy – maybe I'll just keep swelling and swelling. What if it doesn't stop and I explode? No man will ever look at me again!"

"Why don't you do the test?"

"No. It's out of the question. I never had unprotected sex with Phil. I am not pregnant – I can't be!"

Pressing the point was useless. Isobel was fast becoming completely irrational.

"Tell you what," said Sophie in an effort to change the subject, and conveniently forgetting her recent vow to confront her fear of flying: "I'll drive us down in your car. You won't even have to drive. And as a birthday treat, I'll book us both into Ashford Castle for the two nights. How does that sound?" She hoped it sounded all reassuring and mumsy.

Isobel shrugged like a truculent teenager. "I suppose so," she murmured.

"Great then, that's settled," Sophie said cheerfully.

And every cloud had a silver lining. It meant she wouldn't have to fly.

But in the morning Isobel called with disturbing news. Her lovely little Mazda sports car wouldn't start and had to be towed off to the garage. The mechanic said it would most likely need a new engine. It was going to cost a fortune – about exactly the amount of money she'd saved for her holiday this year.

"We'll hire a car. I'll pay," Sophie said quickly.

"I've already thought of that and it can't be done. There are no cars available because of some big international conference on all weekend."

"There must be a car available somewhere. Did you try the internet?"

"It's just too short notice. I've tried everywhere. Anyway, I don't think I'm up to a long car journey. A quick flit across the country by plane is just what I need. We can rent a car at the other end."

"We might not be able to get flights. Have you thought of that?"

"Yes, I have. We're booked – eleven o'clock tomorrow morning – ErinAir flight FA 31."

The next morning, Sophie, who had all but cured herself of smoking, felt overcome with the urge to light up several cigarettes all at once. To suppress the craving, she applied an industrial-strength nicotine patch to the under part of her upper arm. The craving persisted. She applied another patch to the other arm – just in case it was a blood-circulation problem. For further Dutch courage, she washed two Valium down with a stiff brandy and ignored Isobel's catty remark that anyone smelling of alcohol before one o'clock in the day ought to be attending some sort of treatment programme. At the airport they checked in and while Isobel sat in Departures trying to quell the worst of the nausea with sips of bottled water, Sophie took herself off to the bar.

"Damn the man who first dreamt up the daft idea of flying!" she muttered wildly. "A mountain of curses on Isobel's car! A plague on all car-rental companies! A month of biblical-type plagues on Daniel Fielding!"

"Who's Daniel?" said a voice from behind and further along the counter.

She turned slowly, her elbow slipping from the counter, her head wobbling, her eyes struggling to focus on the owner of the voice. It was the flight steward – the one who had been on her previous flight to Castlebar.

"He's nobody really!" she said sharply then instantly regretted her rudeness, especially when she remembered she'd been in a similarly embarrassing state the last time they'd met. Now he probably had her down as one of those bunny-boiling, permanently narky, substance-abusing women. Not that it mattered so much – but it was annoying when people got the wrong impression of her.

He glanced at his watch, then drank off the remains of

a strong black coffee.

"I'm sorry. I'm just not in the mood for small talk," she said apologetically and then tried a joke. "And anyway – don't you have to go and crank up the engine or something?"

"No."

"Or hold the pilot's hand?" she smiled weakly.

He shook his head, not appearing to see the joke at all.

"If I was piloting that death-trap – I'd want someone to hold my hand."

"He's a total darling and I'm nuts about him – and, of course, I'd love to hold his hand – but – and I know you'll be deeply disappointed to hear this – I've just come off duty."

"That must be a relief. Another morning flying into the horrendous pits of hell safely done and dusted."

He grinned – the briefest of smiles – more of a flicker really – but not the sort of grin a man in love with his pilot would make. It was most definitely a flirty fleeting flicker of a smile and Sophie felt quite disappointed as she watched him disappear into the crowd. There was little chance of their paths ever crossing again.

"Who was that you were talking to?" asked Isobel as they made their way to the little plane.

"Some steward."

"He looks vaguely familiar. I'm sure I know him. Are you feeling OK now?"

"Yes – just fine!"

But inside the plane, seated as far away from the pilot as possible, Sophie quickly realised she wouldn't be at all fine. Foolishly glancing out through the tiny window, she noticed that all the runway workers looked dishevelled. Their eyes were scrunched up. They struggled to hold their footing on the ground. And even before the pilot said the one blood-curdlingly terrifying word that Sophie Flanagan dreaded more than any other word in the entire English language, she just knew from looking out at the gusting winds that they were in for some robust *turbulence!*

"Quick, quick, Isobel, say a prayer!"

"What?"

"Let's just join hands and promise God that we will never ever do anything sinful again. We'll devote the rest of our lives to caring for the less fortunate. I'll give up smoking. You'll give up bitching. We'll go to Mass every Sunday."

"I have no intention of giving up bitching and you've never been to Mass in your life!"

It was true. Sophie's mother had raised both her children as atheists.

"I can start."

"You're being silly."

Sophie's knuckles had bunched into tight fists, nails cutting into the flesh of her palms. The plane shook and trembled. The pilot babbled on blandly about altitude and blustery conditions in Knock and estimated time of arrival. Outside on the runway the wind had picked up speed and she watched horrified as someone lost their uniform cap and it careered off in mid-air at a terrifying speed.

"I can't do this. I want to get off."

But it was too late. The plane was ready for take-off. Sophie tried to convey her distress to the stewardess who regarded her with icy distaste.

Trembling, rattling and shaking violently, the plane rose up into the air. The stewardess stumbled against a panel. The plane climbed and dipped.

"We're going to crash. I know it."

She reached for her mobile and decided to send all her loved ones a final text message. But which loved ones? Tess obviously. Cian probably. But who else? Daniel? Oh God, why had she left Daniel? He was a perfectly normal, decent man and she'd gone and ditched him over a minor dalliance with Faye Brewster. Now it was too late.

"I'm sorry, madam. But mobiles must not be used while the flight is in progress."

"It's an emergency."

"I'm afraid I must insist. It's company policy."

The plane dived and the hostess lunged forward. Then came the laid-back caramelly voice of the pilot – like he was presenting a late-night jazz show on TV, instead of hurtling them all to their doom.

"Just a bit of turbulence there, ladies and gentlemen. Nothing to be alarmed about and perfectly routine. Though for your convenience it's probably best to keep the old safety belts fastened for the rest of the journey."

And so it continued for forty of the longest, most terrifying minutes Sophie had ever experienced. The little plane juddering and shuddering, the hostess staggering and lunging and the pilot babbling and gabbling. There was little comfort in his announcement that they would shortly be landing. Landing where? The way things were going, they would most likely land in a ditch – if they were lucky. If not – there was the Atlantic Ocean to break their fall. When the plane finally touched down, having taken a couple of test-bounces on the runway, Sophie declared that she would never ever get up in a plane again.

In the arrivals hall, she rummaged for cigarettes.

"You promised to give up."

"I will. But not just now." She made a bee-line for the exit and joined the shamefaced little huddle of smokers near the taxi rank.

Checking into Ashford Castle restored their spirits. Isobel's nausea had abated and Sophie was over the worst of post flight-from-hell stress. They drove down the long winding avenue, through lush wooded parkland and a perfectly manicured golf course before passing over the narrow little drawbridge and pulling up outside the grand entrance. Sophie parked between a Porsche and an Aston Martin. A porter took their bags and led them through the oak-panelled reception rooms and up the grand old wooden staircase. Even Isobel was impressed.

When the booking had been made, only one room remained – the second most expensive – the *Quiet Man* Suite overlooking Lough Corrib – complete with two separate ensuite bedrooms, four-poster beds, a granite balcony, bathrooms the size of dance halls and a drawing-room big enough to accommodate the entire wedding party, with grand marble fireplace and delicate early Georgian furniture.

"Are you sure we're in the right place?" Isobel enquired when the porter had left.

"Just enjoy. It's your birthday present."

"I've never stayed in such a grand place." Isobel dashed about, pulling open drawers, munching on a bowl of seedless grapes, examining the label on a bottle of chilled champagne, stuffing her washbag with little complementary toiletries from the bathroom.

"Are you going to call in on your parents?"

"No!" said Isobel turning pale at the thought. She would see them at the wedding in the morning and hopefully they would be so excited by the occasion that they would not notice their daughter's growing distress – not to mention her growing belly.

"Well, I'm for the bath," said Sophie. "And then I'm going to see Tess. "

But when she returned from her grandmother's a few hours later, it was with a growing sense of alarm. Maeve had taken her aside and given her some very disturbing news. Far from being the most sensible woman on the planet, Tess O'Meara seemed to have taken complete leave of her senses.

Chapter 19

Sophie lay awake half the night, uneasy about what she'd learnt from Maeve. Horrible! And shameful! And criminal! And foolish!

Tess's foolishness upset her almost more than anything. She'd always regarded her grandmother as the font of wisdom and common sense – a woman of intelligence, a woman of wit and sharp insight into the follies of others.

Something would have to be done and quickly, to steer Tess away from certain disaster. So in the morning, before the wedding, Sophie showered quickly and drove to the old family home. Her grandmother was putting the finishing touches to her make-up at the dressing-table.

"You look lovely, Gran. You always do."

"Thanks. Though something tells me you're not hovering at my dressing-table to tell me how lovely I look."

Sophie leaned on the side of the dressing-table,

struggling to find the right words, anxious not to hurt her grandmother.

"What Maeve told me yesterday about you and Robert Franklin – is it true?"

"Is what true?" Cool blue eyes held hers in the reflection of the mirror.

"Have you been giving Robert Franklin money?" The severity of her own voice startled her.

"What's it to you?" said Tess, gracefully sweeping a powder-brush along her smooth cheekbones.

"I don't want anyone taking advantage of you."

"The only person trying to take advantage of me is Kenny."

"You're dodging the question, Gran." Sophie tried to soften her voice. "Did you give him money? I won't be cross. I promise I won't judge."

"Judge all you want and be as cross as you like."

"Gran – just tell me the truth."

"Yes, I did."

"How much?"

She thought that at this point, her grandmother might at least have the decency to look a bit embarrassed, or even slightly ashamed. But she raised her chin, swept her fingertips along the line of her neck and reached for her perfume atomiser.

"Let me see – I seem to remember a bank draft for five thousand euro."

Sophie gasped but for the moment decided to ignore the possibility that there might be other bank drafts.

"Why?"

"That, young lady, is none of your business. Now if you'll excuse me, I need to finish dressing."

When Robert arrived, Sophie had awful trouble resisting the urge to pick up a broom or a gardening fork and chase him from the premises. His idea of wedding attire was a pair of brown corduroy trousers, a denim shirt and a Harris Tweed jacket and Hush Puppy shoes – hardly standard gigolo attire – but then he was probably a master of the "harmless eccentric" disguise. She was about to haul him out into the garden for a full confrontation when his brazenness astounded even her.

"I was trying to persuade Tess to book into Ashford Castle for the night – so that we could make a good night of Katie and Ronan's wedding."

Not content with seducing and embezzling, he even had the nerve to suggest that they book into a hotel together – in broad daylight in front of the entire neighbourhood.

"You can't seriously think . . ." She was so shocked that she couldn't even finish the sentence.

He smiled easily and rested his hand lightly on Tess's shoulder for a fleeting moment.

"But we decided it wasn't such a good idea in the end," he said and settled himself languidly into an armchair.

Sophie couldn't stay a moment longer. She shot her grandmother a worrying look and drove back to the castle to finish preparing for the wedding. More and more she felt inclined to agree with Kenny and Maeve. Perhaps it really was time for Tess to stop living alone.

The Brehony family of Hollymaine were well liked in the village. Somehow they had the gift of treating everyone with the same warmth and respect, whether it was Tom Rooney who swept up the leaves in autumn or billionaire hotelier Peter Kennedy who could afford to buy up half the county. Through family disappointments and achievements, the Brehonys always managed to stay the same. It meant that on top of a worldwide circle of friends and family, virtually everyone in the parish was invited to celebrate the wedding of Katie to Ronan and so the old Augustinian abbey was packed to capacity. The parish priest, well used to his church being a popular venue for weddings, had added rows of extra seating to the rear of the regular pews. Baskets and sprays of flowers were festooned everywhere and a little orchestra played incidental music as everyone waited for Katie to arrive. Sophie and Isobel sat in the row behind Tess and Robert, Kenny and Maeve. Isobel was dressed in a plain black suit which partly hid her expanding waistline. There was some colour back in her cheeks now and she looked more like her old self, but she was even more waspish than usual. She eyed up the more fashionably dressed ladies with barely concealed envy. Then her eyes came to rest on Maeve.

She leaned over and whispered pointedly in Sophie's ear: "Dear me!"

"What?" said Sophie who was boring holes into the back of Robert Franklin's handsome head with her eyes.

"Look at Maeve. What an extraordinary outfit for a wedding!"

"Don't be nasty. I think it's rather eye-catching."

"If you like lace and feathers and beads and suede fringes. You don't think she's got Red Indian blood in her, do you?"

Sophie pursed her lips and grimaced. "I'm not going to laugh – so don't make me. It's a perfectly nice outfit and you shouldn't be so critical. Maeve spent a small fortune on it."

"She looks like Minnehaha."

Isobel would have spent longer analysing Maeve's origins except for the fact that out of the corner of her eye she spotted Regina and Jim Kearney on the far side of the church smiling and waving over at her. She smiled back half-heartedly at her parents, gave a tight little wave and mouthed the words "Talk to you later" to them. It wasn't a complete lie. She did really intend to spend some time with them later, but maybe not just later today.

Ronan waited nervously at the altar, the best man by his side. Then Katie arrived a fashionable fifteen minutes late. With her arm laced gently through her father's, together they walked down the aisle to the sounds of the little orchestra playing the wedding march. She looked beautiful in a classic fitted white gown and a flowing organdie veil. Beautiful, serene and happy – as a bride should look – walking steadily towards the man she hoped to spend the rest of her life with.

"God help her!" whispered Isobel waspishly.

"She looks stunning and I know they'll be very happy," Sophie replied.

Back at the castle, after the banquet and the speeches,

the crowd had begun to mingle. Ronan led his new bride onto the dance floor and soon others followed. Kenny made such a big show of asking Sophie to dance that she couldn't really refuse him. In any case it was an opportunity to express her concerns about Tess and Robert. Kenny was not one of nature's dancers and close up she found it hard to make any kind of eye contact with him. He kept looking over her shoulder or at her chin.

"Do you think it's time we took the matter of Tess in hand?" he said loudly into her ear over the music

"How do you mean?"

"I mean she's vulnerable on her own. And she's old – or at least not young any more. I'm not saying she can't cope or anything – but it would be awful if someone was to take advantage of her if you know what I mean. I'd never forgive myself."

The word 'old' seemed wrong somehow. Tess wasn't old, not even close. But now was not the time to scold Kenny for his tactlessness.

"What do you think we should do?" she asked.

"She should stay with us for a while. Then she'd see the house is just too big and isolated for one old person living alone. There's plenty of room in our place and she'd be safe from – well, from people like Franklin."

"Tess is fiercely independent. I'm not sure she'd agree."

Kenny's thin lips spread into something approaching a smile. "Leave that to me and the power of subtle persuasion, When the builders turn up, Maeve and I will whisk her over to our house. She won't even know what hit her. And I can guarantee you," he said glibly, "once she's been with us for a few days, Tess will never want to go home again."

Sophie had her doubts about Kenny's subtlety and his plan which sounded plain tactless. But she knew she would have to keep her mouth shut about it – if there was to be any chance of getting Tess away from the clutches of Robert Franklin.

She extricated herself from Kenny's waltzing arms and glanced across uneasily at her grandmother. Tess was sitting with some of the Brehonys and she didn't look even the slightest bit vulnerable or old. If anything, she seemed more like a woman in her fifties. With her customary grace and handsome features, Tess was still capable of turning heads. She chatted easily with her companions, and almost everyone from the parish made a point of talking to her. Sophie felt disloyal suddenly, as if she was betraying her grandmother by even listening to Kenny and Maeve's side of things. Wasn't it crude and tactless of them to be talking behind Tess's back about moving her, to be referring to her as old, to be implying that she was no longer independent? Perhaps her grandmother was right about them after all. But on the other hand – where was the evidence? There was only concrete evidence on one thing – Robert Franklin who was a clear and present danger.

Coming back from the luxurious ladies' bathroom she bumped into him.

Time to act. To take the bullshitter by the horns!

"Robert, can we talk for a moment?"

"Sure," he said, indicating a cosy panelled little nook

to the side of one of the enormous fireplaces.

They sat. She looked into his clear brown eyes, trying to read his face for signs of shiftiness and unease. She opened her mouth to speak but found she couldn't. What could she say about him taking money from her grandmother that wouldn't be rude or presumptious? She grabbed two glasses of champagne from a passing waiter's tray and offered one to Robert.

"Cheers!" she said clinking glasses with him.

An uneasy silence descended as she wrestled to find the right words.

"About Tess," she began finally.

He held her gaze steadily. It was unsettling, almost hypnotic, like something in her heart wanted to melt towards him. But she took a deep breath and tempered her voice with steel.

"Why are you taking money from her?"

Sophie thought she noticed him shifting uneasily as he struggled to find words. He took a few gulps of champagne and stared at his knees intently for a few moments.

"Tess wants me to have it. Like I say, we're friends."

"Taking money from a lonely widow is hardly what I'd call being a good friend. It's the sort of despicable thing I'd never have expected from you. I never thought you of all people would stoop to such slippery deceit."

"Slippery deceit?" he said, raising his voice slightly and giving a masterly display of appearing confused and perturbed.

"Don't play the innocent with me, Robert! I know exactly what's going on."

"Do you? Tess has explained it to you then." he said, smiling easily.

"Just leave her alone."

To give him his due, he didn't try to defend or excuse himself. In fact, she thought he looked even slightly shamefaced. At last, after a lengthy silence he spoke.

"I'm not sure you fully understand and perhaps it's because you are still quite young. But I can't leave Tess alone. I just can't."

He stood up and carefully placed the still full glass of champagne on the table.

"Excuse me," he said and ambled back towards the bar.

Despite her row with Robert, and despite Isobel's intermittent nausea – the wedding proved very enjoyable. There was no shortage of invitations to dance, the floor crowded with guests from eight months to eighty years, plenty of time to catch up with people she hadn't seen since she was a child, lots of good champagne and appetising foods.

During a lull in the proceedings, Isobel, who wasn't drinking, rambled over to one of the vast leaded windows overlooking the sweeping lawns and let out a gasp.

"Oh Sophie! Look who it is! And in his own helicopter!"

A helicopter had landed outside on the vast lawn and a figure with head bent had emerged, dressed in formal wear, accompanied by an elegantly suited, slender dark-haired woman. Sophie glanced briefly at them through the window.

"Well, don't you know who it is?" Isobel said excitedly.

"Haven't a clue. Care less."

"I'd completely forgotten he'd probably be here. He's some sort of cousin I think. Wonder who the dark lady is?"

Sophie tried to look interested – but her thoughts were still on Tess and Robert.

"Who is he?" she said at last.

"You don't know!"

"I've been out of the country for quite a while remember."

"It's Paul Brehony!"

"Is he someone I should know?"

"Everyone knows who Paul Brehony is. You can't open a newspaper without seeing his face."

"What does he do? Is he a film star or a Riverdancer or something?"

"No, silly! He owns ErinAir Airlines and a whole load of other stuff. What you'd probably call a rough diamond. And by all accounts definitely not to be trusted! He used to be a teacher and then he was an alcoholic. Then his best friend helped him to buy an airline. Then he swindled his best friend who went to live in Marbella. And now apparently the best friend has completely disappeared off the face of the earth. Some people say he's living rough in Dublin and others insist that he's dead. It was all in the papers a few months back. Now there's talk of some kind of hostile takeover bid from one of the big European airlines – so he's not having a great year."

Sophie was half-heartedly digesting this information

when she looked out the window again to examine the subject under discussion.

"Oh my God! It's *him*!"

"I thought you said you didn't know him."

"I don't! I mean I do! But it can't be!"

She looked again to check. And there he was, resplendent now in an expensive black-tie outfit. But there was no mistake. "It's the steward! The one you saw me talking to! But if he's the owner of the airline, why was he dressed up as a steward?"

"It's his thing. You know like the chain-store owner working at the check-out desk. He gets to see problems from the ground – so to speak."

Sophie wasn't sure why, but she felt uneasy, embarrassed, like a naughty schoolgirl. As soon as he came through the door, a crowd quickly gravitated towards him, drawn by the potent allure of wealth and hard-earned success.

"I think I'll go for a walk. Don't fancy bumping into him again. He must think I'm an alcoholic and a head-case."

"I doubt that Paul Brehony even remembers meeting you," said Isobel.

"No, of course he won't remember me, but I'll go for a walk all the same. Will you be all right?"

"Don't worry about me."

Sophie escaped quickly through the grand front doors and took the path which ran alongside the little river. She walked for a while, until she found a wooden bench beneath an oak tree. The day was warm. Sunshine flickered and splashed through the rich green foliage and glinted on the water. A light breeze rustled and mingled with the sound of water rippling over stones. The first of the mayfly hovered in the air. Trout glistened and darted beneath the surface of the water.

She felt soothed, calm. She congratulated herself on booking into Ashford Castle – it wouldn't be financially possible again for a while – perhaps never. But now here for Katie Brehony's wedding, back near her grandmother, Sophie realised that, in spite of all the current uncertainties in her life, she was deeply contented to be home. She leaned her head back and closed her eyes, listening to the soothing rhythms of nature. Soon, an easy grogginess swept over her and she drifted off into semi-unconsciousness.

"Are you awake?" said a familiar voice.

It was Paul Brehony. Sitting next to her.

Sophie jumped, embarrassed to be found snoozing on a bench with mouth half open. She sat up straight. "Yes, of course. I was just meditating."

"Sorry if I disturbed you."

"That's OK. I'm finished for today." She hoped he wouldn't ask about which particular form of meditation she was practising – because she didn't have a clue.

"Nice spot you found here." He pointed at a trout which jumped to catch a mayfly beneath the shadow of an overhanging bough. "That lad would make a grand meal."

"He would?" she said, swallowing uncomfortably. Sophie had trained herself to believe that all meat came from a big supermarket somewhere in a remote part of the countryside. She was convinced for instance that the fillet of beef which she'd so enjoyed at Katie and Ronan's wedding had been manufactured in Aberdeen by a family called the Anguses. The cattle, sheep and lambs peacefully grazing in the lush fields of South Mayo were for purely ornamental purposes only. Nobody actually ended up eating them. Did they?

"Yes. Nothing like a bit of freshly landed trout – baked in foil with a dash of lemon, a sprinkling of herbs and some butter. A meal fit for a king."

She pulled a face and was silent for a while, hoping he would go and leave her to enjoy the peace of her own company.

"You don't like flying," he said.

She noticed now for the first time the strong Dublin accent, noticed also a certain hard-edged attractiveness in his face. What had Isobel called him? A rough diamond! She wondered why he wasn't with his elegant companion.

"I hate it," she said at last.

"It's a very safe way to travel."

"Oh please! I've read all the self-help manuals. I've tried hypnotism. I've even tried therapy. Nothing works. From now on, I'll only get into a plane if my life depends on it."

"Don't you think that's a bit like cutting off your nose to spite your face?" He grinned at her, then added: "And that's always a pity when there's a pretty nose involved."

He stretched out his legs, leaned his head back and

closed his eyes against the sun.

She stole a sideways glance at him and frowned. He was undoubtedly handsome, something dark and brooding and disturbingly unrefined about him. She stirred restlessly on the bench, the closeness of his large frame making her warm and oddly dizzy at the same time. But Isobel had said something else about him, something unpleasant and she'd only been half listening. She tried hard to recall what it was but couldn't and returned to admiring the river and the woodland. Her eyes were drawn to a pair of birds perched on a lichened stone by the edge of the river. They were squabbling over some juicy morsel. Then she remembered what Isobel had told her about Paul Brehony. He'd stolen the company from his best friend. She stood up abruptly and swept miniscule dust from her silk dress.

"Well, it's been nice meeting you again," she said coolly.

He opened one eye lazily and saw with some surprise that she was leaving. He stood up and grinned crookedly at her. "Nice to meet you too. Paul Brehony, by the way." He extended his hand.

She gave it the briefest contact and then said evenly: "Sophie Flanagan – and I wouldn't count on my business in future if I were you." There was a note of both mockery and dismissal in her voice which he seemed to ignore completely.

"I'll bring the matter of your future business to the attention of our company accountant – let him know that our profits are in for a sharp fall this year."

He smiled again, half expecting a response. But she said nothing.

"Enjoy the rest of the wedding." She turned to go.

"I'll try," he answered and for a brief moment she glimpsed something absolutely forlorn about him.

When Sophie got back to the hotel from driving Tess home, most of the wedding party had dispersed. The bride and groom had long since left and now all that remained in the old panelled foyer were a few stragglers, a couple of old country bachelors propping up the bar and reminiscing about the making of *The Quiet Man*, a young couple deeply immersed in each other, and the band who had provided the music, now off duty and making up for lost time. Not yet ready for sleep, she ordered a cup of tea and sat into a quiet corner behind a pillar, leafing through a pile of magazines. She tried to concentrate but her mind kept wandering back to Tess and Robert Franklin.

She heard a low murmuring voice from the other side of the pillar and recognised it as Paul Brehony. Now he sounded irritable and completely different to the laidback man of nature she'd met on the bench earlier. His companion also sounded cross. Sophie noticed her very refined accent and a touch of shrillness about her voice. It quickly became clear that they were having some sort of argument. If Sophie tried to leave now, it would be very obvious but on the other hand she didn't like to eavesdrop. She tried rustling the magazine pages to alert them to her presence. She rattled the cup noisily in its saucer. But it seemed they were in a little battle zone all of their own, and oblivious to everything and everyone else. She couldn't help hearing the tail end of it.

"Let's not spoil the evening," he said and Sophie thought she detected a note of tenderness in his voice.

"You are the one who has spoilt it," replied the dark-haired woman.

"Marina . . ." he said softly with a trace of remorse, like he was apologising for something, "I'll make it up to you somehow."

"I'm going to bed," came the icy response. "This whole wedding business is exhausting, so much emotion everywhere, and ghastly people one must talk to. Are you coming?"

Sophie, much to her own annoyance found herself straining to hear his reply.

There was a brief silence before he mumbled something which earned the hot retort:

"Fair enough. Suit yourself," from his companion.

In spite of her luxurious surroundings Sophie tossed and turned all night, unable to find restful sleep. In the early morning light she stumbled onto the balcony and looked out over the lake. Nothing much was visible beneath the heavy mist. Showered and dressed, she went to settle the bill at reception.

"There's a message for you, Miss Flanagan," said the receptionist holding up a white envelope.

Over breakfast she opened the envelope and found inside Paul Brehony's business card, a handwritten note scrawled on the back: "*How about lunch sometime? Give me a call – PB.*"

She was surprised and quite annoyed. But then self-made men like Paul Brehony, not all that well schooled in the social graces, probably strode through the world thinking they could click their fingers and any number of eager women would gladly fall at their feet. The casual arrogance of sending her such an informal familiar note rankled, particularly as he was so obviously with some other woman, a woman he evidently wasn't treating very well either, if last night's overheard conversation was anything to go by. What did that say about him? It seemed that loyalty wasn't high on his list of virtues. She finished her breakfast and dropped the card in a waste-paper bin on her way out. Yet when she went for a walk in the balmy morning mist, she found herself smiling unaccountably.

Isobel emerged from the shower, briefly examined the breakfast-in-bed menu and decided on a glass of water. Alone in the palatial *Quiet Man* suite of Ashford Castle, she pulled out the pregnancy test. With careful deliberation she unfolded the sheet of instructions and examined the contents. She glanced out the window. The mist had lifted and across Lough Corrib, the Twelve Pins looked splendid in colours of mauve and pale amber and green. She savoured the beauty of the scene. It might be her last time to pause and admire the beauty of nature. If she wasn't pregnant – then she must be dying. It was the only solution. If she was pregnant – then she would end it all.

Either way she wasn't long for this world. She had made up her mind.

She turned the lock in the bathroom door and prepared to meet her fate.

Chapter 20

Len Crolly knew that he had been born to manage and destined to lead. He was a man well skilled in managing excellence into the future. His life's dream had always been to run a company and put his own unique stamp on it. As part of that strategy, and in his new role of General Manager of The Athena Club, he decided to call in a management consultancy firm. He announced his plan at the weekly management meeting, which this week happened to fall on Isobel's day off.

"But Colman left everything in excellent shape. All you have to do is make sure it stays that way," said the duty manager, Kevin Gleeson.

"No, we need wholly independent feedback. There's a lot of dead wood in this company, too many chiefs and not enough Indians. We should have a flatter management structure with everyone answerable to one person. And what do all those girls in the office do? Read fashion magazines and discuss men as far as I can see. We could shed at least two jobs there."

"I wouldn't advise that. The girls work hard, often overtime without pay. They are the public face of The Athena Club. They're in the front line with the clients and they do a great job."

Crolly was insistent. He wanted a lean, mean personnel machine.

"The consultants arrive this afternoon. It's all arranged."

"What if they say everything is grand the way it is?"

"They won't. I'll brief them fully about what is wrong with the company, give them my recommendations and let them draw their own conclusions."

"That's a bit dishonest surely and doesn't it defeat the whole purpose? Shouldn't they be making a fully independent report?"

Crolly made a perfect steeple of his hands and smiled warily at Kevin. "Their report will be entirely without bias – I guarantee you that. Besides, there are things about the present state of the Athena Club which only I can explain to them."

"Have you spoken to Isobel about this? She is second in command."

"No need to. I don't want to burden her further. She's already struggling under her present workload. Being second in command to me is a responsibility she probably doesn't need. Besides, it's confusing to the other employees. I am the sole boss. Everyone should answer to me. It's more efficient."

"I don't follow."

"Flatter management structure, Kevin – it's where all the major companies are at right now. People getting hung up on titles and status – that's a thing of the past. We all have to muck in here and make the Athena Club the envy of organisations everywhere, so that we can maximise our flexibility with regard to future decision-making scenarios."

Kevin wasn't entirely sure what Len Crolly meant though he was wise enough not to pursue the matter. But he knew two things for sure. Colman would never have risked alienating his senior staff so tactlessly. And Isobel Kearney was in deep trouble.

It was Monday evening, the day after her return from Katie's wedding, and Isobel was in the Merrion Centre, stocking up on the week's groceries. She was absolutely starving. She bought apples, bananas, strawberries, and lots of salads and vegetables. At the meat counter she ordered free-range chicken breasts, organic low-fat mince and organic lamb cutlets. She selected two glisteningly fresh pieces of plaice and a plump salmon cutlet for storing in the freezer. Mentally, she ran quickly through her low-fat, high-protein, high-vitamin diet for the week. Steamed salmon with vegetables, baked plaice with tomatoes and basil, roast chicken breast with Mediterranean vegetables, lamb cutlets with minted greens and new potatoes, aubergines stuffed with lean savoury mince. Fresh fruit salad to finish each evening topped off with a dollop of low-fat fromage frais. She paused briefly at the dairy produce section, gazed longingly at the slabs of gold, foil-wrapped Kerrygold butter but forged onwards to low-fat spreads and organic, free-range eggs. She'd found a wonderful low-fat recipe for baked omelette. If she used two eggs and lots of herbs and tomatoes, it would make a tasty and satisfying meal for a mere two hundred and fifty calories. A slimmer's dream!

She was like a woman on a mission, or an Olympic athlete – obsessed, totally absorbed, driven, and blind to everything and everyone around her. It was a form of self-hypnosis, a type of auto brain-washing. If she concentrated very hard on a well-thought-out dietary regime, a basket full of healthy, non-fattening food, and a list of suitable recipes, then she wouldn't have to confront the other little matter of the pregnancy test.

The day before, she'd disappeared into the vast bathroom of the *Quiet Man* Suite, locked the door and stood for a good ten minutes psyching herself up in the mirror. Then she slid the slender tester from its box and crouched over the luxurious toilet, waiting for nature to take its course. But nerves had clamped up her bladder and though she squeezed and strained, nothing – not one drop of liquid fell on the tester. Perhaps it was her position. She straightened up, sat down, stood up, and leaned forward. Still nothing! She retrieved a magazine from the bedroom, returned to the bathroom and seated herself once more, hoping that reading would provide the distraction she needed.

If she wasn't in such a state of desperation, she would have laughed. Isobel's bladder generally had a life of its own. She had, as her mother put it, a fine healthy pair of kidneys which never had any trouble functioning – any time, any place, anywhere. Childhood journeys by car were frequently interrupted because Isobel needed "to go". Doing her final exams at college, she'd nearly driven one of the supervisors mad – with her constant calls to be accompanied to the loos. She'd learned to avoid drinking beer, more than one cup of coffee and as for the seventy-nine glasses of water a day that the latest health regimes dictated – it always seemed to her to be a bit of a joke.

Now here she was in the palatial bathroom of the *Quiet Man* Suite – seized up, dried up, out of order completely.

She found a picture of a waterfall in the magazine and concentrated hard on that to see if it would do the trick – or even the trickle. Nothing! In desperation she tried turning on first the steady flow of the hand-basin tap and then the powerful, gushing, tumbling, rushing bath tap. Nothing! The shower next – splashing, spilling, cascading in glistening streams of moisture – nothing!

She drank a tumbler of water and then another tumbler.

Throughout the flight back to Dublin and taxi ride to her dockland apartment, she waited, her stomach painfully bloated, increasingly anxious for nature to call.

It didn't.

It didn't even leave a message.

The following day, her stomach was so swollen that it looked like she was about to deliver twins. Anxiety gave way to anger and rage. She went for a swim in the almost empty pool of the Athena Centre and practically clocked a man who swam into her lane. In the changing rooms a teenage girl cut in at the mirror to touch up her already flawless complexion, leaving Isobel hovering menacingly on the sideline like an old hag wielding a mascara brush.

By the time she reached the Merrion Centre it seemed like all the world was cutting in on her – the man in the BMW who took the parking space that had her name on it, women with babies in buggies who ran over her toes, an elderly lady at the meat counter, several shoppers and their industrial-size trolleys. She tried heroically not to yield to feelings of negativity or rage, forcing herself to concentrate on the magnificent array of healthy foods she'd assembled.

At the check-out she stood in line as patiently as she could, carefully packing her groceries as she listened to the check-out girl going diligently through the same old rigmarole, under the watchful eye of a supervisor.

"Do you have a club card?"

"No."

"Are you collecting the stamps?"

"No, thanks."

"Are you in the monthly prize draw?"

"No!"

"Would you like to register for our on-line shopping facility?"

"*No!*"

"Are you collecting the Wedgewood?"

"*No, I'm not!*"

The assistant gave her a beseeching look that said she

was only doing her job.

"Sorry," said Isobel, noticing the supervisor and smiling apologetically at the girl on the check-out.

"Will you be paying with cash or credit card today, madam?"

Then it happened. Isobel Kearney's healthy bladder and kidneys kicked suddenly and violently back to life and she was overcome with an overwhelming urge to get to the ladies' – *quickly*!

"Excuse me – but I have to go."

"Cash or credit card, madam?"

"You don't understand. I have to go."

Without waiting to explain further, she abandoned the pile of healthy foods and half-packed bags, dashed to the pharmacy across the corridor, grabbed a pregnancy test kit, ran from the shop and barged into the ladies' where she found two women before her.

"I'm terribly sorry but I really have to go," she told them, crossing her legs and wincing in the hope that they would be sympathetic.

"You'll have to wait your turn," said the first, a dour-looking woman intent on keeping order in the ladies' convenience. She darted quickly into the only cubicle.

Isobel turned to the second woman.

"Please!" She was close to tears and the woman took pity on her.

"Go ahead. You must be really in a bad way."

"Thanks," she said with a mild sense of relief. But there was still the matter of the woman in the solitary cubicle – and by the sound of things she was checking through an entire month's shopping. After what seemed like an age the dour occupant emerged grinning broadly.

"Got it!" she announced. "Thought I'd lost my lipstick." She held up the little metal tube. "It's a very hard colour to find –"

Isobel swore under her breath, hurtled past the woman and barged into the cubicle, ripping the tester from its box in a frenzy of impatience.

Shortly afterwards the entire shopping clientele of the Merrion Centre were frozen in shock at the blood-curdling howl which emanated from the ladies' powder-room.

"*I hate fucking blue!*"

Later in Donnybrook Garda Station, a friendly young guard from County Offaly tried to make sense of Isobel's deranged behaviour in the shopping centre.

"The thing is, Miss Kearney – I know that you're not a criminal – but you did leave the supermarket without paying."

"But I didn't take anything!"

"And then sure didn't you go into the chemist and rob an item without paying for it either?"

Isobel nodded glumly. "I know."

"Then, of course, there's the matter of the woman you assaulted in the ladies' powdering convenience."

"Did I?"

"'*Get out of my way*,' you said and then you called her a lewd name and then you physically manhandled her and used foul language."

It wasn't quite how Isobel remembered it but she was in no position to argue.

"I didn't mean to."

"Lastly, Miss Kearney – there's the matter of behaving in a way which disturbs the peace."

"How do you mean?"

"The screaming and the foul language is what that refers to. So it's a terrible state of affairs really. I don't know what we're going to do with you at all."

Isobel wasn't exactly brimming with ideas herself. At that moment, it would have been quite nice if they had arrested her and thrown her into a cosy peaceful cell for a few weeks, or even a few months. After all, she was going to be a prisoner for the rest of her days now anyway. She sat in the little room sipping water and giving her details to Sergeant Moore.

"I have to ask you, Miss Kearney – are you now or have you ever been under the influence of an illegal substance?"

She was dazed, confused, shocked beyond belief to discover her condition, more terrified than she had ever been in her life, and sick – pale and trembling, drained of all energy. It was an obvious conclusion for the guard to draw.

"I'm sorry – could you repeat the question?"

"Have you been taking illegal drugs, Miss Kearney?"

She shook her head. "No, but I wish I had!" She leaned her elbows on the table and buried her face in her hands.

Garda Moore shifted his ample frame awkwardly on

the little stool, leaned forward and dropped all formality from his voice.

"Are things that bad?" he asked gently.

"About as bad as they can be, Garda Moore," she said, tears flooding down her cheeks. "I don't think things can get any worse for me."

"That's a terrible state of affairs. Wait there till I get you a cup of tea," he said, bolting from the room.

He returned quickly with a big mug of steaming hot tea and a Snickers bar, which he informed her he'd borrowed from the communal fridge. Sophie sipped the tea gratefully and munched hungrily through the chocolate as she told him the whole story. In the end he let her off with a caution, looking like he might burst into tears himself at any moment.

Sophie collected her from the police station and sat up with her late into the night discussing the options. Never before had either of them confronted such a paralysing moral dilemma.

"If you decide to have an abortion – that's your decision. People don't need to know. Not your mother, not Phil, not any of your friends or colleagues. And I'll stick by you whatever you decide."

"The thing is I haven't had sex for weeks – which means I could be two months gone already."

"Do you want this child? Will you love this child? Will you let this child become the most important little person in your life – until the day you die?"

"Certainly not! I detest babies. They're revolting."

"Then is it right to have the baby at all?"

"I could have it adopted."

"That's a possibility. Do you think you would be OK with that?"

Isobel lay on the sofa, her face buried in a green velvet and tapestry cushion. It was not how she had planned her life, not at all. She hated moral dilemmas. She was no good at them. Up to now, her usual approach to moral dilemmas was to walk or even sprint swiftly in another direction. There was no walking away from this though. Could she give a baby up for adoption? Definitely! Why did people get into such a state about babies anyway – squeaky, squawky, pukey things – that couldn't talk or walk and did their most intimate bodily functions in their pants?

"Of course, I could give it up for adoption. I definitely wouldn't want to keep it."

Sophie tried not to look too relieved. Abortion was too upsetting an option.

"If you decide on adoption, remember you'll be carrying the baby for nine months. There will be a bond – whether you like it or not. You need to be aware of that."

"Bond, my foot!"

"It's true. The strongest bond there is, stronger than friendship, stronger than romantic love. People die for their kids, for God's sake! Doesn't that say it all?"

Isobel gnawed at the cushion, wrestling with the big issues – issues she'd never had to confront in her life before – life, death, responsibility for another human being, thinking further ahead than her next summer holiday.

"Maybe I will go for a termination after all. It's awful. I hate it – but in this case maybe it's the only decent thing to do."

So it went on for hours on end, Isobel going round and round in circles, making and breaking decisions in the space of a few minutes – until her head swam from the trauma of it all.

Chapter 21

Isobel went to see her doctor the next day at lunch-time, simply to confirm her condition and to get the best professional care that she could. She had a little speech all prepared, rehearsing it over and over in the waiting-room. At last the receptionist called her name and she walked purposefully down the corridor into Doctor Gibson's surgery.

He smiled pleasantly at her over half-moon glasses. "What seems to be the tr–"

"I'm pregnant!" Isobel started off at a canter and quickly broke into a gallop. "I've broken up with my boyfriend. I don't want the baby. It would be cruel and immoral to have it. The world is full of unwanted babies whose parents didn't care enough for them not to let them be born but this baby will be different. I'm not going to inflict bad parenting on this child. And another thing – the world is over-populated already. People only want babies because of some primitive urge to reproduce themselves – it's the height of vanity. So I've given the matter a great deal of thought and I've decided to have a termination. That's all I want to say."

Doctor Gibson listened carefully and took a few notes.

"I see," he said finally.

There was a sudden and awkward silence.

"Well, that's it. When can I go to England?"

Doctor Gibson ignored the question.

"Are you on the pill?"

"Yes, up until a month ago, and before you say it – I never missed taking it."

"First date of your last period?"

"What does it matter? I've made up my mind."

He waited patiently with pen poised.

"Ages ago. I'm irregular and sometimes they're very light."

"Even a vague idea?"

"Hardly nine weeks, maybe less."

"Sure?"

"Yes, I'm sure."

"Right then. Pop up on the couch and I'll have a look."

"What's the point? I'm not going to have it."

"It's my job. I need to know how far gone you are."

Isobel sighed impatiently and climbed up onto the couch, submitting herself to pokes and prods and generally trying to pretend she was somewhere else altogether. Dr Gibson hummed and hawed and took more notes and scratched his sabled beard.

"Less than nine weeks you say, since your last period? Are you sure? Think hard."

She thought as hard as she could. Perhaps she'd had one since then. Maybe she was only a few weeks gone after all. That would make it all so much easier. A termination at six weeks didn't seem so bad.

"I'm not sure. Maybe I had a small one a few weeks ago. To be perfectly honest I can't remember. It's been a rough couple of months for me."

He poked and prodded some more, frowning and in some confusion.

"The thing is – and it's important that you know – but you're over sixteen weeks gone – nearer seventeen – by the feel of things."

Isobel stared up at him in silence for some moments.

"Don't you mean six weeks?"

"Sixteen is what I said and sixteen is what I meant," he said returning to his desk. She felt like she'd been hit by a whole convoy of speeding trucks.

"You're mad! I can't be!" She sat up and glared at him. Honestly, doctors didn't have a clue. How could he tell from prodding her abdomen anyway? It was complete nonsense. She fixed her clothes and reached for her handbag. "Humph! Well if you think I'm paying you for this piece of quackery – you've got another think coming."

"Isobel – I'm telling you the truth. I'm sorry if it's not what you want to hear – but I've been at this game for over thirty years – and I rarely get these things wrong.

You can have a scan – but it will simply confirm what I'm telling you."

"Seventeen weeks? But that means it's got arms and legs and everything."

He nodded.

"And most likely she's got a little face and a nose and toes and tiny little fingers and ears."

"Yes, that's right."

She sank down on the chair, choked with emotion. "But how could I be over four months gone without knowing?"

"It happens all the time. I've even had women on their third or fourth child, going into labour, not knowing they were even pregnant in the first place. And accidents happen even with women on the pill."

"Oh God – what am I going to do?"

Doctor Gibson left the room and reappeared with a cup of tea. It must have been Men Brew Tea Week or something.

"Now drink this – you've had a big shock."

Isobel sipped obediently while he wrote down a list of names and telephone numbers.

"Only you can decide what the right thing to do is. Though I would strongly advise against an abortion after sixteen weeks – so you'll have to make your mind up quickly. I've written out the names of some counsellors and organisations who help people in your situation. Let me know what you decide and mind yourself."

Back at work, she functioned in a daze, picking up the phone to call her mother several times and then replacing the receiver. She was barely conscious when Laura strolled into her office and cast a despairing look at the mounting mess of papers on her desk.

"The management consultants were looking for you earlier."

"What? Who?"

"They're waiting for you now – in the boardroom. I wouldn't keep them waiting if I were you."

Laura's tone bothered her slightly. And then suddenly a little corner of her brain clicked.

"Laura, there's something I want to ask you."

"I'm really busy, Isobel. Can't it wait?"

"No, I don't think it can," she said evenly. "At first when I realised Len Crolly had somehow got hold of my plans for the five acres – I thought it was Colman. I was dead sure of it, in fact, mainly because you and I have always been such good friends. Remember – we even went away skiing together last year. But then when I confronted him about it – I knew he couldn't have. He's just too decent. Then I thought Crolly, slimeshit that he is, might have taken them himself. You know – sneaked in here and downloaded the file onto a disk. But when I thought about it – he's too cunning to make that sort of obvious move. So there's only one other explanation."

Laura stared her down coldly.

"Did you steal the file, Laura?"

Laura smiled fleetingly and shook her head in disbelief.

"Did you, Laura? It makes no difference now anyway. So I'd like to know the truth – call it basic curiosity if you like."

"Well . . . I wouldn't call it stealing. I look on it as more – self-empowerment. Anyway you left the disc lying around. How was I to know you didn't want people seeing what was on it. It wasn't actually marked *Private*."

Isobel thought she might explode with fury – but something was happening to her. For the first time in many weeks, she felt strangely calm. There was no urge to give Laura a long and withering lecture on loyalty and betrayal, or several smacks in her heavily lipsticked gob. She didn't even feel inclined to ask why.

"I suppose he's going to promote you."

Laura smiled ruefully.

"Then I have only one piece of advice for you."

"What's that? Not that I need any advice from you."

"My advice is simply to be careful who you trust. It's not a nice feeling when people you care about let you down."

The management consultants were a pair of wannabee gurus. They came armed with degrees in psychology and Human Resource Management and MBAs from the Smurfit Business School and Doctorates from the Harvard Business School. They sat around a little circular table sipping water and being relentlessly friendly – talking about the weather, admiring the gymnastic facilities of the Athena, ruefully rapping themselves on the knuckles for not being more diligent with their own keep-fit programme. They complimented Isobel on her achievements to date, made special mention of her hands-on management style and her excellent relationships with staff. They asked her opinion about management structures, staffing levels, future deployment of resources. It was all pleasant smiles and even little jokes at their own expense of the "my wife says I'm too familiar with the wrong sort of six-pack" type. In the end they smiled some more and offered her what amounted to a humiliating demotion and a big reduction in salary or voluntary redundancy.

"So what do you think?" said one – as if he was offering the crown jewels.

"We're anxious to get your feedback. This is a consultative process," added the other.

"How many others are to go?" said Isobel.

"We plan to do this in stages. Naturally because of your senior role, we're consulting you first."

"What if I just want to stay in my present post?"

They winced and shrugged and fiddled around with documents and shook their heads sadly, as if to say that she would be making life unbearably difficult for everyone by indulging in such selfishness.

"Then I quit!" She gathered up her things calmly and shook their limp hands vigorously.

"For the record," she said coolly, and then paused to indicate that they should write, "I think you are making a big mistake and this company will be advertising for a new man in less than a year – if it survives that long. And if you don't believe me, just check out a simple little matter like the laundry facilities. Already the clients are complaining about the threadbare little tea cloths Len Crolly has seen fit to provide in place of proper towels –

all part of his penny-pinching approach. Still, it's not my problem any more. Goodbye."

"You quit! And you're pregnant! And you're going to keep the baby! Isobel, are you thinking straight?"

Sophie was stunned, worried, anxious, shaking with trepidation. Isobel – well, she sat curled up on the big old sofa in the sitting-room of Raglan Road as if she'd announced that she planned to get highlights or change her car.

"Where's the money going to come from? How will you support the child? They're very expensive. Mary Doran has a teenager and he spends more in a day that I spend in a week."

"How much can a baby cost? A few clothes, nappies, some pureed vegetables, a cot and a push-chair – what else is there? I'll get some severance pay and benefits and maybe I'll go home to Mum for a while."

"Does she know?"

Isobel turned pale at the thought of telling her mother. The rest of Ireland might have become a trendy liberal hotbed of lust and cocaine-snorting and rampant sex in broom-cupboards and on football pitches – but Regina Kearney and her circle of friends were a beacon of light to those who still hankered after the old ways. Sex outside marriage was something rather unpleasant that happened but was rarely discussed. Sex within marriage was what happened in the ten minutes between sliding under crisp cotton sheets after a warm sudsy bath and rolling over to indulge in the real pleasure of Maeve Binchy.

"I'll tell her when I'm used to the idea."

"You'll need to start talking to adoption agencies."

Isobel nodded absently. On the way over to Sophie's she'd scurried into Easons and spent half an hour lurking in the Mother and Baby section, furtively studying pictures of babies ranging from seventeen-week foetuses to three-month-old infants. The plan was to bombard herself with so many unpleasant baby images that she would be able to psych herself up for adoption – a kind of cheap form of aversion therapy. Up to now, babies were all ugly, looked like Gollum in *Lord of The Rings* and merely inspired feelings of slight revulsion. She pulled a book from the shelf and found some pictures of newborn infants. "This is exactly what I want," she mumbled to herself and set to examining them. They were scrunched-up and wrinkled for sure, did not have nice hair and their heads were funny shapes. Then the week-old infants. The expressions on their faces were plain idiotic. She smiled pityingly at them. Where was the attraction? What possible appeal could such a crumpled-up little creature have? "Aaaahhh, isn't he gorgeous?" A blonde woman, who looked slightly older than Isobel's mum, examined the pictures over her shoulder. "You never forget the smell and the feel of them when they're babies!"

"I'm sorry – did you say smell?"

"Four I had. All grown up now – but every time I see a baby I still get that funny tingly feeling running through me."

"You poor thing! That's awful!"

The woman didn't seem to hear her. She took the

book and began leafing through it.

"Aaaaaah, will you look! My Eamonn looked just like that – a little turned-up nose and those big blue eyes. He's thirty-five now. Has little ones of his own. Is it your first?"

"Who, me? Oh no! I'm just looking for a friend."

When the woman was gone, Isobel riffled through the book until she came to the picture that looked like baby Eamonn – now thirty-five.

Only now, for some strange reason she couldn't fathom, the baby in the picture looked not wrinkled and ugly – but beautiful and magical. Knowing that such a being was right now living and breathing inside her was not horrible any more – but exciting and deeply moving. At that moment it dwarfed absolutely everything else in her life. She forgot Phil Campion. She felt indifferent to Len Crolly and his paranoid empire-building. All the fight and energy and commitment that she'd channelled into her career seemed unimportant for the moment.

And just at the moment when she replaced the book on the shelf, she felt her stomach flutter gently – like butterflies on a warm sunny day.

Chapter 22

Joe and his two assistants had taken Sophie's house and garden in hand and quickly became a big feature of her life – clambering about the house in muddy boots, making tea in the kitchen, occasionally showing flashes of genius in the way they salvaged what looked like bits of useless timber but turned out to be crucial segments of Edwardian panelling, or a scrap of brass that was in fact an irreplaceable part for the lovely old tap fittings in the bathroom.

Money was getting tighter by the day. The renovation work had gone way over budget and Sophie was beginning to wonder if she might have to get a job to make ends meet. Though she wasn't sure how she was going to have the time to do a job, what with travelling down to Tess almost every week and, of course, being best friend to Isobel – which at the moment looked likely to blossom into a full-blown career option.

She had intended to spend the afternoon finding someone to do something with the garden but when she got back to the house from her grandmother's, Isobel was sprawled across the front steps, in jog pants and trainers, shovelling a Big Mac into her mouth as if she hadn't eaten for a month.

"I thought you were going home to Mum."

"Norgmh!" said Isobel through three layers of bun, two layers of minced meat, one layer of cheese and one layer of pickle.

"I take it that's a no."

"Yesgrmh."

"Can you stop eating like that? It's making me ill. Come inside at least."

Isobel followed her into the hall and dispatched the last of the burger, washing it down with the remains of a large Coke.

"Sorry, Sophie – but I was absolutely starving."

"I told you not to skip breakfast and to make sure you have little snacks every two hours or so."

In the kitchen Sophie disposed of the Big Mac wrappings with saintly tolerance as she munched virtuously on a crisp green apple. "That's what I do – and then I never feel the need to stuff my face." She had the high moral eating ground and she wasn't letting go. "Five helpings of fruit and vegetables every day, a reasonable portion of calcium-enriched milk, cheese, etc, baked or grilled meat or fish – it's not expensive."

"But I did eat breakfast."

"I mean a proper breakfast!" Sophie said, lighting a cigarette.

Isobel would like to have begged her not to – to explain candidly that she was coming close to the point where she could detect the nauseating smell of stale tobacco even if it was only the one cigarette, smoked ten years ago, in a remote corner of Munster, through a half-open window in a gale force wind. But she couldn't face even a mild argument right now, especially not after the morning's events.

"I had orange juice, cereal and two slices of wholemeal toast with tea," she said, coughing lightly instead.

Sophie didn't seem too impressed.

"Then a couple of hours ago, I had a yoghurt and a banana."

"I don't believe you. Last week you couldn't even eat a cream cracker."

"But I feel different this week. I don't feel sick any more. I keep wanting to eat all the time – and fruit and vegetables just don't hit the spot. I want burgers. I want curries. I want dirty big doner kebabs. I want greasy fish suppers."

"Stop it! You're being disgusting."

"I want catering blocks of banana icecream. I want giant bags of marshmallows. I want enormous cream buns with lashings of chocolate sauce. I don't seem to have any control."

She looked at her friend pleadingly, hoping for some kind of sympathy. Her life was going down the tubes. Her figure was going down the tubes. And now she didn't even have a roof over her head any more. As and from this morning! Effective immediately! Or as soon as she could pack up her things! In all the turmoil of the past three months, she'd fallen badly behind in the rent and the lease was due for renewal. The landlord had written to remind her but she'd had more important things to worry about. Now she didn't even have enough money to pay the arrears.

The landlord Packy Barron, a stocky ginger-haired chicken farmer from Westmeath, told her with his usual stunning originality that he wasn't running a charity. Then he added something about a man paying a piper to play some tune or other – but she hadn't the energy to listen. And what had it got to do with paying rent anyway? But desperate as she was, Isobel was still at the stage where sleeping in a doorway was much less frightening than going home to Regina Kearney and friends. So here she was now – a friend in need – on Sophie's doorstep. And wasn't there a saying about a friend in need being a friend indeed?

"Let's go for a walk," she said chirpily, trying to show that even though she was eating for her country, at least she was up for a bit of brisk exercise.

"There's not much point in hanging about here, I suppose," Sophie said, looking round her.

Everywhere was covered in dust. There was no floor in the living-room and it was barely possible to move in the kitchen for the amount of builders' tools and equipment, or for that matter builders. They were nice and pleasant and everything but she felt like a foreigner in the house, like she was really in the way.

The afternoon was fine. The last of the May blossom was falling in pink drifts along the footpath. Along the road they passed fine houses, large, red-brick, some still in offices and apartments, but many reconverted into sumptuous family homes. Sophie surveyed the family homes with envy. Their roofs were perfectly tiled in salvaged blue Bangor slates. The brickwork was cleaned and repointed. Cast-iron gutters and pipes were in pristine condition and painted in glossy black. If decaying doors and windows had to be removed, they were replaced with finest quality timber fittings, expensive sashed windows and richly stained glass, in keeping with the Edwardian style. She knew that even with Joe's repairs, her house would still end up looking scruffy and bedraggled next to these beautifully restored edifices. She stopped to admire one house in particular. The side gates were open and it was possible to see into the carefully manicured and lovingly tended garden at the rear.

"Now that's what I want my garden to look like – but with a patio area and maybe a nice secluded decked pergola down at the end."

"That sounds lovely." Isobel tried her best to sound interested.

"Then I'd love one of those Japanese gardens of tranquillity as well – you know – just gravel and rocks and a few bonsai trees."

"It sounds amazing. It really does. Japanese! That's just amazing."

Isobel wondered if they might go round by the little row of shops. Of course, she wasn't hungry any more, not after the Big Mac. But it was a warm day and she thought it would be nice to have an ice cream to cool her down – a nice big thick creamy slab of banana flavour between two crisp wafers. She was on the point of raising the subject when she remembered the reason she'd landed on Sophie's doorstep in the first place. What was wrong with her? Isobel was generally the sort of woman who didn't sleep easy if her burglar alarm wasn't set, who didn't sleep at all if bills weren't paid six weeks in advance. And that had been quite a challenge in the Phil Campion days. But here she was, completely forgetting that she soon wouldn't have even a roof over her head, and obsessing about ice cream instead.

"Sophie, there's something I want to tell you . . ."

"Look, I'm sorry I slagged you about the food. It came out wrong. I know nothing about being pregnant – though I know you have to watch your weight and your diet and in my own stupid way I was trying to help. But I spoke out of turn and I'm sorry. You are my dearest, bestest friend and I wouldn't hurt you for anything."

Oh God! What was happening! Isobel felt big globules of something forming somewhere in her stomach and heaving up through her. Maybe she was having a miscarriage. Her head pounded horribly. Her body began to tremble and her hands shook uncontrollably. Next thing her face went into some kind of muscular spasm – then big streams of water came pumping from her eyes and streaming down her face, forming large puddles on her cheeks and chin.

"Oh, Sophie! That is the sweetest thing anyone has ever said to me!" She flung her arms around her friend – just at the busy junction of Raglan Road and Baggot Street – fastened her in a clinging embrace and sobbed her heart out.

"Hey – what's this?" Sophie said, touched by her friend's affection but also a little embarrassed.

"I don't know . . . I mean . . . that thing you said about not hurting me for anything . . . that is so sweet ... and it just made me want to cry."

She stopped sobbing just as suddenly as she'd started, straightened herself up, looked around her and blushed crimson red. People on the street were giving them very strange looks.

"Sorry about that. Don't know what came over me!" she said brusquely. "I was going to tell you something important. Only now I've forgotten what it is. Oh well! Never mind! Let's go and get an ice cream."

By the time they got back from their walk, the builders had left for the day – leaving the house a bit like the *Marie Celeste*, smoking teacups, half-eaten Jaffa cakes, sugar-coated spoons and everything. Sophie wondered if Isobel should go home to bed – but she'd already put her foot in it once.

"Are you tired from the walk?" she asked gently.

"Me? Not at all! Fit as a fiddle. Let's do a bit of a clear-up."

There wasn't much point in doing any cleaning since

it would all be one big mess again in the morning – but they washed and dried the dishes and swept the worst of the dust from the kitchen floor. Isobel had been straining to remember what she needed to tell her friend and just as she was on the point of remembering, the telephone rang. Sophie ran to answer it.

Isobel yawned. The day's events were catching up on her – trauma, exercise and housework. The very important thing that she had to tell Sophie had slipped from her mind once again and all she could think of was lying down. She'd never felt so tired in her whole life – not even when she'd gone to Crete with a gang from the Athena Club and done without sleep for three days. She yawned again – her mouth stretching open so widely that she thought her lips might split.

"Do you mind if I have a lie-down?"

"No. Excuse the mess though."

Isobel slid beneath the duvet on the bed in the spare room and fell into an instant slumber. Night-time came and Sophie didn't have the heart to wake her, so she slept on until a clatter and banging and general stomping about the place announced the arrival of the builders in the morning.

Sophie had prepared a wholesome breakfast – freshly squeezed orange juice, scrambled eggs, wholemeal toast and piping hot tea. They settled down to eat, huddled around the little kitchen table while the builders bustled and shuffled about them. Tiger had positioned herself on Joe's jacket which he'd slung in a corner chair and she surveyed the odd human behaviour with a certain degree of feline contempt.

"Now I remember what I wanted to tell you. I've to vacate my apartment before the end of the week."

"But that's tomorrow."

"Yes, I know."

Then she explained about falling into arrears after she'd thrown Phil out, and about forgetting to renew her lease and Packy Barron who couldn't wait to get her out of the apartment so that he could charge an even more extortionate rent for it. And though she begged and pleaded and threw herself completely at his mercy, he didn't seem to be even slightly moved by her plight. "I'm a simple chicken-farmer, Miss Kearney – not Mother Theresa of Calcutta," he'd told her with heart-rending honesty.

"So – I don't know what I'm going to do. It feels as though my whole life is in ruins. Got any nice marmalade or apple jelly?"

"Marmalade? Apple jelly? It's time you stopped thinking about food. Set about sorting out the priorities. What will you do?"

Isobel squeezed past Joe who was smoothing plaster onto one of the walls, stepped over loose planks of wood and tins of paint and rummaged through cupboards until she found a pot of strawberry jam. She plucked a clean spoon from the draining-board and tucked in. The ritual of spooning jam into her mouth was oddly comforting and she would have remained quite happily in her strawberry-jam-induced trance if Sophie hadn't insisted on pursuing the matter of where she was going to live.

"Isobel – put the spoon down. We need to talk about this. We need to talk about this now. What about going home for a few weeks – just until you get sorted?"

"No way! Anyway I don't know what you're worrying about. It's not such a big deal. Bound to be loads of places for rent at this time of the year. I'll just have to get a slightly smaller place in a slightly less fashionable part of town. I still have some money my grandmother left me and if needs be I can live on that until I get sorted."

Sophie's heart sank. She knew there was only one thing to do – but she was torn. Isobel was her closest friend. It was just wonderful how they'd been able to take up with each other as if they'd never been parted. They hadn't gone their separate ways. They hadn't found intolerable faults in each other. If anything, she felt closer to Isobel now than to anyone, except possibly Tess. But the fastest way to kill a friendship stone dead in the water was to have a friend move in. She'd seen it before and when friends set to squabbling about who put out the bins, or whose voice to leave on the call-answering service, or playing loud music in the middle of the night, or deciding exactly what magnets were OK to put on your fridge, or when it was time to change the potpourri – well, unlike lovers, they didn't have the useful and delightful device of sex to put things back on an even keel again. When live-in friends fell out, it was frequently terminal. She took a deep breath.

"There's only one solution."

"What?"

"You have to move in here. Now don't shake your

head, and don't for God's sake have one of those weepy wobblies. You have to move in and that's all there is to it. It's the only sensible thing to do."

Isobel relinquished the jampot and spoon and said nothing. Clearly mulling over the idea, she ambled across to the window overlooking the garden and stood there for a long time gazing intently at a badly gnarled tree.

"It's a very kind offer," she said at last.

"Then it's settled. You'll stay? You can take the spare room. It's pretty basic but we can get Joe's crew to give it a lick of paint. There's plenty of wardrobe space for clothes and stuff and you can have it rent free until . . . until . . . well, until whenever."

If Sophie expected Isobel to burst into tears and fling affectionate arms about her, it was not what happened at all.

Isobel simply nodded and turned to face her. "I don't think so. But thanks. I know you mean well." She gathered up her things and moved swiftly towards the door. "And don't worry about me – I'll be fine."

She was through the hall and halfway down the steps before Sophie caught up with her.

"Please, Isobel! You're being foolish. You're in a bad way, not thinking straight. Please, please say you'll come and stay here – for a while anyway."

Isobel rounded on her angrily. "Foolish? Not thinking straight? I can manage perfectly well without your Ballsbridge charity, Sophie Flanagan. I suppose you get some kind of thrill from offering to help poor foolish Isobel Kearney who can't think straight and has got herself into the worse possible mess that any girl could get into?"

Sophie stared at her. A couple of the builders edged past them carrying buckets of plaster.

"No . . . it's not like that at all. You're my friend and I . . ."

It was no use continuing. Isobel had bolted across the front garden and stormed off down the footpath to her car.

Chapter 23

Isobel was in a state of complete turmoil. Pregnant, jobless, and now without her closest friend. And it was all, every single bit of it, including the ridiculous argument with Sophie, entirely her own fault. She sat amid the increasing chaos of her apartment eating a fried-egg and brown-sauce sandwich and prepared herself for the most terrifying ordeal of her life – the panic-induced call to her mother. Since leaving home to go to college at the age of nineteen, Isobel had proudly proclaimed her self-sufficiency. There was nothing her mother could teach her, nothing she couldn't handle on her own. She'd silenced Regina Kearney on almost every issue, rejected her sad matronly attempts to cling to her daughter, to hold on to whatever little shreds of influence she still held. Occasionally, as a diplomatic sop, Isobel would call her mother for a leek-and-potato-soup recipe or the name of a little seamstress who could actually alter the Chloé dress without hacking it to bits. Once for her birthday, Isobel had even taken her mother away to London for the weekend. They booked into a nice hotel overlooking Hyde Park, did all the shops, strolled around Kew Gardens, went to a show and had dinner in the OXO Tower. It had all the ingredients for an idyllic mother/daughter weekend but by the end of the three days, Isobel was relieved to see the back of her mother.

Now Isobel finished the last of her fried-egg and brown-sauce sandwich and picked up the phone to call her mother. But where should she begin? Mum – I've lost my job. Perhaps not. How about – the landlord is refurbishing and won't be renewing my lease. No. She had gone to such pains over the past few years to show that she was entirely self-sufficient and independent, could handle any little set-back life might throw at her, that her mother would rightly feel disinclined to interfere now. Or how about: I've dumped Phil and I'm going to have his baby in twenty weeks! If the very thought of alcohol didn't still make her stomach churn terribly – this last thought would have been enough to send her guzzling quickly through several bottles of wine. She dialled, sweating, trembling, dry throat – classic panic symptoms.

"Mum?"

"Issie – what a lovely surprise! It's lovely to hear from you. Is everything OK?"

"Mum – I'm fine."

"Well, any news?"

"What do you mean? No – nothing much. I've just

been very busy – with work and everything."

"And how's Phil?"

Well, that was one bit of news her mother would be genuinely delighted to hear. Perhaps she could start with that and just say that she wanted to come for a few days to recover.

"It's all over between us."

She could hear her mother straining with all her might not to gloat or say something controversial.

"Oh dear! I am sorry. But plenty more fish –"

"Mum!"

"Sorry – I shouldn't say that. Anyway, at least you weren't married and there are no children to think of."

No children to think of! With a tiny being fluttering away in her belly, the dear little thing limbering herself up for life! There and then Isobel realised it was naïve to think of telling her mother about the baby, foolish to imagine she could enlist her mother's support.

She quickly ended the conversation and once again called Packy Barron to throw herself at his mercy. It was pure humiliating, but she begged, she pleaded, she told him she'd never met a fairer, kinder landlord, and being the big-hearted chicken farmer that he was – he said yes, she could stay on in the apartment – for an entire week – if she paid all her arrears – at the increased rate. He couldn't say fairer than that! He wouldn't see her out on the street! He wasn't a complete bastard!

Relieved that she had bought some time, albeit very expensive time, Isobel trawled through the papers looking for affordable apartments in a nice part of town. She circled one or two that looked promising, then phoned Sophie to apologise about her angry outburst.

"I'm sorry too," said Sophie. "I was tactless."

"You were just being what you've always been – a true friend. I understand, Sophie – I really do."

"You know you're welcome to stay – as long as you like."

"Thanks. I appreciate the offer."

"Have you told your mother yet?"

"I tried to, over the phone – but I couldn't – not yet."

"You'll have to tell her soon. It would be awful if she heard from someone else."

The thought of someone telling her mother about the baby was a new and unexpected worry.

"The landlord's given me another week."

"He broke his heart."

"I'm starting to look for somewhere else – somewhere more homely. Like I said – I'm sure I'll be installed in a lovely little bijou apartment in no time at all."

Sophie insisted that they look together and that afternoon they sat in a quiet corner of Searson's pub on Baggot Street poring over the Apartments to Let section, circling the ones which sounded most promising. They found three.

They drove across the city to Stoneybatter, past the lovely Orthodox church, and into a very pretty development of houses built in the walled garden of an old hospital. It was the perfect set-up – delightful red-brick town houses in an area with loads of atmosphere, and people of all ages and stations. The house itself was a little jewel –

decorated tastefully and with a lovely sunny decked garden to the rear. The owner, a teacher, was going to live in New Zealand for a year. And the rent was well within Isobel's budget. She was on the point of telling the owner that she'd take it, when Sophie tugged at her sleeve and pulled her aside.

"What's that under the coffee table?" she said pointing.

The young man from the rental agency laughed nervously.

"One of the kids next door probably. It's probably just a bit of Hallowe'en nonsense."

"But it's early summer!"

"I'll just get a dustpan and sweep it up," he said and disappeared into the kitchen.

"Very life-like, isn't it," said Isobel bending to take a closer look. It was a massive black plastic spider – the kind that would put the fear of God into David Attenborough.

"Amazing what they can do nowadays," Sophie said as she leaned forward to examine it.

Quite soon afterwards – in fact immediately afterwards, Sophic and Isobel found themselves scrambling frantically through the front door, and clambering hastily into the car, checking their ankles in case they'd picked up any unwanted passengers.

The young fellow from next door appeared, looking quite upset. "So you've found Mahatma Ghandi. There's no need to shout. He doesn't like loud noise."

It turned out that Mahatma the Tarantula didn't live alone. Young Brian from next door made sure he had lots of exotic company. There was Florence Nightingale, the Lizard and Thomas Jefferson, the Grass Snake. He was just that week expecting delivery of Queen Victoria – a rather dangerous-sounding reptile from Australia. Clearly the boy had a keen grasp of famous historical figures and at least it explained the incredibly low rent.

Isobel tried not to be despondent. After all there was still the "*One-bedroom bijou apartment in a period building, quietly secluded and oozing old-world charm. Apartments in this road rarely come up for rent.*"

In almost every respect the advertisement was, strictly speaking, telling the truth. The building was attached to an old Victorian warehouse, but it was a jerry-built lean-to sort of attachment – and the use of the word "attached" could only be taken loosely. The quiet, secluded road was in reality the sort of laneway that even a hardened drug-peddling mass murderer might shy away from. And it was fair to say that apartments in this road rarely came up for rent – mainly because it was the only apartment. Every other tumbledown building was a back-street business of some sort or other. And yes, it did ooze old-world atmosphere – great big masses of the sludge-grey stuff that sprouted from the walls inside and out.

It was getting dark when they rolled up at the last of the three apartments. This one sounded the least promising: "*Small one bedroomed basement flat to rent.*"

They walked past a greasy takeaway, turned the corner and three doors down they descended dank steps through a door that had seen plenty of action, if the number of nailed-on pieces of timber was anything to go by. The owner was a dour lady called Mrs Clabby. She had very flat very black hair, a thin mouth and darting little eyes. She showed them round quickly – the living-room, with a two-ring gas stove and a grimy brown sofa that sat menacingly in the middle of the room. "It's antique!" she chirped. "More like ant-heap!" mumbled Isobel. The woman pointed out the very nice carpet from pre-famine days with its very own built-in curry and unwashed sock odour, and the ancient fridge that had its own personal hole in the ozone layer.

The bedroom wasn't much better. But at least it was dry and warm and the bathroom could be cleaned up with a few gallons of household bleach. Sophie's heart sank when Isobel said she'd take it. She felt horribly low and mean for not having been more insistent about the room in Raglan Road. But it wasn't too late. It was still possible to put the situation right.

"Isobel, you can't stay here. It's just awful. Please come to Raglan Road!"

"No, I've made up my mind. And it's just temporary. I'll soon be back on my feet," Isobel said vehemently.

Phil Campion, like Pythagoras, was a man of unerring mathematical instinct. For instance he could locate a free bar from a probable radius of seventy-five kilometres. In any given room occupied by an average of two hundred people, Phil was able to calculate without the use of quadratic equations exactly who the ones with money were – and more to the point – exactly who were the ones he could subtract money from. And this was especially true with women. His sensory detectors, his antennae, his base animal cunning, guided him intuitively to women who would let him into their hearts. He never wasted his time on street-wise women who were well able to play hard-ball. But, like the common tick, he instinctively found the tenderest sweetest spot and clung there until he found a more vulnerable sweeter spot somewhere else.

Right now, he knew that whatever defences Isobel had built up against him were crumbling. He'd bided his time after his expulsion, waiting until he'd find the crack in the wall which would lead him quickly back to his warm, easy life of sex, money, food and no responsibility.

Being a self-employed man was turning out to be a slightly more complex situation than he'd imagined. For starters, the process of having to tout for business was humiliating to say the least. It was disappointing to realise that people didn't actually know off the tops of their heads what an amazingly gifted video-maker he was. And they didn't seem to put any great value on his charm or his deep understanding of the misery of the human condition. They wanted facts and figures, dates and deadlines, samples of his work to date – and it was useless for him to point out that a true artist such as himself could not give fully of his astounding array of talents under the petty restraints of time and budget.

But he had managed to persuade a small warehouse on the Greenhills Road of the necessity for a 'safety and health in the workplace' video. It wasn't exactly Scorcese – but at least it was a start. The only awkward thing was that to realise his full artistic vision, he would need cash.

Since Isobel had gone pure stupid and hysterical on him that night a few months ago over a little fling he'd had with a girl on his most recent video-production course, and playing one of her stupid games had turfed him out on the street, he'd been shacked up with Billy who was a fireman. Billy lived in a nice house in Templeogue but now Billy's girlfriend was moving in and they would want the house to themselves. All along it had been his plan to return to Isobel, give her time to lick her wounds, come to her senses – and then close in for the reconciliation. He knew she couldn't live without him. He had that kind of irresistible charm.

Now, what with urgently needing a bed and more urgently needing cash to realise his artistic vision, the time was right. He finished up his pint. He would go home to Isobel. The woman loved him, for God's sake!

Chapter 24

Finding someone to put her garden in order had turned into a bit of a saga for Sophie. For one thing all the people recommended to her were booked up solid for the next six months, not to mention the fact that she'd have to take out a small mortgage to pay them. She left messages with several landscape gardeners who had been recommended to her by the neighbours, then tried one or two listed in the *Yellow Pages*, but they'd never even bothered to get back to her. In the end, she rummaged through drawers until she found Nick Lynch's crumpled-up business card, the "dead sound . . . all-round good person," that Cian would most trust with his life. It didn't sound promising at all.

But now Sophie sat in the garden, browsing through a pile of gardening magazines she'd borrowed from Tess, awaiting his arrival. He was almost an hour late. At last he arrived and she was briefly silenced as she came face to face with him on the doorstep. The one thing Cian had forgotten to mention was that Nick Lynch was startlingly attractive, the sort of bloke you'd see in an ad for jeans – unkempt in a sexy, rugged outdoor sort of way and not an ounce of spare flesh.

He had a mane of coppery brown hair, intense David Ginola eyes and a wry unsettling smile. He was armed with sketchpads, plans and maps, photos and even a couple of videos. He beamed with enthusiasm when he saw the garden. It was a rare delight these days, he told her, to get such a large garden in such a nice road. And he intended to give it the make-over of a lifetime. He'd done bigger projects but never one with so much real potential.

It was a blazing hot day and because workmen were clambering all over the house, he carried an old trellis table and two chairs to the bottom of the garden and set them down beneath the dappled shade of a tree.

Sophie provided cold beers and they quickly became immersed in the garden design, heads close together as they worked.

"This is a really exciting project," he repeated, sweeping a lock of coppery hair back from his face.

"I hope you're not going to come up with some dreadfully trendy thing full of mirrors and bits of steel," she said playfully.

He laughed, his healthy tanned face creasing up with delight. "No. I like to combine traditional with modern."

"That's a relief."

"Although I have some lovely yellow moulded plastic sculptures – could I interest you in those?"

"No, thank you!"

"Pity. Now tell me your hopes and dreams for this garden – what do you see yourself doing in it?"

She tried to explain her ideas and though it seemed to her like she was babbling incoherently about light and shade and colour and harmony, he seemed to take it all in.

"I think that's it," she said finally. "It probably all sounds very garbled and dull to you."

"On the contrary, you've got taste and style, Sophie Flanagan."

Hmmm! Was that a little flirt? Using her full name so playfully? She wasn't really ready yet at all for flirting. It felt a bit like trying to do some very intricate dance for which she had once been well schooled but was now long out of practice. The one-night stand with Hendro was the quenching of a pure physical need. There was little flirtation involved. She neither regretted it nor longed for it to happen ever again. But Nick Lynch was quite cute and maybe she could practise a little flirting with him – just to stop herself going completely rusty. Perhaps she'd invite him along to Hendro's party.

"Another beer?"

"Yes, please," he said and spread out a large sheet of graphed paper on the table.

When she returned he held up the paper for her to look at.

"What do you think? Of course, I forgot to include the yellow plastic sculptures – but you get the general idea."

It was quite impressive. He'd incorporated almost all of

her half-baked ideas into the drawing. Only he'd put shape and style on them. There were deep herbaceous borders, winding brick paths, little secret dappled corners of shade, screened off with trees. Along one of the long old red brick walls, he'd incorporated three terracotta wall fountains half hidden amongst the scented jasmine, deep blue clematis and climbing white roses. She was completely taken aback – it was as though he'd read her mind. Close to the patio he'd drawn a little Japanese-inspired garden and even written in the type of rocks and colours of gravel to be used.

"I don't know what to say."

"Don't you like it?" He beat his hand against his head in mock horror.

"I love it. When can we start?"

She was delighted when he said he could start work on the garden straight away. She'd been half afraid he would tell her that it was the wrong time of year and that all he could really do for now was the structural work.

"You'll be sitting in the garden of your dreams in less than a month's time," he promised her and slid a piece of paper across the table with the estimated costs roughly outlined.

She looked at the piece of paper and gasped. She'd imagined half that amount and even at that she'd intended to beat, cajole and flirt him down to a manageable few hundred. How could it possibly cost that much? More to the point – how could she afford it? She couldn't afford it. Best to bite the bullet now, pay him something for his time, and tell him she'd be in touch.

"A bit more than you were expecting?"

"It does sound like a lot."

"To be honest – I'm giving you a good price."

"I just can't afford it."

He smiled and scratched his head and looked genuinely disappointed, like a little boy who'd been promised a go at driving the train and was let down at the last moment.

"I'm not giving up on this one. Perhaps you could come up with the money somehow. And think of the beautiful garden you'd have – like one vast open-air room. That's worth a lot more than five thousand euro. And believe you me – most of the people on this road would consider spending five thousand euro on their gardens as just annual maintenance."

"Now you've made me feel bad."

"I didn't mean to – it's just such a beautiful garden – could be such a beautiful garden. Tell you what – I'll have a think about it and I'll call you in a few days. Maybe we should have a chat with Kinvara Budd – she supplies my raw materials. Please say yes."

He was determined not to be defeated. Anyone else would have turned on their heel and gone off muttering about people wasting their time. But not, it seemed, Nick Lynch. Perhaps, after all, Cian was a better judge of character than she thought.

"OK," she said reluctantly and then added quickly, "I hope you don't think I'm being very forward but . . ."

"Forward? I like the sound of this already."

"Only I'm invited to a party in the mews on Saturday

night – and I was wondering if you'd like to join me? Oh dear, that is very forward – just the sort of thing a returned Yank would do. I don't even know if you're married or anything."

"I'm very single," he said, smiling easily at her.

That afternoon Sophie helped Isobel move to her new apartment. By late evening they had made three trips to the basement flat in Isobel's Mazda sports. And a sizeable pile of boxes and small bits of furniture still remained to be shifted. Isobel was refusing to leave any of it behind. No, she could not live without her selection of cookery books – not even *The Usborne First Cookbook* or *One Hundred and One Egg Recipes*. No, it was not possible to survive without every single CD in her sizeable collection. Not Lisa Stansfield, Enrique Iglesias or Kylie. And no way was she leaving Gabrielle, Whitney Houston, and Eternal or Take That. They symbolised her youth – just listening to them would bring back forever her teenage years of carefree abandon – and Isobel's carefree days were well and truly over. No, she would not part with Extreme singing "More Than Words". No, it would not be right to callously bin the portrait of Ryan Giggs that she still kept at the bottom of her knicker drawer.

At last, having reluctantly parted with the soundtrack from *Bodyguard*, the *Mister Vain* single and a '*Greatest Dance Hits Ever*', she and Sophie flopped down on the ant-heap sofa in her new home.

"Cup of tea?"offered Sophie.

"Please," said Isobel and promptly fell asleep.

Which was just as well. Because soon after the kettle was plugged in – it made a sinister hissing sound, followed by a muted bang, before completely giving up the ghost.

The following afternoon Sophie went to the DIY shop with Isobel to buy some things for her new flat. It might be possible to brighten up the place by painting over the Neolithic-period wallpaper. They could scrub the sofa down with a strong cocktail of cleaning agents and cover it with a nice new chenille throw-over. A good hard scrubbing and a couple of cheap and cheerful rugs would hide the worst of the pre-famine carpet. And furniture polish, bleach and lemon-scented freshener would surely put paid to the curry/sock odour. It was a fine theory – but having worked steadily on the living-room for several hours, exhausted all cleaning agents and air-fresheners, spent their supplies of elbow grease, they were forced to draw the following conclusions:

Pre-Neolithic wallpaper could not be scrubbed clean of centuries of grease and grime, or covered up with two coats of extra thick Sail White satin finish paint.

Nothing short of total immersion in a vat of acid would kill off the wide selection of bugs and insects and fungi that had set up home in the sofa.

If a carpet smells of curry and unwashed socks, shampooing it with a cocktail of cleaning agents will somehow have the odd chemical effect of inversely heightening the bad smell.

But at least they got the bathroom clean.

When they got back to Raglan Road to prepare for Hendro's party, Sophie checked the garden, fully expecting to see his offending little boat still blotting her landscape. But she was pleased to note that the dinghy was gone. It was the first really good thing that had happened to her all day and she allowed herself a little smile of satisfaction at how her remarkable powers of persuasion had worked to such good effect on Hendro. She felt awash with good will towards him and overcome with fondness for him. He would make the perfect neighbour!!

They cleaned and made-up and dressed in smart-casual party wear. It was a bit of a struggle for Isobel – but in the end she leadenly pulled on a pair of ivory draw-string linen palazzo pants and covered her swelling belly with a loose mulberry-shaded lace-over-silk top.

"I look awful – like some pathetic old hippy."

"You look fine. That colour really suits you."

"Don't patronise me. I already look about thirty-three months pregnant and every other woman at this party is going to be flashing their flat tummies right in my face. It's obscene and lewd. In some countries they'd be flogged for going around like that – and proper order too."

Nick Lynch arrived with a little bouquet of hand-picked flowers for Sophie and all three set off down the lane to the party. As Isobel had glumly predicted, Hendro's mews was bursting at the seams with stunningly beautiful women – the trim leggy sort, with firm, curving breasts and offensively flat stomachs, glittering manes of blonde hair, impossibly blue eyes and unbelievably full, bee-stung lips. They stood around languidly, sipping spritzers and generally looking horribly gorgeous. Isobel was pure livid at the sight of them and because she was well and truly off the drink, she went to work sublimating her anger and feelings of deep inadequacy with the platters of delicious finger-food which the caterers had scattered liberally about the place.

Hendro moved among his guests with a languid grace and charm, a glass of wine in his hand, putting his friends at ease and flirting idly with virtually every woman in the room. Almost the entire team had turned up and since they were on a break from training, they were getting stuck into the copious supplies of beer and champagne and food that Hendro had provided. He made sure that Jim and Stephen, two shy newcomers on the team, were introduced to Emerald and Honey from Vicenza Model Agency. He was pleased when they all hit it off instantly.

He even found time to sit in the conservatory and chat to Clementine Barragry who had brought along one of her nephews for company.

"Now you mustn't worry," Clementine chirped. "I won't be staying long. But my mother always told me it was bad manners to turn down an invitation."

"Stay as long as you like. Pretty ladies are always welcome in this house." He grinned broadly at her.

Clementine blushed and preened herself and fluttered her lilac-shadowed lashes and rearranged her pink chiffon dress across her knees.

Everything was going just perfectly. He loved parties – especially his own. He enjoyed being the centre of attention, liked to be surrounded by people of his own choosing, loved the buzz of seeing unacquainted friends getting to know and like one another.

Then in the corner of the lounge he spotted Sophie, Nick and Isobel. He pushed his way through the throng to talk to them.

"Thank you for removing the dinghy," Sophie said, unable to keep the smug grin from her face.

"Not at all. My pleasure." His green eyes twinkled and he leaned forward to give her a peck on the cheek, then planted a slightly more lingering but totally wasted token of affection on Isobel's face.

Isobel responded with a tight grimace and a grudgingly muttered "Thanksforinvitingme".

If she'd known Hendro better, and because she was becoming quite fond of him, Sophie might have taken him aside and told him that, as far as Isobel was concerned, he was definitely barking up the wrong tree. But she couldn't say anything because it would be betraying a confidence. So she held her peace, concluding that it would be rather entertaining to watch a smooth operator like Hendro making a horse's ass of himself over Isobel when he could easily have virtually any other woman in the room.

Hendro offered to fetch Isobel a drink.

"Don't bother. I'm off it," Isobel retorted bluntly.

"Diet?" he asked, blundering on.

"No!"

Stung briefly by her rudeness, Hendro remembered that Isobel had only recently lost her job. No wonder she was in such bad form. He didn't blame her one little bit.

He felt oddly protective towards her in fact. And as for her bluntness, it was rather sexy. At least she wasn't trying to make small talk about exotic holidays and darling little restaurants and exquisite designer boutiques.

Sophie introduced Hendro to Nick hoping to deflect attention away from Isobel's rudeness.

"He's doing my garden – well, *maybe* doing my garden. So just as well you got rid of that dinghy – he might have paved over it," she joked.

That was the cue for talk about gardens and, when Nick heard about Hendro's garden, he just had to cast his professional eye over it and the two men disappeared to check it out. Left alone with Isobel, Sophie rounded on her.

"You don't have to be so rude to everyone."

"If people keep asking me dumb-assed stupid questions that are none of their business I'll answer them any way I want."

"Hendro is the host, don't forget. And besides he's only trying to be nice. He doesn't know the extent of your problems – the dilemmas you're facing."

"Nice! Guys like him are only ever nice for one reason. Right now he's probably out there in the garden struggling with a really big dilemma of his own."

"What do you mean?"

"I mean the only dilemma a guy like Hendro will ever face – which one of these depressingly beautiful, loathsomely lovely women will he take to bed tonight."

It was on the tip of Sophie's tongue to retort that whoever Hendro took to bed would at least be assured of glorious pleasure for hours on end and deep, deep satisfaction at the end of it, that on a scale of one to ten, Hendro would undoubtedly score somewhere around fifteen and three quarters. However, she quickly bit her tongue. The less Isobel knew about her encounter with Hendro the better. Though she didn't intend to make a habit of it, she wasn't one bit ashamed of her night with him. Just that once, sex was just sex – a purely physical need – like hunger or thirst, or a need to dance or dive into the sea. She had simply needed to quench it. In a sense it marked the true end of her emotional involvement with Daniel. She'd hardly even thought of him since. And lucky for her that it had been Hendro. But Isobel wouldn't see it that way. She didn't approve at all of casual sex.

"Let's get out of here," said Isobel. "I feel like a hippo."

"Don't be silly. You look lovely. At least Hendro thinks so. He couldn't take his eyes off you."

Isobel rolled her eyes to heaven. Looking around her, there was quite an amazingly handsome assortment of men – and lots of them. But all she wanted to do was take flight, run away and never see another man again. Her heart was broken, snapped in two, destroyed for ever – and besides she'd found that in the past few days her waking hours were filling up with thoughts of someone completely different – the child she was carrying. Every solitary moment she had was given over to thinking about it.

Well, it wasn't an "it" for starters. It was a girl. She'd seen it on the ultrasound scan when she'd gone to the hospital. "No sign of a little willie in the scan, Miss Kearney, so almost certainly not a boy," the nurse had chirped. So it was to be a beautiful little girl that she could dress in pretty clothes and bring for jolly walks in the park. Isobel found herself thinking of very uncool things – feeding the ducks, finger-painting, making marshmallow buns. Snatches of long-forgotten nursery rhymes came back to her and songs her own mother had sung to her. One morning in the shower she'd been shocked to find herself humming the tune of "Never Smile at a Crocodile", and even more stunned to discover that she remembered all the words. And right now, thinking about the child inside her was about the only thing that was keeping her sane.

"Stay another while," Sophie pleaded. "It will do you good. Help to take your mind off things."

Then the lights dimmed, the thumping loud music stopped suddenly and the unmistakable crooning sound of Barry White singing a smoochy, schmoozy, 'you are the only, perfect, beautiful, clever woman for me and I am a sex-machine sort of love god who is going to make passionate love to you forever and never let you go' type of song. It was the cue for couples who had been flirting with great diligence and concentration for the past hour, to somehow manoeuvre onto the little dance floor and slink into each other's arms in a climax of eye and skin contact and little knowing looks and smiles.

Sophie looked on tolerantly, mourning her own lost romance, but enjoying the scene nonetheless, glad she wasn't really putting herself out there, setting herself up for excitement, fulfilment, disappointment and despair in that order. She felt oddly detached from it all, like David Attenborough observing the strange mating rituals of some rare species. She stood watching the scene contentedly until Nick returned, took her hand and led her onto the dance floor.

Isobel was close to throwing up. The last thing she needed to witness at this precise moment in her life was the nauseating spectacle of couples embarking on a night of romance-filled and sexually charged excitement. Didn't they all know where it would end? Did those horribly beautiful girls not realise that those impossibly handsome blokes were all merely trying to get into their knickers and steal all their money and demolish their self-esteem and run off with their best friends and their mothers and their sisters and their cousins and their aunts? Would they not just stop and think before hurtling themselves with foolish abandon into a situation that was bound to end in tears and tragedy? And whose bright idea was it to play Barry White? Unable to stop herself now, she sidled over to Hendro's elaborate sound studio, edging her way carefully along to the rack of CDs, shiftily rummaging through them – looking for something more appropriate, something that would reflect the truth about love and romance and in particular about men.

Sophie got to her just in time and before she replaced Barry White with the rather less romantic-sounding Atilla and The Muck Demons singing "Love is for Sad-assed Losers".

"Maybe it's time to leave," said Sophie, doing her best

to steer Isobel away from making a fool of herself. "Let's go into the garden and say goodnight to Hendro."

Disappointed to be interrupted in her plans to stamp out romance, Isobel traipsed after her like a truculent child and mumbled a sour thanks to Hendro, whose arm was casually draped across the shoulder of one of the lovelies, who was looking up at him with feline hunger, basking in the casual warmth of his smiles, sunning herself in the delightful closeness of his body.

Isobel glared in a hostile fashion at the lovely. "We'll leave you to *it*," she said, putting a fair amount of withering emphasis on the last word.

"Yes. Thank you. It was a lovely party, Hendro. We really enjoyed ourselves," Sophie added warmly.

"It's a pity you have to leave." Despite being draped over Katarine the fabulous feline, Hendro's eyes lingered on Isobel's sullen face, willing her to look into his eyes, wanting her to smile and flutter her lashes at him, like virtually every other woman in the room. But she was definitely not playing. She was mad as hell about something, giving off waves of hostility and rage all night. Was it simply about losing her job? Who could tell? Women were a complete mystery – and perhaps, he concluded as Isobel scowled one last time at him before leaving, perhaps after all his mother was right. Romantic entanglements were a complete waste of time.

Isobel went home and Sophie, unwilling for the night to end just yet, invited Nick in for a nightcap. She found a nice bottle of Burgundy which she'd been keeping for a special occasion and they sat on the terrace drinking it.

He told her that he had drifted into garden work and now he operated from home which was a partially restored Victorian bungalow facing onto the seafront in Clontarf. But that his real ambition was to be an artist.

"How about you?" he asked.

Sophie talked about her mother and the promises she'd made to her during her final illness – and then her work in the States.

"Why did you give all that up?"

"I just fancied a change. Working with money is boring really."

"Half the people I know these days work in some kind of banking and finance. They don't seem to mind it."

Sophie struggled to explain her choice without bringing up the subject of Daniel. Though she was enjoying sitting in the dark chatting with Nick, she wanted to steer well clear of talking about personal stuff. She did not want any hint of cosy intimacy to creep into the evening. He sensed her reserve.

"I didn't mean to pry," he said apologetically and asked her instead about going back to college.

"I'm looking forward to it but also dreading the fact that virtually every other woman in the place will be ten years younger than me. And *look* ten years younger than me!"

"Why do women get so hung up on that stuff? You look fine to me."

"Thanks but they'll all have smoother skin and smaller waists and smaller bums for starters."

"Like I said – you look fine to me." He smiled across the table at her and there followed one of those awkward little silences. Their conversation had reached a kind of crossroads. And what with the wine and the moonlight and everything, she was quite tempted to flirt a little more eagerly with him.

"Thank you," she said smiling warmly at him.

"And I'm sure you'll do very well," he answered, deflecting her smile and standing up suddenly. "I'm really sorry but I have to go. Early start in the morning. Thanks for a lovely evening."

"Yes, of course," she said, slightly taken aback and uneasy suddenly that she might have made a fool of herself.

The ways of men are strange, she reminded herself as she tumbled into bed.

Chapter 25

A few days later, Sophie drove to Kinvara Budd's garden centre in Isobel's car and met Nick as arranged in the foyer. He kissed her fleetingly on the cheek and she definitely didn't imagine the initial awkwardness of their conversation.

"You found the place OK? No problems with the directions? Good. How are you?"

Three rapid questions followed by an uneasy silence. What was that all about? She didn't even fancy him. Not really. If she were to set her mind to fancying any of the men she'd met since her return home, Sophie knew with disquieting certainty that it would be Paul Brehony. But he was way out of her league. And he had an unsavoury reputation. And, of course, in spite of his tacky lunch invitation, he was clearly not available.

"Fine. No problems," she said easily to Nick.

They stood around awkwardly in the herbaceous

plants section. Nick was definitely ill at ease and not much in the mood for small talk, it seemed. It was another scorching hot day and she was glad she'd opted for a T-shirt, and a cool hip-skimming denim mini. She'd lost weight since her return home and her legs looked quite sleek beneath the short skirt.

"Hot, isn't it?" she said with a blinding flash of originality.

"Yes," he answered, idly examining pots of hellebores, then added: "Sorry, it's just that I'm expecting an important call."

"A client?"

"Yes. A client."

Luckily at that moment, Kinvara, a tall, amply proportioned woman, emerged from the Portakabin office.

Nick greeted her with a warm smile and a light kiss on the cheek.

Kinvara turned quickly to Sophie. "And you must be the girl with the garden? Lucky you!" And she beamed, a perfect little cupid-bow smile, framing white even teeth.

Sophie took an instant liking to Kinvara who chattered away about gardening as she led the way through the dining-room and onto a little paved south-facing patio. Nick strolled behind them, busily texting someone. When Kinvara offered lemonade Sophie half expected glasses full of the sticky, Day-Glo orange, fizzy stuff of her childhood, the stuff that was one hundred per cent guaranteed to make you throw up on the back seat of the Ford Anglia. But Kinvara's lemonade was a cool, refreshing delight, the colour of creamy buttercups splashed over crushed ice – not too sweet, not too tangy. Nick drank his quickly, checked his mobile once more and pulled out his car keys.

"Sorry about this, have to go," he said easily and placed a folded sheet of drafting paper on the table.

"What's this?"

"It's a revised plan and shouldn't cost too much with imaginative planting. I'll leave that to you."

Sophie noticed the way Kinvara looked at him rather oddly as he was leaving, a curious, and not entirely warm look. She was also troubled with a vague sense of personal annoyance about him. Was he playing silly games with her? Why was he warm and flirtatious one moment, distracted and distant the next? What was going on? And more to the point why the hell was she bothered? After all, only a few days ago, she'd been quite happy not to have to think about men or romance or flirtation or any of that time-consuming, energy-sapping, brain-fuddling nonsense for a long and unspecified time to come. Now it felt as though she was being sucked into a will he/won't he/does he/doesn't he situation, without really even wanting to be there.

But she pushed those thoughts to one side, started on a second glass of delicious lemonade and became immersed in conversation with Kinvara who bubbled with enthusiasm and radiated easy, unforced warmth.

Some time later, Sophie drove out absently through the gates of Kinvara Budd's garden centre. Distracted by thoughts of plants and flowers, she just about remembered to indicate that she would be turning right. There was hardly any traffic on the road and she pulled out to the other side, shifting up into second, then third gear. She still found the gear-change awkward and when she tried to move into fourth, the stick jammed and the car stalled for a moment. Just then she saw a dark blue Mercedes pulling out from a large old gateway to her right. She shoved the gear-stick into first and accelerated out of the way – but swerved and ended up in the ditch.

Her first instinct was to jump out and let the other driver have it. It was clearly his fault. If he'd bothered to check, he would have realised that he didn't have clear passage onto the road.

"Damn!" she murmured and then winced with sudden pain. When the car tumbled roughly into the ditch, her left leg had rammed into the steering column.

Looking in the rear-view mirror she noted that her motoring assailant had also ended up close to the ditch. "More haste – less speed!" she muttered to no-one in particular as she rubbed a throbbing and rapidly swelling knee. She opened the door and tried to ease herself out onto the soft grassy verge. One leg dangled clumsily from the driver's seat as she squirmed and twisted trying to shift the other leg. But it was no good. Each time she attempted to move it – all hell broke loose on the pain front. She let out a few yelps and howls, then sheepishly pulled her one good leg back into the car.

"Are you OK?"

She looked out and came face to face with a pair of

tanned knees. And to be fair, as men's knobbly, hairy knees go – they were quite – presentable.

"I don't know," she informed the knees. "You could have killed me!" She was damned if she was going to admit that the incident had been her fault, even though she knew perfectly well that she'd ended up in the ditch because she still wasn't used to driving a car with a gear-stick.

She twisted and wriggled so that she could make eye contact with the owner of the knees, give him the full extent of her annoyance, possibly even a short lecture on the rules of the road. After all the best form of defence is attack.

"You!" she squeaked with what she hoped was just the right amount of righteous indignation when she saw who it was.

"Well, well! This is a nice surprise."

"Nice surprise! Not exactly the words I would have chosen."

"Come on! Let's get you out of there."

"I can manage!" she said, frantically trying to wrestle her left leg into action and howling again with sudden pain.

"Why don't you move the seat back? You've got it pulled too far forward anyway."

"You're hardly in a position to lecture me about my driving skills," she hissed as she searched around for the lever to release the seat. At last she found it and slid backwards several inches.

"Before we do this, can you feel anything broken?"

She shook her head, haughty as could be, desperately trying to salvage some last scraps of dignity from the situation. And let's face it, there wasn't much in the line of dignity left. Her face was streaked with water-proof, tear-proof, tidal-wave-proof mascara. Her hair had rearranged itself into something suspiciously like a capsized bird's nest. Her slinky little denim hipster skirt was up around her waist, revealing a perfectly cool but perfectly immodest little blue cotton thong. Her left knee was now swollen to about twice its normal size reminding her of the thick shanks of well-fattened cattle her grandfather used to farm.

"I have advanced First Aid training – if it makes you feel any better. This sort of situation is routine in my business. So don't worry. Now let's have those legs!"

She briefly considered warning him not to go anywhere near her legs, but quickly realised that she didn't have much choice. For the time being at any rate, Sophie was entirely at Paul Brehony's mercy.

Conversation over the next ten minutes mostly consisted of "*Owowowowowowowow!*", "*Oooooouuuuuuucccccchhhhhh!*" and "*Mindmykneeithinkit'sfallingoff!*"

"There now!" he said at last as both her feet rested gingerly on the grass. "Now stand up and let's see if you can walk."

She could! Just about! At least if she put her entire weight on her good leg and hung the rest of herself out of him like a drunken nymphomaniac.

"That's it. Take your time. Now can you lean against the boot just until I get my car out of the ditch?"

She nodded and watched in a painful daze as he revved the engine of his car until it almost jumped out onto the road. This time he scooped her up and slid her into the back seat of his car. By this stage, Sophie was feeling quite light-headed and confused what with the shock and pain. He could quite easily have carried her off in one of his nasty little sewing machines of planes and flown her through an electrical, tropical storm to his underground lair at the bottom of an active volcano somewhere near Java and she would hardly have noticed.

She was about to suggest he call for an ambulance when he draped a cashmere wool blanket over her legs, placed her handbag beside her, gently closed the door and slid into the driver's seat. He turned the key in the ignition and the engine hummed smoothly into life.

"What do you think you're doing?" said Sophie.

"You need to see a doctor. I don't think anything's broken – but it would be best all the same."

"You can't drive away from the scene of an accident," she said, trying to seize control of the situation. While she fumbled in her bag for the mobile phone she said as curtly as she could: "I'm calling an ambulance and the guards."

"That could take hours. A lot easier if I drive you up to my house. I can have my own doctor here in much less time."

Sophie barely noticed the drive up the long winding avenue to Fernmount House, distracted as she was by the throbbing pain in her knee. She didn't heed the grand-pillared portico that graced the front entrance, could barely hear Paul's footsteps as he half-carried, half-dragged her across the marble-tiled hallway to a sumptuous drawing-room facing west onto a grand sweep of lawn.

Sophie felt herself being eased onto a sofa, pillows placed beneath her head and one to support her knee. She heard him ask if she wanted tea or a painkiller and she heard her own voice, mumbling thickly that she didn't want anything – that there wasn't a thing wrong with her and if he could just drop her home she'd be fine. But somehow she took the painkillers anyway, washing them down with a few sips of water. Gradually the pain receded as the pills did their work and she began to feel very drowsy indeed . . .

When she woke up, Sophie hadn't the slightest idea where she was. She tried to piece together what had happened but she could only remember snatches. She'd gone to the garden centre to meet Nick and Kinvara Budd. Nick had behaved oddly towards her. Kinvara had spent quite a long time going over planting arrangements. Then someone had come speeding onto the road and caused her to career into a ditch. Paul Brehony! Driving like a madman! Why did she keep bumping into the man? Was there some supernatural being, some powerful tide of destiny throwing them together?

She opened her eyes and looked around the room. Newly restored and, unlike her own penny-pinching efforts in Raglan Road, with absolutely no expense spared, the expansive drawing-room of Fernmount House was like the blueprint of how such a grand old Georgian room should be – high ceilings with delicate mouldings, swathes of shot-silk curtains, the walls housing a collection of fine paintings – tastefully mixing classic and modern styles. And the furniture reflected this as well – a subtle mix of the classic and modern, though there were one or two items that looked oddly out of place. On the mantelpiece at one end next to a very expensive-looking antique vase sat a perfect model of a yellow Renault 4. At the other end was a large garish blue vase in the shape of a fish. In the corner resting up against a very seriously expensive-looking antique bureau, was an old red corduroy bean-bag – for a dog perhaps.

"How are you feeling?" Paul said as he edged his way through the door with a tray laden with tea and Jammy Dodger biscuits.

"I've had better days," she mumbled plaintively..

He set the tray down on a table and, slipping his arm behind her, sat her up on the sofa. Then he poured a cup of tea and set it into her hands.

"I haven't had a Jammy Dodger for years," was all she could think to say.

"Drink the tea while it's hot. I've sent for the doctor. He'll be here in a while."

"There really was no need. Just get me home and – damn! I've just remembered – Isobel's car!"

"It's all sorted."

"How do you mean sorted?"

"They've towed it away to a garage. There's only a few scrapes. It will be as good as new in a day or two. You really should stay here overnight once the doctor has looked you over."

Sophie ought to have been pleased about the car and the offer to stay. But she wasn't. Who did Paul Brehony think he was? Did he think he could just click his fingers and everything would be all right again? What about the trauma and distress he had caused her? What if her leg was irreparably damaged? She might never walk again . . . never dance again . . . never play tennis again . . . never golf again! She didn't actually play golf but she might at some point in the future take it up and would he care if her back swing was permanently impaired?

She began to cry and he offered her a hankie. Then just as she was working herself up into a nice warm lather of self-pity, the doctor arrived. He was a kindly-looking man with ruddy cheeks, blue eyes and greying curly hair.

"Does any of this hurt?" he said, pressing on various parts of her knee and doing various swinging things with her leg.

"*Owwwwww . . . ouuuccchhh!* "

"Hhmm!" he said, doing some more knee-jerks.

"Is anything broken? My knee-cap could be broken."

"Nope! Bad bruising though – let's call it tendonitis."

"Are you sure?"

"We can get it X-rayed just to be on the safe side – but nothing's broken – take my word for it."

He gave her an anti-inflammatory ointment and made a call on his mobile arranging for her to have an X-ray in the Blackrock Clinic the following day.

"I can't afford that! I'll go home now and take my

chances with Accident and Emergency."

He scribbled a note. "You can if you like – but they won't see you for at least twelve hours."

"Why not? I'm in pain. I might have broken something. I've had an Accident! It's an Emergency!"

He smiled as if to ask where she had been for the past ten years. "This may come as a shock to you but a swollen knee is not an emergency. Even a broken patella, which you don't have, is not an emergency. If you're lucky – some kind nurse will take pity on you and get you a chair in the waiting-room. And if you're really lucky – and I mean like lotto-winningly lucky, some good-hearted young intern will slip you past the man who had fifteen pints and thinks he's dying, past the DIY expert who has a nail lodged in his thumb, and get you on a trolley-bed. And then you'll still be behind all the real genuine and deadly serious accidents and emergencies. But I guarantee you one thing – it will be at least twelve hours before you get an X-ray."

Sophie looked pleadingly to Paul for guidance.

"He's right," he said. "The most sensible thing to do is to stay here overnight and go to the Blackrock Clinic in the morning. And don't worry about the bill – it will be taken care of."

Sophie wasn't too keen on staying overnight under Paul Brehony's roof but perhaps it was the only sensible thing to do after all.

She nodded her assent weakly and then Doctor Killen left, leaving her alone with Paul.

"There's a bed made up in one of the spare rooms. You

can sleep there and you'll probably feel much better after a good night's rest."

"Thanks," she mumbled, suddenly uneasy at the thought of being all alone in a house with him for the night. She barely knew him but from what she'd heard and seen so far, he wasn't exactly the sort to be trusted. There was a contained roughness about him, as if there was a wild animal in him, threatening to burst out at any minute. She didn't know whether the idea thrilled or frightened her. Besides all that – there was Marina.

He picked up his laptop and flopped into a leather armchair. "Sorry but I must answer a few emails – excuse me."

"Oh – fine!"

Sophie took the opportunity to phone Isobel – she didn't get her but left a message – and then, from her prone position on the sofa, she couldn't resist secretly watching Paul, immersed in work, as if she wasn't even there.

"It's getting late," she said at last. "Maybe I'll turn in for the night."

"What!" he said looking up from his laptop in surprise. "But I was enjoying your company. Stay a while longer."

"You're working – I don't want to distract –"

"You're a very welcome distraction," he said, snapping the lid of his laptop shut and putting it back in its case.

Then his eyes locked with hers for the briefest of moments and she saw that same forlorn look in his face. But it was gone in a moment and she wondered if she'd imagined it.

"Glass of wine?" he offered and before she could

answer, he'd uncorked a bottle and poured her a glass. She noticed he poured a glass of water for himself.

"To destiny – who has seen fit to throw us together for so many interesting encounters!" He raised his glass and smiled teasingly at her. "Let's hope she keeps up the good work," he added.

God, he was flirting with her and she was liking it – really liking it, suddenly wanting to know every last thing about him, his family, what kind of music he liked, who his friends were, whether he slept on his back or his side, if he wore PJs in bed or if he went naked. She swallowed and turned away.

"Wine OK?"

"Yes, thanks, delicious. Haven't had anything like this since the expense-account days. It must be nice to be able to afford such luxuries whenever you want them."

He shrugged dismissively and there followed an awkward silence.

"You never took up my invitation to lunch," he said suddenly.

Sophie thought about launching into a lecture about how presumptuous and vain and tacky his business-card lunch invitation had been, but she realised there wasn't much point in wasting her breath. It was all very well for them to be alone in this lovely room, flirting and generally edging towards a close encounter of the romantic kind. But one simple fact remained.

"You were very definitely and very obviously with someone else," she said coolly.

He didn't say anything for a few moments, just twirled

the tumbler of water in his hand.

"But you see that's where you're wrong. There's nothing between Marina and me."

"It's over? I'm sorry."

"Nothing to be sorry about."

"Yes, but the end of any relationship is sad," she said trying to look as earnest and sympathetic as she could, while inside her heart was doing Olympic-standard somersaults. He was free after all and he clearly liked her and she was also free to start liking him.

He came and seated himself on the edge of the sofa. He was careful not to cause her knee any pain but he was close enough for her to feel the warmth of his body and she got the faint musky woody scent of him. Yippeee! said her heart as it danced about in a state of tremulous anticipation.

"So now that you know," he said quietly, "maybe you'll accept an invitation to dinner this time . . . or if not dinner, whatever you like. Name your dream date. Say yes."

Yes! Yes! Yes! Yes! she chirruped inwardly while she tried to frame a cool and measured response. "I suppose – maybe – and destiny and all that, like you said – I mean – now that you've asked me properly . . ." She stumbled on, struggling to accept in a way that wouldn't look too eager. But she never got to the end of the sentence.

She heard the front door open and the unmistakable sound of stilettos click-clacking across the marble floor. Then the door into the drawing-room opened and Marina stood there elegantly poised.

"I'm so sorry. I understand you've had an unfortunate

incident," Marina said, surveying them across the wide expanse of room and then somehow moving across the room towards them without appearing to touch the floor.

Sophie's heart had plummeted. More than anything in the world, she wanted to just disappear. How could she have been such a fool, allowing herself to be so easily taken in by him? Everything he told her had been a lie. And even though she knew already that he wasn't to be trusted, she'd let herself be led along like some kind of pathetic sheep. Were her brains turning to sludge? Had she lost all sense of good judgement and insight into people? She had to get out of Paul Brehony's house right now.

Marina walked over to Sophie and extended a slender, perfectly manicured hand.

"Marina Weber Hyde, how do you do?"

"Sophie Flanagan," And I don't do very much very well at the moment, she felt like adding.

"But you poor dear!" Marina exclaimed. "You're obviously in a lot of pain. Lying here on a sofa with all of us peering at you can't be helping either. You need to be resting that knee in bed. Paul, what were you thinking, darling? This poor girl needs to go home – not spend the evening hunched up on a sofa in some stranger's house. Why don't I arrange for a nice comfortable taxi to take her home in comfort?"

Marina arranged herself in a magnificent armchair and instantly took matters in hand by swiftly leafing through a leather-bound phone directory.

"Thanks – it's really kind of you," Sophie said, quite

impressed with Marina's no-nonsense concern for her welfare, and lightning efficiency.

Paul, whose face had clouded over as soon as he heard Marina's footsteps in the hall and who hadn't spoken one word since her arrival, stirred himself to action now.

"It's hardly the proper thing to do under the circumstances. Sophie needs a comfortable night's rest. She can have one of the bedrooms upstairs."

Marina shot him a look that would liquefy rock. She then brushed her lovely little hand across her perfect brow and winced ever so slightly.

"Oh dear!" she said fretfully. "You see, I'm working. Coming up the driveway just now – I was struck by this marvellous insight . . . something truly new . . . quite unique . . . such a blinding moment of discovery . . . I'm just amazed no-one has ever thought of it before . . . I've only just this instant realised that the pain of romantic love transcends its ecstasy . . . I simply have to get it down, explore it, tease it out, put the very essence of it on the page . . . and I must have complete silence and solitude to do it."

She sank her slight frame into the vast armchair, visibly exhausted from the internal struggle of framing her thoughts.

Sophie didn't even bother to look at Paul but she sensed he wasn't happy. No doubt he was kicking himself that Marina had arrived just at the wrong moment, just when things were getting all hot and smoochy with Sophie. His cosy little moment of seduction spoiled! It was just pathetic and poor Marina undoubtedly had a lot to put up with. He didn't even seem to be interested in all the hard work she clearly put into her writing.

"I was on the point of asking Paul to call a cab when you arrived," she said hurriedly.

Marina nodded distractedly. "That's fine. I hope you don't think I'm being rude – it's just – well, the Muse doesn't keep office hours."

She smiled ruefully at Sophie.

Some time later a very comfortable limousine taxi deposited Sophie home and the driver helped her hobble up the steps. The swelling had gone down considerably and there wasn't even that much pain. The biggest pain Sophie was suffering from now was shame at her own foolishness for almost being taken in by Paul Brehony's pathetic attempt at seduction.

She should really ring Isobel and let her know she had come home after all – but what was the point of telling her now so late in the day? Better to leave it and talk to her first thing in the morning. She curled up on the sofa and tried to make herself comfortable, trying to force the memory of her encounter with Paul from her mind.

Finally she hobbled off to bed where she slept fitfully.

In the morning she hobbled around, trying to stay out of the builders' way. She was beginning to feel quite sorry for herself when Clementine Barragry arrived and, seeing Sophie's condition, quickly took up shopping duties. Not long afterwards, and because Clementine had passed the word around, Hendro arrived with an enormous box of chocolates and a bottle of champagne and some of his favourite CDs. Then he disappeared and quickly reappeared with a very well-upholstered garden chaise which he set up on the timber deck. He wanted to know all about her accident and that led to a conversation about sports injuries and his own catalogue of hamstrings, groin strains, ankle sprains, smashed cheekbones, sciatic nerve pains, torn ligaments and shoulder problems. He listed them off cheerfully like he was naming his favourite movies. Then there were the long physiotherapy sessions, hours with the masseuse, nights in Casualty, and afternoons in X-ray theatres. It all made Sophie's little knee swelling look insignificant in comparison.

"But why do you bother?" Why anyone would go out into a mucky field and routinely expose themselves to such a terrible catalogue of injuries was completely beyond her comprehension.

"It's a bit of fun, isn't it? Anyway what else could I do? I don't see myself working for my father – and honestly I'm not all that bright."

He sat opposite her, in loose T-shirt and shorts, his broad shoulders dwarfing the chair that did its best to support him, strong muscular legs spread across the deck, his knees supporting his elbows, a hint of sweat glistening on his skin.

"Hey," he said huskily, leaning forward so that she could feel his breath on her skin, "you're looking very pretty today – even with a bandaged leg."

She pushed him away with an affectionate tap on the shoulder.

"We've had our thrilling moment together," she said

fondly. "Let's not spoil the memory of it by trying for a repeat performance."

"Fair enough," he said, leaning back and taking it in good spirits. "Just never forget how pretty you are – and how damned sexy. Soon some bloke is going to lay claim to you – and he's going to be one lucky guy."

"You're such a charmer, Hendro Sayers," she said, trying to sound light-hearted.

"I mean every word," he said simply and for some reason that she couldn't really fathom, Sophie suddenly felt close to tears.

Chapter 26

In spite of her injury, the next few days passed surprisingly pleasantly. The doctors in the clinic had told her that it was just a bad bruise and that it should be completely healed in a few days if she just rested it as much as possible. But far from being isolated and alone, Sophie found herself besieged with callers and well-wishers. Kinvara Budd sent a bouquet of flowers and an open-ended lunch invitation. Joe was very attentive and even offered to postpone the final building work if it made life any easier for her. Nick Lynch called several times laden with gardening books and magazines. He was once again warm and flirtatious and Sophie tried to respond warmly to him, forcing thoughts of Paul Brehony from her mind. Isobel stayed over and helped her in and out of the shower, painted her toenails and was thrilled when her car was returned in mint condition with the added bonus of a service and valeting as well. Hendro took Sophie for long leisurely drives on his free afternoons.

On the third day, a courier delivered a simple bouquet of pale cream roses, with just the merest blush of pink near the base of the petals.

"Who from?" Isobel sniffed with post-romantic scorn.

Sophie examined the card. "It says: *I hope you are feeling better. Sincere Regards – Paul Brehony.*"

Isobel, now deeply suspicious of any kind of romantic gesture no matter how innocent, stuck the flowers unceremoniously into a glass vase and set them on a table in the dining-room – where she hoped no-one would see them or feel obliged to comment on them.

He called round in person the following day. Clementine led him through the long mess of unassembled kitchen units and out onto the deck where Sophie lay languishing in the warm sunshine on Hendro's plush lounger.

Her heart sank when she saw him.

"Hi," he said squinting against the sun.

"Hi," she replied coolly, unsure of what else to say.

"How's the knee?"

"It's fine."

He sat, facing into the sun, lazily surveying her leg.

"How's Marina?" she asked pointedly after a brief silence.

He shrugged indifferently. "Marina is Marina. We don't –"

"Thanks for the flowers," she cut in quickly. "They're pretty. And Isobel says thanks for getting her car into such good shape."

"It's no big deal," he said, realising she wanted him to leave. He stood up. "Anyway – good to see you're on the mend," he said, making for the door. "I'll see you round sometime I suppose," he added before letting himself out.

It was the first evening she had to herself. Her knee was healing nicely and she could walk with only one crutch now. The work on the house would be finished the very next day and a sense of calm was returning to her life at last. She lay on the sofa reading a gardening magazine, listening to Coldplay. Isobel was at her ante-natal class. Hendro was training. Clementine was at the theatre and Nick was away in Holland. She had pushed all thoughts of Paul Brehony from her mind and had even managed to laugh at her own foolishness. Now there was absolutely no reason in the world for them ever to see one another again. A couple of embarrassing moments at the airport, an oddly pleasant interlude by the riverbank in Ashford Castle, that arrogant business card and then the unfortunate car accident and his clumsy attempt to seduce her afterwards – an unusual sequence of encounters – but probably now at an end.

When the doorbell rang, she hobbled across the newly polished wooden floors hoping that whoever it was didn't stay long.

She half expected that it might be Hendro, or Nick back from Holland, but it was another man entirely – a much older man – perhaps in his sixties – nicely dressed, with a look of Harrison Ford about him.

"Sorry to disturb you. I'm Ed Thorne."

"Yes?"

"The guy upstairs."

She looked him over quite closely – and could see no hints of any kind that he might be an axe murderer. But appearances could be very deceptive. Her thoughts flew back to the night she'd searched the apartment upstairs. This Ed Thorne person might look perfectly harmless and friendly and quite handsome in an older-man kind of way – but could she be really sure that he wasn't just here to have her guts for garters? There was something awfully sad and forlorn about the expression in his eyes – but that meant nothing! Don't crocodiles weep before they devour their victims?

"What can I do for you, Ed?" she said, hoping he wouldn't notice the nervous wobble in her voice or that her leg was gammy and she wouldn't stand a snowball's chance in hell of escaping – should he decide to take out his axe and chase her across her newly polished floors.

"I should have called before – it must seem odd – me coming and going at all hours of the day and night. I hope it hasn't disturbed you."

This was it. He'd soften her up – and then lunge. She held on tight to the door in case she had to slam it in his face quickly.

"Me? Disturbed?" she squeaked. "No – just curious – technically the landlady and all that."

"I do consultancy work for a big bank. They pay for the flat. I come to Dublin so often, it's cheaper than hotel bills. I live in Kilkenny."

"Consultancy work?"

"Yes – staff development and training mostly."

While he was talking she made the mistake of looking down and there at his feet, as brazen as you like, not even hidden from her or anything – was the proof positive that he was an axe murderer.

Ed Thorne had a suitcase – one of the old-fashioned kind with reinforced leather corners and stickers from all corners of the globe. It had to be full of axes and whatever else axe murderers needed. More axes – probably different sizes. Maybe he had a titanium axe – like the new stuff in golf clubs. He'd probably now make some pretext for bending down to open the suitcase and then he would whip out his axe and that would be the end of her.

"Anyway – sorry for disturbing you and pleased to make your acquaintance," he said with a slight American twang. "Better go or I'll miss my flight." He bent down and took hold of the suitcase.

"Flight?" she croaked.

"Yes, off to Frankfurt for a day or two. Well, goodbye now."

"Bye," she said after him as he climbed into a waiting taxi and disappeared.

Of course, she got on the phone to Isobel straight away with the latest thrilling instalment of the mystery, what he looked like, what he talked about, how he had this big suitcase and how she'd let her imagination run away with her – but that there was still something strange about him. Isobel didn't seem all that interested.

"So what's his name – this consultant?"

"Ed Thorne."

Isobel laughed. "Eddie Thorne! You thought Eddie Thorne was an axe murderer!"

"What's so funny? How do you know him?"

"I've worked with him. He did some training programmes with us in the Athena Club. He's quite well known – almost a bit of a guru! In fact, we used to call him Guru Eddie sometimes just to wind him up."

"That doesn't prove anything. And how come a man like that doesn't have family? Don't you think that's a bit weird at least?" She was slightly miffed that Isobel had burst the bubble of her dramatic tale of mystery and suspense.

"He has family – a daughter who's married with two children and a son who's gay and lives in San Francisco. His wife died of cancer a few years ago and he's never got over it – he's had a lot of difficulty coping – so I hope you weren't rude to him or anything."

Sophie felt that horrible sinking feeling – a nasty stab of guilt – how she'd nosed about in his things, pried into his private life, even planned to go to the agency about him. Thank goodness she hadn't had the time to follow it up. She wondered if he knew and then she remembered how she'd fallen asleep on his sofa and woken up to find a blanket had been placed over her. Of course, he knew. Alone in the kitchen, hobbling around to fix herself a sandwich, she blushed hot bright scarlet with shame at how foolish and insensitive she'd been. How could she have been such an idiot?

Chapter 27

Isobel lay on the dingy sofa in her basement flat. Scattered about the pokey room were plates bearing the congealed remains of several greasy fry-ups and the sticky remnants of take-aways. She rubbed her hand across a taut swollen belly, feeling the child within stirring, flexing her little limbs. She'd spent the past few days sinking into a mire of self-pity and hopelessness. The love of her life, her glamorous lifestyle, her smart little apartment in the docklands, her wardrobe of designer clothes, and her job in the exclusive Athena Club – it had all disappeared overnight.

She knew she wasn't coping. But there didn't seem to be any point in even trying. Down at the bottom of the pit where she now found herself, Isobel could see no way out. Too proud to confide in Sophie how awful everything was, she put on a great show of being in control and wonderfully positive whenever they got together. And she still hadn't told her mother. It would be the last straw. They would disown her, or worse still, be full of showy tolerant pity.

She watched soap operas but then the storylines became too distressing. It was all adultery, murder, family rows. She tried listening to classical music to soothe her spirits – but the music was hauntingly sad. The news of wars and famines and poverty and social injustices caused her awful distress, as if she was personally involved with every single tragedy on the planet. In the end she vowed only to watch comedy shows – but then she realised that there wasn't much to laugh at. Ordinarily a great fan of *Sex and The City*, now she found Carrie and friends silly and pointless, found amiable *Father Ted* deeply irritating, thought the people in *The Office* should all be put down humanely. Even the ads disturbed her – the road safety ones in particular. At last she found a programme on the Hobbies Channel about a man who was building a model railway in his garden and since it didn't arouse any emotions at all in her, since it had much the same effect on her as watching paint dry, she spent most of the evening watching that.

When the model-railway programme was over and though it was still daylight, she changed into cotton pyjamas and climbed in between the sheets. Not really tired as such, but just tired of being awake, she began to drift off into a glum sleep.

When the doorbell rang, she didn't even consider answering it. Since moving in, she'd discovered that the entire population of flatland Rathmines seemed to think they had a God-given right to ring her doorbell – people selling things, people looking for directions, people wanting to talk religion, politics, the environment, drunk and drugged people, lost people . . . she didn't want to see any of them.

The doorbell rang again.

"Go away!" she wailed. "Leave me alone!"

But the ringing persisted and in the end she had to answer – just to make whoever it was stop. She mooched over to the door and yanked it open.

"Hi, babes. I'm back. It's been quite a struggle finding you – but here I am."

Her heart leapt, somersaulted, bungee-jumped and then plunged down to the soles of her rapidly swelling feet.

"You'd better come in."

He sidled in behind her, a rucksack slung over his shoulder. "Are you hungry? I've got some takeaway from the Chinese round the corner." He cleared a space on the tiny table in the corner and set out a few cartons of food, and beside them a half bottle of whiskey.

"Got a couple of forks?"

She pointed at a drawer and watched in amazement as he tucked into his food – like he'd been there all his life. She picked half-heartedly at a tinfoil dish full of prawns and noodles. When he'd eaten his fill, he cast his expert eye around the room.

"Bit of a change, isn't it? From the old place I mean! This is terrible!" He seemed distraught at her new accommodation.

But Phil Campion believed in rolling with the punches. So he rolled himself a joint, made himself a hot punch with some of the whiskey and put his feet up on the sofa. He gave Isobel the benefit of a reassuring smile.

"We'll manage for a while. I've finished my course and there are a few contracts in hand now – so as soon as we're sorted I'll buy us a nice little apartment in Ballsbridge."

Apartment in Ballsbridge! He couldn't afford a shoebox in Calcutta. She barely listened. Phil was always full of plans and schemes – all of them grand, every one of them doomed to failure. What she was really thinking about was how long it would take him to notice the bump. She'd made no effort to conceal it.

"God, I've missed you, Isobel – I really have. Can't sleep thinking about you. Come here and give us a kiss." He pulled her towards him and only then did he notice her new shape. "Putting on a bit of weight, aren't you? Not been keeping yourself fit? Letting yourself go in my absence?" He pulled her tighter to him and nuzzled against her ear. "It's OK though 'cos right now I gotta have your lovin'." Phil often spoke in song lyrics.

Isobel was in a frightful state. The nearness of his body to hers, the feel of his arms around her, was sending her chaotic hormones into overdrive. She wanted quick hot sex like she'd never wanted it before and at the same time she wanted to be hugged and petted and nursed like a child and at the same time she wanted to take a rusty bread knife to him and also at the same time she wanted him to get out of her life and never come back. What happened in all the hormonal confusion was that she began to cry – great big sobs – splashes and dollops of tears – incoherent ramblings – piteous moans and strange strangling choking noises from the back of her throat.

"Don't cry," Phil said. "I'm here now. I should never have let you send me away. I knew you wouldn't be able to manage alone."

He held her tight and led her into the tiny cupboard of a bedroom.

"Lie down here and let me cuddle you and mind you," he said coaxingly and Isobel obeyed.

Perhaps this was a new and tender side to Phil. Perhaps throwing him out had been the right thing to do after all. He'd gone away and decided to mend his ways and come back to her. His arms felt so good. His body smelt so good. His pale blue eyes gazed directly into hers, bringing on a new bout of sobbing.

"I love you, Isobel. How could you ever doubt it? I've changed and I'm sorry for letting you down before but I'm ready to commit to us now. I really am. Don't cry, baby. Phil's here now."

He kissed her matted hair affectionately and stroked and caressed her. She felt safe for the first time in weeks. She felt that if she could face the world with Phil at her side – then having a child and getting her life back together again would be easy – a cakewalk. Yes, he had been unfaithful – but now he'd made the decision to come back and that had to count for something. Yes, he had been a drain on her purse, but all that could change now. Didn't he say that he'd finally finished his course?

Granted it was three years after everyone else in his class – but he was finished now and that was the important thing. And he said he had some contracts in the bag. Isobel felt herself relax beside him and she nuzzled her face into his chest.

"That's more like it, Babybel," he said, his hand sliding across her shoulder, kissing her now on the neck, exploring her.

She could feel his erection hard against her thigh and she really wanted him.

Later he brought her a cup of tea in bed and sat up beside her, told her how much he'd missed her, how he loved her and would never ever leave her again. Then he talked away about his big contract – the *Safety In the Workplace* video for the company in the Greenhills Industrial Estate. He was so excited about it all that she didn't want to shatter the moment by mentioning the baby. She'd tell him in the morning. If he'd tried this hard to find her and get her back, he might be quite pleased at the idea of being a father.

"I have some good ideas for it. They're all in my head still – as you know, babes, true genius takes a bit longer. First I want to use U2's music. Now the rights are going to cost big bucks – but it has to be done properly. And I was thinking about getting a well-known actor to do the voice-over – maybe Colin Farrell. I know a bloke whose cousin used to go to school with him – so that could be a good place to start. Course I've been busy out looking for interesting locations – I thought perhaps Newgrange or maybe some place in the docklands – I want to give it an arty feel. I mean I know it's just a safety video – but it's a chance to show what I'm made of. Also I think the story line should be dramatic – you know, to reflect the true bleakness of the human condition. I feel it's important to make a statement about that. Safety in the workplace is a global issue – a universal theme if you like."

Isobel was asleep, curled up beside him in the cramped bed, in spite of everything happy to have him back, someone to share her problems with, safe in the loving protection of his arms, dreaming of houses and weddings and nurseries and christenings and happy-ever-afters.

In the morning she woke suddenly. Phil was standing over her, not looking one bit loving or protective. He was brandishing a book in his hand.

"What's all this about?" he banged his thumb on the cover of *The Single Mother's Guide to Pregnancy*.

Isobel rubbed the sleep from her eyes and sat upright in the bed.

"Don't be angry with me. I was going to tell you – only I didn't want to spoil the moment last night."

"It's not mine, is it?" He gazed in horror at her bump.

"Yes – of course, it is."

"Fuck!"

Not quite the response she was expecting – but she could see he'd had a shock and in fairness his mind was distracted with worries about the video. She decided to tread carefully and play it as cool as possible. It wouldn't do to frighten him away. He needed time to get used to the idea. She knew he'd come round eventually. He'd often said that when he became a father, he wouldn't make all the disastrous mistakes his parents had made in raising him. It only needed time and encouragement for him to recognise the great opportunity life was putting in front of him now.

"I know it's a shock. It's been hard for me to adjust to the idea. And if you hadn't shown up – you might never have found out. But you're here now – and, though I didn't think so at first, talking to you last night and the closeness between us – I do believe we can work things out between us after all. We just need to give ourselves time to get used to the fact that we're going to have a baby."

"No, Isobel – *you* are going to have a baby. I can't afford at this crucial stage in my career to be held back just because you forgot to take your pill or something!"

This wasn't going quite as she'd expected. But she realised her best chance of winning him over would be to stay calm and highlight all the positive aspects of becoming a father.

"You've always said you wanted a daughter. Think of that – you'll be able to go for walks together, show her how to use the video camera . . . er . . ." She'd run out of things they could do together. In fact she couldn't remember much else that Phil did apart from going for walks, rolling joints and drinking pints. "Discuss the meaning of life together," she added hopefully.

He sighed and ran a worried hand through his hair. "Isobel, this was a really stupid move. You know that, don't you?" But he said it gently and put his arm around her shoulder affectionately.

"I didn't plan it," she said, her voice rising in spite of herself. "And I never missed taking the pill. The doctor said it can just happen – a chance in a thousand or something. The very last thing I need in my life at the moment is a baby. I even thought about getting rid of it."

"There'll be no abortions round here."

"But the two of us together – maybe this is what we needed all along."

Phil was in a state of acute anguish. She could see he was completely torn.

"Look, I went to a lot of trouble to find you so that we could put the past behind us and make a new start. And I also thought with a bit of financial backing from you – well, this safety video would be a sure-fire winner and we could plan for the future . . . the nice little apartment in Ballsbridge . . ."

Isobel slipped from his arms and turned to face him.

"Where did you think I was going to get the money?"

"You have that nest-egg your grandmother left you – it's still in the bank. Well, knowing you, you've hardly spent it. What's the point of it being there? Interest rates are so low now that you might as well spend it on something worthwhile before it devalues."

He said it like he was advising her to invest in a sensible pension fund, like he was advising her to put a deposit on a nice little house.

It was for Isobel a moment of final and shocking insight into the man she'd loved so truly, so madly and so foolishly. She stared at him, too angry to cry, too shocked to speak, horrified that in her vulnerable state she'd allowed herself to be so stupidly taken in by him – yet again. As if he hadn't used her and hurt her enough already!

"No!" she said finally, battling her tears, hurtling between anger and despair.

"No? What do you mean no?"

She opened her mouth to speak but thought better of it. And in any case what could she say – that she hadn't already said when she'd thrown him out in the first place? She could even script his answers. "*Yeah, yeah,Babybel – I've heard it all before – throw me out today – and bawl for me to come back tomorrow . . .*"

Instead she went about quietly packing his few belongings back into the grubby rucksack. He followed her pleadingly around the cramped living-room.

"Look – give me time to get used to the idea of a baby. Let me stay. I'm sorry for what I said. I wasn't thinking. Forget about the money. I'll get it somewhere else. And I do love you."

"It makes no difference anyway," she said, tying up the straps on his rucksack. "You can't have that money – because – because I've spent it."

"On what?"

"Just bits and pieces – things for the baby – a holiday – a health-insurance plan – just stuff. Anyway it's all gone – so there's not much point in you staying."

She handed him the rucksack and held the front door open as he walked out, his face clouded with a mass of emotions: disappointment, shock, annoyance, worry and complete disbelief.

Chapter 28

Sophie showered and climbed into bed – but sleep wouldn't come. She was worried and fretful. She hadn't been out and about much, mostly because she couldn't afford to do much socialising, at least until she'd finished the course. And that was starting in a matter of weeks. She'd paid the builder and there wasn't a whole pile of money left in the kitty. I'll manage somehow, she told herself repeatedly. Still, working out how she would survive on very little money was beginning to keep her awake at night. Then there was the matter of Tess. A few days earlier Kenny had called Sophie to tell her the news.

"Just calling to give you a bit of good news," he said and then added with a dramatic flourish: "The eagle has landed, Sophie! Now isn't that great news?"

Sophie wasn't quite sure what he meant.

"Tess has moved in with us," he added by way of explanation.

She felt relieved that her grandmother had been rescued from the clutches of Robert Franklin but more than a little surprised that she had decided after all to stay with Kenny and Maeve. What had caused her change of heart and was she happy with the move?

Sophie fretted about her, made several attempts to call her at Kenny's but each time Tess appeared to be out, either on the golf course or playing bridge with friends. Now she tossed and turned in bed, fretting about her grandmother too.

Lastly there was Isobel, whom she hadn't heard from in days. Now Sophie felt deeply concerned. She had made several phone-calls to the basement flat but the phone would ring out and then the line would go dead. She began to worry in earnest. What if Isobel was unwell? What if someone had broken into the flat and attacked her? She considered calling Isobel's parents, telling them the whole story. It was time for them to know anyway. It wasn't right or fair to keep news of a baby from them any longer. But it wasn't her place to do that. If she hadn't managed to contact Isobel by the next evening she would call a taxi and go straight to the Rathmines flat.

She was about two hundred pages into a book, usually guaranteed to hold her attention until she slipped away into sleep. But tonight she couldn't concentrate. She tried *Hello* magazine that Clementine had brought – but not even photos of the 'fabulously happy and impossibly glamorous, never been happier, destined to be together forever' celebrity marriages held her attention. It was almost midnight now and she was wide awake. At last, too worried to sleep, she dialled Isobel's number again.

This time, Isobel answered. Well, answered might be putting it strongly, though there was something like a response. It sounded like "*Glurgh!*" A word Sophie hadn't heard since she'd given up reading the *Beano* comic. It was time to adopt a firm, matronly, concerned-parent approach. Damn! She hated any form of intense emotional experience late at night. It always kept her awake.

"Isobel – I've been trying to call you for days! Why didn't you answer?"

"*Grnlgh!*"

"What? Are you drunk? You can't be drunk! Think about the baby."

"*Nosrlgh!*"

"You're not making any sense at all! Pull yourself together and try talking properly!"

"*Wishwasdead . . . wannakillmyself!*"

Sophie thought frantically. She knew in an instant that she had to get her friend out of that horrible dump. She struggled out of her PJs and pulled on a track suit while she talked into the phone.

"Don't be silly. You can't be dead and that's that." She sounded a lot more bossy and in control than she really felt. Inside she was close to panic. What if Isobel really was serious? What if she didn't get there in time? And, of course, she felt guilt. Why hadn't she insisted on taking her friend in – when she was in trouble and needed it most?

"If you kill yourself – I will be very cross," she said, jamming her stockingless feet into a pair of trainers and hastily tying her hair into a ponytail.

"Think of all the fuss in the newspapers – photos, details of your private life, analysis of your state of mind. Would you really want that? And detectives going through your knicker drawer for forensic evidence? I don't think so, Isobel Kearney!"

She hoped her shock tactics would work, or at least stall Isobel until she got there.

But what should she do? Go round in a cab and bundle Isobel into the back seat and bring her to Raglan Road? That would be too difficult to manage alone. And now it was past midnight. Who could she call that would understand? And what if Isobel was stroppy and refused to move? This was a job for a strong discreet man. Ed Thorne might have fitted the bill but he was in Frankfurt. Nick was still in Holland.

In desperation she tried Joe's mobile phone. It was switched off.

She called Isobel again.

"Are you still there?"

"Yeah."

"Well, stay put! I'll be there as soon as I can."

"Don't bother. No point."

"Isobel – I'm coming! Just wait there! Please!" Sophie begged and slammed the phone down.

Through her bedroom window she caught sight of a light in Hendro's house.

"Of course," she said and let herself out the front door, galloping down the side lane to the mews. She rang the doorbell three times before he answered, sleepy-eyed and half naked. She swallowed and averted her eyes from the broad expanse of chest that met her at eye level.

"A bit late for jogging. Hope you don't expect me to join you. Come in, why don't you?"

"No. Thanks. This is an emergency. I need you to help – right now."

"Sure but just give me a few minutes to get in the mood," he said, misunderstanding the cause of her urgency.

"It's Isobel. We have to help her. She's in big trouble."

Despite his large and languid frame, Hendro could move swiftly when the situation demanded it. Like a Ferrari, he could do nought to sixty in less than ten seconds. In the space of two minutes, he'd dressed, found his car keys and his wallet and was sitting into his BMW sports revving up the engine.

"So what's this all about?" he said, screeching down the quiet moonlit mews and disturbing a few foraging cats. "It sounds more serious than just losing a job."

Sophie hesitated about revealing the extent of Isobel's problems but at last she told him everything – about the job, Phil Campion and the baby. Lastly she told him about Isobel's saying that she wanted to be dead..

"That's not good," he said grimly as he negotiated half empty streets at three times the speed limit, slamming over ramps, swerving to avoid one or two late-night revellers, even crashing one or two red lights.

"Why are you driving so fast? We'll get there just as well at a safe speed."

"If someone like Isobel talks about killing herself, I

wouldn't hang around to see if she really means it," he said angrily, hurtling up Charleston Avenue.

They parked about three doors from Isobel's, and Sophie led the way to the basement flat. Hendro was horrified when he saw the roughly patched-up front door, the grimy, grease-coated and barred window, the crumbling steps and the blackened corners filled with empty cans and bottles.

"What sort of place is this?"

"She moved here a few weeks ago." Sophie was about to embark on a strong defence of her own attempts to have Isobel move in with her – but Hendro brushed her aside and rapped as loudly as he could on the barred window.

"Isobel! Are you in there?"

There was no reply. Everything was in darkness and Sophie suddenly felt horribly queasy. Hendro banged loudly on the door and both of them called in to her.

"How could you let her stay in a dump like this?" he said angrily.

Sophie opened her mouth to explain how she'd offered, how Isobel insisted – but she knew he was right. Any explanation now would sound miserably hollow.

"She's not answering," he said, pulling off his sweatshirt. "Coach will kill me if he hears about this. So let's just hope I don't do my shoulder in. Here goes."

He gathered all the force he could into his six-foot-four frame, and, with his best side-tackling manoeuvre, lunged his shoulder at the door. It gave way quite easily and he went crashing through into the gloomy living-room. Sophie followed quickly and when there was no sign of Isobel she darted into the bedroom.

It was a mess, clothes everywhere, half-empty glasses of milk, biscuit crumbs, orange peel and apple cores. In the middle of it all on the narrow unmade bed lay Isobel.

She was quite still.

Sophie sat gingerly on the side of the bed. At that moment she realised how much Isobel meant to her – a sister without the baggage, a true and loyal friend from their very first days in nursery school. They'd played together, sat together in class, had teenage sulks together, gone on double dates, studied together, shared clothes, make-up, deep deep secrets, gone clubbing and partying, taken holidays with each other. And the friendship had survived all that, had survived separations, arguments, petty jealousies – even one another's boyfriends.

"Oh, God!" she croaked. "Isobel – please don't be dead!"

"Not dead! Goway."

Hendro, who had been stunned into silence by the horrific state of the room and by an unwelcome sharp pain in his shoulder, jumped swiftly into action. He gently brushed Sophie out of the way like she was nothing more than a little kitten and sat on the bed beside Isobel. Beneath the weight of his sixteen stone of pure muscle, the bed creaked and sank almost to the floor. He felt for a pulse, pressed his palm to her forehead and then spoke very loudly.

"Isobel – can you hear me?"

"No need to shout! I'm pregnant – not deaf."

"Good." He lowered his voice. "Listen carefully. Have you taken anything?"

"What?"

"Taken anything? Like – well like – pills? Or any kind of drugs?"

"No. Now go away and leave me alone."

"You sure you haven't taken anything?"

"Last night's Chinese take-away – does that count?"

"What was in it?"

"He said it was prawns with noodles – but the stingy cheapskate wouldn't buy proper prawns. It was probably one of those miserable bargain-basement 'seafood' things. Oh God, I feel awful. Please just let me die in peace."

Stingy cheapskate! It could only be Phil Campion. No wonder Isobel was so distressed – and suffering from food poisoning as well by the looks of things.

"Come on, we're going," said Hendro, rummaging through her things for a coat and shoes.

Isobel moaned pathetically and begged to be left alone. He ignored her pleas and hauled her up to a seating position. Then with a lumbering gentleness that surprised Sophie he slid Isobel's arms into the sleeves of the coat and eased the shoes onto her swollen feet.

"Wait – I need a toothbrush, my washbag, clothes . . ."

"We'll come back for the rest of your things tomorrow," he said as he scooped her up into his arms and carried her out to his car.

The journey home was a little uncomfortable – Hendro's flashy two-seater, soft-top BMW had been designed, engineered and purchased for speed, seduction, posing and for showing off to his mates. To date it had not been involved in any mercy missions – except a few late-night trips to the off-licence for parties. Now Sophie was jammed in behind the two seats, with half of her rear end in the boot, while at the same time leaning forward trying to keep Isobel in an upright position with her two hands – all the while nervous that her newly healed knee might be damaged again. Whenever she let go, Isobel would keel over, capsizing into Hendro's lap. And though Hendro generally speaking never refused a lady who wanted to bury her face in his lap, on this occasion he was quite worried that Phil Campion's bargain-basement seafood noodles might end up all over him. Besides he seemed to be in foul humour. Perhaps he'd had to leave some lovely lissom blonde alone in his bed. Perhaps he didn't like the abuse his car was getting. Either way, Sophie felt it would be better not to aggravate him any further. So she held onto Isobel as best she could despite the awful body contortions it required and the risk to her unfortunate knee.

At last they reached Raglan Road and once again he scooped Isobel up and bundled her into the house. He set her down on a bed in Sophie's spare room and they propped her up with cushions and spread a duvet over her. She moaned and mumbled a little – but was asleep in a matter of minutes.

"I think she'll be OK," he said.

But Sophie called a doctor just the same. She wasn't taking any more chances.

Later when the doctor had left, having diagnosed a

touch of food-poisoning, she and Hendro sat out on the deck, relieved that Isobel was going to be all right, and glumly sipping white wine. There wasn't much conversation. It was almost two in the morning.

"That was quite impressive – what you did. Thanks," she said.

"It's no big deal," he said, rubbing a hand over his aching shoulder.

"No, really. I couldn't have managed without you and I'm very grateful."

Hendro was quiet for a few moments, then he rounded on Sophie.

"What I don't understand is how you let her stay there in the first place? When you have this massive place here?"

"Don't. Please. I feel guilty enough as it is. I did try to get her to stay here – I know I should have tried harder – but I suppose I was really hoping she would do the sensible thing and go home to be with her parents while she sorted things out."

Hendro didn't seem to hear her. "What good is a place like this – if you can't share it with your mates? How could you live with yourself – with all this refurbishment, a lovely new kitchen, everything – knowing she was struggling to cope in a miserable hole like that? What kind of Sheila could get so worked up about my dinghy cluttering up her back garden – when her best friend is reduced to surviving on last night's cheap take-away?"

"What can I say? You're right and I'm very ashamed," said Sophie, now racked with guilt and remorse. "My only excuse is that the past few months haven't exactly been easy for me either and maybe I was thinking a bit too much about my own space for a while."

"How much fucking space do you need, for God's sake? Christ, if I'd known she was in such dire straits, I would have insisted she stay with me. I wouldn't have taken 'No' for an answer!"

It made it even worse that Hendro was so angry with her.

"Look you've made your point," she said trying not to let a full-blown argument develop. "And Isobel will stay here for as long as she needs. This time – I'll chain her to the bed if I have to. I can't bear to think of her in that place again and worse than that, I can't bear to think of her at the mercy of that slithering worm, Phil Campion. There ought to be an island somewhere in the middle of the Atlantic for him and his kind – where they could all be together like a colony of leeches and sponge off one another, and boast about their dazzling and unrecognised talents, and dream up elaborate schemes for world-wide success over endless joints and endless pints of beer, and seduce one another's partners behind their backs."

"Is he that bad? What did she see in him?"

"Who knows? What did I see in Daniel? Why do you sleep around so much? How many hearts have you carelessly and casually broken?"

"That's different!" he said, horrified to be mentioned in the same breath as someone like Phil Campion. "I never mislead people. I make it clear that I will not be falling in love. I don't sponge off people and I don't manipulate people. So it's very different. And to answer your question – why do I sleep around so much? It's called being a man."

He grinned sleepily at her.

Sophie rolled her eyes to heaven. She was too tired to argue any more with him and besides, she was grown terribly fond of the lumbering Hendro Sayers.

In the morning, Isobel was a slightly less sickly shade of green. Sophie brought her a breakfast tray with tea and plain toast and the daily paper, sat her up against a mountain of pillows, forbade her to leave the bed, and absolutely forbade her to go back to the basement flat. She listened in horror to the latest evidence of Phil Campion's sponging, predatory behaviour. It could have been prevented so easily. A transparent jellyfish of a man like that wouldn't have had the balls to come lurking round Isobel if she hadn't been so vulnerable and alone. Sophie vowed to build a ring of steel around her, to protect her from any further unwanted attention from him. And in that much at least, she had Isobel's full co-operation.

"I never, ever want to see, hear or even think about that man again as long as I live. It doesn't matter that he's the father of my child. He doesn't deserve to be anyone's father. When this child starts to ask about her father – I'll tell her it was a one-night stand with George Clooney."

In the afternoon, Hendro and Sophie drove over to the flat and packed up Isobel's things into cardboard boxes and Hendro arranged for them to be delivered to

Raglan Road. Sophie took some photos, CDs and books etc back with her and while Isobel slept off the worst of the 'seafood special' food poisoning, she set about making the room as homely as possible. Joe had painted the walls a warm porcelain colour. A large window framed in pale lilac muslin curtains faced out onto the back garden. Sophie washed and ironed some of Isobel's clothes and hung them neatly in the wardrobe. Hendro brought flowers – lovely big stargazer lilies and a massive box of handmade Belgian chocolates and he set them down on the Victorian chest of drawers beside Isobel's bed.

By the time she awoke again to her new and comparatively luxurious surroundings, Isobel was feeling much better. She had a warm, scented bath, wrapped her freshly washed and conditioned hair in a large towel and padded into the kitchen in Sophie's dressing-gown and slippers.

"Feeling better?"

"Lots thanks. That smells good – what is it?"

"It's nothing much – just a shepherd's pie. Comfort food – probably what you need most right now."

"I think I'll call Mum and Dad in the morning and tell them I'm going to visit."

"I'm glad," said Sophie carefully.

"It's time to tell them and now I'm ready to face the music. Anyway what's the worst they can do – cut me off and never speak to me again? I can live with that. I'll have my own child now – and together we'll get through anything."

"I'm sure it won't be as bad as all that. They probably won't be delighted – but they'll come round."

She set the steaming dish of shepherd's pie down in the centre of the table and set out two plates with savoury baked potatoes and some greens. Isobel had some colour back in her cheeks and her appetite was better. After tea, they curled up on the sofa to watch an old movie and tucked into Hendro's Belgian chocolates. It felt a little bit like old times.

Chapter 29

It was high summer. Which in Ireland meant that the temperature had plummeted suddenly to forty-nine and that sinister black clouds hovered overhead, constantly threatening to burst and dump their entire contents of exceedingly wet rain on the unfortunate little country below. The sun hadn't been seen for days, not since the end of May to be precise. It would undoubtedly reappear in September when all the kids were back at school and when it wasn't safe to sunbathe any longer because of swarms of wasps driven insanely sadistic by the prospect of their own imminent death.

Isobel was driving west to see her parents at last – to let them know about their impending grandparenthood. Sophie sat beside her, staring up miserably at the black clouds.

"Instead of getting a children's allowance, Irish people should get a sunshine allowance," Sophie observed morosely as little spits of rain on the windscreen thickened into a steady flow and then a torrent.

"Another daft notion you picked up in the States, I suppose?"

"Nope! I thought this one up all on my own since I came home. You have to admit it makes sense. Think of all the medical and psychiatric services and replacement windows and doors grants and central-heating grants that would be freed up if the government only channelled some of that money into giving us all sunshine holidays instead. It could be means-tested or something."

Isobel turned on the windscreen wipers and sighed deeply. The weather was not top of her agenda right now. She was horribly apprehensive. In ordinary circumstances there might have been a knot in her stomach – but this baby was getting so big that there wasn't any room for knots. She'd spent the past two weeks in Sophie's being spoilt and cosseted and a sense of calm had returned to her life. She was facing resolutely forward. Phil would never feature in her life again – that was carved in stone across her heart. Even her humiliating treatment at the hands of Len Crolly in the Athena Club was fading in memory. Each new day she woke more and more focussed on the new life inside her. She was bedazzled with strange new questions – things which had never before entered her head: Why have babies such big heads and no teeth? Why do people allow their babies to cry so much? Why do people sit up half the night talking gobbledegook to babies? When can you introduce a baby to seafood pasta? What is colic?

And it was no good asking Sophie. She hadn't a damn clue. She had offered the following information: babies sleep in cots and only drink goat's milk. Their teeth are hidden in their gums. They have holes in their head. You have to change their nappies every hour. Most babies can walk at six months.

Isobel didn't believe any of it. Her mother might be able to answer some of these pressing questions – though she seriously doubted it. As for her father – he farmed sheep for God's sake. Just as soon as she returned to Dublin, she intended to enrol in Motherhood classes and she planned to seek out Mary O'Connor and become initiated into the Divine Secrets of The Playdough and Mashed Banana Sisterhood. But for now she had to face her parents and deal with their shock, their anger, their feelings of betrayal, their shame, their disappointment, their humiliation in the face of the neighbours. It would require huge reservoirs of patience and inner strength. Above all, she needed to be able to break the news to them and bolt for cover immediately afterwards. For this plan to succeed she had enlisted Sophie to get the key of Tess's house so they could stay there for the night, Tess being still at Kenny's.

So as they drove westward, she rehearsed her speech. It went something like this:

Hi, Mum and Dad. How are you? You're both looking great. Isn't it a shame about the weather? Still next month is promised fine. Is that a new flat-screen telly? God, it has a great picture, doesn't it? I bet the News looks brilliant on the wide screen. Speaking of news – I suppose I'd better tell you

– I'm pregnant. That's right – going to have a baby. Well, I just thought you'd like to know. Thanks for taking it so well. By the way it's a girl – I'm going to call her Flora and Regina after you, Mum. Well, I must be off. I'd love to stay for the tea but I promised poor Sophie I'd stay with her tonight – so she wouldn't be alone. Byyyyeeeee!

Jim Kearney farmed a hundred acres of fertile South Mayo pastureland. Neatly constructed, well-maintained stone walls enclosed rolling rectangular fields of lush grass. His solid farmer's house was always brilliantly whitewashed, his driveway and paths neatly gravelled. Regina tended a large sloping garden to the front of the house and an even larger domain to the rear. There were two goldfish ponds, a tiny hump-backed stone bridge built over a stream at the far end, a heather garden, a bog garden, and her pride and joy – the rockery, a perfectly proportioned miniature replica of the limestone mountains, valleys and wild flowers of the West of Ireland.

Isobel parked in the driveway and stepped out awkwardly from the driver's seat. She'd worn a large navy-blue sweatshirt over baggy combats and if she maintained a certain round-shouldered slovenly pose, it was hard to notice the growing bump.

She trailed round to the back of the house with Sophie closely in tow. She instantly caught sight of her mother pulling weeds at the far end of the garden, waved quickly and dived in through the back door. Her father was in the kitchen bustling about, whistling tunelessly and talking to himself. For the briefest of moments, she was catapulted right back into childhood again – where everything was safe and wonderful and the worst tragedy was not being allowed to get banana wafers from Brehony's on the way home from Mass.

"Dad?"

"Isobel – you made it!" He spun round and wrapped his arms about her in a warm bear-hug of an embrace like she was still a little girl. It felt comforting and disturbing at the same time. She longed for the comfort of being his little girl again. Yet the longing made her feel vulnerable and needy – like she'd never really grown up. And of course she'd grown up. She'd flown the nest many years ago, turned away from the glad, happy days of childhood and strode off valiantly into adulthood – never until this moment looking back. Perhaps it was the baby dredging up all these strange and conflicting emotions. But the God's honest truth was that at that precise moment, Isobel Kearney would have liked nothing better than to sit on her daddy's knee and sob her heart out on his shoulder and tell him all her miseries and for him to say "There, there, Bella pet. Here, let's see if a gigantic banana wafer will put a stop to those tears. I think a banana wafer might just do the trick."

Instead she slipped stiffly from his embrace and breezed over to the kettle – which was by the range where it always was – and set about making a pot of strong tea. Sophie quickly made her excuses and left to visit Tess at Château Kenny-and-Maeve, leaving Isobel floundering about in her slovenly pose, trying to make small talk with her father. In the end it came down to the weather and how awful it had been for the past fortnight and how the lower field was still sodden and how Regina had lost an entire bed of delphiniums to the slugs.

"And how are things in Dublin?"

"Great thanks."

"Work going well?"

"Yes. It's fine."

"And the social life?"

"Couldn't be better."

Her mother was still working in the garden. Isobel watched her through the kitchen window, totally absorbed in work, kneeling daintily on a little green mat, a sturdy fork and two neatly cotton-gloved hands busily rooting out weeds and piling them all into a plastic bucket to throw on the compost heap. She looked up and waved at Isobel, then quickly returned to her work. It felt like she really wasn't interested in seeing her only daughter, like she was more worried about the weeds. Which was quite strange and a little annoying since Isobel had gone to all the trouble of driving for four and a half hours to see her. Why wasn't her mother fussing about and asking awkward questions and generally putting her foot in things?

"Is Mum not coming in?"

"She's just finishing off that border. She'll be done in five minutes."

"How do you know?" Isobel asked, slightly unnerved.

"She's just texted to tell me. She says hello by the way."

Isobel was disappointed somehow. She was all geared up for a big family show-down over an elaborately prepared and fussily presented dinner, weeping and gnashing of teeth, wringing of hands, hysteria and mayhem. And what was all this? Her father whistling and pottering, her mother tranquilly weeding the garden – and the pair of them texting one another like two lovestruck teenagers. It unsettled her deeply. Her most recent memories of life with Jim and Regina Kearney revolved around angry spats concerning the length of her skirts, the smell of drink, the lateness of the hour, body-piercings, the unsuitability of the man, the state of her room. It felt like she was in a different house altogether. She half hoped her father would settle into a nice reassuring lecture about the evils of drink and the dangers of drugs and the need to invest in a good pension fund. Instead he poured himself a brandy, settled into his favourite armchair and insisted she have a drink too. She sipped half-heartedly, waiting in what she felt was the terrifyingly still calm before the storm.

At last her mother appeared, smiling apologetically.

"Isobel, darling! Welcome home! Sorry for the delay – but if I don't get those weeds when they come up – there's hell to pay later. Oh, Jim's got you a brandy – that's nice. Now I thought – instead of me fussing and foostering over dinner – we'd eat in Leonardo's. In fact, I've already booked. Is that all right?"

"It sounds lovely," Isobel mumbled weakly.

But it didn't really suit her at all. She couldn't very well announce in Leonardo's Italian restaurant on Main Street, Hollymaine, that she was almost thirty weeks pregnant. And besides, she didn't intend to hang around long enough for dinner. Sophie had promised faithfully to call back for her in a couple of hours, vowed not to leave her at the mercy of Jim and Regina. As well as that, she couldn't really turn up in a restaurant in her sweat-shirt and combats. And on top of all that some neighbour was bound to notice her bump and comment on it before she got a chance to tell her parents.

"Yes – he does delicious saltimbocca. He's originally from Sardinia apparently – but he met a lovely Irish girl and here they are – right here in Hollymaine – bringing us the finest Italian cuisine."

"I think your mother fancies him – to be honest," Jim said mischievously.

"What?" Isobel was horrified that her father would talk so casually about her mother lusting after some Italian waiter. But Regina simply laughed girlishly and said she didn't think she'd have the energy for a toy boy.

Perhaps aliens had come and spirited away her ultra-conservative, killjoy, hideously sensible parents and replaced them with two mad look-alike chilled-out Martians. God, she would have to say something quickly – to shock them back into their normal selves.

She completely forgot about the little speech she'd rehearsed on the drive down and rapidly blurted out: "I've got a bit of news."

"Good news, I take it?" said Jim.

"Eh . . . yeah . . ." Well, not for them . . . but she herself could hardly label Flora bad news.

"You can tell us in the restaurant – over a nice bottle of Barolo."

"No!" she said quite crossly. "I have to tell you now – because – because Sophie's picking me up soon and I really can't stay long. And I'm only here to tell you my news – that's all."

She'd half expected her mother to look hurt at being slighted, her father to fix his steely grey eye of disapproval on her.

Instead her mother said mildly: "That's fine. The tables in Leonardo's are a little cramped anyway. Your father and I will go alone. We can all eat there another time. Tell you what – I'll just shower and change quickly because we are running a little late – and we'll hear your news then."

Without waiting for an answer, Regina disappeared and returned some agonising twenty minutes later in a rather voluptuous dark-green jersey-silk dress, with her ash blonde hair swept elegantly from her face and wearing a pair of surprisingly glamorous black satin slingbacks. Isobel was stunned. She never remembered seeing her mother's legs before. Well, she'd seen them – but they were the legs she'd swung out of as a child, the legs she'd clung to in moments of crisis, the legs she'd pinched, scratched and on one occasion bitten in fits of temper, legs she'd drawn on with marker, legs she'd propped her dollies and teddies against. So it was quite a shock to discover that Regina Kearney had a fine pair of legs, slender, graceful and bloody hell – elegant! Distracted by the startling discovery, Isobel momentarily forgot the purpose of her visit. It was as if all the foundations and certainties of her life to date were trembling and threatening to collapse beneath her.

Regina put a pair of sparkling diamond studs in her ears and applied one last coat of lipstick.

"So, dear – what's this news? Good news, you say?"

Isobel gulped. There was nothing "badder" than the news about to break. She took a deep breath, a larger than necessary sip of brandy, and prepared for the inevitable barrage of violent abuse.

"Here goes," she said, standing up, so that she'd be in a better position to make a quick getaway in the event of her father flying into a violent crockery-flinging rage.

"Yes, dear. Well, what is it? We are running late, as I said. Leonardo will be waiting," Regina said a little tetchily.

"Oh, fuck Leonardo! I'm sorry – scratch that. I mean this is important and you don't seem to be the slightest bit interested."

"Sorry."

"OK. As I said a moment ago – here goes."

"Yes?"

"Well I – sorry about saying 'fuck' by the way. I know how you both despise bad language."

"It seems everyone says 'fuck' nowadays. I've even heard your dad saying it when he misses an easy shot on the golf course."

"Yes – I suppose – and, well, I'm pregnant."

Once she'd uttered the words, Isobel froze like a statue. There was a terrible silence. Then her mother sprayed some perfume behind her ears. Her father took a loud gulp of his brandy.

"Are you sure?" said Regina.

"Yes – I'm sure." She tugged up her navy-blue sweat shirt and patted the large bump beneath. "Couldn't be surer."

"I thought you'd put on a little weight but didn't like to say. Being pregnant explains it though," said Regina, carefully replacing the perfume cap and returning the bottle to a cupboard by the window.

"When's it due?" Jim asked.

"Two months."

There was another ghastly silence before her mother spoke again. "You left it late to tell us, love. And how are you feeling with it all?"

"Fine. I feel fine."

Eerie – was the only word for it. Only Martians posing as Jim and Regina Kearney would react so oddly. She couldn't stand it a moment longer.

"OK – you two – I don't quite know what's going on here – but something's going on – and I'm not stupid – I'll get to the bottom of it. Where are my real parents?"

In fairness – that seemed to shock them a little bit.

"What do you mean?" said her mother.

"I mean all this! It's not real. This ridiculously fake 'chilled out' routine, eating out in Italian restaurants, flirting with Italian waiters, texting one another from the house to the garden, drinking during the week, and since when did you start showing off your legs, Mum – and knees as well? But most of all don't think I'm one bit fooled by this spookily cool reaction to my pregnancy. So come on out with it! What's going on?"

"Don't follow you," said Jim, always at sea when women let loose with their emotions.

"You've both changed. You're different. I want my narky old mam and dad back."

Regina smiled and slid into a chair next to Isobel, then carefully applied a final coat of nail varnish as she spoke.

"Darling – you're twenty-eight. Your life is entirely your own. We let you go many years ago. It was tough at the time – but we got through it."

"What do you mean let me go? Don't you two love me or care for me any more?"

"Yes, of course we do," said Jim. "I hope you never think otherwise. But like your mother just said – your life is your own. We're always here for you. We'll always stand by you – but you're not eighteen any more, Isobel. You're a grown woman and your worries and responsibilities are yours and not ours. And as for 'the chilled-out routine' as you call it – it's just that we've got our own lives too and we don't stop existing and making the most of life – just because you're not around. Also, I'd like to add on a personal note – your mother has always had a fine pair of pins – one of the first things I fancied about her."

"I don't understand. I was expecting you to fly off the handle, to screech and wring your hands, to banish me from the family home."

"Then perhaps it's you who's having trouble letting go of us," said Regina. "Look – why don't you tell Sophie we'll drop you over later? Come and have dinner with us in Leonardo's. We'd like that very much."

Regina rested her hand lightly on Isobel's and the

touch shot through her, unlocking wells of emotion that had lain dormant for a very long time. Of course the hormones that were sloshing around in her system added to the intensity of the moment and, before she knew it, Isobel was bawling her eyes out at the kitchen table as her mother hugged her and patted her hand. Out it all tumbled – Phil Campion, the job, the apartment – and her initial horror about being pregnant. Jim and Regina listened sympathetically and then her father decreed it was a situation that definitely needed to be slept on and the best thing they could do for now was to go and eat saltimbocca and drink Barolo at Leonardo's.

Sophie was quite relieved not to have to go back to Isobel's. She wanted to see how Tess was getting on in Kenny and Maeve's. She hoped that the move had put an end to the bizarre business with Robert Franklin but she was still anxious about her grandmother's wellbeing. She drove the short distance to their two-storey house with the Rennie-MacIntosh-style stained-glass windows and the Grecian porticoed doorway flanked by rows of neatly clipped topiary in huge stainless-steel pots.

Maeve welcomed her profusely, clip-clopping across the oak floor in a pair of slinky designer mules. Tess was out visiting. Would Sophie care to see the work they'd done on the house, while she waited? Maeve bustled about opening doors with looks of childish anticipation as she watched her guest's face closely.

"And this is the master bedroom with lounge area, en-suite dressing-room and en-suite bathroom in glass, all

Kenny's own ideas," Maeve said reverently.

"It's amazing," said Sophie, stumped for words. Kenny had taken to heart every single article of faith in the Minimalist bible. The low-slung Japanese-style bed was resplendent in pure white linen. Not a solitary sock, knicker or lipstick case could be seen scattered about the bedroom. Not even a toothbrush in its mug was on view to offend the eye.

The toilet itself was a vitreous china thing of simple grace and elegance. And there standing proudly in the middle of the bathroom, resting on its own glass-tiled plinth – was the glass bath.

"What do you think?" Maeve asked eagerly.

"Very tasteful," said Sophie, anxious not to offend.

Maeve showed her Tess's room and indicated all the special touches she'd added to make Tess feel at home. There were the new curtains, the brand new matching duvet cover bought specially in Moon's of Galway, a selection of books for her to read and, Maeve emphasised – loads and loads of storage space for clothes and papers and mementos.

Sophie asked how Tess was settling in. It was clear that in her muddled way Maeve was doing her best – but the chances were that Tess was feeling suffocated and restricted in her new surroundings.

"I'm sure she's happy. Strictly speaking she's only here until the work is done on her house – but between you and me Kenny's trying to persuade her to sell up and move in here for good. Of course, he has her best interests at heart – but I don't mind telling you, Sophie, that

Kenny can be a little overbearing sometimes." Maeve bit her lip and frowned distractedly through the window for a moment. "Though, of course, he's only being practical. I mean she still goes to see Robert Franklin most days. And what's to be done about him, I ask you? It's a very peculiar state of affairs and between you and me and the wall Kenny lies awake some nights worrying about it. Then if he doesn't get his night's sleep . . . just between ourselves . . . he can be quite demanding."

Sophie felt a sudden burst of sympathy for Maeve – struggling to make life pleasant under Kenny's oppressive regime. Perhaps it really was time to do something about Robert Franklin once and for all.

When Tess arrived home from a day's golf, she hugged her granddaughter warmly but Sophie thought she looked gaunt and miserable. Maeve made tea and served it up on her best china in the drawing-room. When Maeve left the room to refill her Wedgwood china teapot, Sophie snuck across to Tess and squeezed her hand.

"Are you having an awful time here?"

Tess smiled grimly.

"I thought you said you wouldn't agree to stay with them ever – that you'd rather live in a tent."

"Yes – well – Robert told me I was being silly and that there wasn't a thing Kenny and Maeve could do to me as long as I stood up to them. So here I am – trying to make the most of things and stay out of their way."

"You're better off here until the house is sorted," Sophie said reassuringly, trying to ignore the mention of

Robert Franklin. "Kenny and Maeve are company at least and you're safe from intruders or robbers – or anyone else that might try to take advantage," she added pointedly. "And you're always welcome in Dublin. You know that."

"Thanks, Sophie, that's a kind offer. I'm doing my best not to be a troublesome house guest but they're driving me bananas. I am sixty-nine years of age – not ninety-six – which is how they treat me. Kenny shouts at me like I'm deaf and stupid and she treats me like I'm a resident in a nursing home. And I'm not old."

"It's only for a few more weeks and they mean well."

"Do they?" Tess said, an uncharacteristically hard edge to her voice.

Sophie didn't know how to respond to that.

She promised to meet Tess for coffee in the village the next day, kissed her warmly and left – using Isobel as her excuse not to linger.

The sun was setting a deep red on the horizon, beneath billowing pink clouds, as Sophie drove along by the river bank, past the hulking ruins of an old cavalry barracks, now home to flocks of sheep. After a while, the sun slipped behind purple-smudged mountains and it grew dark and chilly suddenly.

A pair of enormous crumbling Greek-style pillars came into view. The gates which must have also been huge had long since rusted and decayed. Bits of them lay tossed in the unkempt verge grass. The car rattled and bumped along the long winding avenue, flanked with dense trees, the remnants of last year's autumn leaves still lodged in pockets on the roadside. Then Robert's ancestral home came into view. Though ancestral was putting it strongly. His father had made a bit of money in South America and sunk it all into Firthland House. Regrettably he didn't actually have the money to maintain it and Robert and his sisters had grown quite used to the sight of architectural salvage merchants arriving on their doorstep – loads of doorsteps really – and carting off bits of the house to pay some bill or other. By the time Robert inherited the property there were no fireplaces or fixtures or fittings of any kind and virtually no furniture.

Sophie parked the car on the bedraggled driveway and climbed the stairs of the grand entrance. She was angry. She was resolved. She was entirely focussed. This man, this *gigolo*, would pay dearly for trying to take advantage of someone she loved very much. She rapped loudly on the door, feeling a bit like a character in an old Victorian ghost story. Robert appeared instantly and for a brief moment she almost forgot the purpose of her visit. His chestnut-brown hair was swept back from his face and he wore a frayed but brilliantly white cotton shirt with the sleeves rolled. Warm brown eyes smiled welcomingly at her.

"Sophie – this is a lovely surprise. I'm just in the middle of some tedious work – and this is a great excuse to stop."

He seemed to have completely forgotten about their conversation at the wedding. And what a bloody fine actor – as if butter wouldn't melt in his mouth.

"Come in, come in! But excuse the mess. I can't seem to keep the place in any kind of order."

Even if she was a girl on a mission to pulverise, annihilate and destroy – the strange living arrangements of Robert Franklin still took her breath away. The hallway was a vast marble-pillared room – oceans of black and white marble flooring, marble everywhere in fact. Overhead, a domed portico with a circular fanlight, and all about – tall elegant windows clean and neatly painted. Doorways led off to other floorless, fireplaceless and in some cases windowless rooms – but the hallway was a palace in its own right. In the middle of it all was the most surprising feature of all: a slightly raised wooden platform, about thirty feet by fifteen, and fastened to the platform was a neat, well-maintained Nissen hut. It was painted sky blue and white and it had windows, proper electricity and even plumbing.

He led her inside and she was surprised by the cosiness of the place – it was like something a hobbit would live in – with two old armchairs, a gas stove, and masses and masses of books and manuscripts about his archaeological interests. To one end of the room was a desk, cluttered with papers, a laptop, a phone, fax and printer, beyond that a door leading to a bedroom.

"Tea?"

"No, thank you. Quite a nice little set-up you've got here. Laptop and everything. That must have cost a few bob."

"Yes, but very useful for research nowadays. Lucky for me Tess paid for the laptop."

She was stunned by his cool arrogance. He disappeared into a little kitchen. She couldn't resist peeping. It was untidy, of course – but clean and it smelt of basil and mint and fresh fruit. There was a vase full of wild roses on the little table.

He reappeared with two mugs. "I made you some anyway," he said, placing one on a little table in front of her. He then went and fetched a plate of biscuits.

"How do you like being back in Dublin?" he asked as he sat down.

He held out a plate of biscuits and because she was still ravenous, she tucked in.

"I'm not here to make small talk, Robert. In fact I'm sure you know full well why I'm here."

Robert raised an eyebrow, sipped his tea thoughtfully and said, "Have you been to see Tess?"

"Yes, I have." She was amazed that he would raise the subject so blatantly. "Things are working out well for her. Kenny and Maeve couldn't be nicer."

He sipped his tea quietly, his head bowed in thought. Perhaps he was ashamed. And he ought to be ashamed. If he was so strapped for cash why couldn't he just sell off some of his land? It was fertile and rich – bound to fetch a good price. Come to that, he didn't even need to live in this ridiculous set-up. All he had to do was sell off a few acres of land and build a sensible little bungalow. Perhaps growing up in a house like Firthland had given him the notion that living in a regular house like the rest of the parish was somehow beneath him.

"May I show you something?" He jumped up and began rummaging in an old pine dresser.

"Robert – you must know why I'm here." She tried to

sound firm and disapproving – but something about his manner made it difficult to give full rein to her anger.

"Got it!" he said, rescuing a large brown envelope from the bottom of a raggedy brown-envelope pile, then sat opposite her and once again gave her the benefit of his candid brown eyes.

"Look – no offence – but if this is about dolmens or passage graves – frankly I'm not interested right now. I only called to tell you –"

She stopped mid-sentence. What could she say next? Tell him to what? Watching him as he withdrew the contents of the envelope, it was hard to imagine he could seduce or steal from anyone. He just wasn't the sort. He'd always given off an air that he didn't care what the world thought of him – and the way he lived was a visible expression of that. Yes – but you should never judge the book by the cover, she reminded herself. He might look like an honest, intelligent man of integrity – but that meant nothing.

"To tell you to leave Tess alone."

"I figured that was the reason for your visit. Here, have a look at these."

He handed her a sheaf of papers – mostly bank statements – sums of money, including two lodgements for five thousand euro, made over the past few months. She thought she might just stand up right there and then and clock him until she looked at the name on the account.

"I don't understand."

"This is all the money Tess has been giving me."

Sophie looked at the paper again to make sure she

wasn't mistaken. "But it's in her name. Why would she give you money to put into her own account?"

"Kenny's been trying to get her to draw up a joint account with him – that would give him access to all her money – her life's savings."

"But why doesn't she just refuse – tell him to get lost?"

"Because he's a bully. I'm sorry – but it's the truth. As far as I can see, even Maeve is half afraid of him. I know your grandmother is a tough woman but Kenny's been wearing her down for years. She was thinking about giving in to him – just to keep the peace. It wasn't something she could discuss with her friends here. You know how small the village is really."

"Why get you involved?"

"I'm an outsider. I know I live here – but I've always been an outsider. We've been friends for a very long time and she trusts me. Knows I have no need of her money. I've never been interested in the stuff. It always complicates life. As long as you have enough to live on, to enjoy your interests – and to pay the bills and have a little holiday – what more do you need?"

"I thought –"

"I know what you thought. Anyway about a year ago she hit on this scheme of opening up an account in Dublin that he wouldn't know anything about. She couldn't transfer the money directly – because he would find out from checking the bank statements – yes, he's capable of that. So she asked me to help. She's been withdrawing it in dribs and drabs and I've been lodging it to the Dublin account."

"But didn't he ask what she was doing with the money?"

"Constantly! Finally in a fit of mischief she told him she had a much younger boyfriend who was a bit strapped for cash. Which wasn't exactly very helpful for me – but what could I do. He nearly came round here with a shotgun when he heard it was me. Tess thought that was very funny. You know – she's got quite a kick out of Kenny and Maeve thinking she was having an autumn romance with a man almost half her age. Sophie, I've never taken a penny from Tess. No, I tell a lie. She insisted on the laptop as a reward for helping her out."

It began to make a certain amount of sense, though she still wasn't convinced that Kenny was the bully that Robert described.

"You know what I think?" she said finally. "Maybe Tess got the wrong end of the stick with Kenny. I mean I'm grateful and everything for you trying to protect her interests – but don't you think it's all a little bit overdramatic? I've never actually heard him threatening her or being nasty."

"He's not a very obvious bully. He's never threatened her. He's never been nasty to her. He's too sly for that. But he has brought the auctioneer round to her house several times – just for a chat about 'options'. He's bombarded her with property supplements, brought her to meet an architect, a solicitor and a bank manager on various occasions. He knows he can sell her place and get planning permission to build a nice little development of houses. He has even shown her brochures for two old people's homes in the area. Look at all that in one light – you simply see a nephew trying to help his aunt maximise her assets and give her a worry-free old age. But turn it another way – and it looks a bit more sinister."

"I didn't know. At least I didn't see it like that. But why didn't she tell me?"

"She has tried to tell you – but you didn't seem to want to hear. She was hurt that you thought her foolish enough to really squander her money on a gigolo – but then she was afraid that you'd tell Kenny and Maeve and the game would be up. Anyway, I'm glad it's all out in the open. She's had a good laugh all along – but I was beginning to feel pretty miserable about it."

"So you're not – I mean you haven't – that is to say – you and Tess . . ."

He smiled, his nut-brown face crinkling up warmly. "She's a beautiful lady, your grandmother . . ."

Sophie swallowed, sorry she'd asked the question. It didn't sound after all like she'd want to hear the answer.

". . . but nothing like that. We are very good friends though. And she calls me her 'best man-friend'. Besides – I know you think I spend all my time down passage graves – but I have a romantic life of my own. Her name's Catherine and we're planning to be married next year."

Sophie felt very small suddenly, mean-minded and judgemental. Why, for all her smartness, had she not been open to the truth all along? How could she have been so quick to condemn her grandmother when everything she'd known about her up to this point proved her to be wise and sharp and absolutely nobody's fool? And hadn't she also always known that when God had been giving out decency and sense of fair play, Robert Franklin must have been very first in the queue – and had probably come back for seconds. Catherine, whoever she was, was a lucky girl.

He rested strong tanned forearms on his knees and leaned forward.

"You know – one of the things I hate in this life – is having to explain myself to people. It's such a complete waste of time. Because half of them won't believe you and the other half won't listen anyway. I love Hollymaine and most of the people in it. But they all have their own perceptions about me – about who I am and how I live my life. And they're wrong about most of it. They really haven't a clue about me. I suppose the reason I'm so fond of Tess is that she's one of the few people who know what I'm really like and take me just as I am. You were quite happy to believe I was a gigolo until a moment ago. In this village, I am variously considered to be a miser, an opportunist and a raving lunatic – because I live like this, I'm friends with your grandmother and I won't sell off the land to improve my own standard of living."

"You can't blame people for thinking that though – I mean if you don't spell it out for them – and anyway why don't you sell the land? You'd get a fortune for it – and then you could set yourself up very nicely."

"You're as bad as the rest of them," he said smiling. "I have no intention of selling the land because I don't want to see it built on. When I die – which Catherine and I hope won't be for decades yet – I intend to leave it to the state to make into a public park."

"Very noble, I'm sure. But why don't you sell just a few acres and get a decent house?"

"Because I like it here. No-one else in the world lives like this. And anyway I don't suppose it will be for much longer. Much and all as she loves me, I couldn't ask my future wife to start her married life here."

There was no arguing with that, no arguing with him anyway. He was not the kind you could argue with. She thanked him for the tea and he saw her across the marbled floor to the door.

"Are you going to tell Kenny and Maeve?"

"I don't think so though I don't really feel comfortable being a part of your little conspiracy. I'll have to think about it. And if Kenny's bullying Tess – I'll have to think about that too."

Next morning, she met Tess as arranged in The Hot Griddle, a coffee shop attached to Garrivan's Select Bar, where Mrs Garrivan let her imagination run wild with scones – the regular plain ones, rhubarb scones, savoury cheese and bacon scones, strawberry scones, blackcurrant scones, and the house special – black olive and caramelised-onion scones. Tess ordered a plain scone with home-made lemon curd and Sophie couldn't resist the sound of olive and onion and since she'd had no breakfast, and since the scones were truly, madly, deeply delicious – she'd polished off three before they got round to much conversation.

"I owe you an apology, Gran."

"That so? Wouldn't be the first time. Probably won't be the last."

"About Robert."

"What about him? He's great in bed. And he says he really doesn't mind about my wooden leg and my false teeth."

Tess had perfect teeth. She'd always minded them and had gone off to London a few years ago to spend a few thousand on keeping them that way.

"There's no need any more to wind me up. He's told me all about the account in Dublin, about Kenny and the bullying – and I'm really sorry for ever doubting you. I guess I've been away for so long, it's taking me a while to get my true bearings with people. Of course, you would never be foolish enough to take up with a man half your age."

"How do you know? And if I did – whose business would it be but my own? Anyway, it's about the only bit of fun I've had lately – watching Kenny cringing with embarrassment and greedy worry every time Robert showed up. Of course, they don't know that he's very happily engaged to Catherine."

"You are really very wicked. Don't you care about your reputation – what people think of you?"

"No, I don't. More tea? Last night Kenny made me watch a horrible programme about an old woman who lives all alone in a house in the country and who's attacked and robbed. It was supposed to frighten me."

Sophie picked at the last crumbs of Mrs Garrivan's olive scone.

"Why don't you come to Dublin for the few weeks, just until this place is finished?"

Tess eyed her sharply across the table.

"Gran – I really mean it. I'm not just asking for the sake of appearances. You gave me a home when I was a little girl – now it's time for me to share my home with you. Please – say yes – I know I haven't always been the best granddaughter – but now is my chance to make it up to you . . ."

"That's very kind of you, Sophie, but I couldn't. It's only for another few weeks – I'm tough enough to stick that out. And besides, you have enough on your plate with trying to make ends meet, going back to college and Isobel and the baby – and how are you going to find a nice man with an old trout like me hanging round the place? I'm very grateful and deeply touched – but no."

Tess squeezed her hand affectionately and Sophie could see tears sparkling in her clear blue eyes.

"I'll be fine," she said and smiled resolutely at her granddaughter.

Chapter 30

Flushed with excitement and nerves, Sophie bustled about the kitchen gathering up notebooks, pens and books and packing them into her rucksack. She made two rounds of chicken sandwiches and packed them into a lunch box with an apple and a bottle of water. When everything was ready, she poured herself a fresh mug of coffee and sat at the table studying her timetable one last time. Today was to be an induction class – meet the class-mates, meet the teachers and get the hang of the place. It all sounded easy enough. But still she fretted. What if everybody else was eighteen and beautiful? Maybe no-one would like her. Maybe it was all a big mistake. Maybe she should just get sense and find a well-paid job in a bank – just like the one she'd had in the States. What could she possibly hope to achieve by sitting in a lecture room and learning about English Literature? What had she been thinking of? To spend so much time just reading stuff and then writing essays about reading stuff. And then sitting in a room talking about stuff that she'd written about reading stuff – with no money changing hands at all, with no massive deals to be clinched, with no high-powered board meetings, no smart business lunches, no conferences, no exciting bonding weekends in luxury hotels in the Caribbean. Suddenly she desperately wanted her comfortably meaningless old life back.

She pushed thoughts of the course aside for a moment and examined a gold-embossed invitation card that had arrived a few days before. *ErinAir Literary Awards* – at the Merrion. Paul again. Why had she been invited and should she go or not?

Isobel waddled into the kitchen in slow motion, her belly enormously great with child. She eased herself down into a chair and tucked into a bowl of cereal. Sophie made toast and tea and set them down in front of her.

"On the off-chance that Nick might call round . . ." She looked out despairingly at the ploughed-up quagmire that had once been a perfectly acceptable garden. She hadn't seen or heard from him in weeks – neither for gardening or flirting.

"I reckon he's done a runner with your deposit and he's probably married as well. He looks just the sort. So forget about him," Isobel said between mouthfuls. "All set for the big day?" she added, changing the subject.

"I've changed my mind. I don't want to go. Besides I

can't leave you here alone in your condition. You might go into labour. As a matter of fact – you look like you're about to go into labour any moment now. No – I really should stay at home and look after you."

It was worth a try – but Isobel wasn't swallowing it.

"What would you know about labour? Besides, I have seventeen days to go at least. Now get going. I'll cook the dinner and clean the house."

"No! No cleaning! I beg you."

"Please don't make me not clean! I couldn't bear it. Do you have any idea how dusty and grimy a house gets even in one single day? Don't you know there are germs lurking in every corner? I thought I might do the kitchen today – tidy out the cupboards, wash down the presses, and throw out the stuff that's past its sell-by date. And the oven could do with a good scrub – and behind that dresser looks definitely dodgy . . . "

"But it's a brand-new kitchen!"

"It doesn't matter. Germs have a nasty habit of building up anyway."

There was no point in arguing. Isobel was a pregnant woman on a mission to cleanse and was liable to burst into inconsolable tears if she didn't get her way.

"By the way, fancy coming along to this thing on Thursday?" she said, placing the invitation card on the table before Isobel.

Isobel picked up the card, glanced over it briefly and tossed it to one side. "No, thanks! I don't feel like being all sociable and glamorous right now."

"I'd really like you to come. I can hardly go alone and

we could keep each other company."

But Isobel shook her head adamantly and waddled off to clean the bathroom.

While she waited for classes to begin, Sophie sat on the grass beside the lake and pulled a book of Yeats's poetry from her bag. She tried to plunge herself into the emotional depths of his soul. But it was no good. Schooled and trained in every business method and economical theory and financial strategy that had ever been thought of, the mere sight of a poem brought her out in a cold sweat of fear and incomprehension. Trying to decipher Einstein's Theory of Relativity in ancient Chinese would be less frightening.

She gathered up her things, slung her rucksack and trudged into the building, up the crowded stairs to a little lecture theatre on the third floor. She made a quick bolt for the back row but it seemed like everyone else had the same idea and Daphne Joyce, the professor with the frizzy grey hair who had interviewed her a few months earlier, shunted them all up to the front – just like at school. Sophie found herself sitting next to a woman in a pink hoodie who introduced herself as Lucy Lonergan, spinster and ex-nurse.

When everyone was settled, Daphne went round the class asking everyone what they were reading.

"*Bridget Jones's Diary*," said Lucy.

"*The Beano*," said a scruffy-looking bloke called Dennis who was leaning on a radiator at the side of the room.

"*Lucy Sullivan is Getting Married*," said someone else.

Sophie sat up stiffly and said nothing, waiting for Daphne to pour scorn on their vulgar reading habits.

"All great books," Daphne began, her stern-looking face crinkling into a warm smile. "with the possible exception of *The Beano* – though I must admit I was rather a big Minnie the Minx fan when I was a little bit younger. During this course we'll take a look at all of them – and see why it is that they are so popular. I want you to forget this nonsense about literature and popular fiction. It's an invention of intellectual snobs who like to feel they alone have control of the high literary ground. Some of the most highly regarded 'literary' works of previous centuries have sunk without a trace. Why? Because most people didn't feel inclined to read them. Literature, it is said, is a luxury. Fiction is a necessity. And what makes a classic piece of fiction survive? A true classic reaches us all – no matter how humble or exalted – whether we are the king or the beggar. A true classic can change with the times which is why we still watch Greek tragedies, why passages from *The Bible* and *The Koran* still have the power to move and comfort us, and why many of the plots of Shakespeare's plays have been 'borrowed' by Hollywood . . ."

Sophie relaxed and sat back in her desk, captivated by Daphne's easy command of English and her obvious love of books. She knew she had done the right thing after all in taking on the course and by the time Daphne came to the end of her lecture, Sophie felt the urge to go out and read every single book mentioned during the lecture.

Daphne spent the last half of the session outlining their work for the coming term. It would be quite demanding, with a long reading list, a regular programme of essays and assessments and, of course, an exam at the end for those who wanted to move onto the degree course.

A few days later in the crowded, smoky student restaurant, Sophie sat huddled around a tiny table with Lucy Lonergan and some others. The conversation and the company were easy – plenty of warm laughter and a general air of fun and edgy anticipation. They had only known each other for a few days and yet it seemed as though they had been friends for years.

The table was littered with polystyrene cups, mobile phones, study pads, hefty text books and a copy of the day's paper, the front page featuring yet another article about Paul Brehony being in trouble with the Revenue Commissioners. There were also rumblings of a hostile takeover, whisperings of unorthodox business dealings, and the old chestnut – the mystery surrounding the whereabouts of his ex-friend Dermot Stenson.

"God, he's everywhere that fella," murmured Lucy, slipping the photo a discreet admiring glance.

Sophie said nothing, not wanting to bring her various encounters with him to everyone's attention. Then she turned pale and hastily began to gather her things.

"I have to go. Sorry – I been invited somewhere. I've just remembered. In all the excitement I'd forgotten. I'd better go."

"It's a man, isn't it?" Lucy grinned. "Let him wait!

Finish your coffee."

"No! It's bad manners not to be on time. I'm supposed to be at the hotel in half an hour."

"You're not going to make it, honey!" said Lucy. "Let him stew. It will only whet his appetite even more. Treat 'em mean – keep 'em keen. That's my motto."

"Oh no! It's nothing like that," Sophie said. "It's not a relationship – it's – it's Paul Brehony – that article reminded me."

Everyone at the table looked at her oddly.

"But how do you know him and where are you meeting him?" asked one of the other girls, enthralled by the glamour and mystery of it all.

"We met at a mutual friend's wedding," said Sophie evasively. "And the venue is the Merrion Hotel."

"Humph!" snorted Lucy. "We all know what he'll want to get up to there! You poor girl – to be taken advantage of by some middle-aged playboy. It's pure criminal."

"No, it's nothing like that," Sophie said, laughing. "Look, Lucy, why don't you come with me? It's some kind of sponsorship reception. I wasn't even going to go myself. In fact, I'm not Paul Brehony's biggest fan – but it will be free food and wine for us poor students if nothing else."

Lucy pulled a face, glanced at the lecture timetable for the afternoon, saw that it was Lucinda Tarpey talking about obscure religious poetry of the Middle Ages and decided it was no contest.

"OK – count me in," she said. "But I hope they don't throw me out for being in a track suit."

"Leave that to me," said Sophie and they sped out the door.

It took a while to find a parking space and by the time they had raced several streets to the hotel, both were bathed in sweat and city grime.

"Come on! In here." Sophie tugged Lucy towards the plush rest-room off the foyer.

"We don't have time."

"There's always time for a dash of lip gloss," Sophie said, steering her companion into the restroom.

They freshened up as best they could and made their way to the reception room where the presentation was to be held. It was jammed with journalists and photographers, people from the publishing world, portly men in fine suits who exuded wealth and power, and impossibly glamorous and elegant women.

Close by, Paul Brehony was deep in conversation with some men in suits, not looking all that bothered about the imminent demise of his business and his reputation. Sophie's heart leapt in spite of herself until she noticed that Marina was hovering with elegant smiling menace in the background. Lucy spied the generously laden table of canapés and hurried off to fill two plates.

A large notice board in the corner was decked out in a very tasteful poster which Sophie examined with interest:

ErinAir Literary Awards

3000 Euro Bursary and publication

This year's recipient:

Billy Flynn for his book of short stories

Waiting in The Wings

Guest Speaker: Marina Weber Hyde

Champagne & Canapés Reception

"Champagne?" said a voice beside her.

It was Paul.

"Thanks," she said taking the glass and instantly found herself floundering in a tense silence.

"Glad you could make it," he said at last.

"Thanks for the invitation. Though you shouldn't have bothered. I wasn't even going to come, only I mentioned it to my friend Lucy and she insisted. She's mad into books and literature so I didn't want to disappoint her."

"I wasn't sure you'd come – well, after that silly card that I left for you at Ashford and then the accident in the car and . . . and everything. Well, how are you?"

"Fine thanks," she said awkwardly and they fell into an another uneasy silence. She took a couple of gulps of champagne.

"I suppose you're kept busy with the airline," she said at last trying to keep the conversation on a business footing.

God, it was a really stupid thing to say.

He responded with the merest hint of a tic at the corner of his mouth. Possibly it was the beginnings of a smile.

She felt like she had tumbled into some kind of conversational quicksand! She could feel herself sinking further into it. Best thing to do was stop talking altogether and then he'd get bored and go back to Marina. After all, the last thing he probably wanted to talk about now was business.

"I'm sure you'll have plenty of business come Christmas. Ryanair are doing very well, aren't they! I see EasyJet are running flights to Eastern Europe now. There must be loads of opportunities in those parts. If I was you I'd check it out . . . and then there's North Africa –"

God, why couldn't she stop? And why was he letting her babble on?

"Have you flown down west lately?" he said at last.

"No time," she replied a bit too quickly. "I've started a foundation course in English Literature for a few months. That's how I met Lucy. She's taking the full degree course. I wanted to take the degree course but –" she stopped suddenly. She had no intention of discussing her financial dire straits with him. "But I have a short attention span," she added quickly.

There was another edgy silence and she was glad when he excused himself and crossed to chat to Marina who had been beckoning coquettishly from a far corner of the room. Today she was dressed in yet another slim-fitting black suit. She certainly had all the moves. Sophie noted her perfectly slender manicured fingers which she curled and flicked elegantly in front of Paul, like a pair of miniature Japanese fans. She had a way of shifting from one foot to the other which drew attention to her tiny waist and slender sheer-stockinged legs, a kind of side-on, heavy-lidded smile which didn't so much hint at sexual promise as positively cast-iron guarantee it. Paul Brehony appeared to be quite enthralled by Marina's arsenal of heavy-lidded, finger-flicking, foot-shifting weapons and Sophie felt an odd pain in her chest as she watched the pair of them.

Marina had now taken a seat on the podium, crossing one leg elegantly over the other and dangling a dainty little ankle with careless charm. Quite a few men in the room were mesmerised.

The young man who'd won the ErinAir fiction prize came and sat next to her looking like he'd rather be somewhere else far away.

"Are you nervous?" Sophie overheard Marina asking him. "Don't be. It must be tremendously exciting to see your very own book in print – a great privilege to see one's name cascading down the spine of even the slightest volume. It was such a clever idea of the ErinAir marketing people to think of it."

At last Paul stood on the podium said a few words about how sponsoring new writers was something very close to his heart – since he'd once been an English teacher himself.

"And here to present the award is a renowned writer in her own right, the first person ever to have written a novel set entirely in St Kevin's Round Tower at Glendalough in which the main characters are a Swedish accountant and an Irish water diviner. Regrettably I haven't yet had time to read it myself."

Of course it was only natural for him to select Marina to present the award. It was his money and he could spend it however he wished. But looking over at the shy young lad who'd put his first book of short stories together, Sophie couldn't help thinking that Marina wasn't exactly putting him at his ease.

"So without further ado, ladies and gentlemen – I give you Marina Weber Hyde – author of *Dagmar in the Divine Glen*."

Marina beamed a dazzling smile at Paul – a pair of fleshy pink lips framing perfect little rows of even white teeth – and gracefully took her place at the microphone. She looked about the room, establishing eye contact, smiling with the heavy lids, nodding humbly to the applause.

"Thank you. It's a delight to be called upon, a privilege to be asked to speak."

She paused and smiled again, her brilliant beam lingering at last on Paul Brehony. She tucked one sweet little ankle behind the other – so that her legs now formed a graceful twisting swaying curve – impossible not to notice. Sophie was beginning to have a number of not entirely nice thoughts about Marina.

"Writing is an agonising and tortured vocation and I'm sure Billy here would agree. So first I'd like to talk to you all about my own personal literary voyage."

Sophie glanced over at Paul whose face was expressionless.

Marina went on. "The idea for *Dagmar in The Divine Glen* first came to me as I walked my dogs, Ted and Sylvia, on the broom and heather slopes of the Connemara Mountains, one gloomy indigo-clouded evening some years ago. Then, of course, it was just the germ of a bothersome idea. I hovered over it menacingly.

I wrestled with it – tried to banish it from my mind. Dear God, let this chalice pass! I prayed. But my mind accepts no boundaries – it is as open and boundless as my beloved mountains. And Dagmar's struggle with his father's coldness and his ultimately tragic but life-affirming fate – would not leave me in peace. At last I yielded to my literary vocation and I'm glad of it. For in Dagmar I have discovered a hero of our times."

Sophie felt dangerously close to throwing up, especially as this was meant to be poor Billy's big moment.

Marina flicked her hair back and continued.

"But, of course, this is Billy's big day – so congratulations, Billy, on your win."

She quickly held out the little Newbridge silver plaque and a white envelope and planted a small '*mwaw*' type peck on his cheek which made the poor lad blush horribly.

"What did you think of yer one's speech?" Lucy said to Sophie afterwards as she loaded up her plate with a small mountain of prawns.

"She must be very talented," said Sophie straining to be tactful and kind, though she found it difficult to inject much sincerity into the words.

"I thought it was a load of shite!" said Lucy, munching on a prawn filo parcel.

Sophie suppressed a giggle.

"Her speech was shite and I bet her book is even more shite. Look at her with that airline bloke – she's practically got her hand down his Y-fronts. She's probably only after his money."

"I don't see Paul Brehony in Y-fronts somehow."

"Whatever! The thing is Whatserface is a complete slapper from what I can see. And wouldn't you think a man like him would have more sense than to be taken in by her?"

"She's probably OK," Sophie said, anxious to change the subject. She didn't think it would be a wise move to speculate any further on his love life. And after all, it really was none of her business. "Look, sorry, but I have to go. Must get back to Isobel. I promised her I wouldn't be late. But you stay if you like –"

"No – I've had enough, " said Lucy, swallowing down the last crumb of the prawn filo parcel.

"Right – I'll go and thank Paul. Meet you in the foyer."

She made her way across the room to where Paul stood with Marina.

Marina looked her over, taking in the baggy combats, the T-shirt and the trainers.

"Have we met?"

"Yes – the day I had the accident – I hurt my knee – I was on the couch . . ."

Marina looked puzzled for a moment. "Ah yes – I do have a vague recollection. But how sweet of you to invite her, Paul – and how thoughtful."

Paul seemed to be completely lost for words.

"Anyway I have to go," mumbled Sophie. "Thanks again for inviting me."

"I'll walk you to the door," he said quickly, and before Marina could object he led Sophie across the room towards the foyer. As they crossed the room she thought he muttered something about wanting to speak to her. She hoped to make a quick getaway when they reached the foyer but there was no sign of Lucy and she realised she'd have to wait.

"I don't want to keep you from Marina," she said, hoping he would leave.

"Now that's what I wanted to talk to you about, though I can see you're rushing off and it's probably not the time or the place anyway," he said, looking around the busy foyer gloomily. "But I do want you to know that I –"

He didn't get any further because just at that moment Lucy returned and announced that she had just met a Hollywood actress in the ladies' powder room.

"And she has very bad breath," said Lucy gleefully. "And she's a complete slapper," she added, looking pointedly in Marina's direction.

At home in Raglan Road, Isobel had been busy. The place smelt of furniture polish and freshly laundered sheets and baking. It smelt like home in fact.

They tucked into a deliciously tender beef and dumpling casserole as Sophie chattered away, filling Isobel in on the day's events – the dash to the hotel, the prize-giving, Marina's dreadful speech, Lucy meeting the Hollywood actress in the rest-room, and a fleeting afterthought mention of Paul Brehony, as in: "Oh, and, of course, I met Paul Brehony." Then she changed the subject quickly. "So apart from cleaning and baking – what did you get up to?"

Isobel clattered her knife and fork noisily onto the dinner plate.

"Just who do you think you are?" she said, flushed with sudden anger.

"What? What did I say? I only asked what you did today. What's wrong with that?"

"What's wrong with it? You've been swanning around town talking about poetry and sipping wine with all sorts of glittery people, and I've been stuck here all day – trying to keep this place clean, making sure there's a decent dinner on the table, putting fresh sheets on the beds . . . how could you be so tactless?"

"That's just not fair. I invited you along! You can't blame me because you refused to come!"

Isobel gathered up the plates noisily and shoved them in the dishwasher.

"Why don't you let me do that?"

"No, it's OK. I can manage."

"You shouldn't be bending too much."

"I'm fine," said Isobel and promptly shed enough tears to wash and rinse the dishes. Sophie took her by the hand and led her into the drawing-room. Then she made her lie down on the best sofa propped up with cushions and a rug. Her first instinct was to tell Isobel to stop being silly and pull herself together – but just at that moment her eyes were drawn to Isobel's bump.

"Oh my God – will I call a doctor?"

"What for?"

Sophie pointed in horror to the bump. "It moved!"

'Moved' was actually an understatement. Isobel's

stomach was shifting, stretching and sticking out in all directions. Isobel didn't seem at all bothered. In fact she smiled tenderly, patted the moving belly and said softly: "It won't be long now, Flora sweetie – just a few more weeks."

Sophie winced as Flora seemed to go through an entire range of Pilates stretches inside Isobel's womb. It suddenly dawned on her that Isobel was dealing with some fairly life-shattering changes – the complete and utter annihilation of life as she'd known it up to now, the strangeness of loving an unseen infant that without even being born had already casually and without any kind of warning, inflicted cramps, piles, chilblains, heartburn, excruciating headaches, sore breasts, constipation, swollen feet and agonising backache. To say nothing of the agony yet to come! And then responsibility for another human being – forever more! To manage all that with a loving partner on hand to mop up all excess hormones was a feat in itself. To do it alone was a bloody miracle.

"Sorry – I'm not much use."

"You're plain hopeless, Sophie Flanagan. It's a good job it's me having this baby – because I don't think you'd be able to cope. As you're sitting there – just scratch my toes, will you – bloody chilblains – can itching drive you insane, I wonder?"

Sophie scratched and rubbed as best she could.

"By the way," said Isobel, settling into a drowsy state. "Nick dropped by and promises to have your garden sorted by next weekend. He asked for your mobile number – said he'd lost it – so I gave it to him – hope that's OK?"

"Yes, it's fine," she answered a touch wearily. But Isobel didn't notice. She was fast asleep.

A few nights later, Sophie had dinner with Nick. She didn't really want to go – had promised herself not to leave Isobel alone for any longer than necessary. But it was Isobel who had insisted, who had practically driven her out of the house in fact.

"At least keep on his good side until he sorts out the mess he's made in your garden. And besides – you can find out if he's married or not."

"He's single! He told me so!"

"OK – but check his hands for ring-marks."

"OK. Now, call if you need me. And Hendro's back from Melbourne. So I'll ask him to check in on you – just to be on the safe side."

Isobel scoffed and pointed out that if she was short-taken, Tiger the cat had more proven experience in the matter of delivering babies than Hendro the rugby player.

Nick took her to Reef, a rather trendy little place which styled itself as a South Pacific Fusion Eatery. Conversation flowed quite easily.

"You look very pretty tonight, Sophie Flanagan."

She was wearing a delicate turquoise chiffon-silk skirt with tiny sprigs of pale yellow daisies on the background and a simple white cotton top. The skirt was about five years old – and probably slightly dated – but it was one of the things that suited her and she liked the light feel of silk against her legs.

"Thank you. I seem to be living in jeans lately so it's nice to get the chance to dress up."

"Then we must organise more dressing-up opportunities for you. How is college?"

"Not as bad as I thought."

She chatted about the course, and the book-prize event, and he appeared to listen intently to everything she said.

"Sorry, I'm babbling on," she said finally. "Why don't we change the subject and talk about you?"

"What about me?" He reached for the wine and topped up her glass.

"Any turning points in your life yet? I mean – sorry – that sounds nosey."

"There's no need to apologise. I suppose starting up the business and seeing the Grand Canyon were both fairly big moments. And of course – did I forget to mention meeting you?"

Sophie laughed and met his eyes which tonight were full of frank admiration.

He reached across the table and took hold of her hand. "How about a moonlight walk?"

Yes – it sounded like just the ticket – a moonlight walk, a bit of harmless flirting, nice conversation. She'd examined his fingers for signs of ring marks and found none. So she was pleased enough to stroll around the town with him, though he didn't set her heart on fire, though she found her thoughts swerving off at the oddest times to Paul Brehony who was definitely not available and, if Marina had her way, would never be available again.

Outside, he slipped a coat over her shoulder and they rambled slowly through the crowded cobbled streets of Temple Bar, beneath the obligatory starry sky.

"May I hold your hand, Sophie Flanagan?"

"You may."

"Thank you – because it's quite a lovely little hand – like its owner."

"Now you're teasing me."

They were on the boardwalk now and it was quieter. The harvest moon cast a trembling reflection in the black water beneath them. She felt enveloped in a warm wrap of ease, savouring the bustle and chatter of the night city. It was all perfect really.

"I suppose you're the sort of girl who doesn't believe in kissing on a first date?"

"You suppose right," she said, and then to soften the blow added, "Though I may allow you a modest peck on the cheek if you behave yourself."

He did, told her stories about his childhood, made an amiable fool of himself trying to name some of the stars, moved protectively closer to her just long enough to pass a gang of rough-looking youths, said several times what a wonderful time he was having, talked at length about how he was going to transform her garden.

He took her home in an open horse-drawn carriage and put his arm about her to provide warmth.

"Thank you," she said, rummaging for her key. "It's been a lovely evening."

"Let's do it again. How about next weekend?"

"I'd like that very much."

He bent and kissed her on the cheek – a soft, winning kiss. "I'll call you during the week."

She smiled sceptically.

"No! I mean it! I can't call you before Thursday – because I'm really busy. But I will definitely call you Thursday. And I'll begin the serious garden work on Friday – I promise."

Chapter 31

Time seemed to have stopped for Isobel. She had never felt so impatient in all her life. Every day she trudged about two miles round the neighbourhood because her mother said it would speed up the arrival of the baby. As far as she could see, the only effect it had was to crucify her feet – which let's face it weren't the most fabulously beautiful feet in the world to begin with. At the best of times, Isobel felt deeply ashamed of her feet. Somehow, despite her mother's dainty girlish size fours, Isobel had ended up with broad workmanlike spades. The only advantage was it meant that she never had much trouble with keeping both her feet firmly on the ground, or even with calling a spade a spade. Now, to her absolute consternation and horror, they'd grown even wider and she was beginning to feel like Daffy Duck. But more horribly worrying was the fact that they'd grown longer as well. It wasn't possible. It couldn't be possible. But now they were a monstrous size seven. What if they didn't stop? And wasn't there a Spanish proverb about never marrying a woman with big feet? What if she had to wear men's shoes for the rest of her life? How would Flora cope with a disfigured mother?

Unexpectedly the easiest part of her pregnancy had been getting used to the idea of the new person inside her. Less easy to handle were the strange and sudden shifts in her attitudes to things. Until recently a strong supporter of the Children Should Be Not Even Seen and Certainly Not Heard movement, she now found herself eyeing other people's babies and infants with moist-eyed endearment. Where once she'd scowl disapprovingly at the sight of a gurgling dribbling baby in a restaurant, now the shoe was on the other foot – or in Isobel's case – the spade.

Most of all, the gradual realisation that she would soon be responsible for a tiny vulnerable human being unsettled her long-held opinions of Regina and Jim Kearney, who up until recently in her opinion had lived on the far side of a very sad planet, beyond even the Pathetic Galaxy, and who most definitely should only be heard and not seen. Since her return from Hollymaine, they'd called almost every day to make sure she was taking things easy. Jim had booked her into a private room in the maternity hospital which was probably costing him a by-pass and a hip-replacement. Regina had cleared out a spare room and was busy stripping the walls and floors and riffling through interior decorating magazines for ideas. Baby would need a bright and comfortable nursery, she said. She and Jim had more money than they needed. What better way to spend it than on a grandchild? And they had plenty of room. Where was the sense in Isobel struggling by alone when between the three of them they could provide a warm and loving home for Flora? Isobel had to wonder, could she possibly have misjudged them in the past?

Some afternoons were taken up with ante-natal classes and practising the breathing exercises for a completely natural birth. The way the young nurse explained it made the whole business sound terribly easy and Isobel wondered why women got into such a state about giving birth. "Just get the hang of the breathing and there will be relatively little pain – nothing more than a mild period cramp," the nurse had said cheerfully. That didn't sound so bad and Isobel didn't think it was at all fair when one of the other older women asked the young nurse just how many babies she'd had. "None so far," the nurse had replied and then the woman, who was on her fourth child, exchanged knowing glances with some of the others and left. But Isobel felt sure the young nurse was right. She made a mental note to send her a nice big box of chocolates once Flora was born.

One afternoon, Hendro bounded in. She hadn't seen him since he got back from Melbourne. His face dropped visibly when he saw her grand bump. She'd grown quite a bit since the last time he'd seen her. Typical man! Isobel thought.

"God, that's huge!" he said with mauling tactlessness.

Her face crumpled and she turned away.

"I mean that's a good thing, isn't it, because it shows you're going to have a healthy baby. What if I'd said you were tiny – wouldn't that have made you feel sort of inadequate? But you look blooming! Radiant! Serene! Beautiful in fact!"

He placed a flat parcel on the table in front of her.

"I brought you something from Melbourne. I saw it and thought of you instantly."

"What is it?"

"Open it and see while I make us a cup of tea."

Isobel fumbled with the wrapping paper. She didn't know Hendro all that well – but she knew that not all rugby players were renowned for their sensitivity or tact. What if it was some awful blokey type sex-shop joke? She'd completely lost her sense of humour. It seemed to have utterly vanished the night Phil Campion had slunk around to the basement flat with his poisonous takeaway meal, to borrow money and bedroom facilities from her. To be honest, she didn't think she would ever laugh again. What was there to laugh about in any case? Life was full of treacherous, self-serving, two-faced bastards. From now on, Isobel's life would centre round one person only – baby Flora.

Hendro set two mugs of tea down on the table and noticed the still unopened parcel.

"What's this? Don't you like opening presents?"

"Maybe later."

"Then I'll open it for you."

Before she could stop him, he'd ripped the wrapping paper away to reveal – a small painting. The colours were warm rich deep earthy blues, reds and browns. The painting was of a young Aboriginal mother nursing her infant. Isobel was stunned. No-one had ever given her a painting before.

"Don't you like it?"

She held it out in front of her, studied the face of the young mother looking down at the baby. She could imagine what the girl was thinking. Her face was suffused with love and protectiveness and a little tinge of regret. Maybe she'd been left high and dry by some bastard like Phil Campion too. But it didn't matter because she held something far more precious in her arms. The clever artist had put it all in.

"Thank you! It's lovely." She hauled herself up from her chair and kissed him on the cheek. The sudden movement caused a twinge at the base of her spine and she sat back quickly wincing. She'd been getting little twinges like that for the past few days and the doctor had warned her to expect them and not to panic because the real thing would be a lot sharper and not likely to happen for a few weeks yet.

"You don't look too hot all of a sudden. Is it the painting? I'll take it away if you like."

"I'm fine now. And the painting is lovely."

The pain disappeared as quickly as it had come on.

"I know what to do to take your mind off things. Come and watch me train."

"I couldn't think of anything less appealing."

"Come on! You can have a laugh if nothing else."

"Well . . . OK then."

The day was breezy but warm. Isobel knew that loads of girls would give their eye teeth, their right arms, their mothers, their grannies and their friends' grannies, just to sit into a BMW sports with a man like Hendro – and drive through town with the hood down to watch a group of half-naked men in prime physical condition do their exercises.

Hendro was in training gear, and his long muscular limbs filled up the car. His tanned and rugged face and sun-bleached hair drew admiring and envious glances from women passing by in modest Ford Fiestas. He was like one of those Greek gods – slightly haughty – and horribly handsome and well-built. Stopped at traffic-lights, two girls in an adjoining red VW Golf rolled down their window and whistled and winked at him. Just as the lights were changing, a little white card came flying onto his lap.

"It's a couple of mobile-phone numbers," Isobel said examining the card.

"The things girls do," he said and tossed the card onto the back seat. "Now let me explain the rules of rugby to you . . ."

At the training ground, she eased herself from the car and waddled penguinlike into the little club house with him. He ordered a cup of tea for her and was instantly swallowed up in a rowdy, energetic knot of team-mates in black and white striped jerseys. Like a herd of mad zebras, she mused scornfully.

Hendro came in for a great deal of slagging.

"Hey – Sayers – how's the shoulder, you daft bastard?"

The speaker was a very large red-headed person with a squashed-looking neck and horribly swollen ears. Isobel shifted uncomfortably. Because of his shoulder heroics in her basement flat, Hendro had damn near lost his place on the team. And worse still, the team had lost a crucial match. Coach Gary Burton had been furious. Isobel prayed he wouldn't finger her as the reason for his injury. She didn't fancy drawing the anger of this lot. They looked quite friendly now and some of them had welcomed her and shook her hand. One had even asked when her baby was due, and was she hoping for a girl or a boy and wished her luck. But the fact remained that they were all built like army tanks and they spent their days training to tackle and maim and wrestle other gangs of equally huge men to the ground.

Hendro laced his boots and took his team-mates' comments in good spirits.

Gary Burton called them to order and then gave a short pep talk to his troops.

" . . . and I don't need to remind you lads that this weekend's match is the big one. We face relegation to the second division if we lose. Fortunately for us – and barring training injuries – we now have our full team back. Hendro's shoulder is fine. Kieran's groin strain has sorted itself out. We've got to win this match– so let's get out there today and train like we mean it."

They marched out onto the pitch, faces blank with concentration, bodies stiff with determination.

Mad! Isobel concluded, as she watched them leave and Flora took the opportunity to do some more Pilates stretches in the womb. They're all mad. Really, what was the point of men at all – if this sort of thing was all they could get really passionate about?

She found an old newspaper and took her tea out onto the veranda to watch them train. She hadn't the slightest interest in seeing any of it but at least it would while away an hour or two. So while they practised scrums and heaves, crouching and engaging, binding and driving, throw-ins and lineouts, passes and tackles, she looked on with mild interest and thanked God that she wouldn't be rearing a son. But as the afternoon wore by, something odd happened. She noticed how they passed the ball so skilfully to one other, how sometimes a player would take hold of the ball and duck and dive his way through waves of opponents, and she became caught up in it. By the end of the session, she was sitting on the edge of her seat, hollering her lungs out every time Hendro got the ball.

"I quite enjoyed that," she told him on the way home.

"You sound surprised."

"I am surprised. I thought I'd be bored out of my skull. But I wasn't. I forgot about my own worries completely."

"Why don't you come to our next game?"

"I don't know."

"I mean it. What have you got to lose? Apart from anything else it will help you pass the time."

One of the marvellous things about being in the late stages of pregnancy, Isobel realised, was that she was completely immune to the attractions of men. And it was just as well because Hendro had spent the whole day being pleasant and charming – the present of the painting, the invitation to the training session and his easy concern for her wellbeing. But right now, he could shower her with gifts and compliments for an entire week and it wouldn't make the smallest bit of difference. And it was really just as well, she thought, stealing a longing glance at his hulky frame.

Chapter 32

On the way home from her afternoon lecture, Sophie checked her mobile for messages – but there were none. She popped into the Merrion Centre and bought a few groceries including some of Isobel's latest food craving – apple jelly. At home, these days, Isobel was in quite good form, and even cracked jokes about Hendro and the effect he had on women and spent ages talking about her trip to the training session. She seemed calmer somehow, less inclined to furious bursts of energetic cleaning, less prone to torrential floods of tears.

Sophie realised she was dreading the moment when Isobel's parents came to collect her. The house would feel empty and quiet. They were sisters in all but name. Together they had travelled a long way in the past few months, both of them hurtling through some momentous changes. And if anything, the experience had cemented their friendship even more firmly.

They went for a walk. It was more of a slow and stately procession really as Isobel couldn't manage much else. The evenings were closing in and the night air smelt of decaying leaves, the first log fires of the winter and the last sweet grass cuttings of the year. They strolled in companionable silence for a while then talked about the baby and what Isobel planned to do in the future.

"I told Phil a lie, you know. About my money."

"Good for you – give him a small taste of his own medicine."

"He really means nothing to me now. I never thought the day would come. And it's awful how I kept on loving him even when I discovered just what a complete lying, cheating disaster he was. Now I feel like I've had a bad tooth pulled or a painful growth removed. I'm free of him, free of even wanting to think nasty thoughts about him. In the matter of Phil Campion – I am truly, madly, deeply – indifferent."

"There's nothing in the world quite like the sublime bliss of indifference."

Sophie remembered many of Phil's lies, the worst being the lies he'd told about his family and which Isobel had only recently uncovered. His father, far from being an alcoholic wife-beater, was a mild-mannered accountant. His mother, a kindly and well-liked woman, ran a playschool. His brother did not live in a drain in New York – but in a nice house in Blanchardstown with a lovely wife and two children. Yet, smart as she was, Isobel had believed it all for a while. He'd told her that his fiancée had left him at the altar on their wedding day and that his heart was broken. But it wasn't true. In the first place, he had been the one to cruelly ditch his fiancée a week before their wedding. In the second place, Phil Campion had no heart. In place of a heart, he had a bottomless chasm of needs that he satisfied diligently and with an almost religious fervour: the need to be liked, the need for quick sex, the need to seduce other women – which he explained was part of the burden of a true artist – the need to dine out in fancy restaurants, to drink expensive wines, to spend weekends in luxury hotels, the need for endless lines of cocaine which he informed Isobel were essential for the releasing of his most profound creative talents. "Do you honestly think Michelangelo was inspired to paint the Sistine Chapel by drinking camomile tea?" he once said by way of justification. He had endless reservoirs of self-esteem. He was a living monument to the power of positive thinking. He had limitless quantities of love – for himself – and truckloads of confidence in his own stunning abilities. Except that he didn't have any talent. Yet Isobel had tolerated him for years, ignoring his faults, imagining his virtues.

"You know that money my gran left me – I told him I spent it – because he would only have wheedled it out of me otherwise. But I still have it. I'm going to put a deposit on an apartment and rent it out until Flora and I decide where we want to live and how I can support us both. Mum and Dad say we can stay with them for as long as we like."

"Sounds good," Sophie said, sneaking a look at her phone for messages.

"So in case I don't remember to say it another time – thanks for everything. Thanks for steering me through the break-up. Thanks for holding my hand when I lost my job. Thanks for taking me and Flora in. I wouldn't have survived the past few months without you."

"This isn't leading up to one of those weepy wobblies, is it?"

"No – at least I don't think so. Who can tell with these bloody hormones? Anyway you've been a true friend and I will never forget it."

"Yes, well – the truth is I'd have been lost without you these past few months. So let's just leave it at that." She glanced at her mobile again and explained that Nick had promised to call.

"As if I hadn't noticed!" said Isobel.

"Noticed what?"

"You've only sneaked a look at your mobile about twenty times since we left the house. I didn't know you were that keen."

"I didn't know myself – but it is half past seven – and you would think he'd have called by now."

"You know men and time. They see it completely differently. They measure it differently. When they say 'See you soon' they generally mean sometime in the next five years. When we say 'See you soon' we usually mean sometime in the next five hours."

Isobel yawned, dragging her feet the last steps of the way. In her present condition, the romantic turmoils and yearnings of others didn't interest her one tiny bit. What she most deeply yearned for was a big warm bed, a mug of cocoa and magazines about babies and nurseries with loads of pictures and no writing apart from the captions.

Sophie pushed thoughts of Nick from her mind, took a long hot bath, sent off some emails, tried to engross herself in composing an essay on *The English Patient*, gave it up as a bad job and clambered into bed. It was past midnight when she was forced to conclude that he wasn't going to call.

Daphne had been under strict orders from Lucinda Tarpey to arrange a personal development, goal-setting, life skills, life-coaching morning for her students. It was to be facilitated by Karl Sigmund O'Connor. Daphne had said to her students "It's college policy to run these things. Take what you can from it. Who knows it may be of some use. Unfortunately I have to go to a meeting!" It didn't sound very promising and Sophie had attended enough staff-development days in her Stateside banking career to know that the mystic gurus who ran these courses had a gospel to preach and a particular path towards enlightenment to share – and dare anyone disagree. She picked her way reluctantly through couples strewn on the dew-drenched grass by the lake and made her way to the Meeting Room.

Inside, the chairs were arranged in a large circle. There were two flipcharts, a cluster of scented candles in the centre of the room and in the corner two bags of what looked like rags. Some of her classmates had already arrived. Lucy had pinned Dennis to the wall and was filling him in on some of the more grissly episodes of her nursing career. A couple of younger girls were busy swapping notes on American poets of the twentieth century. The rest sat about leafing through newspapers, sent text messages or grumbled quietly about the traffic and the awful queue at the photocopier.

"Have you ever been to one of these?" Sophie asked Lucy.

She hadn't and she was quite excited. Could there actually be a formula for helping them to get more out of life? Would it really change their lives? Make them happier or more successful?

"We might leave here at lunch-time and be an entirely new bunch of people," said Lucy, full of enthusiasm. "I might go out and find the man of my dreams. Dennis could become a famous poet."

"What about me, Lucy?" Sophie asked trying to enter into the spirit of things. "What's in store for me – since you're in fortune-telling mood?"

Lucy surveyed her new friend from top to toe. She closed her eyes tight and pressed her hands to her temples like a fortune-telling mystic.

"You will find your bearings," she said suddenly.

"What do you mean?" Sophie was stunned – even a little annoyed that Lucy had chosen the very same words Sophie had used to explain herself to Tess. What bearings? Of course, she had her bearings. Didn't she have a nice home, great friends, and a worthwhile few months of learning ahead of her which in turn would lead to endless possibilities? What other bearings were there in life? Lucy was making her out to be a rudderless ship, a plane without a pilot, back in Dublin without a map or even a man!

"I don't know why but it just came into my head," Lucy said, biting her lip anxious that she might have offended her classmate.

Sophie would have taken her to task on it but just at that moment a small, lean man with floppy blond hair and rimless glasses bounded into the room juggling three balls in the air and wearing a smile bright enough to light up the dark side of the moon. He wore baggy denims and an alarming purple paisley-print shirt.

"Hi! All set? Good! Because today is the first day of the rest of your life. You have the power to change. You have the power to be You – the You you really want to be. By the end of today – you may be an entirely different You."

Sophie's heart sank as he frolicked over to the flipchart.

"Raising the bar of your life!" he said loudly and with great emphasis as he drew a straight thick black line across the middle of the board with a squeaky felt-tip pen. Rembrandt he wasn't.

Dear God, was there a remote village somewhere in California where they secretly cloned these people. She'd seen the exact same performance by a Mexican and a Texan in the past two years.

"I'm Karl Sigmund O'Connor of the Win Win Foundation."

Then a juggling ball was passed around and everyone had to say their little piece.

"I'm Dennis and I'm a complete and utter waster."

"I'm Lucy and I'm an unclaimed treasure."

"I'm Jenny and I'm really looking forward to the next year."

Sophie's turn. What would she say? 'I'm Sophie and not really interested in hearing just another meaningless feel-good message'? How about 'I'm Sophie and you should be ashamed of yourself taking money for this crap'?

"I'm Sophie and I've just moved back to Ireland."

It was as bland an answer as she could muster but it seemed to satisfy Karl Sigmund.

He gambolled energetically into the centre of the room and spread his arms in some kind of quasi-evangelistic pose.

"Children! Have you ever noticed children – fearless – they'll do anything. Somersaults! Swimming under water! Telling Granny she has a hair on her chin! But we lose that fearlessness, don't we? What's our biggest fear?"

Various people offered suggestions – failure, death, losing control, getting old . . .

"Spiders," said Lucy.

"I'm scared of bleedin' birds," said Dennis.

Sophie would like to have sung dumb but it was clear that if she didn't join in the discussion soon she might as well go home. What was the sense in being here at all if she wasn't going to leave herself open to some kind of change in her life? After all, she was paying for the privilege of hearing Karl Sigmund – she might as well get some value out of it. She took a deep breath.

"Fear of flying," she mumbled like a sullen teenager.

"What's that?" said the guru pouncing on her. "Out loud so the group can hear."

"Fear of flying!" she repeated.

"And what have you done about it?"

"Nothing. I just live with it."

"But you have the power within you to change. You don't have to live with it. What if I were to tell you it could be cured?"

He drenched her in the cascading brightness of his glistening feel-good smile.

Sophie glowered at him. She didn't really fear it that badly. She was well capable of getting up in a nice big sensible jumbo jet and flying halfway round the world. So in a sense it wasn't a real fear and she instantly regretted mentioning it to the glistening guru.

"It's easy!" he said with enough optimism to power a space shuttle. "Just let go of those old preconceptions about flying. Let them float out through your toes. Those thoughts are holding you back. Let them go."

"OK. I'll try," she said – in an attempt to get rid of him.

But he was having none of it.

"I'm not going to let you off that softly. Let me guess? You always look at the hostess doing the safety procedure – not because it's polite but because the plane will crash otherwise. You tank yourself up with alcohol. You get sudden bouts of severe religious fervour when you're flying which disappear just as soon as the plane hits the ground – sorry bad choice of words . . ."

Plenty of people in the room laughed at his little joke. Lucy thought it was hysterical and kept repeating the phrase "hit the ground" and laughed for ages which annoyed Sophie even more. She sank even further into her chair, half afraid that he would single her out to show off his ability to work miracles. But luckily he'd only been paid the group rate and one-on-one healing sessions weren't apparently included in the package. At last he got bored with her fear of flying and her sullen refusal to warm to his fabulousness. So he moved on to a woman who had a bizarre fear of books.

The rest of the morning was spent drawing little positive-thinking charts and making happiness pictures from the collections of rags. A couple of girls joined together and did a picture of a kind of Paradise Island with palm-trees and a beach and what was meant to look like people having a good time. Dennis assembled some black felt and put a little scrap of cream silk fabric on top. "Guinness!" he proclaimed fondly. Lucy made a house from scraps of ribbon and put a nice garden in front with flowers and a green cotton lawn. Sophie fiddled half-heartedly with a handful of coloured strips of linen. At last just to get the glistening guru off her back she made a vase of flowers which brought on an unwelcome reminder of Paul Brehony . . .

Then they played silly survival games like: You have been marooned on a desert island with five others. You have only a Phillippe Starck lemon-squeezer, a pound of mouldy carrots, an old bicycle pump and a compilation disk of Celine Dion's greatest hits. How will you survive?

Guru Karl zip-zapped about the room with endless reserves of irritating, grinning, in-your-face, "ain't I awe-inspiring" enthusiasm. By lunchtime, everyone in the room was punch-drunk from all the wisdom, advice, insight, meaningful little stories and shiny, happy energy that he had rained down on the group.

"OK – last thing!" he said and produced a bag of juggling balls. "Can anyone juggle? I mean really juggle? No? OK then – let's give it a go."

She tried hiding behind Dennis – so that she wouldn't have to take part – but it was no good. Karl Sigmund sought her out and wouldn't leave her until she'd made a jolly good effort to juggle. Being sullen and rude to him didn't seem to have any effect so very reluctantly she took the balls in hand and set about teaching herself a completely new skill.

Soon, in spite of herself, Sophie was completely engrossed. The secret he explained was not to throw and catch but to throw and throw. And he was right. In the space of five minutes she had mastered juggling and would quite happily have stayed practising for the rest of the day.

So in a sense and though it stuck in her throat to even think it, he was right and she did come away a different person. She might very well bury Guru Karl Sigmund's juggling balls up his bottom if she ever saw him again – but at least now she could juggle with them first.

Chapter 33

It was drinks all round in Kealy's Bar and there was definitely that Friday feeling of everyone being in high spirits – jokes, slags, talk of what club they'd go to.

"I wouldn't be let into any club," said Lucy.

"Why not?" asked Sophie, who was already collecting money for cabs and entry.

"I'm too old."

"Don't be daft! Who says you're too old?" said Dennis.

"I just am. And that's all there is to it."

"Well, we're not budging without you," said Sophie.

"Suit yourselves," said Lucy dismissively.

But Sophie could see that inwardly she was quite chuffed.

They finished off the last of the drinks and gathered outside in the darkness to wait for taxis. Sophie called Isobel and was told to stop fussing and to go and enjoy herself. Then just as she was putting her mobile away, it rang again.

"Hi – sorry I haven't been in touch."

She resisted the urge to remind him that he'd promised

to call the day before, to point out to him that they had actually made a date. That it was a bit late calling her now. Instead she played it cool.

"I'm out on the town with some friends."

"Are they special friends?"

"How do you mean?"

"I mean – supposing I told you I had a table for two at Patrice Languedoc for nine o'clock?"

Sophie swallowed. She wasn't especially into posh eateries and definitely not now that she couldn't afford them. But Patrice Languedoc was the classiest, trendiest, most exclusive restaurant in Dublin. Now that she was practically broke, it might be foolish to turn down that sort of invitation – even at short notice.

"I'll call you back."

"Don't be too long."

In deeply apologetic tones she explained the situation to her companions.

"Can we all come?" asked Lucy.

"You have to go," said Dennis.

"But I'm here with all of you – I can't just leave because I've got another invitation. And anyway he only called at the last minute."

"Patrice Languedoc with hunky gardener Nick Lynch or The Pink Giraffe with us lot? No contest! And if you don't go – I'm going in your place," said Lucy tartly.

And that was it. She took a cab home, showered quickly and dressed in an elegant black trouser suit with silver strappy mules. Less than an hour later she sat opposite Nick at the best table, in the best restaurant in town.

A waiter, who seemed to be trying to locate something at the end of his nose, hovered like a shop-window mannequin. Another waiter whose cheeks seemed to have somehow got stuck together between his teeth stood poised with a napkin. Nick poured some champagne and proposed a little toast.

"To you. You look beautiful. Doesn't she?" he said turning to the waiters. They nodded disinterestedly and one of them relieved him of the bottle to replace it in the ice bucket.

"Thanks," she said, blushing slightly.

"I should apologise for not calling sooner . . . "

"You should," she said lightly.

"It's just the business – so much to do – new clients – it's chaotic all the time. Anyway I'm really sorry. But you knew we had a date. I wasn't going to stand you up – if that's what you were thinking."

He reached over and rested his hand on hers.

What could she say? Never waste your energy sulking with a man, the nuns of Perpetual Caution used to advise. And never, ever sulk with him in public. She decided it was too nice an occasion to spoil so she smiled her warmest smile at him and told him there was nothing to forgive.

"I suppose we should order," she said indicating the waiters who were now standing sadly to attention like pallbearers about to wilt at a funeral.

After that, he was charm itself, ordering the best wine in the house, admiring her hair, her dress, her easy sense of style. He talked about books he liked to read and how he was a regular theatre-goer. He told her he had ambitions to some day build up a collection of art. Almost everything he said made her like him even more.

But she had no thoughts beyond the evening and the delicious food which a whole fleet of waiters delivered to the table with reverential care. She hadn't eaten such good food since her expense-account days in the States. She dispatched a melt-in-the-mouth crab brûlé and then started on some heavenly sole. Nick had ordered rack of lamb which was mouthwateringly tender.

"I'm sure you're looking forward to having your garden sorted out," he said.

"Yes! I can't wait for it to be finished, and for spring to arrive so that I can go out there and enjoy it all."

"Sophie in her garden . . . I can picture you so well in it. I promise it will be all sorted in a month."

He was leaning on the table, his head bent towards her, his eyes lingering over every contour of her face. It was not a good time to remind him of his earlier promise to do the work in a matter of days so she bit her tongue and said nothing.

"I've never met a woman like you before," he was saying. "Something is happening – a moment like this is so rare – you must feel the same. It's like I'm falling in love . . ."

"Steady on! It's only our second date!" she protested uneasily. Besides, there was still the frozen berries and the cheeseboard to look forward to.

"True. But something special is happening, don't you feel it?"

Since she'd been off the dating scene for quite a while, Sophie had completely mislaid her bullshit detector and she found herself floundering about, wondering whether she should feel nicely flattered or mildly alarmed.

"Can we just go a bit slower?" she said to Nick. "We hardly know each other."

"Very sensible. I'm just an incurable romantic – and I can't help myself around you. Let's change the subject altogether. Tell me about your time in the States."

With a gasp of relief she galloped through a potted history of her career, her job, her home and her friends in New England. She even managed a brief and coolly detached mention of her relationship with Daniel. As the wine flowed, they soon found themselves swapping silly jokes. Then, with the desserts and coffee, it was on to their most embarrassing moments and she laughed out loud when he told her the story about his first kiss and how he'd been so enthusiastic that he'd given the girl of his teenage affections a nosebleed.

"You're making that up!" she said, laughing.

"No. It's the truth. She never forgave me. I ruined her best white blouse."

She was rummaging desperately in the back of her mind to find the least embarrassing most-embarrassing moment that she was prepared to share with him, when an insignificant movement to the side of the room caught her attention. Some woman was talking to her companion – explaining something with her hands. They were perfect little things – slender and fabulously manicured. And they seemed to almost dance about in the air like they had a flirtatious life of their own. It was impossible to ignore them. And then she recognised the slender, tastefully groomed and expensively dressed figure of Marina Weber Hyde. And across her shoulder, sitting back easily in his chair, his eyes fixed on Sophie, a glass of mineral water in his hand was Paul Brehony.

How hadn't she noticed them before? He had probably been watching her and Nick all the time. Not that it bothered her – but dinner for two was an intimate business and it always spoiled the effect if there was some other uninvited, half-acquaintance hovering in the background.

Paul raised his glass in a salute. Then Marina turned and gave them the benefit of a little finger-fanning before turning again to her dinner companion.

God, that woman! Sophie was not the sort to take a quick dislike to anyone, but Marina Weber Hyde was making her stomach churn – the sort of woman who had to make a conquest out of every man she met – who would pulverise him with a stockpile of weapons of mass-seduction. Sophie guessed she was the kind to have crimson silk sheets on her bed but no food in the fridge, a complete arsenal of Lejaby underwear and no walking shoes.

"That's Paul Brehony. Do you know him?" asked Nick.

"Not really."

"He seems to know you . . ."

She wanted to leave now but stuck it out, chatting as energetically as she could, unwilling to betray her unease to Nick.

At last, it was time to leave and Nick disappeared

behind a screen to settle the bill, leaving Sophie alone twirling her glass. She was conscious of the fact that Marina had risen and gone to the powder-room a few minutes before, and now, out of the corner of her eye, she saw a tall figure approaching.

"We meet again. Do you think it's fate?"

Paul Brehony smiled lazily as he loomed over her. She still found his gravelly Dublin accent quite sexy but wondered how plum-voiced, vowel-strangling Marina could even tolerate it.

"May I?"

He didn't wait for an answer and slid casually into the chair just vacated by Nick.

"Enjoying your meal?" she asked.

He cast a slightly anxious look in Marina's direction. "To be honest – I'm more of a meat and two veg man. You can take the man out of the bog and all that. Marina raved about this place and she insisted on coming here. But I've never been in Patrice Languedoc before."

"I'm surprised. Don't you nouveau riche people have to be constantly proving your status or something?"

"I'm not that rich. I don't even make it into The Rich List."

"Don't tell that to your dinner partner."

"Don't tell me what?"

Marina had emerged from the powder room – splendidly re-preened and ready for a further assault on the wallet of Paul Brehony. She rested her tiny hand lightly on his broad shoulder. If that hand could speak it would have screeched quite forcefully with strangled vowels:

"*Mine! So back off, lady!*" Sophie suspected that Marina would be a dangerous and vindictive woman if crossed in matters of love or wallet. She didn't plan on hanging around to find out.

Nick reappeared and after the briefest of introductions they left Paul and Marina – who though very much on the wrong side of thirty-five clung to his side like a schoolgirl coquette, fluttering her eyelids and pouting in a way that did not entirely flatter her collagen-enhanced lips.

"Coffee in my place?" she offered to Nick as they hailed a taxi.

"I would drink coffee all night with you," he murmured and planted a soft kiss on her hair.

In the kitchen, she tried valiantly to rustle up coffee but he wouldn't let her be. And she didn't mind too much – but her heart wasn't on fire either – nor did she feel the desperate hunger she'd sated with Hendro.

"Maybe we should stop," she said.

"Why?" he whispered as his fingers began to slide down beneath the loose fabric of her trousers.

Sophie slipped from his arms. "I'm not at all ready yet for anything like that. I'd like to take this a bit slower if it's OK with you. And Isobel's in the house."

"What's Isobel got to do with it?"

"It just wouldn't feel right and where's the rush anyway?"

"Fair enough," he said easily. "I'll call you Thursday."

Then he kissed her lightly on the lips and left.

Chapter 34

Tess O'Meara's hands trembled as she made several valiant efforts to put her keys in the ignition. The car was a navy-blue, ten-year-old Toyota Corolla. She'd bought it the year after her husband's death. At last she steadied one hand with the other and slipped the key into its housing. She heaved a big sigh of relief when the engine chugged into action, and putting it swiftly in gear she drove the five miles to Robert Franklin's house.

In all the seventy years of her life, she'd never felt so alone, so humiliated. Strange to say but for a woman who had exuded an easy good-humoured confidence all her life, suddenly she felt catapulted back to the hesitant, fearful days of her teenage years. She felt awkward, not in control, full of self-doubt.

When Thomas her husband was alive, they'd stood together against all adversities and his strong if rakish presence by her side had given her the strength to tackle anyone and anything. Since his untimely death and especially when beset by the ups and downs of life, Tess now confided in the close circle of friends she'd had since childhood. They had held each other's hands through the loneliness of their children leaving home and through the traumas of death and separation from their husbands. But now she couldn't even turn to them. Annie had found new love with an old flame and was living it up in Florida. Bridie was visiting her daughter in Boston. And Phil, who was always the most concerned with her appearance, was having her veins done in the Blackrock Clinic. It briefly crossed Tess's mind to call Sophie and take her up on the offer to stay. But she knew it would sound whiney and pathetic. She wanted Sophie to know that she was strong and independent. So Tess had no other option than to throw herself at Robert's mercy and she hoped he'd understand.

On the back seat, curled up in fluffy, canine oblivion was her dog Stevie, clearly relieved to be escaping Maeve's strict dietary regime of two less-than-square dog meals a day.

Beside her on the front passenger seat was her weekend case, hastily packed with nightdress, change of clothes, toiletries and some private papers. It was the papers which had caused the row with Kenny. The Will, to be precise. Over breakfast he'd asked her to hand it over – to give it to him for safe keeping – in case anything should ever happen.

"God forbid, Tess – sure you're only a teenager, God bless you," he'd said and it particularly annoyed Tess the way he always dragged God into it. God, if he existed, would have more sense than to waste his divine energies on such a phoney. She had refused to hand over her will – and told him very pointedly that it was none of his business and it never would be. She'd never seen her nephew in a rage before – though she'd always suspected him of having a fearful temper. But when Tess had refused to hand over her Will, he'd shouted at her and told her she was a stupid old woman.

She knew then that she couldn't tolerate his bullying for one second longer. So she'd finally made it clear to him that he wouldn't be getting his hands on even one square foot of her land. And it was a prize he greatly coveted. He behaved as if he, her only living relative in the parish, had a divine right to her seventy acres of lush rolling pasture. But he didn't. Tess was leaving the farm to the most beloved of all her family, the one most like her own girlish self, the one she argued with most fiercely, indulged most fondly, the one who always showed up when Tess needed her – Sophie.

She drove along the bumpy, neglected avenue to Robert's house and brushed tears from her smooth cheeks.

Stevie bounded across the marble hall and into the Nissen hut, and as usual made directly for Robert's bed. Tess wondered vaguely if the dog had been some sort of pampered courtesan in a previous incarnation. Robert made peppermint tea and offered her some shortcake while he listened calmly to her story. Even sitting with him made her feel less fretful and distressed. He immediately suggested she call Sophie. But Tess was adamant. She didn't want her granddaughter thinking she couldn't run her own life.

"I'm her granny. What sort of example would that set? She has no mother so I'm a kind of role model and I need to always bear up with dignity and good humour for her. Show her how to grow old with strength and good grace. If I turn up on her door now like some pathetic old woman who can't manage alone, I'll be letting her down."

"You're not pathetic and you've never let anyone down. It's only for a few more weeks. Barring any major problems, Brady the builder has the roof sorted now and next week they're rewiring the place. Soon you'll be back on your own turf and beholden to no-one."

"I'm afraid, Robert."

Being afraid was not something she could admit to easily. But why did she find it so easy to be honest with him? She smiled now ruefully at him. It was her seventieth birthday. No-one knew but herself and somehow, though she didn't mind being old, it had thrown up a whole new bunch of fears and concerns. She was frightened – not of growing old but of becoming unimportant – surplus to requirements. She desperately missed her husband today of all days. He would have made her put on her best suit and taken her out shopping and for a nice meal afterwards. He would have told her she was still the most beautiful woman in Mayo, would have kissed her and held her hand like an eager teenager as they strolled along the prom in Galway. She knew she would never have that kind of love again – both separate – both together – like sturdy pillars in a church.

She smiled again, warmed by Robert's open good looks. It was one of the delights of growing old – to be able to admire handsome men with utter indifference. She admired Robert's good looks in the same detached way that she admired George Clooney on the big screen, because it was just reassuring to know that there would always be good-looking men in the world. She dreaded ending up in a life that included no men. Probably if Kenny had his way he'd stuff her into the women's ward of that new old people's home. Tess really believed that a world without men was a lesser place, a duller place, and in some ways a more treacherous place. Always excepting Kenny, of course!

"Well, I'm going to call Sophie whether you like it or not," said Robert.

She begged, threatened, pleaded, said she would book into a hotel in Westport for the two weeks, could even rent a little house somewhere. He agreed reluctantly and got on the internet, checking out hotel deals and houses for rent. Everything was horribly expensive. It was late autumn and Westport was booked out with conferences and literary festivals. All the nice houses were either taken or too far away. There was one old cottage for rent – several miles from anywhere, halfway up a wild heather-purple mountain near Partry.

"I'll take it."

"It's very remote. What if you got sick or someone broke in?"

"I'm a tough old bird. I've survived worse. And anyway it's only for a couple of weeks. What do I need other than a television, a few basic items of food and a telephone?"

She knew he wasn't keen on the idea, could see him wrestling to come up with some better solution.

Robert had the picture of the little cottage up on screen and was clearly playing for time. "I don't like it, Tess. The windows don't even look very secure. And it says nothing about central heating."

She scoffed. "'Tis far from central heating I was reared. Here's my credit card. Book it."

He was halfway through typing in her details when the phone rang. He listened carefully and his face grew childishly animated. "But that's wonderful. Where?"

He scribbled something on an old scrap of paper. "When did you discover it?"

He looked like a little boy suddenly, grinning and patting his chest with excitement.

"Thanks, Cormac. You have made me the happiest of men. I'll get over there tomorrow first thing . . . today is tricky . . ."

She knew without him even saying. Only one thing could set his deep brown eyes dancing with such delight – some old archaeological ruin or other. But it was evident from his behaviour that this was something very special indeed.

"That was Cormac Hanley up in Ballina. He's doing some drainage work on the lower fields and he reckons he's found a completely untouched passage grave. I'll drive up there tomorrow."

She could see him straining at the leash, longing to go and do the thing he truly loved. She pitied Catherine because in some ways she'd always be in second place to his love of ancient things.

"But why don't you set out now? Be the first there. Don't you know that in a few days it will be crawling with experts from every museum in the country? And you're our local expert and curator of the local museum – so it's only proper you get to see it first."

"But what about you?"

"Just book me that wretched cottage. I'll be fine."

Robert hesitated for a moment, clearly torn between duty to his old friend and excitement in the new discovery.

"I know," he said, an idea suddenly dawning on him. "Forget that dingy cottage! You can stay here. It looks like I'll be away for at least a week. You can mind the house for me. It's perfectly safe. There's even an alarm if you feel the need to switch it on. As a matter of fact you'd be doing me a favour."

It had never crossed her mind that she could stay here – but now that she thought of it, Robert's place was perfect. And wouldn't it make Kenny really mad to think of her staying there. Yes, that was an added bonus! She could go for walks in the woods with the dog every day and maybe tidy Robert's papers which were in a terrible mess. Then when Robert came back, she'd call Sophie and tell her she was planning a short visit to Dublin. Sophie wouldn't mind putting her up for a few days.

"OK," she told him, trying hard to hide the relief in

her voice. Lonely hillside cottages had never been high on Tess O'Meara's list of ideal places to live. "I'll stay and mind the house till you get back. But on one condition – you let me buy you lunch in the village now before you go."

"What's the rush? We can have lunch when I get back."

"It's my birthday," she said shyly. "And I can't think of anyone in Hollymaine I'd rather have lunch with today."

Chapter 35

A blustering gale blew across the grounds of Old Rathgar Rugby Club. The team stood in a huddle at one end of the pitch as Gary Burton the coach psyched them up for the match. On the sidelines a sparse gathering of supporters scrunched up their faces against the wind and called out half-hearted cheers of encouragement to Hendro and his team-mates. They'd barely survived relegation in the last season and the word on the street was that they wouldn't even make it past the first match this year. Today they were against Barnfield, a team from Limerick – the biggest, toughest bunch of players in the country. In Barnfield, the game of rugby was more of an extremist religion than a sport and it seemed to Sophie and Isobel that the entire population of the little place had made the journey to Dublin to support their heroes. And heroes they were. Sophie swallowed when she saw the massive specimens of Munster manhood jog onto the pitch. Each and every one of them, even the slightly less huge scrum half, made the Old Rathgar team look like a bunch of half-grown teenagers. Apart from Hendro, of course. He stood out, tall and fair, in his black-and-white striped kit, and smiled easily at a little cluster of blonde, bare-midriffed and heavily made-up young admirers.

"Hiya, Hendro!" they called out eagerly to him.

"How's it goin', girls?" He waved and smiled laconically which made them capsize into fits of hopeless giggling and some kind of group jigging.

Sophie sat alongside Isobel on a hard, uncomfortable bench. In her present state Isobel probably wouldn't be able to stay long and it was just as well because Sophie had lots of assignments to catch up on and wanted to have an early night because she was expecting Nick to call round and get started on her garden the next day.

"Just say when you want to leave," she told Isobel.

"Maybe we'll go at half time."

Hendro stopped to talk to them, thanked them for coming, and said they should come round to the clubhouse afterwards – for a really wild party.

"I don't think so," said Sophie, wondering how he could be so thick.

The last time she and Isobel had attended any kind of football match together, they had been eighteen, not much younger than Hendro's little army of admirers along the bench. Gaelic was a passionate tribal religion of its own in Hollymaine. At the end of the village stood the entrance to the pitch and on Sundays during the warm summer months, crowds would flock to support their home team. On those sunny days, shops would close and the entire village would empty. Sturdy farming men, old men walking slowly with the aid of sticks, women with their weekend hair-do's, wearing their smartest summer frocks, teenagers in skimpy T-shirts and jeans, young boys wild with excitement, infants in buggies sucking lazily on ice lollies – all made their way through the village to the Hollymaine pitch. Only the very sick and the very old stayed at home. In common with most of the girls in their group, Sophie and Isobel chiefly attended to spot the talent. And there was always plenty on the Hollymaine team. Sophie remembered a procession of handsome ruddy-faced, sandy-haired youths, in the peak of physical condition. Neither of them knew the first thing about Gaelic. But as far as muscular prowess and good looks went – they were the very best of talent spotters.

"Do you remember Danny Blake and how much you fancied him?" she said now to Isobel as both teams went into pre-match huddles at either end of the pitch.

"I never fancied Danny Blake. That was you – I think you even went out with him – for almost a month."

"Did I? Oh yes – so I did. He was absolutely divine but he had this awful habit of scratching. Anyway it was only a summer thing."

"No – I fancied Colm Munnelly."

"Did you ever see him again?"

Isobel pulled a face.

"Bald and fat and sweaty with chewed finger-nails. He has a wife, three children and a drink problem. Lucky escape for me I'd say. God, Sophie, when I think of all the blokes I've been nuts about – every one of them turned out to be a waster or a bastard or both. But Flora will be different. She won't make my mistakes. I'll put her wise to the ways of men."

"I'm sure, like you, she'll want to make her own mistakes."

Isobel patted her stomach and then frowned suddenly.

"What is it?"

"Nothing. Well – not nothing exactly but I've only just realised – she's been very quiet today – no kicking at all. Maybe she's just having a nap."

Sophie said she was probably right and they turned to engross themselves in the match. She couldn't make head or tail of it. Every so often the game would stop and two lots of the really heavy players would face one another like two rows of prize bulls and then they would bend down and one crowd would start pushing the other with their heads and shoulders.

"What's happened? Are they fighting? My God, someone could get hurt. Is no-one going to stop them?"

"Calm down," said Isobel. "It's called a scrum. See the scrum half – that's the fellow holding the ball there – he'll put the ball between the two front rows and the hooker – that's the bloke in the middle of it all – he'll hook the ball back to his team-mates and then the ball will pop out at the back and then the scrum half will grab it and pass it backwards to the out half . . . then . . . "

"Enough! How did you get to be so much of an expert all of a sudden?"

"Hendro explained it."

Sophie tried to keep up. But just as soon as she thought she'd figured it out – something else peculiar would happen. One of the Old Rathgar players kicked the ball right off the pitch which seemed to her a completely stupid thing to do – but for some reason the crowd cheered and shouted *"That's the stuff, Rathgar!!"* Then some of the players from both teams formed two lines like they were waiting for a bus or a glass of orange or something. Then Jack, the Old Rathgar hooker, shouted out *"Twenty-one Holland!"* and instead of handing out refreshments, he threw the ball at them. Someone lifted Hendro high up into the air so that he could catch the ball, and then everyone cheered again and then he threw it backwards to George who threw it backwards to Colin who threw it backwards to Liam. But Liam must have spotted that they were all passing the ball in the wrong direction because when he got hold of it he hurtled forward, sweeping aside a bloke from Barnfield who'd tried to pull him to the ground. Then he ducked and dived past several other opponents and charged onward. He was heading towards the goal-post now and Sophie became quite excited. What if he scored? Isobel had told her Barnfield were a sure cert to win the match – but maybe Hendro's team could pull it off in spite of everything. Then to her horror, Liam seemed to get a rush of blood to the head, and instead of kicking the ball into the goal, selfishly held onto it, then seemed to trip and crashed headlong across the white line about two yards to the right of the goal-post.

"You stupid eejit! You could have scored easily!" she shouted out, unable to stop herself.

But all the Old Rathgar supporters were on their feet, jumping up and down now and cheering and hugging one another. Even Isobel was on her feet with hands in the air cheering the team on.

"Why are they all cheering? He messed it up."

"How could you be so clueless? He's just scored a try – which is five points. And it will be an easy conversion – so that will be another two points."

So the game went on. At half time the teams were level. Sophie felt she'd given the game of rugby enough of her time and was seriously disappointed when Isobel said she couldn't leave now because it was too exciting. If Old Rathgar beat Barnfield – it would be the turnaround of the season. They simply had to stay – it would be bad manners, bad luck and bad sportsmanship to leave now.

"I don't think our absence will make one bit of difference," said Sophie.

"Still – we should stay. Besides – I haven't had so much fun in ages. I can shout as loud as I want and no-one will even notice."

Where exactly was the fun in that? thought Sophie.

The second half was hard going for Old Rathgar. The Barnfield players seemed to have stepped up a gear and had control of the ball more often. It was the only way that Sophie knew Hendro's team were losing the struggle – because every other thing about the game was a complete and utter mystery to her. Two minutes from the end, one of the Limerick players burst forward through the defence and hurtled with a strange ungainly grace across the white line, to score their second try.

Isobel gasped in horror and let out a string of curses. Barnfield were in the lead. With less than two minutes to go, Old Rathgar would never catch up now.

The players seemed to just run out of steam. Tired and exhausted, they trudged about, half-heartedly tackling their opponents. Great! thought Sophie. It will all be over soon and we can go home! She looked sideways at Isobel who had turned grey with what she hoped was disappointment. Sitting on the sidelines of a rugby match on a rock-hard bench, in a blustering October gale, was really not the best place for someone who was about to have a baby. Old Rathgar got the line out. Jack held the oval ball above his head, a look of grim determination on his face. He called out "*Thirty-eight Sweden!*" and Hendro rose up in the air like a Greek god and caught the ball.

Isobel couldn't stop herself. She stood up, cupped her hands to her mouth and shouted out so loudly that her voice probably carried halfway across the country:

"Come on, Hendro Sayers – you Aussie bastard! You're about as much use as a lighthouse in a bog! Show us what you're really made of!"

Whether he heard or not, Hendro seemed to get his second wind. He surged forward, swiping away Barnfield players like they were little flies until he was only ten yards from the line.

The Barnfield centre Larry O'Mahony tackled him, almost bringing him to the ground. But Hendro stayed on his feet, battling onwards. Now he was an agonising five yards away from the try line. O'Mahony tried to bring him down again and Hendro inched onward as he wrestled to shake off the full weight of his opponent. But the Limerick man clung on like a limpet and Hendro could hold no more. The crowd gasped with despair as they watched all six foot four of him topple forward like an oak-tree crashing towards the ground in a storm – the ball still miraculously in his hand. Then in a moment of what his team-mates later called 'sheer athletic poetry", he stretched out his long arm and with barely an inch to spare before his body connected with the ground, in one single move he touched the ball down over the line for the winning score.Then his huge frame collapsed in an exhausted heap.

"*Yeeees!*" roared Isobel, jumping or at least trying to jump up and down.

"*Yeeees!*" roared the Old Rathgar supporters who were now dancing a wild frenzy of joy. Hendro rose awkwardly to his feet and took the embraces and "well-dones" of his team-mates with uncharacteristic humility.

Amid the scenes of jubilation, the tears, the cheers, ecstatic youngsters charging onto the pitch, Hendro being carried off the pitch held shoulder high by the fans, the exchanging of jerseys, the squeals of admiration from young girls, the name of Hendro Sayers called out over the tinny tannoy as "Man of the Match", sweet papers and empty chip cartons and plastic bottles swirling across the pitch, the autumn breeze stiffening and cooling, Isobel suddenly felt rather strange – as if someone had swiftly stuck a stiletto knife in the small of her back and pulled it out again just as quickly.

"God, my back is killing me."

"I told you we should have gone at half-time."

"We have to go behind and congratulate Hendro."

"Are you crazy? It will be animal in the clubhouse. All dirty socks and naked men – mud everywhere and filthy rugby songs into the bargain."

"All the same – it's his big day."

"Hendro doesn't expect us to go in there." She regarded the scruffy-looking clubhouse with a mixture of horror and scorn.

"Come on," said Isobel. "We'll just congratulate him, then all I want to do is lie down and put my feet up."

The clubhouse was jammed with friends and family in jubilant mood, all buying celebratory drinks or tucking into the sandwiches that Gary Burton's wife had organised. But there was no sign of the players.

"Hendro's not here, so let's go home," said Sophie.

"Wait a minute."

And before Sophie could stop her, Isobel had slipped down a dingy tiled corridor, following a murky trail of mud, boots, socks and jerseys. From inside the shower room she could hear Hendro singing out loudly – not exactly perfectly but definitely giving it loads. It was some old-fashioned song – like "Summertime" or "Amazing Grace". She'd never associated him with singing. He was not the sort of man you'd look at and say – God, he must have a powerful voice! But standing in the muddy muddle listening to his voice soaring above the shower room noise, she felt oddly moved.

She was beginning to feel very tired and needed desperately to lie down – but she wasn't leaving without at least congratulating him.

"Hendro! It's me! Isobel!" she called loudly into the shower room.

A loud chorus of predictable locker-room-type remarks followed and then Hendro appeared at the door – wearing quite a small towel – which barely covered his privates. His sandy-golden hair was damp and ruffled. His smooth hard body glistened with moisture, his smoky green eyes sparkling with the pure joy of winning. Although she'd seen it all a thousand times before in the Athena Health and Fitness Club, she was briefly mesmerised by the sheer beauty of him.

"I just came by to say . . . " Her back was really acting up now and she leaned against the wall to steady herself. " . . . to say . . . well done. Great match. You were . . . "

"Isobel, are you OK?"

"It's nothing. Backache. I just need to lie down for a while. So I'm going to have to miss the party, I'm afraid."

"Disappointing – but no sweat. There'll be other parties, other celebrations . . . are you sure you're OK? You look kind of green."

She was now glued firmly to the concrete block wall, the cold firmness of it giving her odd relief. The smell of sweaty socks and boots, combined with the smell of mud and wintergreen, was closing in on her. Fresh air – that would do the trick. She'd done what she came to do. She hadn't let Hendro down. Now she could just slip out and go home to bed. She took a step away from the wall and felt the quick and horrible stabbing pain once more.

"I'm calling the hospital," he said as she swayed and turned a sicker shade of green.

He led her gently outside and sat her down on a chair while Sophie rushed to her side and gave her a glass of water to sip. In a matter of minutes, Isobel was her old self, a bit of colour back in her cheeks, the pain completely gone.

Meanwhile Hendro was calling the maternity hospital and explaining the situation. The midwife asked Hendro if Isobel was still in pain.

"Tell her I'm fine," said Isobel. "It's nothing. The pain's all gone. Just get me home."

Hendro explained to the midwife and she told him to watch out for when and if the pain came again. It was probably just a false alarm but she advised him not to go too far until things settled down. If the pains began to come every fifteen minutes or so – he was to bring her straight to the hospital. Otherwise she should stay at home and rest. Under no circumstances should he call an ambulance or bring her to the hospital unless he was sure she was in labour. They didn't have the room and would just have to send her home.

"But I'm not the – that is, it's not my – we're not a –" Hendro stuttered, "I mean, it's not my responsibility –" meanwhile thinking: and I've just scored and my team expect me and it's going to be the biggest night of the year and do you have any idea how many babes in the clubhouse want to be with me right now?

The midwife told him sharply to get his priorities right

and hung up, no doubt thinking he was the most despicable father-to-be she'd ever spoken to in her life.

Isobel decided to take control.

"I'm just fine, everybody. Hendro, go and enjoy the party. You deserve it. Sophie will drive me home. And thanks for calling the hospital but there was really no need as you can see."

The cluster of young lovelies stood in the clubhouse doorway and called longingly to Hendro.

"We've saved you the best seat at the bar, Hendro! Come on! It's party time!"

He looked across at Isobel – her feet large and swollen, face bloated, shapely body lost in a large tank-like shape, with two spindly legs holding it up. Isobel – soon to be a mother – with a life of pure drudgery and responsibility ahead. Then he looked around at the cluster of beckoning blonde midriffers. It was no contest. He was Hendro Sayers. He had scored the winning try. Women loved him. Women wanted him. His body was a temple – a temple of pleasure. Life is short and no man is an island.

"Sorry, Isobel." He smiled apologetically. "They want me." He grinned helplessly and added: "Are you sure you're OK? I'll stay with you if you like."

If she wasn't in such pain, Isobel would have completely cracked up at the sight of him being so hopelessly torn. And, of course, she was just a tiny bit hurt that he wanted to rush away from her so quickly. But – he was a man – what more could you expect?

"I'll check in on you tomorrow," he said and melted into the awaiting blonde honey-pot.

Chapter 36

Back at the house, Sophie made her a cup of tea and disappeared into the study to do some work, while Isobel sank gratefully into the sofa and put her feet up. For a while she became engrossed in an old Ingrid Bergman film that was showing on TV but it was not long before she found it just too tiring to concentrate. She was just about to drift off to sleep when another sharp pain shot through her as if someone had impaled her on a red hot poker. It was so intense that she almost called out. But then it disappeared quickly and she nodded off.

After what seemed like only minutes later, she was wide awake again and screaming with a new pain – this one slightly longer and definitely more intense. What had the nurse said to Hendro – if the pains were coming every fifteen minutes – or was it twenty? But not to bother them unless she was absolutely sure . . . Beads of sweat formed on her face as she tried to make the short journey down the hall to get to Sophie. She practically fell through the door of the study.

"Call Hendro quickly. Ask him what the nurse said on the phone."

"Why?"

"I think I've gone into labour."

"You can't be! It's weeks yet. Everyone goes overdue on their firstborn. It's probably just a bit of backache from sitting on that awful bench."

"All the same. Call him. I should have listened to him more carefully." She winced again and leaned against the door frame.

"Will I call an ambulance?"

"No. The nurse said not to do that – unless it was a real emergency. And it's not. Even if I am in labour – it will probably be hours yet. I just want to check that's all."

Hendro's phone rang out several times. At last a giggling girl came on the line.

"Hi – this is Hendro's playmate for the evening. He can't come to the phone right now because he's just having too much fun. But if it's urgent you can leave a short message with me and maybe I'll pass it on later when I'm finished with him."

Several minutes later, after pleading, coaxing, explaining and then screeching something quite rude, Sophie finally persuaded the giggling playmate to fetch Hendro.

"Sorry to drag you away, Hendro," she said, "but just tell me what that nurse said again."

"Why? What's happened?"

"I think she's probably just a bit tired – but she's

convinced she's in labour."

"I'll be there in ten minutes," he said and rang off.

When the pain disappeared again and so completely, Isobel wondered if she'd imagined the whole thing and she suddenly felt foolish. Hendro would be furious at being dragged away from the party. And why was he coming anyway? She'd only wanted to ask him what the nurse had said. He could have explained easily over the phone.

Although she insisted that the pain was completely gone, Sophie made her lie down on the bed and sat with her, chatting about any distraction that came into her head. Ten minutes passed and Isobel began to feel her old self again. She begged Sophie to call Hendro and tell him not to bother coming, that she was fine.

"This is silly," she said, sliding from the bed. "I'm going to have a shower and go for a walk."

She made it to the door of the bathroom and was gripped by the horrific sensation that she was about to be simultaneously disembowelled and ripped apart.

Hendro emerged from a taxi as she was in mid-howl, his collar undone and his shirt askew.

"How often are the pains coming?"

"Too fucking often!" she screamed and hollered and gripped her back.

He made her sit on the bed then sat beside her as she practically wrenched his fingers from his hand. At last the pain subsided. He mopped her forehead with a cool, damp cloth and told her to lie back and rest while they decided what to do. He thought it was really time to call the hospital and Sophie agreed but Isobel wasn't so sure.

She wanted to talk to her parents. This wasn't meant to be happening. She wasn't supposed to go into labour until she was at home with her mother who would fuss over her and pet her and make everything less difficult. And her father was supposed to be driving her to the hospital where she would have a nice pain-free labour and then Flora would just pop out and in next to no time she would be sitting up in her bouncing chair in a pretty little pink gingham dress with a matching bonnet and bootees, eating baby rice and making cute gurgling sounds. Isobel began to cry at the thought of her carefully constructed plan collapsing about her.

She'd hardly worked herself up into a good miserable sob when suddenly there was another pain! But it only seemed like five minutes ago since the last one. She gripped the sheets, Hendro's hands, Sophie's hands, and bellowed until her throat hurt. Funny how the pain seemed to last forever and the intervals in between seemed to go by in an instant. Funny how suddenly there didn't seem to be any intervals – just burning, body-splitting, disembowelling agony. She barely noticed Hendro and Sophie exchanging glances and Sophie disappearing into the kitchen where she phoned for an ambulance and begged them to come immediately as the contractions were coming every five minutes. She hardly saw them huddle in the corner whispering frantically as Sophie tried to remember something about hot towels.

"No stupid! That's what you get in Chinese restaurants. Hot water and clean towels is what we need," Hendro hissed, now completely sober.

"But what are you going to do with them?" Sophie hissed back.

"Haven't a bloody clue. But get them anyway. What about the ambulance?"

"They'll be here as soon as they can. It's a busy night with accidents they said "

Hendro took Isobel's hand in his and told her she was doing fine and that they'd called an ambulance – just to be on the safe side.

"Leave me alone. I want my mammy."

"I'm afraid I'll just have to do."

"Where's Sophie? I need her here."

"She's on the phone to your mother."

"Oooooooowwwwwwwww I'm dyyyyyyiiinnnggg!"

"You're not dying. What about those breathing exercises you told me about?"

"I can't remember what the nurse said."

"Try! Short breaths – long breaths – panting – something like that –"

She forced her mind back to the ante-natal classes and the sweet little nurse who had assured her that childbirth was – now what had she called it again – "a doddle!"

"Yes! Now I remember!" she said as the pain subsided once more. The nurse had said that if she just did the breathing exactly as they had practised in the ante-natal classes she'd hardly feel a thing. That the breathing would release natural pain-killing chemicals in her body which would deal with the contractions. That the contractions weren't in fact pains at all but merely muscular movements. She was glad she'd remembered it at last.

Now all she had to do was put the wonderful little nurse's advice into action. She could feel the start of a contraction – a mild gripping sensation to begin with – and she started the breathing, concentrating on her chest rising and falling, slowly drawing in long breaths of air and letting them out in little gasps.

"That's it. Good girl, Isobel! Don't try to talk," Hendro said.

She stared at the ceiling and forced every cell in her brain to concentrate on just breathing. For a brief moment it seemed like she had it under control then came another back-splitting spasm.

"Natural pain relief, my arse!" she screamed as her whole body sank into a mire of agony once more. Then she remembered what it was about the nurse that bothered her. The nurse had never had a baby in her life! "I'll give her 'a doddle' the next time I see her!" Isobel rasped through gritted teeth.

Sophie returned with bad news. The ambulance would be at least twenty minutes. There followed another hissing conversation about whether they should bundle her into the car and drive her to the hospital themselves. Meanwhile Clementine Barragry arrived, all agog, and she quickly set to boiling kettles in the kitchen. In a mad act of desperation, Sophie set up her computer on a table next to Isobel's bed and logged onto the internet. She did a Google search for "*Emergency Delivery Of Babies For The Completely Clueless*".

The contractions were coming every minute now and Isobel was forced to ask a very awkward question.

"Would someone please have a look down there to see what's going on?"

Hendro, ordinarily charmed to be in a position to examine any woman's intimate regions, felt that on this occasion Sophie might have a better eye.

Sophie blanched at the thought of staring her best friend's private parts in the face. Their relationship would never recover from the embarrassment.

"For God sake, somebody take a look!" Isobel wailed desperately.

Sophie shook her head stubbornly and primly held up the sheet for Hendro.

He dived under and then emerged quickly – a look of total confusion on his face.

"Bloody hell – I can see the head, Isobel! . . . I'm not quite sure what the procedure is at this point . . . but I think it's time for you to crouch and engage."

"What?" said Sophie furiously scrolling down through a website on home deliveries. "There's nothing about crouching here."

Through a dense hurricane of pain, Isobel heard and understood. Hendro had bored the maternity pants off her one afternoon with a lengthy explanation of rugby terms. He'd even told her that some psychologists liken the scrum to childbirth. Some bloody joke that was!

"I think he means I'd better push!"

Hendro gazed at Isobel. Her face was not a pretty sight. Sweat-stiffened hair fell across blotchy red cheeks. Her eyes and forehead were mangled horribly with pain and fear, her mouth pinched and twisted in agony. "You look beautiful," he told her.

"*Oooooowwwwwwwwwllllllnnnnrrrrnnnggghhhh!* Don't be so bloody stupid! That is a really stupid thing to say to a woman in labour."

"Yeah – well, it's true whether you believe it or not. Now bind and drive!"

"What?" said Sophie once more.

"I mean push!" he said quickly.

Childbirth and motherhood were quite abstract principles to Hendro. How he came into the world or how any of his friends or girlfriends had come into the world was of little interest. He found it hard to believe that he himself had once been a tiny defenceless infant – even though his grandmother often showed him photos. Yet he'd never identified with the grainy pictures of a small wrinkled thing in a blue bonnet and jump-suit. Real live babies and the people who had babies didn't normally enter into his sphere of existence. Even watching Isobel these past few months as the child grew in her womb, he'd never actually considered the fact that the end result would be a completely new human being. Until now that is! Suddenly the whole awesome, agonising miracle of birth hit home and it seemed to him that Isobel was engaged in the most heroic struggle, the noblest self-sacrifice of all. Hendro felt his heart swell with affection, admiration, pride, deep concern and an instinct to save and protect. It was a strange moment to fall in love. Not that he recognised it as such at the time.

Things were progressing very quickly now. With one last piercing shriek and a final push, the baby emerged into Hendro's waiting hands.

He could barely contain his shock or his excitement.

"Hey! We've done it! I mean you've done it! He's a beauty, Isobel. Well done!" He beamed down at the tiny infant in his hands. Sophie and Clementine bustled about clumsily attempting to follow instructions which had been downloaded from the net and Ed Thorne arrived from upstairs with offers of help and advice which merely added to the confusion. Clementine argued that a bath in the last of Sophie's Jo Malone foaming bath oil was probably not the best thing for the newborn infant and quickly took charge of the baby while Sophie tended to Isobel. But by the time the ambulance arrived, the baby had been washed and wrapped in a soft warm towel and was sleeping peacefully in Hendro's arms.

Some hours later, Isobel was comfortably tucked up in a hospital bed, having hungrily gobbled up two helpings of toast and tea. Now she was barely able to stay awake. Her baby had been pronounced fit and taken to the nursery to be weighed and given a proper bath. Her parents were on their way from Hollymaine and the midwife had said that all being well, she and baby could discharge themselves first thing in the morning. Hendro had gone home to bed, too tired and overcome to return to the wild party, promising to join her for breakfast. Sophie had gone late-night shopping for baby-clothes and nappies.

It barely registered with Isobel that she had just become a mother. The whole ordeal was still just a hazy blur of panic, pain and final relief. She drifted pleasantly in and out of consciousness until she woke abruptly at three o'clock in the morning and sat up in bed, alert and suddenly deeply curious about her new child.

She slipped into the white hospital dressing-gown and shuffled awkwardly down the corridor to the nursery. Amazing how all the babies were peacefully asleep. She tiptoed across to the cot with her name on it and felt herself fill up with unimagined tenderness. Then as if sensing her presence, the baby stirred and Isobel couldn't help herself. Overcome with longing, she lifted Flora out and held her close and kissed her and whispered affectionate nonsense in her tiny perfect ear. Then the baby opened her mouth very wide, much wider than Isobel could ever have imagined, and bawled her head off.

"Oh my God! What's wrong?"

The night nurse smiled comfortingly. She was well used to first-time mothers and all their fears and anxieties.

"He's just hungry. You can tell by the cry."

Then because Isobel wanted to have a go at breast-feeding, the nurse led her back to her bed and sat with her while she worked out the mechanics of putting her nipple in the baby's mouth and having it clamped tight between a pair of terrifyingly strong jaws and half sucked to death. The nurse said it would be uncomfortable for a couple of days but she'd soon get used to it.

"Flora is a grand name," the nurse said encouragingly as Isobel fumbled to release her nipple from the vicelike grip of the baby's jaws. "My uncle in Cork is called Flor – which is kind of like it – Flora without the 'A'. There now, see, he's fast asleep."

"Asleep? Your uncle?"

"No silly! Flora – the baby, I mean."

Isobel laughed at the nurse's mistake. "You said 'he' – that's why I thought you meant your uncle."

Nurse Brennan looked at Isobel a bit oddly. "But . . . you know he's a little baby boy, don't you?" she said hesitantly, keenly aware of how emotionally sensitive new mothers are.

"A boy? No, it's a girl. I saw her on the scan months ago. That's why I called her Flora."

"I think you'll find – I mean, if you just check – for your own peace of mind – that is – but he is most definitely a boy."

Chapter 37

Sophie was exhausted, almost as if she'd given birth to the child herself. The past few days had been quite stressful. The sudden trauma of a premature labour was excitement enough. But there was also the sense of helplessness as she watched Isobel's body wracked in perfectly natural but awesomely horrible pain, then the gobsmacking shock of seeing a baby emerge into the world for the first time – it would take her weeks if not months to recover. Then while Isobel settled into hospital, she'd gone off to find baby-clothes and nappies and made a complete fool of herself in the Babycare shop.

The assistant had clearly graduated with first-class honours from the "Only What's Out" Retail Academy. She maintained a scrupulous blank-faced disinterest and occupied herself with busily staring into the middle distance.

"My friend's just had a baby," Sophie said to her, hoping to elicit some interest.

"Babies nought to twelve months, last three rails on the left," the assistant said, pointing vaguely and continuing her examination of the middle distance.

Sophie thanked her and went in search of the three rails in question. She got into a complete tizzy filling a basket with all the things she thought a baby might need – vests, underpants, tights, cardigans, dungarees, bonnets and shoes. She found the sweetest broderie anglaise and silk dress in palest pink and ivory and though it was way beyond her budget, it just had to go in the basket too. Winter was coming in – shouldn't she buy a good warm overcoat as well? She found a lovely cerise cashmere coat, with a black velvet collar – the kind of thing you'd see in old Mabel Lucy Attwell pictures. It said "12 months" on the label – but how different in size could it be?

Luckily a kindly granny-to-be took pity on her and explained that new babies mostly needed lots of soft, pyjama-type things and that they grew so quickly and needed changing so much that it was pointless buying anything like the broderie anglaise and silk dress unless it was for a special occasion.

"No, dear, if it's a newborn baby it won't be needing shoes just yet either. As for that velvet collared overcoat – far better to get her a warm padded anorak with little bunnies or ducks printed on the outside, for strolls in the winter sunshine."

The next morning Sophie arrived at the hospital to find Isobel in floods of tears.

"Cheer up – I've brought lots of lovely things for Flora to wear. She'll be the prettiest baby in Hollymaine."

Isobel sobbed even louder. "It's a boy!"

"What's a boy?"

"The baby, stupid! It's not a girl – it's a boy!"

Sophie thought she might check for herself but there was no sign of the baby in the room. "Maybe you didn't look at her properly. Maybe you're mixing up the cord and the whatsit?"

Isobel shook her head with glum certainty.

"Are you sure?" was all Sophie could think of to say in the end. And she didn't need to hear a reply. The look on her friend's face said it all.

It took a few moments to digest this new and startling information. How had they not noticed? Perhaps because it was all such a complete panic and in any case Hendro had been holding the child all the time until Clementine had washed it and it had never entered Sophie's head to check out if it was a boy or a girl. And then the ambulance had arrived so quickly after the birth. She'd just assumed. Her first thought now was that she'd wasted an entire two hours buying a whole load of stuff which would have to be exchanged and she dreaded going back to "Miss Middle-Distance Daydream", who would be absolutely no help at all in the matter of what to buy for little boys. Apart from that she really didn't much care if the baby was a boy or girl. A baby was a baby after all. But she could see that Isobel was deeply distressed and she had no idea what to say that might comfort or console her.

"Boys are OK."

"I don't want a boy. Boys grow up into people like Phil

Campion. They don't wear nice clothes. They like getting covered in muck. And they only want to play with guns and pretend they're commandos and spacemen and they're always getting cuts and bruises and I can't bear the sight of blood. Mary O'Connor's son is always bringing her worms from the garden and he has a pet frog and his favourite bedtime reading is *The Great Big Dorling Kindersley Book of Spiders!*" She wailed this last accusation even more ferociously.

"I know it must be a bit disappointing – and you're probably very emotional right now," said Sophie. "But you'll feel differently in a day or two. Shall I go and fetch him?"

"No, thanks. The nurses will give him a bottle. There's no point in feeding him myself. I've decided on adoption after all."

"You can't be serious!"

"I can. I don't want him. He'd be better off with two loving parents who really wanted a boy." She turned away and stared listlessly out the window.

Sophie felt powerless, unable from across the great divide of her non-maternal state to reach out to the friend who was struggling with so much that was new and frightening. She'd heard that mothers sometimes rejected their new babies and that it was usually a symptom of some kind of post-natal depression. It would probably wear off then – but what if it didn't? What if, having finally moved on from the horror of discovering she was pregnant, Isobel had built up a whole set of expectations around the baby which were now to be shattered because it was a boy? Isobel was usually such a fighter. Through the thick and mostly thin of the past few months, she'd struggled forwards, refusing to buckle under an impossibly awful set of catastrophes. She might have moments of anger and self pity – but always she would bounce back. Now she seemed suddenly to have given up the fight, to be almost beyond caring. Perhaps the pain and trauma were catching up with her after all. Whatever it was, Sophie had never seen her like this before – withdrawn, uninterested, almost detached from life.

When Hendro bounded into the room carrying a massive bunch of white roses, a rugby ball and a teddy, and looking dazzlingly handsome, Sophie hoped he might lift the dark, gloomy atmosphere.

"Hey – how's the new mum?"

"Fine really," Isobel said, barely looking at him.

He flashed a rakish smile at a passing nurse and was quickly in possession of the biggest vase on the ward. He jammed the flowers in the vase and set them down on her dressing-table. Flower arranger he was not. Isobel stared dully at them.

"So where's Jonah?" said Hendro.

"Who?"

"Jonah! Unless you've thought of another name. But we might as well call him Jonah until you come up with something else."

"Whatever."

"What's up? I thought you'd be delighted to have it all over – and a fine big healthy boy as well! Am I missing something?"

"It's a boy."

"Yeah! Probably a winger by the look of him – maybe an outhalf though – what a kicker!"

Hendro forged clumsily onwards and Sophie wished fervently that he'd shut up and that she was somewhere else. Far from improving things, he was making them worse.

"I don't want a boy!" Isobel said and suddenly she was in floods of tears.

Hendro stood by helplessly for a few moments and then because he couldn't bear to see any woman crying he decided to take matters in hand. "OK – I get it. Back in a minute!"

Then he disappeared down the corridor, returning minutes later holding Jonah in his arms.

"Look, he's opened his eyes. He's staring up at me. I'm going to teach you all the tricks, young man. We can go to football matches and watch *Match of The Day* on telly. And you have to learn to fly a kite and swing a golf club and sail through rough wind. Do you think it's too early to buy him a train set? But isn't he the cutest thing you ever saw?"

"Oh stop! You're making me sick, Hendro. First of all, he's not your child and I don't know what you're getting so excited about. Secondly, it's all very well you talking about bringing him to matches, when you're not the one who'll have to feed him in the middle of the night, change his nappy, put up with him screaming with gripey pains, scrub his mucky knees and be presented with horrible worms. And lastly –"

"Lastly what?" said Hendro, now wondrously absorbed in watching how Jonah's tiny fingers were clutching his big stumpy thumb in a fierce grip.

"I've decided he's going to be adopted. So take him away – I don't need to see him any more."

"You're not serious!"

"Hendro, bring him back to the nursery for now," said Sophie, desperately trying to avert a storm. "Let Isobel rest and get used to the idea."

"I'm not tired. I don't want to rest. And, Hendro, if you don't bring that baby back right now – then I'll just have to carry him down there myself."

"Fair enough. You do that," he said angrily and placed the baby carefully in her arms. "You bring the poor little scrap back to the nursery and dump him there like a bit of lost luggage if you like. Personally I couldn't do that to a stray dog."

"I will too," she said and clambered awkwardly out of bed, trying not to look at the little face which was staring up at her with an expression of earnest scrutiny. Then she strode off purposefully down the corridor. Or at least as purposefully as a woman who's just given birth could.

Sophie had observed Hendro's behaviour with amazement. Overnight, it seemed, he'd gone from being Dublin's most active and eligible stud to every boy's dream daddy. Perhaps it was just a passing fancy. Perhaps the novelty of having delivered Jonah had gone to his head a little – Sophie was well aware that above all things Hendro loved novelty. Having been abandoned by her own father when she was only a child, made her instinctively suspicious of men and babies. Hendro wasn't even Jonah's father and so had no real need to be emotionally involved at all. The brutal reality was that he would most probably come down from his high in a few days. Once Isobel went home to Hollymaine with or without the baby, Hendro would naturally forget all about her. Men like him were genetically programmed not to have hand, act or part in the rearing of children – especially another man's child. Sophie didn't want Isobel building a whole new set of expectations around Hendro only to be cruelly disappointed yet again.

"I know you mean well," she said, "but you're only upsetting her more. It's all very well for you to get excited and delighted about that little fellow – like he's a new puppy or something. But Hendro – there's a lot more to it than that. I haven't the first clue about being a parent – I only know it doesn't begin and end with a few nice presents and promises of matey treats. If you care at all for Isobel, you'll realise that she's in a terrible state at the moment and that she needs our support to help her decide what to do."

"Point taken! It's just so exciting to have been there and I can't believe she doesn't want Jonah just because he's a boy. I suppose I just got a bit carried away. What do you think I should do?"

"I haven't any idea what either of us should do and I'm really worried about her. That's the honest truth."

Sophie hadn't heard from Nick and in the excitement of the baby it hadn't seemed important but now she looked out at her garden and began to feel quite annoyed. They were supposed to have had a date but he'd called at the last minute to cancel. Then he'd promised to call her on Wednesday. That was two days ago and she hadn't heard a word. She told herself he was probably busy and reminded herself that in any case there was nothing much between them. Still, she didn't fancy spending the evening alone. What she needed now more than anything was a bit of social life, a bit of fun, a few drinks and a good night's sleep. So when Lucy called to ask her to go for a drink in her local the Shangri La followed by a meal in the Chinese round the corner, she jumped eagerly at the invitation.

They had a few drinks and then Lucy led the way to the cosy little Chinese restaurant. It was packed to the gills and a small queue had formed outside.

"It's very popular," explained Lucy. "They're in the *Good Food Guide*. But we'll have to wait a while for a table. Is that OK?"

It wasn't really. Sophie was cold and disheartened and she felt like going home and curling up under a warm duvet and sleeping the day's traumas away. But she didn't have much choice now. She couldn't very well leave Lucy in the lurch.

There were about ten couples in front of them and Sophie shifted from one foot to the other, her knees occasionally threatening to buckle under her, trying to conceal the fact that she was not quite sober. If only she could get inside and sit down then the whole world would stop spinning and she could sober up over a plate of

Peking duck and fried rice and some strong black coffee.

After ten minutes it seemed like they'd moved only two feet. Lucy suggested going somewhere else but Sophie insisted she wasn't budging. She peered enviously through the window at the happy, munching diners, hoping that someone would notice the hungry, shivering crowd outside. The people ahead of her didn't seem to mind – but then they were all wrapped up warmly and they weren't in the least bit drunk. And they hadn't spent the previous night delivering a baby.

After another few minutes a very smart Chinese waiter appeared and made his way down along the queue.

He stopped by Sophie and Lucy. "This way, ladies," he told them. "Your party's already here."

"But we're not –" said Sophie.

"This way, please," he repeated politely.

Sophie and Lucy exchanged confused glances but wasted no time in following the waiter. They slunk past the rest of the queue and dived in through the door of the restaurant gratefully. Oh, it was lovely and warm inside! And it was redolent with the smell of delicious sizzling food and buzzing with the sound of people having a good night out.

"Lucy! He thinks we belong to some party or other. We'll have to leave again when he finds out!"

"Say nothing," muttered Lucy. "No way am I leaving now that we're in. Just act innocent!"

They followed the waiter who led them to the best table in the room – a large circular table with seating for ten. There were a few other people at the table but no-one objected as Sophie and Lucy, avoiding all eye contact, sat down or rather collapsed into the chairs which the waiter very courteously held for them. When there was still no outcry from the other diners, Sophie peered to her left. And came face to face with Paul Brehony.

"Hope you don't mind joining us," he said.

She straightened up and tried to stop her head wobbling. She was about to say something smart when Lucy poked her in the ribs.

"He arranged for us to skip the queue!" Lucy hissed in her ear.

Paul introduced every one at the table – his father, who lived just round the corner, an Auntie Olive, a brother Steve and his girlfriend Grainne.

Sophie sat poker straight, desperate to cover up the fact that she was drunk. Not mentally – her brain was working reasonably well – but her body felt like a blob of half-set jelly on a merry-go-round. How was it that every time she bumped into Paul Brehony she was in some sort of embarrassing condition?

She turned to Paul, struggled to compose her face in her best 'I am completely sober and utterly capable of deeply intelligent conversation' manner. She would be grateful but distant. Besides, there was something important she wanted to ask him about – if only she could remember what it was.

Paul's voice broke in on her thoughts. "Bit of a change from Patrice Languedoc though, don't you think?"

The waiter had put shredded duck, pancakes and sauce on the table as a starter and everyone helped themselves.

She tucked in hungrily – she had never tasted such duck in her life. There was no comparison between Patrice Languedoc and Wayne Wong's.

"I think I prefer here," she said, her mouth full of duck and shredded lettuce and pancake.

"Me too! This is the best little restaurant in the whole of Dublin. But don't tell anyone. We like to keep it a secret."

"Where's Marina tonight?"

"She's having dinner with friends. This isn't her kind of place and she finds family get-togethers awkward. I gather it upsets her artistic equilibrium. She's highly sensitive to family tensions and has a weak stomach."

Oddly he didn't seem all that disappointed not to have her around.

"But your family looks like a nice bunch – not much tension in the atmosphere here."

It was true. Sophie felt instantly at ease with them. Paul's father, who had just turned sixty-five and was celebrating his birthday, was full of high spirits and planning a long holiday in America. Steve was like a smaller stockier version of Paul, less guarded and more jovial.

"So how long have you known the brother?" he asked when Paul was outside taking a call on his mobile.

"I don't know him. It's just that I keep bumping into him. It's coincidence really."

"Old Arab proverb says: one coincidence is worth a thousand rendezvous," he said, smiling impishly at her.

"It's nothing like that," she said, nervous that they might put her down as just another gold-digger.

The main course arrived and everyone began dipping into the various dishes. Out of the corner of her eye, Sophie watched Paul talk to his father who was seated next to him. Once again she was struck by how relaxed and contented he looked here away from the intricate web of Marina's formidable charms. Heads close together, he and his father chatted, listening intently to each other, occasionally sitting back in their chairs and laughing. It made a lovely picture – a man and his father – good friends. She didn't often think of her own father – basically because she'd never clapped eyes on him. But on rare occasions, she had a deep longing to know him, to see him even. This was such a moment.

Soon she found herself chatting again quite easily with Paul. He told her about his childhood, how he'd always wanted to be able to travel around cheaply, how he'd hit rock bottom, the drinking, then how his friend Dermot Stenson had bailed him out to start up the airline. Watching him in the company of his family, in his favourite restaurant, away from the starchy humbuggery and funereal waiters of Patrice Languedoc, he was quite at ease, even funny and charming.

"Anyway, that's enough about me," he said. "How about you? Fate seems to have thrown us together quite a lot and yet I still don't know the first thing about you."

"I'm just a girl come home to build a new life and let go of an old one."

"Has that been difficult?"

"I thought it would be so easy. I thought I was coming back to one place and one set of people and I came back to some completely other place and very different people. I came home in search of simplicity, harmony and stability but I haven't found it. Somehow the ground hasn't settled for me yet – like I haven't found my bearings. I feel unsure of myself suddenly – let's call it a minor identity crisis –"

God, what was she doing – pouring out her innermost thoughts to him over the black-bean sauce, confiding things she hadn't even shared with Isobel or Tess? Especially when he clearly wasn't to be trusted, when she'd vowed to push all thought of him from her mind. She couldn't use the excuse of being drunk – because now she was quite sober.

"It takes time to settle into a new life – even if it's a good one. I'm still not used to mine. Marina says I spend too much time here in my old life – and that until I let it go, I'll never fully appreciate my new one."

I'll bet she does, thought Sophie, feeling oddly sympathetic and fighting the dangerous warmth she felt towards him.

He paid their bill and then dropped Lucy home. When Sophie suggested that she ought to get a taxi, since she didn't want to risk being breathalysed, he insisted on driving her. She didn't put up too much of a fight. It was always nice to be driven from door to door.

"You remember the day in Ashford Castle when I left my card for you at reception . . ."

"Yes?"

"That's what I'm talking about – not being used to my new life. It makes me do tacky stuff sometimes. You know, a bit like an awkward teenager who blurts out something really stupid – thinking it will impress everyone. When I was a teacher, for instance, I would never have dreamt of doing anything like that. I guess it didn't make a good impression."

"Not really."

"But – when I saw you in such a comical state over a silly flight to Knock – I thought – I just wanted to get to know you – well, you were funny."

"It's not one bit funny. Getting up in those little planes scares the insides out of me."

"Tell you what – come out to the aerodrome with me on Sunday I usually take my little plane out then – I promise not to frighten you – in fact I guarantee to cure you –"

"I don't think so. I don't think I have the courage – and besides Marina mightn't like it."

Sophie felt a genuine sense of alarm at the thought of crossing swords with the formidable Marina.

"Oh she won't mind. She has no interest in aeroplanes anyway. And besides . . . " he paused as if about to say something, then changed his mind. "Besides, I'd enjoy the company."

"OK," she said, her heart sinking into the soles of her shoes at the thought. She didn't know what terrified her most – getting up in the plane – or drawing the jealous wrath of Marina. And just as his car disappeared down the road, she remembered with annoyance what it was she had wanted to ask him.

Chapter 38

On Sunday morning, she woke bathed in a clammy sweat. What had she been thinking of, agreeing to go up in a plane with Paul Brehony when every sensible cell in her brain screamed out in revolt?

She tried breakfast – some muesli and a cup of strong, hot tea – but could get nothing down. She looked out over the ploughed-up garden and froze when she saw masses of dense low-lying grey cloud and the tree-tops swaying in the cool autumn breeze. Wind meant turbulence. Turbulence meant air-pockets. Air-pockets meant the plane bobbing up and down helplessly in mid-air. Besides, she had an important assignment on American Poets of the Twentieth Century to complete. Professor Daphne Joyce expected it on her desk first thing in the morning and she'd only completed an outline. Just to reassure herself that she was after all doing the sensible thing by not going, she picked up the Sunday paper in the hall and turned quickly to the weather forecast. Storm force winds! Right that did it.

She dialled Paul's home number. Marina answered the phone with a mixture of cold disapproval and existential artistic angst.

"He's not here. I'm alone in the study. I'm struggling with a paragraph that explores the essential nihilism of female friendship . . . "

"Sorry for disturbing you," Sophie said evenly.

"Yes, well, the creative process is easily shattered by irrelevant interruptions. I think of poor old Coleridge . . . I can take a brief message?"

"No – that's OK."

When the doorbell rang – Sophie considered ducking downstairs to hide out in Clementine Barragry's flat, or even throwing herself at the mercy of Ed Thorne upstairs. Perhaps she should plead a headache.

"All set?" Paul said when she opened the door.

"You know – I really wasn't thinking straight yesterday. There is so much work to do for this course and besides I'm a bit under the weather. Then there's my grandmother – I promised I'd call her and, of course, Isobel and the baby, not to mention the fact that my neighbour downstairs has been feeling poorly these past few days and I offered to do her messages –"

It slightly weakened her case when Clementine emerged from the flat downstairs, resplendent in her best Sunday suit and hat, looking the picture of health on her way to Mass.

"Come on!" said Paul. "We need to get up there before the weather worsens."

By the time they reached the little aerodrome near Lucan on the outskirts of Dublin, Sophie was rigid with fear. He barely seemed to notice. He led her into the Portakabin, signed in and confirmed his flight path, joking with the clerk at the desk that it was going to be a bumpy one.

"I said to Mick just before you arrived – I betcha Brehony's the only one mad enough to go up in that!" Sophie overheard the clerk saying to him. "Not many others risking it today."

"It will add to the excitement. We might have to go up to ten thousand feet, that's all."

Somehow, in an effort to make the whole experience more bearable, she'd convinced herself that because it was only a single-engine plane and because he was only an amateur pilot he probably wouldn't be allowed to go higher than a few hundred feet – just enough to clear the tops of the trees might be manageable. Green with nausea and drenched in the cold, clammy sweat of fear, she trudged reluctantly along the little runway after him, past all the other little Pipers and Cessnas until they reached his plane which was parked on a side ramp. It was slightly larger than the others, a Cessna 182 he'd explained as they were making their way from the Portakabin. It was all white with a royal blue propeller and blue wing tips. On the side was a blue fish logo, just like the ornament on his mantelpiece. He saw her examining it curiously and explained.

"It's my lucky symbol. A fish changed my life once – well a poem about a fish to be precise. Sure you want to go ahead with this?" he said as he helped her up into the seat and showed her how to strap herself. "I mean if you really can't face it – I'll understand. It's not too late."

He could have said that much earlier and let her off the hook. Now she'd look like a total eejit if she unstrapped herself and walked the whole way back along the runway to the little building. Everyone would know she was just too scared. And, of course, he would have a right good laugh.

"Let's just do it," she said, gritting her teeth.

He spent a few minutes explaining all the dials and switches but she lost concentration after the third dial and he wisely decided not to continue.

She shut her eyes tightly, and tried to ignore the way the little plane was rattling, the wind lifting the wings before he'd even started the engine. Why hadn't she at least taken a stiff drink or ten? As for her resolution to give up the fags when she started the course – it now seemed a bit impetuous.

Then she heard the controller's crackly voice over the loudspeaker.

"Clear for take-off,"

"Thanks, Jimmy! Here goes!"

She could hear the engine revving up and then the unmistakable feeling of the plane jolting along the bumpy concrete taxiway before turning onto the runway. She chanced opening one eye. It was a mistake. As the plane left the ground it rose hesitantly and laboriously, like a big old seagull in need of a hip-replacement. The wings dipped on either side and the engines roared angrily as they climbed unsteadily upwards. Now they were higher than the trees, heading out across the Liffey valley.

"I suppose we'll just fly over the bay and back again. That will be enough to cure me. I'm sure of it," she said.

She calculated that would take all of thirty minutes. She could stick it for thirty minutes, distract herself by picking out landmarks and keeping a careful eye on the horizon in case it slipped or anything.

"We've arranged a more interesting flightpath than that. I thought we might stop for a spot of lunch somewhere," he said, quite absorbed in finding a comfortable cruising level.

"Honestly, I'm not hungry. I had a huge breakfast," she lied.

"Still though – we might as well make a little expedition of it."

As they passed over high ground, the plane banged suddenly and dipped a couple of hundred feet. The impact of the turbulence was so strong that Paul's headphones were knocked off. Dear God, the whole machine was going to fall apart at this rate of going! And what was that he just said about an Expedition! He made it sound like they were going up the Amazon rain-forest for a month to find a lost tribe. Perhaps, in spite of his earlier promise, he was just trying to frighten her. She tried a different approach and fixed a broad smile onto her face.

"It's fantastic! Thank you so much for bringing me up. I really don't know why I was so scared. But do you know what? I'm completely cured. I could fly to Australia now and it wouldn't knock a feather out of me."

Whatever about frequent flier she was definitely becoming a frequent liar.

"Afraid Australia is out of the question – this is a single-engine aircraft and we've only enough fuel for a four hundred miles round trip. So the farthest we could go is Eastern France. What about Deauville?"

"Not really my cup of tea."

She swallowed, deeply worried now that he might just take it into his head to chance France. He, on the other hand, had never looked more relaxed. He pointed out Glennstown and his old school and the family home. Then he curved out over the water and she could see Howth Head and Lambay Island. She tried to smile and look excited but was mightily relieved when he headed back across the city towards the aerodrome – until he got on the radio to Air Traffic Control.

"Alpha, Yankee, Juliet – confirming flight path to Portaferry . . ."

"Roger that. Hold this frequency," said the crackly voice.

Sophie felt increasingly helpless, anxious and forlorn. He smiled across reassuringly at her.

"OK," he said. "Are you ready?"

"How do you mean?" she said swallowing hard.

"I mean ready for a little adventure. We've been up more than twenty minutes – so you're used to it. Let's fly a bit."

She smiled weakly at him and sank back into her seat. Trapped! No escape! No hopping out at the next red light! No pleading for an emergency pit stop at the nearest Spar or petrol station! He banked up towards the clouds and suddenly they were invisible. At least the rest of the world was invisible and they were horribly alone in the isolation of grey-white murkiness that swirled around them. The plane began to tremble. The engine sounded like it was stalling and he seemed to be having difficulty holding the controls, like he was trying to rein in a contrary stallion.

"Don't worry – it will stop when we get above the clouds. When we get to ten thousand feet – it will feel like floating." he said calmly.

Ten thousand feet! That was miles. Some sort of strangulated animal sound escaped from her.

"Just think of it as a bus driving over potholes or a car bumping along across a few cobblestones. A bit uncomfortable – but harmless!"

Harmless!

It was time to stop being nice. Being nice and polite and trying to play it cool had got her absolutely nowhere. She wondered should she try to grab hold of the phone and contact Jimmy at ground control.

"Hello, Lucan!! We have a problem!!"

And then what could she do? Nothing! It wasn't as if she knew the first thing about the controls. There was an array of dials and switches in front of her – but none of them made any sense. She wished now that she had listened more carefully to his pre-flight demonstration on what they all meant.

"Put me down!" she said trying to sound bossy and in

control. "I mean let me down! I mean I want to get down!"

The fuselage rattled so much she thought it was about to disintegrate. What if she fell from the sky and landed in someone's back garden – bang and splat! *BALLIVOR WOMAN'S DREAM COBBLE-DOCKED PATIO COMPLETELY WRECKED IN FREAK FLYING DEBRIS ACCIDENT!*

Life seemed deeply precious suddenly and here she was, sitting side by side with the man who was about to put an end to it – to shatter all her hopes and pulverise all her dreams. They plummeted through the dense cloud and it felt like her stomach was heading on upwards to the ozone layer while the rest of her was plunging inexorably towards a ghastly blood-spattering premature death. She could see the forlorn little headline now – on the bottom right-hand corner of page four in the *Evening Herald* – just above the advertisement for an exotic holiday in Mauritius and beneath a failsafe recipe for low-calorie Christmas cake. And she would never see another Christmas, never lovingly pack her future children's stockings with silly novelty toys like wind-up walking teeth and whoopee cushions, never serve up that perfect Roast Turkey and Ham dinner with all the festive trimmings to her dearest friends and family.

Well, if she was going to die, she'd let Paul Brehony know exactly what she thought of his silly boyish prank before she went splat on the Ballivor woman's patio.

"I knew I shouldn't have trusted you! I hope I never see you again! I wish I'd never met you –"

He didn't get a chance to reply because Jimmy came on the radio sounding quite concerned.

"You OK up there, Paul?"

"It's a bit bumpier than I thought it would be – but we'll be out of it soon."

"Roger that. Just as well you've got clearance and a flight path through the clouds. We wouldn't want any jumbo jets bumping into you. Keep in touch. There's a fine thunderstorm blowing down here."

"Will do."

The reminder that there could be other much larger, much faster planes stumbling about blindly through the dense cloud only added to Sophie's conviction that she was not long for this world. The fact that he had his own flight path with Air Traffic Control was hardly any consolation. What could they do to save her now? There was nothing for it but to close her eyes and start praying for a quick and easy end. She wondered if it would hurt. Her only hope was to be knocked out and tumble unconsciously to her doom.

But suddenly the rattling and buffeting stopped. She half-opened one eye to discover that they had somehow drifted into a wide blue space – dazzling, aquamarine, azure blue – and everything was smooth and they glided along as if they were drifting on a placid lake on a warm summer's day. It took Sophie's breath away. It felt like they had the entire world to themselves.

If this was being dead – it wasn't so bad after all.

"I'm sorry. What were you saying?" he said, relaxing at the controls once more. She reached over and touched the fabric on his jacket and then her own face, her own skin. Not dead! Not even slightly dead! Alive actually! More tinglingly alive than she'd ever felt.

"Nothing. It doesn't matter. This is amazing. I never thought . . . "

"I was afraid for a moment you wouldn't like it."

They cruised through the sky, pillows of softly billowing cloud beneath them, and the pure blue all around. They sat in companionable silence. There was simply nothing that needed to be said.

"I could stay up here forever," she said after a while.

"Me too. It puts the world and all its problems into perspective somehow. I thought we might have lunch somewhere in the Ards Peninsula – there are some nice little seafood places there. We could grab lunch, have a stroll on the beach and then fly back in time for dinner at my place.."

"It sounds lovely – but I won't stay for dinner," she said, worried that Marina might regard her as some sort of rival. Which she certainly wasn't.

"I insist," he said.

In Portaferry, they found an inviting little seafood bar. He chatted quietly to the head waiter who swiftly led them to a secluded table in the conservatory that overlooked the bay. Outside the view of sea and rolling green hills was idyllic, though chilly autumn breezes blustered about and the sea waters were choppy. But inside it was warm and cosy and Paul Brehony didn't look at all like a man whose company was about to collapse. As she tucked into her second glass of champagne and the conversation flowed easily, Sophie had to remind herself that like it or not, he'd lied to her once before and he was still in a relationship with someone else. Besides, there was the business of cheating his best friend. Her head buzzed in confusion. She wanted to tackle him but maybe with all his current business worries, the time wasn't right. After all, strictly speaking, none of it was any of her business.

"I'd like to explain one or two things about me, things I've tried to tell you – but it's never the right moment," he said halfway through the main course of grilled sole and as if he'd read her mind.

"How do you mean?" she asked as casually as she could.

"You've probably heard all sorts of rumours."

"Rumours?"

"The papers are full of stories about me. And then there's the 'small' matter of Marina."

"It's none of my business really," she said trying to sound totally disinterested.

"But I'd like to tell you. I want you to know. Things are not all as they seem."

God, she was bursting with pure curiosity now.

"Well, if you really want to confide in me, if it means that much to you . . ."

He took a sip of water and was just about to begin when his mobile rang and he went into the foyer to take the call. When he returned he seemed to have forgotten all about their recent conversation and he paid the bill quickly and suggested they take a short walk on the beach before heading for home.

The beach was deserted except for a few hardy stragglers walking their dogs. He set off at a rapid pace and she struggled to keep up with him, occasionally making stabs at conversation, and dropping hints that she'd like to hear what it was that he was so anxious to tell her over lunch. But he seemed preoccupied now and she began to long for the walk to end. The flimsy windcheater she'd brought was no match for the sharp breezes blowing in from the North Sea and the wind stung her ears.

"Look!" he said at last. "The sky's clearing and the wind has died down. We should have a smooth flight home."

Once or twice on the return walk to the village, her shoulder glanced off his. At one point, he held her hand to step over a little rivulet of water. She retrieved her hand quickly. Then there was an awkward moment where they stood facing one another And he quickly took her hand in his once more, gently tugged her towards him, bent his face to hers and brushed his lips ever so lightly against her cheek. It lasted a mere fraction of a second and Sophie was left wondering for the remainder of their walk on the beach, if it had been an accident or a mere trick of the wind, or an actual kiss.

Sophie felt like a complete interloper, the proverbial gooseberry, the spare maid at the wedding when Marina greeted Paul at the front door of Fernmount House with effusive doses of affection and some particularly graceful twirls of her exquisite hands.

"It's good of you to join us, Sophie."

Her petite figure was emphasised beautifully in a stunning black dress that was slit from the nape of her neck to the base of her spine. It made her look deeply alluring and when she moved the material seemed to caress her. Not really hard to figure out what Paul saw in her after all. Sophie felt large and ugly suddenly – in her chunky woollen sweater and denim jeans, her hair tumbling down haphazardly onto her shoulders, her nails cut short and unpolished.

Feeling grubby and unwashed she jumped at the offer of a shower in one of the guest bathrooms. She tried her best with a little emergency make-up kit – but looking forlornly in the mirror was less than impressed with the result. It was one of those deeply depressing mirror moments. She gazed and looked, searching for something in her appearance which would match Marina's dazzling blend of sophisticated grooming and smouldering sex appeal. But all she could see was straggly hair, highlights long since faded, eyebrows that in all the college and baby excitement she'd forgotten to pluck for almost a month, a nasty little spot, a face that hadn't seen a proper facial since she'd left Cape Cod. It wouldn't have mattered so much if Marina wasn't such a walking paragon of everything that makes men go weak at the knees, drool at the mouth and do rash things with their credit cards. Sophie who had once been quite a fan of grooming and looking her best now observed herself and saw a dowdy shadow of her former self.

Oh well! She wasn't on a date. If Marina wanted to

play silly little "I'm the fairest one of all" games, that was her problem.

When Sophie returned to the drawing-room. she could feel Marina's dark beady eyes looking her up and down and taking sadistic delight in her tired blue cotton sweater, her faded jeans, and her unmanicured hands. They had drinks. Marina insisted on pink champagnes and fired several quick questions at her about the flying experience, designed, Sophie felt, to humiliate.

"You see, I find fear so hard to understand because nothing frightens me," Marina declared when Sophie tried to explain why she didn't like flying.

"That's amazing," was all she could politely reply.

"Yes – but I don't think of myself as amazing," replied Marina, completely getting the wrong end of the stick. "On the contrary – I believe I'm quite ordinary – people tell me I have this marvellous gift for writing – but I'm quite humble about it. One must be humble I believe."

It amused Sophie to see how easily the conversation had shifted to Marina's favourite topic – herself.

"And did you write well this morning?"

Marina frowned and crossed one beautifully slender knee over the other. She straightened her half-revealed and sensuously curving back, twirled her ankle and considered Sophie's question while tilting her whole body provocatively in Paul's direction..

"I'm compelled to do it, you see – whether I'm having a good day or not – that is the true writing vocation. Did I write well this morning? Let's just say – that I believe I didn't write badly. Exploring the depths of the human soul isn't easy and it burns me up. It drains me. Sometimes I can barely talk."

Not that you'd notice, thought Sophie.

Paul contributed little to the conversation. Once or twice Sophie accidentally caught his eye and looked away quickly, feeling strangely guilty.

The atmosphere didn't improve over the fillet of beef.

Marina, her tongue loosened even further by the very palatable wine from Paul's cellar, droned on for ages about how she'd first discovered her vocation as a writer.

"Is your beef all right?" Paul asked Sophie.

"Yes – just lovely, thanks."

Paul had insisted on driving her home which made Sophie feel terribly uneasy. Marina had shot her dagger looks as she was leaving, looks which carried with them all sorts of dire and unspeakable threats and accusations. An "All's fair in love and war" kind of look, a look which meant that if Sophie so much as fluttered an un-mascaraed eyelash at Paul, the least she could look forward to was a slow and painful death by rusty tweezers.

"Marina was right. There was really no need to drive me home," she said as they hurtled along the Kildivor Road towards town.

"It's no trouble," he said and fell into a gloomy silence.

The previous night in Wayne Wong's, the afternoon piloting her over land and sea, the easy, lazy lunch in Portaferry had shown her a very different Paul Brehony – one who was alive, intelligent, warm and above all considerate. But since their return, he'd sunk further and further into gloom and though she made several brave attempts to strike up a little light-hearted conversation, he didn't appear to be interested. Not surprising really. Who could compare with the carefully honed and studied appeal of a woman like Marina? Sophie felt a deep sense of regret. All the same, she stole a longing look at him in the cosy darkness of the car and wondered fleetingly again what it would be like to be really kissed by him.

"Right," he said abruptly as they approached the suburbs, "no time like the present. You've got the complete wrong end of the stick about Marina. There never was and never will be anything between us."

"Yeah, right," she heard herself say, her mind racing in all directions.

"Marina is a friend of a friend. That's all. She may like to give the impression that there's something between us – but there isn't. She's just staying with me until she gets a place of her own. As soon as that happens, she's out of my life and without being ungallant, I can't say that I'll miss her very much. I hope that's clear."

She stared at him blankly for a few moments, trying to make sense of what she'd heard. No – she couldn't make sense of it – because it was yet another pack of lies – obviously.

"So why don't you just ask her to leave? A rich and powerful man like you should have no trouble getting rid of an unwanted house guest." She couldn't keep the sarcasm from her voice.

He nodded as if he'd been anticipating the question. "Unfortunately it's not as simple as that. She kind of has my head over a barrel – but that would take too long to explain just now. But please, Sophie, you've got to believe me – there's nothing between Marina and me."

Her mind raced in several directions at once. How could Marina have his head over a barrel? What hold could she possibly have over him? It just didn't make sense. She was about to tackle him about it further when her mobile buzzed with a text message. Her heart sank when she saw that it was Nick.

"Where are you? I'm parked outside your house."

She deleted the message.

Another appeared immediately. *"I really need to see you and explain. I've let you down and I hate doing that and I'm really sorry."*

She deleted that too.

"Excuse me," she said to Paul.

"No, don't worry. You carry on," he said.

"OK. I get the hint. Just want you to know that I really like you and that I was running around like a blue-assed fly all week. I think we had something special going."

She couldn't resist it.

"What does a blue-assed fly look like when it's running?"

She knew it was a mistake to engage with him at all – as soon as she sent it.

"That's more like it. Knew you weren't really mad at me. When will you be home? I'll wait if you like."

Oh well, at least he might do something about her garden.

The car swung into the driveway of her house and there was Nick, looking none too pleased to see who she was with.

Paul took his cue and left so quickly that she didn't even have a chance to thank him for the lovely time.

"What were you doing out with him?" Nick asked once they were in the kitchen.

"Nothing much. We went flying. Then dinner."

"Are you seeing him?"

"No! His girlfriend was there. He was just being nice."

"Will you be seeing him again?"

She felt like he was giving her the third degree and it annoyed her. He'd promised to call and never showed. Now he'd turned up three days later, full of remorse and acting like he was her husband.

"I don't think that's any of your business," she said curtly. "Glass of wine?"

She wasn't prepared for what happened next.

He buried his head in his hands and uttered a strangled sigh.

"You're right. I've blown it, haven't I? I have no right to ask your business – but I just get so jealous to think of you with anyone else. I like you so much, Sophie – if it meant taking on someone like Paul Brehony in a fist fight – I'd even do it. That's how much I feel. That's how much I want to be with you. That's why I stayed away – to give myself time to explore those feelings fully."

His face was a storm of emotion – waves of despair, longing, fear and hope all battling away inside him. He was in such distress that she figured it must be genuine. But she wouldn't let him off that easily.

"All you had to do was text that you couldn't see me for a few days. I wouldn't have minded. It's not like we're engaged or anything. But I hate when people make arrangements and then don't show up. It's just plain bad manners. And what about the garden? It looks like a war zone out there!"

He wrung his hands remorsefully and then his face clouded over.

"The garden?" he snapped angrily. "That's all you can think about at a time like this! Have you any idea of the pressure I'm under? I made all this effort to come and see you. Doesn't that mean anything?"

"I'm sorry if you're under pressure and I certainly wouldn't like to add to it," she said, smiling anxiously and trying to defuse the squally atmosphere that had erupted out of almost nothing.

"This isn't going very well, is it?" he said, running a hand through his hair once more. "I'm tired and narky. Maybe I should just go."

She was inclined to agree with him but at the same time he seemed to be all tangled up and she felt a bit sorry for him.

"Stay and have a cup of tea. I don't have any wine, I'm afraid. Shoestring budget at the moment."

"OK," he said, "and thanks. I'm sorry for overreacting."

"No worries," she said easily.

"Let's go out on Wednesday – somewhere nice," he said, the squall completely past.

Sophie smiled reassuringly at him. She wasn't quite up to refusing him outright, though some persistent little voice at the far back corner of her subconscious was telling her that she ought to have no further dealings with Nick Lynch.

There was a new Martin Scorcese movie he wanted to see. They could go to that on Wednesday and then maybe on Thursday night he'd bring her to Moscow – a Russian restaurant which had a resident balalaika player. She ignored her vague qualms and agreed to go.

Chapter 39

Over the next few days Sophie hardly had time to think about either Nick or Paul Brehony. There were several assignments to catch up on, and a lengthy session in a recruitment agency to prepare herself for a swift return to the workplace as soon as the course was over. Clementine was travelling to Brussels to visit her nephew and Sophie helped her pack and brought her to the airport.

But true to his word for once, Nick arrived on Wednesday after tea and they drove to the cinema. It was a dark murky evening, cold drizzle falling and the unmistakable scent of winter in the air. The cinema in contrast was warm and cosy and they had good seats to the rear. Sophie looked longingly at the buttered popcorn, but decided to be disciplined, especially when Nick mumbled that he loathed people munching and rattling sweet papers around him. She'd never noticed before, even considered munching and paper-rattling and drink-slurping as part and parcel of the whole cinema experience. Now as they settled in to watch the trailers, she was suddenly conscious of two teenage boys in the seats nearby who were munching loudly and chattering away to their hearts' content.

Nick glared at them and said he hoped they wouldn't carry on like that when the main feature started.

"Sorry," he said then. "You must think I'm very intolerant."

"Not at all," she said, willing the two boys to stop making noise.

They didn't. Ten minutes into the feature, Nick leaned over and asked them to stop talking, that they were spoiling other people's enjoyment of the movie. They apologised and stopped talking instantly. She heaved a sigh of relief and Nick sat back to savour the broad sweep of gangland war in twentieth century America. But the boys continued to munch noisily and Nick quickly tensed up again, his shoulders stiffening, his body leaning forward.

"Is something wrong?" she asked.

"Bloody popcorn!"

"Can't you just ignore it? They don't mean any harm. They're only young."

But he wouldn't be placated. Even to Sophie it now felt like the only noise in the cinema was the sound of the boys munching. As for the film – she could barely concentrate and quickly lost track of the plot. Nick said "*Ssshhh*" a few times. But the boys, though happy to stop talking, continued to munch away. Nick, it seemed, couldn't take any more and excused himself. She was afraid he'd gone off to make a scene and have the lads ejected but he simply returned a few minutes later and resumed his seat. He continued shifting about restlessly for another half hour, making occasional comments about Scorcese's directorial style, and then disappeared again. It went on like that to the end of the film and Sophie felt she would be quite happy never to see another mafia or gangland film again. It was far too violent for her taste anyway.

As far as dates went, it had been pretty much a disaster so far. She concluded that if they were to continue seeing each other, then it might be best to avoid the cinema altogether in future. Afterwards, they went for a meal and he talked almost non-stop. She could barely keep up with him and by the time they got back to her place, she was reduced to merely nodding and making the occasional meaningless reply.

"I'm talking too much. How about you? To be honest I'm under huge pressure with the business at the moment. I've got ten projects on the go which have got to be completed by the end of the month – and they're all fairly big – a hotel in Malahide, some rock star's place in Dalkey, a block of apartments out in Citywest . . . I've had to take on new people just to get through the workload and there's always cash-flow problems in this line of work. But I haven't forgotten about your garden, I promise."

"It must be stressful," she said, "but look on the bright side – you're doing something you love and giving pleasure to people at the same time."

He took her in his arms and planted a moist lingering kiss on her lips. "I haven't been great company – but I'll make it up to you tomorrow night."

Where was she going with this guy? She didn't know,

could not get any handle on him. He was like mercury, slipping through her fingers, one moment paying her passionate attention, the next coldly giving her the brush off. She didn't know if she even liked him. Every time she met him he seemed different. Was that what intrigued her? She loved puzzles, cryptic clues, mystery novels. Might it be plain old-fashioned curiosity and nothing else much? Surely at her age, she should have more sense.

Later, when he'd left, she lay awake in bed for a long time. What was it Lucy had said? Something that annoyed her deeply – that Sophie would find her bearings in the end. She knew at the time why she'd been so annoyed – because it was the truth. She did feel all at sea, rudderless. She'd talked to Paul Brehony about it the night in Wayne Wong's – but what was the good of talking to him? What was the good of even thinking about him? In spite of his declaration that they weren't lovers, it was plain that he was with Marina. She didn't for one minute believe that daft tale of Marina having some kind of hold on him. So perhaps she should stop looking over her shoulder wistfully and put more effort into the man who was currently paying her the most attention – Nick. He was good-looking, successful, hard-working, interesting and clearly liked her. She ought to be feeling quite pleased with herself. But she wasn't.

The next evening, she decided to prepare for dinner with Nick by having a long, lingering, candlelit, scented bath. She filled the tub, poured in the last sachet of her Jo Malone bath-oil, lit lime-scented candles, rubbed the remains of a Clarins facial on her skin and sank into the warm, frothy water.

She was just slipping into a balmy slumber when the doorbell rang. It was too early for Nick. He wasn't due for at least another two hours. It rang again, this time more insistently and she climbed out of the bath crossly. She pulled on an old towelling dressing-gown, and tied her dampened hair up in a towel. She slipped her wet feet into a pair of old trainers and padded across the hall to the front door. If it was Hendro – she'd clock him!

"Tess!"

"I'm sorry. I should have phoned ahead – but I made up my mind at the last moment."

Sophie hugged her grandmother, then led her into the kitchen and made her sit in the rocking chair by the range.

"It's lovely to see you, Gran," she said as she put the kettle on, "but is something wrong? Is it Kenny?"

"I've had enough of him, Sophie. I really have."

She told Sophie all about Kenny's bullying and how she'd ended up staying in Robert's while he was away. There had been a hold-up on the repairs on her house in Hollymaine and now it wouldn't be finished for another week. She couldn't bear to go back to Kenny's and would Sophie mind awfully if she stayed?

"Gran," Sophie jumped up and hugged her, "there's nothing I'd like better."

Sophie swept aside the pile of books and notes that littered the table and served up a hastily assembled salad with tea. Since Isobel had left, things on the domestic front had deteriorated sharply. And strictly speaking what she served up to Tess wouldn't pass as a salad. There were a couple of tomatoes, a slice of curled up Cheddar cheese, a spoonful of very tired roast pepper hummus and some olives she'd found in a jar.

"Sorry, Gran. I've been so busy lately – I don't remember to shop. But at least the bread is fresh."

"It's lovely," Tess said diplomatically.

The evening was chilly and after Tess had eaten they lit a fire in the sitting-room. Sophie poured Tess a gin and tonic and they sat in companionable silence for a while. Something strange was happening and she wasn't sure what. But it seemed as if the house was filling up with memories and experiences – even though they were only sitting quietly.

Tiger came in and checked out the newcomer and when she'd established that Tess had no nice titbits, went prowling around the room doing some kind of sentry duty as if to say "Am I the only creature round here who does any work?"

Sophie dried her hair and slipped into jeans and T-shirt and wondered what she should do about Nick. It wasn't really very welcoming to leave Tess alone on her first night in town. The only decent thing to do was to cancel. She felt sure he would understand. But Tess wouldn't hear of her staying in.

"Go out and enjoy yourself. I'm fine!"

"Are you sure?"

"Sophie – I'm perfectly capable of looking after myself. Stop fussing."

Tess was still up when she arrived home. She'd emptied the dishwasher and swept the floor and worked her way through a pile of ironing that had been building up for several days. Sophie scolded her and then told her about Nick and what a pleasant night she'd had. It wasn't entirely the truth. Everything had been going quite well until she had gently introduced the subject of gardens as they were strolling home along a quiet street.

"Just leave it for now," he said smiling tensely.

But she wasn't prepared to leave it any more. It was her garden. He'd ploughed it up. She didn't want an argument but fair was fair..

"I'm sorry but it really is time something was done about it. It's been nearly two months now. The whole summer has gone and I haven't been able to move beyond the decking."

He rolled his eyes to heaven and tucked in his chin. It made him look almost peevish.

"Perhaps if you were to pay the going rate, I'd be able to do it all on demand," he joked edgily. "But you know perfectly well I have cash-flow problems. I'm doing you a favour – remember?"

Sophie didn't especially want an argument and she had to admit that in a way he had a point, so they walked the rest of the journey in an uneasy silence. She invited him in to meet Tess but he declined saying he had a busy morning.

He did make a quick dash to her bathroom though. "Wine always does it to me," he explained. Then he kissed her affectionately and left.

"I hope he treats you nicely," Tess was saying now.

"Gran, stop worrying. He's a nice man and I'm perfectly capable of looking after myself."

In the morning when Sophie got up, the breakfast table was laid and the smell of freshly baked croissants filled the air. There was fresh orange juice and even the daily paper.

"You know I'm an early riser. I can't seem to stay in bed. So I decided to pop round the corner and get a few messages."

"Thanks, Gran. It's a real treat."

"But, Sophie – that cat of yours is behaving very oddly."

"What do you mean?"

"See for yourself."

They both looked outside through the half open sliding doors and watched as Tiger tore round the garden in circles and sprinted and tumbled and chased her tail and darted off haphazardly in all directions.

"She shot out of the bathroom a few minutes ago and through the doors into the garden and since then she's been behaving like that," said Tess.

Sophie shrugged dismissively and told her grandmother the cat was pure daft anyway and didn't belong to her.

"All the same – I think there's something wrong with her. You ought to bring her inside – see if she's injured or anything."

"Damn cat!" said Sophie, sorry she'd ever agreed to mind it while Clementine was away. If anything happened to Tiger, Clementine would be devastated. So there was a good few minutes of chasing round in the ploughed-up soil and calling and coaxing with a piece of tinned tuna. It was Tess who finally managed to shoo her into the house.

In the kitchen, Tiger continued her mad rampage totally unabated.

"See how she's pawing at her nose?" said Tess. "Maybe something stung her?"

"She ran out of the bathroom, you say?" asked Sophie.

"Yes – perhaps you should check in there?"

A minute later Sophie emerged from the bathroom with a piece of folded paper in the palm of her hand.

"I found this on the ground," she said.

Tess examined the paper. "It's some kind of powder."

Sophie held up the paper gingerly to her nose and then she noted neat folds in the paper – it was like a little flattened home-made paper cone.

"Oh shit!" she said, dabbing her finger in the powder and tasting it just to be sure.

Tiger was now doing the feline equivalent of skipping the light fandango and dancing cartwheels across the floor.

"Well, what is it, dear?"

"Nothing. She needs to see a vet straight away."

"Well, that's OK. You go along to your classes. I can take her. But tell me what it is first."

Oh hell! Gran was a grown-up.

"It's cocaine."

Tess looked horrified. "How did it get here? Sophie! You don't –"

"No! Of course not!"

"Then how can you be sure what it is?"

"A girl I shared a flat with once – she brought some home from a party."

She racked her brains, tried to remember who'd been in her house over the past few weeks. Isobel – who detested even the mention of drugs. Clementine wasn't the sort to even smoke a casual cigarette. Hendro? No, he was too smart – too athletic – enjoyed life too much. Could it have been Joe and his assistants? Somehow that didn't seem to fit . . . Nick? No, she'd have noticed. What about Ed Thorne? He'd been in the flat the night Isobel went into labour. Perhaps with the loss of his wife, he'd taken to drugs as a means of coping.

"Then whose is it?" said Tess, poking at the white powder with pure curiosity.

"I don't know. Unless it's Ed's."

"Who is Ed?"

"He's a widower. He lives upstairs."

"What sort of widower is he – dropping dangerous drugs all over the place? Sophie, you shouldn't have a man like that staying under the same roof!"

"I don't know that it is his! He seems harmless."

While Tess took Tiger off to the vet's, Sophie went to her classes. Over coffee in the crowded canteen, she told Lucy and Dennis about Tiger and the cocaine. Lucy thought it was the funniest thing she'd ever heard and made Sophie go over her story several times, savouring the zaniness of it all.

Chapter 40

The vet had confirmed that the cat had been dabbling in illegal substances. Fortunately as it was only a one-off incident, Tiger would suffer no long-term effects.

When Sophie came home from college, Tiger was curled up on her favourite cushion, pretty much back to her old disdainful self and the kitchen buzzed with Tess's laid-back warmth – a real log fire in the range, the scent of bread baking, a warm hearty Irish stew in the oven, a bunch of flowers on the table, the radio chattering away quietly in a corner. Sophie kicked off her shoes and flopped into a chair.

"Here. This will do you good," Tess said, handing her a mug of soup.

It was thick and creamy carrot and coriander – the perfect antidote to cold winter days.

"Tiger's none the worse for wear. The vet said she'd be

fine. Though I have to say, Sophie, that I'm horrified to think of there being someone about the place that uses drugs."

Sophie remembered that she'd planned to ask Ed if he was the culprit. If he was, she wouldn't judge. There were far worse crimes in the world after all. But she'd have to think very carefully about renewing his lease. Possession of drugs was a criminal offence. She didn't want her home associated with anything like that. After dinner and a hot bath, she went upstairs and knocked on his door. He appeared in a towelling dressing-gown.

"Sorry – I'm just out of the bath. What can I do for you? How's Isobel and the baby?"

"She's fine. Ed, I need to talk to you. It's fairly important."

If he was startled he didn't show it. "I'll be down in five minutes," he said.

While they waited, she and Tess cleared up. Then Tess who was a serious devotee of *Coronation Street*, took herself into the sitting-room with a gin and tonic and the crossword, leaving Sophie alone to confront Ed. True to his word, he arrived in a little over five minutes, now dressed in casual chinos, a smart polo shirt and a navy crew-neck sweater.

"Mmm! Something smells good," he said.

"My grandmother – she's staying over for a few days. While she's here she wants to spoil me a bit. I'm not complaining. It's nice to have the company and wonderful to come home to a properly cooked dinner for a change."

"I miss all that. The worst thing about losing a spouse

is always coming home to an empty house. I still find it hard. I still miss my wife. It's been five years – but sometimes it hurts just as much as it did on the first day."

She poured him a cup of tea and watched him ease into a chair while she picked her words carefully.

"I can't imagine what it must be like to lose your life's partner . . . "

"It's like losing your heart . . ." he said then thanked her for the tea.

She picked her words carefully, anxious not to offend him. "I don't know how you cope . . . I'd probably end up taking to drugs or something . . . "

He laughed and his eyes crinkled up. "Don't ever get into that. It's a mug's game. Take it from me."

"Do you . . . I mean have you . . . "

"Never even smoked a cigarette."

"Are you sure?"

"Of course I'm sure! Look, if you're trying to offer me a joint or something I'm not interested."

Oh God! He thought she was coming on to him. She took a deep breath.

"Only I found a little quantity of cocaine in my bathroom . . . I mean Tiger the cat found a little quantity of cocaine and had to be taken to the vet . . . anyway, it must have fallen out of someone's pocket, possibly the night Isobel went into labour . . . I found it on my bathroom floor . . . I'm sorry . . . but I must ask everyone who's been here . . . I can't have that sort of thing in my house and –"

"Not me," he said and drank back his tea.

He seemed sincere. She bit her lip, at a loss as to how to proceed with her investigation.

"What about that garden chap?" said Ed. "He's been around once or twice."

"Nick! Never. He's far too busy for that kind of non-sense. Besides, I think I'd know . . ."

She blushed and took to examining her fingernails. Of course, it couldn't be Nick. What an idea! He was so successful, so busy, so go-ahead, so confident, so good-looking, so fit, so clean and smart. Exactly the wrong profile for a drug-user!

She didn't know what to say to ease the embarrassment and was grateful when Ed began to chat about general matters. He talked about his family for a while – his wife, his gay son who he'd fallen out with but was now reconciled to, his daughter and his three lovely grandchildren. He worked all the hours God gave – because he hated being alone.

"When I'm alone I read, non-stop, or garden. I have a big garden at home in Kilkenny and that keeps me sane. Sometimes I spend a few weeks with Aoife – that's my daughter. Sometimes I hang out with Donald and his gay friends in San Francisco. It sure is educational and they always make me feel right at home – but as far as I'm concerned it's a different world . . ."

Sophie was just thinking what a nice man he was and ashamed of the way she had so completely misjudged him, when Tess came into the kitchen. *Coronation Street* was over and she didn't like *EastEnders*.

"There's a clue in the crossword I just can't figure. It

says: 'Pay these to do your rounds, five and four letters' . . . oh, I'm sorry, I didn't realise . . . "

She turned to go then stopped and stared at Sophie's guest.

Ed stood up and Sophie smiled at his old school manners.

"Green fees," he said promptly. "That's the answer . . . pay these to do your rounds . . . green fees . . . "

Tess stared at him for a moment, then said, "What?"

"Green fees, that's the answer."

"Yes, thank you," she answered vaguely, dropping her newspaper on the table and continuing to stare at him. Then, her voice trembling slightly, she said, "Sophie, do you know who this is?"

"Sorry, Gran – forgot my manners. Tess O'Meara meet –"

But Tess cut her short. "There's no need for introductions. Edmond? Edmond Thornton?"

They studied one another coolly across the kitchen table for what seemed like ages. Sophie began to feel quite peculiar, as though the room and everyone in it were in the grip of some perplexing magical spell. Then Ed's face broke into a warm crinkly smile.

"Tess, what the hell are you doing here?"

"Sophie's my granddaughter. And you?"

Sophie was mightily confused. These two knew each other? Ed Thorne had suddenly turned into Edmond Thornton. What was going on?

"My company rents the flat upstairs."

"Sophie didn't tell me anyone by the name of

Thornton was living here."

The room had filled suddenly with sparks and electricity. Sophie didn't feel at all comfortable though Ed smiled easily and her grandmother was practically glowing with pleasure.

"I'm still Edmond Thornton. I just use Ed Thorne in my line of work because it's easier. It's good to see you after all these years, Tess," he said and embraced her warmly.

Tess stood back and held his hand and beamed radiantly at him.

"How is your wife?" she remembered to ask.

"She's dead." He still had difficulty saying the words.

"I'm truly sorry to hear that, Edmond – really I am. I lost my husband too – many years ago . . ."

They'd examined each other closely – seeing how the years had marked or marred them. Then they sat at the table chatting about families, a look of fond friendship in their eyes. Sophie quickly felt surplus to requirements and even a little resentful. She didn't know where to look. In the space of five minutes, her grandmother seemed to have become ten years younger and the wary sadness which was so much a characteristic of Ed's conversation had dissipated.

An insistent little bell tinkled in the back of her mind. When she'd come home from New England, Tess had told her about a love affair with a man that she had gone on picnics and God knows what else with . . . Edmond!

Too shocked to say anything, Sophie dived out of the kitchen and before she even realised what she was doing, she was knocking on Hendro's back door.

In his stylish kitchen, Hendro was listening to The Red Hot Chilli Peppers and trying to do something vaguely appetising with chicken and pasta. He was failing miserably. When he realised the chicken was burnt and the pasta all stuck together in a horrible lump, Hendro tossed the lot in the bin and called for a Chinese take-away.

"I thought Chinese food was out. You're supposed to stick to your special diet."

"No worries. I'll order steamed chicken and noodles. It will do just as well. Anyway, what's up? You look all over the place."

She told him about Tiger and the cocaine.

"So who dropped it?"

"I haven't a clue. Don't suppose you'd know? I mean, if it was you, Hendro – you'd better just say."

"No way! I'd never touch the stuff."

"Well, if it's not you, or Ed, or Isobel – I don't know who it could be."

"What about the builders or your gardening friend?"

"Nick? He's far too sensible," she insisted loyally.

Anyway, that wasn't why she had dropped in on Hendro and so she proceeded to tell him about Tess and Ed – or was he now to be called Edmond?

"I mean the whole thing is just too awful. What would my mother say?"

Hendro stretched out careless long legs and leaned back in his chair, shrugging amiably.

"What's that supposed to mean?" she said.

"In the first place it's none of your business what your grandmother got up to in the past. In the second place, by the sound of things they're both very nice and very lonely people. It would be more in your line to be delighted that they've met up again after all these years. As for your grandmother having had a lover – she sounds like my kind of Sheila!"

"Oh, stop being so flippant! I shouldn't have expected you to understand. After all, you have the morals of a tomcat."

"Yeah maybe – but I don't do drugs. I don't sponge off women like Phil Campion. I never fail to turn up for a date like your gardening friend. I'm bloody good in bed and as it happens I'm faithful to all the women I date."

"That's because you never stay around long enough to get bored. How long are you going to go on living like that? Some day, Hendro, I know it's hard for you to imagine right now – but some day, your hair will be grey, your body will start shrinking, your magnificent six-pack will settle into middle-aged spread. The phone will stop ringing. Girls will stop hitting on you. Women will stop making eyes at you at the traffic-lights and then what?"

"I never think ahead. It's a complete waste of time. Nothing ever pans out the way we expect it to anyway. More wine?"

"No, thanks. I'm meeting Nick."

"So is this a serious thing or what?"

"Who knows? What about you? I thought you'd be out on the town . . . checking out the babes in their autumn finery?"

"Maybe later on. Any news from Isobel and Jonah?"

"She's not taking any calls and won't talk to anyone. It looks like she's going to go through with the adoption.

"That's really too bad," he said quite glumly.

Although Paul Brehony had specifically asked her not to mention Wayne Wong's about the town, she couldn't resist bringing Nick there for dinner. It was just too good a restaurant not to visit. Nick wasn't all that keen. He wasn't really interested in dinner at all, he told her. He'd had a bad day.

But she felt sure the homely warmth and mouth-watering food would lift his spirits. When they sat down at a cosy little table for two in the corner, she made valiant attempts to kick-start the conversation. But it seemed the more she tried, the more he sunk into a restless sullenness. He didn't like Chinese food. The tables were too close to one another. The decor was too modern.

"The crispy aromatic duck is scrumptious," she said.

"I hate duck."

"Then how about the sizzling prawns in chilli sauce?"

"I'm allergic to shellfish."

In the end he settled on a green chicken curry and was hard pushed to find fault with it.

Sophie began to feel miserable.

"What's the matter?" said Nick.

"Oh nothing. Tell me about your parents."

There wasn't much to tell. They sounded like a perfectly normal couple, members of the local golf club, both retired but never busier.

She asked him about the rest of his family.

There wasn't much to tell about them either. His sister was a secondary teacher. His brother was in Financial Services. The conversation quickly dried up.

Suddenly, she decided to ask him.

"Oh yes . . . " she said as lightly as she could, "there's something I've been meaning to ask you . . . "

"What?"

"Oh it's nothing really . . . something silly happened . . ." She told him about Tiger and the little quantity of cocaine she'd found in her bedroom.

"What are you telling me all this for?"

"I was just wondering . . . I mean . . . God, don't get the idea that I'm accusing you or anything but . . . and let's face it – live and let live – that's my motto – don't forget I've lived in New York ... only I thought maybe you . . . "

"If you've something to say – you'd better spit it out . . ."

She felt oddly intimidated, which was a first for Sophie Flanagan. The last time she'd been intimidated by anyone was when she was eighteen and a bouncer had threatened to throw her out of a nightclub for dancing in an area that was not a designated dancing area. All of a sudden she couldn't speak, tongue-tied, petrified, struck dumb, in fact totally gobsmacked.

Nick shoved the last of the green chicken curry into his mouth and glowered at her.

"Was it yours?" she said, doing her best impersonation of a mouse with laryngitis.

He rested his fork carefully on the plate.

"What's the big deal?"

"I'd just like to know, that's all. I mean there's an issue of trust here . . . and Clementine's cat might have died . . ."

"Oh, fuck the cat! I've had enough of this." He stood up, quite angry now. "Call me when you've grown up and discovered the real world!"

He threw a bunch of money on the table and stormed out.

Now this was one situation the Sisters of Perpetual Caution had never envisaged. No friend of Sophie's had ever been left sitting in a restaurant because the man of the moment had stormed out in a huff. It had always been and surely always would be a girl's solemn prerogative, duty and birthright to do the storming and the huffing in a date situation. She sank into the red-leather chair, vainly trying to conceal the humiliation and horror of what had just happened. She sipped at her coffee and fiddled idly with the bunch of notes as if it was the most normal thing in the world. At last, when she could feel the worst waves of embarrassment subsiding, she beckoned to the waiter, paid the bill and asked him to call a taxi. Then she scuttled out of the restaurant, and ducked into the ladies' to have a good cry.

Chapter 41

There had been a few reconciliatory text messages from Nick on her mobile, but Sophie erased them all without replying. She never wanted to see or hear from him again.

Now the winter was truly here and it seemed that all about her, people were finding happiness and fulfilment, settling in contentedly for the long, dark days. Tess O'Meara was blooming. Ed had asked her to stay on in Dublin for a few weeks and the pair of them were gallivanting about the town like lovestruck teenagers. Sophie observed their courtship with a steely disapproving eye, until Tess took her aside one evening.

"You're not happy about Ed and me, are you?"

"No."

"I have a right to happiness, Sophie. We all do. Don't resent me just because things on the romantic front haven't been going so well for you in the past year."

"It's nothing to do with that," she retorted hotly.

"Isn't it?"

"Well, Gran, since you ask – it upsets me that you would just take up where you left off with the same man you deceived my grandfather with! It's – it's so grubby! You should be ashamed of yourself!"

"Listen to you! So prim and proper! I never betrayed my husband – not with Ed – not with anybody."

"No? So what was all that about having a lover?"

"I suppose I was trying to shock you a bit. To make you think. You make all these assumptions about me simply because I'm your grandmother and so much older than you – and most of the time they're just plain wrong. You think I should be wiser, that I ought never to have done anything I'm ashamed of, that purely by being old I am some paragon of virtue. Well, I'm not! And what's more I won't be put in that 'paragon of senior citizen virtue' box by you or anyone else! If you must know the truth about Ed and me – we were good friends. I don't deny that we were attracted to one another. But it was never mentioned – not once. Although he did plant a lingering kiss on my cheek, after the Mayo County Final in Castlebar in nineteen fifty-nine – after I bought him a raspberry-ripple wafer."

Sophie had never seen her grandmother so cross. They stared each other down across the living room.

"What is it you young people say? Get a life!"

Much later, when Tess had come back from her night at the theatre with Ed, Sophie slunk into her bedroom and sat on the side of her bed.

"Sorry, Gran. I'm really sorry. I had no right to treat you like that."

"I'm sorry too. See how much I love you – you're the only person in the world who can still make me lose my temper."

Sophie buried her head on the pillow and cried, sobbing that she would never be settled, never be happy, never find a nice man to have children and grow old with. And what a hopeless judge of men she was and what a fool she had been.

"There there!" said Tess patting her head affectionately, for once allowing herself to revert to grandmother stereotype.

Several weeks had passed since the birth of Isobel's baby. Sophie kept in touch by emailing or phoning Hollymaine almost every day. But the news from the Kearney household was not good. Isobel was refusing point blank to have anything to do with the baby, didn't want to see or hear him. And the poor mite was left almost entirely in the care of her parents. Jim and Regina were overjoyed with their grandson, quite pleased to be reliving their child-rearing days – but they didn't exactly want the responsibility of a small baby for the rest of their lives. They had been there, done that and got the puke-stained T-shirts to prove it.

"How old is he now?" Sophie asked Isobel on the phone one evening.

"God knows. A few weeks. I've been on to the adoption agency. They're coming to visit me in a few days. I think they'll take him pretty quickly. Plenty of couples want a boy. It's for the best. Then I can get back to Dublin, get a proper job and put this whole sordid episode behind me."

"Don't rush into anything you might regret later."

"You don't know the first thing about it."

Sophie could see she wasn't getting anywhere. Isobel sounded cold, distant, not at all her old fiery, fighting self.

"I'm coming down at the weekend to see you and – to see you all."

"OK."

"Thought I'd let Tess have the place to herself – on account of Ed – I mean, I don't want to crowd her out . . ."

Sophie hoped that the story of Tess's blooming romance with Ed Thorne would be just the thing to lift Isobel's spirits.

"Yeah – whatever."

"And we might bring Hendro . . . he's been in Ireland for nearly eighteen months and he's never been outside Dublin. Don't you think it's time we showed him the real Ireland?"

"I'm not really in the mood for socialising. None of my clothes fit me. My hair is falling out. One of my nipples has turned inside out and I have stretch-marks."

"No-one's going to be looking at your stretch-marks."

"For God's sake, Sophie, can't you take a hint? I don't want to see anyone. I don't want to talk to anyone. I'm sorry if that sounds hurtful – but it's just the way it is."

Sophie quickly forgot about Isobel's problems when

she was passing through the student canteen the following morning and a tabloid headline caught her eye. It couldn't have been blunter:

BUSINESS TROUBLES WON'T GET IN THE WAY OF TRUE ROMANCE!

WEDDING BELLS AT LAST FOR GLENNSTOWN BOY MADE GOOD!

She thought there must be some mistake. But when she read down through the article, the in-depth profile of "*World-Renowned Author Marina Weber Hyde*" her heart sank. A photo of Marina leaning dreamily against the gnarled trunk of a tree, her eyes a concerto of mystery, sensual allure and longing, her dress a floating peppermint chiffon fantasy – the location the grounds of Paul's home. The picture was accompanied by the caption:

"The woman who has captured the heart of Paul Brehony."

"Marina Weber Hyde , award-winning writer, is not your typical run-of-the-mill author. A beautiful and enchanting lady who is universally adored in literary circles, Marina has had her fair share of tragedy. Her first husband, a Dubliner, abandoned her after only six months. Only two years ago, she suffered the break-up of her third marriage to wealthy Count Helmut Von Weber the well-known German patron of the arts. But Marina is not the sort to lie down under pressure. Her writing has kept her going through a third turbulent divorce and given some meaning to her life. 'It's been dreadfully hard,' she said, 'but I go on even through the bad times because I always believe that things work out for the best in the end.'

Now it appears she is poised to marry wealthy airline owner Paul Brehony. Though he began his career as a secondary teacher, the thirty-eight-year-old from Glennstown has built up quite a successful airline business against stiff competition. Still only snapping at the heels of larger companies like Aer Arann and Ryanair and not yet rich enough to make it onto the Wealthiest One Hundred, sources close to Brehony say that he is nevertheless a man of quite considerable wealth and an attractive catch for any woman. Now it seems his bachelor days may be over as Marina spoke with tremulous happiness about their new-found love.

'I wasn't looking for anyone. Truly I wasn't. But when we met, I felt this extraordinary sense of destiny – a moment in time if you like – of earth-shattering joy and deep significance. Since our first meeting eighteen months ago, Paul and I have had a whirlwind romance and we count the hours that we are away from one another ... like true kindred spirits. He is – my north, my south, my east, my west . . .'

Asked about their immediate plans to marry, Marina smiled enigmatically and simply asked the press to please respect their privacy for a little while longer . . . ."

Chapter 42

Hendro lay back in the warm bubbling comfort of the Jacuzzi in the Athena Health and Fitness Club. He closed his eyes and, as directed by the fitness coach, meditated on his fitness level for about ten seconds! Hendro didn't think much of meditation. He ought to have been quite gobsmacked when Beatrice Heavenly climbed languorously into the tub beside him, legs from here to eternity, a mane of blonde wavy hair and a figure that had "Caress me lovingly with expensive massage oil" written all over it. But he felt quite indifferent.

"Hi," she said, and even smiled. It was a first. She never smiled at anyone.

"Hi."

"I've seen you around here a few times."

"Yes, I train here."

"I'm Beatrice Heavenly ..." She held out a silken smooth and exquisitely manicured hand across the expanse of bubbling froth.

"I'm Hendro . . . how are you?"

"Hendro – such a cute name. I hope you don't mind me asking but have you been swimming?"

"Yeah, a few lengths – why?"

"Well, the water's terribly cold. I wonder did you notice? And all the lockers in the changing rooms are locked all the time – like they've lost the keys and haven't bothered to replace them. And look, the paint is peeling on the ceiling over there. Worst of all is the towel situation."

"The towel situation?"

"Yes, now they'll only issue members with one towel and something that looks a bit like a glass-cloth. Well, how's a girl supposed to dry her hair and her body and have something clean to stand on as well? Standards have slipped since that Kearney girl left and I'm writing a letter of complaint and getting members to sign it. Would you be interested?"

"Sure. Count me in."

"That's great. After all we pay enough membership fees. Hey – do you fancy going for a drink later?"

There was a small bet going among the boys of Old Rathgar Rugby Team on who would be the first person to get a date with Beatrice Heavenly. It was the ultimate score. And who would believe Hendro now that he'd sat in the hot tub minding his own business and that

Beatrice Heavenly had chatted him up and invited him for a drink and that he had said:

"That's quite a tempting offer. But I'm in serious training at the moment."

"What? You dipstick! You're winding us up!" they shouted collectively at him in the changing rooms later that evening.

"True as God!" said Hendro hardly understanding himself why he'd turned down the heavenly Beatrice Heavenly.

Later that afternoon Hendro called round to Sophie's house and announced he was going to see Isobel in Hollymaine.

"She doesn't want to see you – or anyone else for that matter. And if you have some silly notion that you can persuade her to keep Jonah – save your breath."

"I just fancy a trip down the country – to see what it's like. It's no big deal. Why don't you come with me? You look like you could do with a break."

Right now what Sophie needed most was to wallow in some serious misery – alone, in front of the fire, with chocolate and David Gray's *White Ladder* album. But Hendro had a point. A few days out of town might do her good. And, despite Isobel's insistence that she didn't want to see anyone, perhaps a visit to Isobel might take the edge off her own dismal romantic failure.

"Come on," said Hendro. "I need someone who knows the way. Remember I've never been beyond Lucan – and that was only for a game of golf."

Hendro was like a child driving through the countryside.

"Look at that old castle! Do you think I could buy a castle? Are they expensive?"

"Don't be ridiculous – cold, draughty things with too many stairs."

"Where's your sense of romance?"

Somewhere at the bottom of the trash can with the vomit-inducing profile of Marina Weber Hyde – along with her self-esteem, her pride and her sense of fun.

"I'm tired. I think I'll have a nap," she said morosely.

The rolling, constantly changing landscape came as a pleasant surprise to Hendro. Somehow he'd expected the whole of Ireland to be just one big green field with maybe a few nice golf courses scattered around. But he was charmed with the little villages they passed through and fascinated that one tiny country could change so suddenly from rolling green pastures, to eerie marsh and bogland, to lush green fields enclosed in carefully crafted stone walls – and almost everywhere pastel-shaded mountains in the distance. Even in the deepening gloom of a damp winter afternoon, the landscape had a dark, watery beauty of its own.

Night was falling when he steered his BMW sports along the twisty road beneath the railway bridge and emerged on the other side, into the village of Hollymaine. He was struck by the smallness of the place – just the one main street perched on the brow of a low hill.

He woke Sophie. She was in vile humour, uncharacteristically curt and grumpy. Even a heavenly lasagne with rocket salad and a bottle of finest Barolo in Leonardo's Restaurant didn't appear to lift her spirits.

"Nice wine. A good little restaurant," he said, trying to finish their meal on an optimistic note.

"I suppose."

"What is wrong with you? Can't you be a little more pleasant? Come on, be nice! I've just bought you dinner."

"Sorry! Thanks for the dinner! OK?"

Hendro gave up. He had more important things to worry about than whatever was eating Sophie Flanagan.

Baby Jonah lay contentedly in his cot. He was wrapped in a soft blue fleecy cotton blanket, smelling of new baby skin and baby shampoo and lotion. He examined his tiny exquisitely perfect fingers as they waved in front of his eyes. Occasionally a ray of late afternoon sunshine would flicker on the wall and he would track the light carefully with his eyes. There were other things in the room – pictures on the walls, mobiles hanging from the ceiling, box loads of cuddly teddy bears and Fisher Price toys – but for now Jonah was happy with his waving hands and the flickering light. He was blissfully unaware of the raging storm taking place in the living-room down at the end of the corridor.

"Well, that's rich coming from you," Isobel shouted at her mother.

"He's a little human being, Isobel – a person, your son. You haven't even given him a chance. Since he came home, your father and I have done all the loving and the caring. All you've done is to sit in your room and feel sorry for yourself and go on some ridiculous banana and turnip crash diet."

"It's bananas and cheese. And it's my business what happens with that baby – and I want him to go somewhere else. I want him out of here as soon as possible."

Regina drew in a sharp breath and bit her tongue. Her daughter had no idea what she was saying, hadn't even looked at the infant once since she'd brought him home. If she had once seen him, once fallen under the spell of his gummy little smile, once caught his tiny toes between her fingers, once held his perfect slippery body as she soaked him in his little duck-shaped bath, Isobel would not be so chillingly cold about him now. As things stood, she avoided all contact with him, insisted on sleeping at the other end of the house, would not go into the kitchen or living-room when he was there, put plugs in her ears at night in case she might hear him cry. Regina had to admit – from her daughter's point of view – the strategy was working perfectly. Isobel was quite content – once she didn't have to see the baby. But Regina and Jim had quickly grown to love Jonah . How could they bear to think of their own grandchild being loved and cared for by someone else?

"Isobel darling, just come down to the nursery and look at him. He's so beautiful. I've never seen such a beautiful child. If you could only see the way he –"

"Is the local hairdresser any good? I was thinking of getting a trim before I go back to Dublin."

It was just as well that the doorbell rang at that point – because Regina was coming very close to slapping her darling beloved daughter across the face. She bustled Hendro and Sophie into the kitchen where Isobel was making something awful with bananas, cottage cheese and cucumber.

Isobel was totally immersed in her diet, sticking rigidly to the menu for each day. She knew the calorie and fat content of almost everything in the fridge. She knew down to the last milligram how many units of food she was consuming each day. She was obsessed, fanatical in her zeal to return to the shape of the slender girl she had once been. She lay in bed at night, reviewing her calorific intake, planning her next day's menu, inventing new recipes according to the guidelines of the diet. Now she was contemplating an exercise routine – jogging, weights, stretches and swimming – anything which would keep her mind off the little matter of Jonah Kearney.

When Hendro and Sophie came through the door, Isobel was surprised to find how pleased she was to see them. She made them tea, put a feast of her mother's baked scones and apple-pie in front of them, while she herself picked daintily at the bananas, cucumber and cottage cheese. Hendro was infused with enthusiasm for the West of Ireland and couldn't wait to explore the place in the morning. Why hadn't Isobel told him she came from such a wonderful place? How could she bear to leave such a beautiful spot? Why would she want to exist in a crowded grimy city when she could truly live in a place like Hollymaine?

"Are you feeling all right, Hendro?" she asked at last.

"Never better."

He produced presents, told her she looked wonderful and said Dublin wasn't the same without her and when were she and the baby coming back?

It had all been going quite well until he mentioned Jonah. Isobel had found herself looking quite admiringly at Hendro, had been touched by his gifts, and charmed by the fact that he'd driven all this way just to see her.

There was a leaden silence.

"So how is the little critter?" said Hendro. "Is he smiling yet? I'll bet he's a real beauty."

"Here he is. See for yourself," said Regina returning with a restless and hungry Jonah in her arms. "He has his evening feed now and another usually around midnight. Then he sleeps right through till seven – don't you, my darling?"

Isobel had to get out. She couldn't bear to be in the same room. Even the sound of Jonah's tiny baby whimpers felt unsettling and suffocating.

"I have an appointment with the doctor. Got to go or I'll be late," she said quickly, grabbing her coat and darting from the room. She didn't have any appointment. She would drive into the village and just stay there until she knew he was safely back in his nursery and asleep.

Hendro insisted on holding and feeding Jonah who quickly settled comfortably in his arms.

"Is she really going to give him up for adoption?"

"We've tried everything. But you can see how it is. She even refuses to be in the same room as him. The adoption people are coming tomorrow and if all the papers are in order, they may take Jonah immediately."

Regina began to cry and Sophie tried hard to comfort her.

"No way!" said Hendro. "There must be something we can do."

"Like I said, we've tried. We've taken on all the drudgery of minding a baby and left her with just doing the nice things like bringing him for a walk in his buggy or cuddling him on the sofa in the evenings. But she's just not interested. It's like she refuses to acknowledge he even exists. The only time she'll even talk about him is in relation to the adoption."

"But he's so lovely. How could she even bear to part with him?" said Sophie warming to Jonah as he gurgled and flashed his quizzical Kearney smile at them all.

"I have an idea," Hendro said after a few moments' thought.

Regina was horrified when she heard his plan. It was cruel, not to say downright irresponsible and dangerous, she said.

"We have to think about Jonah. What if he became ill suddenly or distressed?" she fretted.

"It will just kickstart her maternal instinct into action. I've seen it at home on my grandmother's farm with the livestock."

"Livestock and babies are two completely different things!" she said indignantly.

She wouldn't hear of anything which would endanger the baby but when Jim came home from town, he listened carefully to Hendro's idea and thought it might just be worth considering.

"What's the worst that can happen?" he said reassuringly to his wife.

Regina didn't even want to think of an answer to that.

Chapter 43

Isobel was tired. It was wonderful how her head had to just hit the pillow these days and she was fast asleep. By the time she got home Hendro had taken Sophie for a pint in a lovely rickety little pub he'd seen on the way into Hollymaine. It struck her that Hendro and Sophie might be getting close to each other. And though the thought unsettled her, she was able to push it to the back of her mind. She had a warm soapy bath and readied herself for bed. Tucked in beneath warm Foxford blankets and her mother's best cotton sheets, she leafed through her dieting book, selecting new recipes for the week ahead. In a few minutes, she felt her eyelids drooping, her mind drifting away. She reached for the earplugs which were kept in her bedside locker. When she couldn't find them, she told herself that it didn't matter, that between her parents and Hendro and Sophie who were staying the night, between the whole lot of them – she wouldn't have to come into contact with the child.

She fell into a deep dreamless slumber from which she was woken suddenly less than an hour later. There was something blowing in the wind outside, a door creaking or a gale whistling through one of the outhouses. The sound rose and fell and subsided, then started up again. She pulled the blankets up around her head and resettled into her warm cocoon. There it was again, like a little sigh, rising almost to a high-pitched howl, which this time barely subsided before starting up again. She sat up in bed. As a child she'd been frightened of the usual night-time spectres – banshees, Grim Reapers and the like. And now for a moment she was catapulted back to a child's fearful nocturnal irrationality. Wide awake now, she listened, trying to identify the sound. Was it Barney, her dad's sheepdog, baying at the moon? But there was no moon and anyway Barney slept in a room at the back of the kitchen.

"Oh no!" she wailed and sank beneath the pillows as she realised that the source of the noise was the baby. But it wouldn't be long now before Regina got up and Isobel would hear her padding down to the kitchen to warm a bottle. Then in a few minutes the howling would stop. She'd have to listen to it until then. Where were her ear-plugs? She searched again frantically. No earplugs. She packed the pillows tightly against her ears and tried to concentrate on breathing calmly and rhythmically. The noise couldn't last much longer. She waited until she thought a good few minutes had passed and very carefully she lifted a pillow from one ear.

Shit! Where was her mother? What was she thinking of? Nothing for it now but to get out of bed and let rip with a right good holler at Regina Kearney.

"*Maaammmmm!*" she shouted down the corridor, barely making herself heard above the awful bawling and screeching that was coming from the nursery. "Mam – you have to give him a bottle!"

She stopped outside her parents' bedroom, listening for the tell-tale sounds of her father's snoring. But for once he was quiet. They were both quiet. Perhaps they'd had one glass of wine too many with their dinner. She opened the door and called again. But nothing seemed to wake them. Now she was getting desperate. This wasn't fair. It wasn't right. They were being very inconsiderate. She switched on the light.

"Right, you two. I've had enough of this. Now which one of you is going to get up and see to . . . ."

She stopped. The bed was unruffled, undisturbed, no parents asleep in it at all. She checked the kitchen, the living-room, even the bathroom. They weren't there. The baby howls could probably be heard in Dublin now and she was just about to work herself up into a real panic when she remembered – dear old Hendro. He could do it. He seemed to like babies. She knocked on his door, tip-toed in, called his name. He wasn't there. And Sophie wasn't in her room either. The house was empty. There was just Isobel and the baby – the screeching baby. What on earth was she to do?

Baby Jonah liked watching his hands waving about and also the light flickering on the wall. He didn't much like the darkness. And besides the big pain in his tummy told him he needed food. And there was only one way to get food and that was to open his mouth and cry as loud as he possibly could until the food arrived. Usually he didn't have to wait long. But tonight he was having to scream much louder than usual. What was happening?

Isobel stood outside his room, paralysed with fear. Her hands shook as she opened the door. But there was nothing else for it. The only way to stop the crying was to feed him. She'd just pick him up, carry him to the kitchen, give him a bottle and put him back in his cot again. It couldn't be that difficult. Anything to stop the dreadful wailing! She turned on the light and the crying stopped. Now it was just a kind of whimpering. But that was almost worst than the wailing because it was giving her a horrible pain in her abdomen.

She edged closer to the cot, reaching in to lift the baby out. He seemed a lot heavier than when she'd held him last. But she supposed that was natural. Once out of the cot, he lifted his head and looked about him, and she could feel his eyes settling very quickly on her face. But she wouldn't look back. Typical man, she thought, as she carried him briskly into the kitchen. Thinks all he has to do is look at a woman and she'll be putty in his hands. In the kitchen, she tried to put him lying beneath his favourite musical mobile in his playpen. But he was having none of it. Each time she put him down, he wailed as if she was abandoning him in the windswept Antarctic Wastes for good. God, was her mother going to pay for this – big-time! To add insult to injury she found a note propped against his bottle of milk. It read:

Warm to body temperature. Test on your wrist first. Don't forget to wind him afterwards. And he probably needs a nappy change. Mum.

"My mother is a complete bitch!" she murmured to herself as she warmed the bottle. Jonah gurgled back, clearly wanting to join in the conversation, but when he finally got the bottle of milk in his mouth, well – nothing else seemed to matter any more. Isobel stood rigidly in the middle of the kitchen, baby in one arm and the bottle stuck resentfully in his mouth, counting the minutes. It was only a few fluid ounces of milk. How long could it take for God's sake? But Jonah, having sucked furiously for about ten seconds, seemed to have fallen asleep by accident. She wiggled the bottle in his mouth and he woke again, sucked for another few seconds and then he nodded off again.

A horrible thought dawned on her. What if her mother didn't come home soon? What if he kept falling asleep instead of drinking his milk like any decent baby? She might be here all night!

Then it was probably best to sit down and at least be comfortable. Standing with a heavy baby in her arms wasn't going to improve her posture one little bit.

She settled into her dad's old armchair by the range and somehow the baby fell naturally into a kind of comfortable curl in the crook of her arm. That at least was something. Maybe now that he was settled, he'd drink up his milk and go back to sleep. But Jonah had other ideas. He sucked enthusiastically for a brief moment and then pushed the bottle from his mouth. Isobel could feel his intense baby eyes burning into her, but she was determined not to look. She slotted the bottle back into his mouth and leafed through Jim's copy of *The Farmer's Journal*. It was not her usual reading material – but she forced herself to become involved in a raging controversy about sheep-tagging in the north of the county. It seemed that there was some skulduggery going on though she couldn't quite make out what.

Jonah pushed the bottle from his mouth again and set to gurgling. He squealed with delight at the sounds he was managing to create all by himself. Isobel struggled to contain her patience, replaced the bottle once more and read another article about revolutionary advances in tractor design. At last the bottle was empty. She held him facing away from her, rubbed his back and felt a small sense of achievement when he emitted a loud burp which set him to squealing with laughter all over again. She changed his nappy and with a much lighter heart lay him down to sleep in his cot once more.

Jonah didn't much like the idea of being alone again. He loved the feel of being up against something warm, the warm comforting sound of breathing and the steady thump-thump of a heart beating. So when he found himself alone in his cot once more, he set to crying about the injustice of it all. He was a good crier, could keep it up for ages, had the energy to keep on going when lesser babies would just have given up and fallen asleep.

Isobel clambered crossly out of her own bed again and once more she went into his room, turned on the light and lifted him from the cot. As soon as he felt her arms he stopped crying and set to smiling and gurgling. Each time she put him back in the cot, he wailed pathetically.

"Right! Mister Baby! I've had enough of this," she said and carried him to her own bedroom. There she laid him down on the bed, tucked him in carefully under the blankets, propped a pillow behind him so that he wouldn't fall out and climbed back into bed. She switched on the lamp on his side of the bed – hoping it would distract him.

"Now, just go to sleep!" she hissed at him and turned away.

It was probably the most thrilling moment of Jonah's short life to date – to discover that there were actually big warm places where a baby could sleep as well as cuddling up against something warm and breathing, and especially this warm and breathing person. He nestled in and had a brief gurgle while he mused on the wonderfulness of it all.

Isobel tried to sleep and was on the point of succeeding when she felt a tiny hand on her ear. She would have to move her body away from the baby. She turned, carefully in case she would hurt him. But in the movement, she couldn't avoid coming face to face with him. He was staring up at her face, scrutinising her intently, scanning her features, the way the chestnut brown hair fell about her face, the shape of her warm hazel eyes, her nose, her chin. Then he smiled his strange gummy smile – beamed it at her, like a million rays of sunshine, like the warmest, sunny summer's day.

"Don't smile at me like that!" she murmured to him and then tears streaked down her cheeks. "How am I supposed to give you up if you smile at me like that?"

"I think it was a really mean thing to do and I will never forgive you," she told her mother and father over breakfast. She was still in her dressing-gown, munching on hot buttered toast and trying to spoon some scrambled egg into her mouth. Jonah lay in her lap, somewhere between sleep and wakefulness. Every so often he would wave a hand up at her and smile, just in case she forgot he was there.

"Well, it was Hendro's idea. So you can blame him," Jim said.

"Yes – but you went along with it. I was against it all along," said Regina, anxious that her daughter wouldn't think that she was a completely heartless bitch.

"Hendro? The guy is full of surprises."

It was time for Jonah's bath. It was Isobel's first time to bathe him and she was terrified that he'd slip, that she'd get shampoo in his eyes, that she wouldn't be able to dry him properly. But she needn't have worried. He was a natural water baby and squealed deliriously when she sponged the warm soapy water down his back.

Suddenly and intensely caught up with her new baby,

she barely had time to talk to Sophie. She'd been so immersed in her own problems that it only dawned on her now that her friend seemed very sad, and uncharacteristically bad-tempered. In comparison to Isobel, Sophie was generally more placid, more capable of controlling her own destiny, less likely to explode in fiery fits of temper, or back herself into silly emotional corners. She would have liked to get to the bottom of her friend's distress But Sophie was gone to check up on her grandmother's house. All she could do was put the matter out of her mind now and try to make up for lost time with Jonah. Sophie's problems, whatever they were would have to wait.

Used to spending hours in rigorous physical training, Hendro was restless to get out of the house, restless to see the countryside, restless to stretch his legs, restless to have a pint. Restless, full stop!

Jonah was asleep. Regina and Jim had promised to mind him for the afternoon. So Isobel brought Hendro to Lough Carra, along hidden windy roads that were barely wide enough for one car to pass, past old whitewashed cottages, past a ruined medieval monastery, past an evergreen forest, with the spectacular ruins of Moore Hall barely visible through the trees that had been planted some years before. The lake was still, the water scarcely rippling, reeds swaying and sighing in the mild breeze. They parked the car and walked along the moss-grown woodland path through an ancient oak forest by the lakeshore. Close by they could hear the water lapping quietly and a soft breeze sighing amongst the branches of the gnarled trees. Hendro picked up a sturdy lichened branch and poked idly at the fallen autumn leaves, rambling along the path lost in thought.

Isobel felt curiously surplus to requirements, trailing beside him in the deep silence of the forest.

"Do you like it?" she asked.

"Yeah. It's a fine spot," he said absently and headed deeper into the woods to investigate a tiny cemetery belonging to the Moore family.

It was clear he didn't want to talk and Isobel felt a twinge of rejection. Watching him clambering over moss-covered rocks and fallen branches, she allowed herself to admire fully for the first time, the remarkable magnificence of Hendro Sayers's body, his tall ungainly grace, his rugged, athletic charm. Since her last encounter with Phil, she'd been completely void of even the slightest sexual feeling. The whole emotional rollercoaster of her pregnancy and Jonah's arrival had banished all other thoughts from her mind. But now, bursting with newborn love for her newborn son, she had time to consider the role of Hendro Sayers in her life. What was he really doing here? Why had he become so deeply involved in Jonah's fate? What was in it for him? He would hardly go to all that trouble just to get into her knickers. He wouldn't need to. There was a constant stream of women ready to fling themselves at him without any provocation. Perhaps he was only trying to be an old-fashioned good guy in his own ham-fisted way and perhaps he was simply curious about the West of Ireland and its hidden treasures. Being realistic about him, what else could she expect? A man like that would hardly be interested in her now – with sore nipples, stretch marks, and most important of all a child to rear.

"It's getting chilly," she said. "Perhaps we should go home. Besides – I said I'd be there in time to give him his bath."

"OK."

She began to walk quickly back through the woods, desperately trying to stamp out the strange emotions and feelings which were bubbling up inside her. She wanted to get away from him now, to hide the sudden realisation that she liked Hendro very much, and that whatever string of floosies he would have in the months and years ahead, she would be horribly jealous, deeply sad, to hide the fact that deep within she felt a warm fluid longing to be kissed, held, caressed, undressed, caressed again and completely and utterly ravished by him.

She speeded up, walking briskly, almost running away. She knew any involvement with Hendro would inevitably end in a broken heart – her broken heart. And it was already broken, shattered, snapped clean in two by Phil Campion. It might never mend in any case. But if she once let Hendro see the longing in her heart – it would be destroyed forever.

The only thought in her mind now was to flee from the strange feelings induced no doubt by the romantic mystery of the woods, to get home to Jonah and her parents and to have a very cold shower. Come to think of it, she shouldn't even sit in the car with him for the ten-minute drive. It would mean driving off and leaving him to make his own way home. But he had long legs and was super fit. Hendro could walk the few miles no bother and she felt sure he wouldn't be the slightest bit offended, might even enjoy the joke. He was that easy-going kind of guy.

Later that evening, after she'd fed and bathed Jonah, after she'd cuddled him for what seemed ages on her own bed, then kissed and hugged him tight before tucking him into his cot, she curled up on the sofa and settled in to watch a movie on television. She was completely immersed in it, when the door burst open and Hendro appeared, his handsome face oddly clouded in some expression she didn't at first recognise.

"I suppose you think that was funny!"

Oddly enough he didn't sound all that amused.

"Who the hell do you think you are – treating your friends like that?"

Not amused at all! Furious in fact.

"Hendro – let me explain –"

"No explanation required! I've had enough! I've stood by you, kept you company, listened to your interminable problems, rescued you from the dungeon of hell in Rathmines, even delivered your baby for Christ's sake, and driven across the country to see you – and all you can do is dump me in the woods as part of some stupid childish prank! When are you ever going to grow up, Isobel? When are you ever going to appreciate the people who really care about you – not the slimy Phil Campions of this world – I mean your parents, Sophie, me?"

How could she tell him that the reason she'd run away in the woods of Moore Hall – was because of her feelings for him? How could she explain that she'd fled out of fear and a basic human instinct for self-preservation? Swamped with feelings she just couldn't handle, Isobel collapsed in a bundle of tears.

"I'd like to feel sympathy for you – but I don't. I'm driving back to town tonight. Take good care of Jonah. Goodbye."

She sobbed and sobbed, thought about chasing after him and telling him how much she loved him – yes, loved him – how much she longed to be with him. But that would have added to her humiliation – and though he certainly wouldn't reject her straight away, he was a man after all, he would reject her eventually, have his fun and then let her go. No! It wasn't worth the risk.

Chapter 44

A few days later Sophie and Lucy sat in the kitchen of Raglan Road, struggling to get to grips with the parallels between *Pride and Prejudice* and *Bridget Jones's Diary*.

"It's ridiculous! They're two completely different books," said Sophie impatiently.

She was rapidly losing interest in English literature, was seriously contemplating chucking in the course and finding a well-paid fantastically important job with loads of shallow, meaningless and absolutely delicious perks.

Tess bustled around the kitchen, humming and supervising a large pot of Irish stew. Ed was coming to join them. Sophie had invited Hendro along as well because he was in such bad form, but he had declined, thanking her but saying that he had a hangover from being out on the town having fun with his team-mates and some girls the night before.

"I think I prefer Bridget to Elizabeth. I can relate to her more," said Lucy. "But they do have lots in common. They both go for the wrong man to begin with. They both misjudge the right man ..."

"Oh men! Men! I'm sick to the teeth of books about girls trying to get their man. It's all a big con. Everybody knows true love and love at first sight and all that meeting the love of your life stuff is crap!"

"I believe in all those things," said Lucy vehemently.

"Poor you!"

The cold and biting winds of resentment and bitterness were blowing big-time through Sophie's life. These days, it was hard for anyone to hold a civil conversation with her. Life seemed grey and leaden. There was little to look forward to, little to hope for. She tried to throw herself into the coursework but found her mind dwelling on her failure with men. How had she got it so wrong?

When Isobel arrived with Baby Jonah in tow to stay the night, Sophie could hardly contain her lack of interest. It was left to Tess and Ed to welcome them and Jonah was passed around the room amid smiles and excitement while Sophie sullenly served up tea and cake.

"I wasn't expecting you," she said to Isobel when they were alone.

"I haven't heard from you and I was concerned. You've been so good to me, Sophie, these past few months – I'll never forget it."

"That's OK."

"I've been completely wrapped up in my own problems

– and now I realise that maybe things aren't going so well with you at the moment. So if you want to talk...."

"Don't be ridiculous. I'm fine."

"I heard about Nick. I'm sorry."

"Don't be. I've completely forgotten about him."

"Then what's wrong? Everyone says you're in terrible humour all the time."

"Everyone should mind their own business. I'm fine, so can we just drop it now, please?"

"If that's what you want? Have you seen Hendro lately?"

"Yes, I was talking to him earlier. What did you do to him? He made us tear back to Dublin like he had a hornet's nest up his ass. And he's been out on the town almost every night since."

"Nothing much," Isobel said, suddenly close to tears as the whole silly story of what happened in the woods of Moore Hall came tumbling out.

"I like him terribly, Sophie – I didn't mean to start liking him – but I've always found it hard to control feelings. I definitely won't do anything about it though. That much I can control. I just can't risk a relationship again. Especially for Jonah's sake – he needs a mother who's sensible and settled and not pining after a rogue of a man who doesn't love her. I can't say it to Hendro either – because it will only give him an even bigger head than he has already."

"But you should go and make it up with him. He was awfully hurt – and Isobel – there's one thing you can say about Hendro – he's straight-talking. He tells the truth.

There's a light on in the mews, so he's definitely at home. Why not go and talk to him now? What harm would it do? He doesn't need to know that you have feelings for him. Just apologise – put it all down to post-natal hormones – and then you never have to see him again."

"No," Isobel said, "I can't take the risk."

Tess packed a few last items into her suitcase and pressed down the lid. She would miss Sophie's company. She was worried about her granddaughter, about what would become of her. But she couldn't live her life. Now it was time to go back to Hollymaine and get Kenny and Maeve off her back once and for all. Then she had all sorts of plans. She was going to Australia with Ed in the New Year and then on to New Zealand. Ed was good company – light-hearted, respectful, and considerate. But who could tell how long their friendship would last? Anything might end it – separation, their respective family commitments, old marriage baggage, conflicts of interest, illness – maybe even death. What struck Tess most strongly since she'd been reunited with Ed was how fragile a thing life is – and how fleeting. Thirty years had passed since they'd seen each other – whole lives begun and ended in between, whole worlds changed forever, entire families brought into being and now scattered and rearing families of their own. As far as Tess O'Meara was concerned, there would be no more growing old gracefully!

Isobel also packed her bag and loaded it into the boot of her car together with all Jonah's baby paraphernalia.

That morning she'd had a long talk with her bank manager and he'd advised her to stay at home with her parents until she secured a new job which would allow her to make repayments on a mortgage. Yes – well – she told herself – it's the real world now – mortgages and babies! She had her head well buried in the boot of the car when she heard a familiar voice behind her and for a moment she froze.

"So this is little Jonah."

She straightened up and came face to face with Colman.

"Nice to see you, Colman? Home on a visit?"

"Back to sort out the Athena Health Club. Len Crolly has made a right mess of the place."

"That's too bad," she said absently, picking Jonah up and cuddling him. The complete decline and fall of the Athena Club was a matter of supreme indifference to her now. It was hard to even imagine how she'd been so completely and utterly obsessed with her job there less than a year ago.

"He's gone. Sacked. You name it – he got it wrong. The last straw came when Beatrice Heavenly organised a protest about conditions. Almost every member in the place signed it. There was practically a riot."

"And I suppose you're back now on a hugely inflated salary . . ."

"Not at all! The wife loves Kent – so I'm stuck there. I'm only home long enough to oversee the appointment of a new general manager. I've recommended you for the job. What do you think?"

Jonah had begun to whimper, coldness and hunger making him fractious.

"Thanks – but I'm really not interested at the moment."

"At least say you'll think about it."

"OK. But don't get your hopes up."

Driving through the traffic jam at the Lucan bypass, and away from the city, she smiled wryly to herself.

"Imagine that, Jonah – they wanted me back. Len Crolly turned out to be a disaster – what a surprise! But I couldn't care less if the whole place fell down about their ears. I've got something much more important. I've got you."

Isobel woke to a loud banging sound that shattered the silence of her parents' farmhouse. It sounded like a thunderstorm or an earthquake. At last she realised it was just someone knocking at the door. Jim and Regina were out and she struggled bleary-eyed into a dressing-gown and shuffled along the hall to the front door.

Outside on the doorstep, looking like he might keel over at any moment was Hendro.

"What are you doing here?"

"I followed you – you stupid woman!" he roared to the villagers of Hollymaine.

He tried to steady against the front door.

"I saw you leaving Sophie's house and I followed you all the way from Dublin. Don't you ever look in your vree-vew mirror?"

"You're drunk, Hendro!"

"Yes, plastered!" he said, grinning daftly.

"I thought you'd have more sense than to drink and drive."

"I didn't. I drove from Dublin and then I went into Garrivan's and got pissed. What do you think of that, Isobel Kearney?"

"I don't think much of it at all. Now go away and sleep it off. I've had a long day and I'm tired," she said woodenly.

She tried to shut the door in his face, but he pushed his foot through the doorway, so that she couldn't close it.

"Let me in!" he demanded, swaying and buckling at the knees.

"Please go away. You're in an awful state."

Isobel was no physical match for Hendro, drunk or sober, so at last she stood aside and watched helplessly as he proceeded unsteadily along her mother's new maple floors. He barely made it to the newly upholstered sofa in the sitting-room, before keeling over and collapsing in an untidy heap. He was instantly asleep. She tiptoed out and found a warm blanket, pulled off his shoes, and tucked the blanket in about him. And she ought to have been able to resist, felt sure she'd banished all feelings for him from her mind, but looking down at his boyish, rugged face, she couldn't resist brushing his cheek very fleetingly with her fingers.

She turned to leave quickly but found her wrist in a sudden vice grip.

"Don't go."

"I have to, Hendro. I have to go to bed."

"Stay and talk to me."

"No. You're too drunk."

"I can get sober. Make me coffee. Please – I need to talk to you."

She pulled the candlewick dressing-gown tight around her and disappeared, returning not long afterwards with a mug of strong black coffee.

"Thanks. Sorry for all the racket outside," he said blearily as he struggled to regain a state of soberness.

"That's OK."

"I want to tell you something. I know you think I'm just talking bullshit now because I've had a skinful – but I'll tell you anyway."

He sat up awkwardly on the sofa and gulped down the hot liquid.

"I'm listening," she said when he promptly went into a silent daze for a few minutes.

"Well, the thing is, Isobel – it's taking me a long time to get it out – because I've never said it before and so I don't have any practice – I'm not making much sense, am I?"

"Not really. I'm sorry about the day in Moore Hall. It was a mean thing to do."

He nodded absently and drained the last of the coffee.

"Do you know how I feel about you?" he said after another long pause.

"You like me. We're friends – mates. You've helped me out and I'm grateful."

"And how do you feel about me?"

She stared into the dying embers of the fire and tried

to rustle up a bunch of convincing words.

"Hey – you're a good guy. I'm dead fond of you – you old rogue."

She chanced a soft matey punch to his chest.

Yes, that sounded convincing. She glanced across at him. He was buying it.

"Fond? You make me sound like a faithful old Labrador or a comfortable old sweater."

"You're sort of like a big brother. How's that?"

"I don't want to be like your brother. I love you."

"Yes, of course. It's love of a kind."

"No! Will you listen? I love you. I love you as in 'I love you'."

"Yes – you've said that."

"I mean I love you and I want to take care of you. I fancy you. I dream about you at night. You know …. you and me naked …. I need you. I can't go on without you. I get jealous when I think of you with anyone else. I want to spend the rest of my life with you . . ."

Yes – it was your typical drunken bullshit verbal diarrhoea … throw enough compliments at her and she would just tumble into bed with him. But she'd been to the school of painfully hard knocks – The Phil Campion Academy of Drunken Bullshit. Consequently, Hendro's words barely registered.

"There hasn't been anyone else in my life since I met you. I really do love you, Isobel. Will you marry me?"

Marry? That was taking the verbal diarrhoea a bit too far – even for Hendro.

"Ask me in the morning!" she said, her voice wobbling

horribly as she bolted from the room in a state of fearsome agitation.

She woke the following morning to more loud knocking on her bedroom door. She slid out of bed and then hesitated, wondering if she should at least brush her hair. Then she shrugged her shoulders and opened the door.

There was no-one there. She looked up and down the corridor but it was empty. Then she caught sight of a little scrap of paper on the floor. She bent to pick it up, saw that there was writing on it and returned to her bedroom to inspect its contents. She held the paper up to the bright morning sunlight to read it.

"I, Hendro Sayers, do solemnly swear that I am now extremely sober and painfully hungover. I feel so poorly that I may not last the day and I ask you now, Isobel Kearney, to make a dying man happy by agreeing to be my wife. If you want to discuss the matter further, you will find me in the kitchen raiding your mother's aspirin supplies.

I love you with all my heart

Hendro."

Without stopping to fix her hair or pull on a dressing-gown, she darted down the corridor to the kitchen. He was leaning against the counter, looking a little the worse for wear but holding in his hand a small bunch of her mother's prized winter flowers. She went to him, kissed him lightly on the lips then pulled away.

"Are you going to hold onto those flowers for the rest of the day?"

"What? Oh – no, wait – stand there – a man's got to do this properly."

In an instant he was down on one knee, had taken her hand in his.

"Marry me, Isobel. Please say yes."

"Oh, get up off your knees, you great big Aussie tart! Of course I will," she said hauling him up and nestling into his arms.

Chapter 45

Sophie found the coffee shop on Liffey Street where she and Isobel had arranged to meet. The little place was brimming with people in cheery festive humour, making their lists and checking their purchases. A woman sitting across from her was engrossed in reading the newspaper. The warm spicy smell of mince-pies filled the air. In the background Frank Sinatra crooned 'Have Yourself a Very Merry Christmas'. While she waited, she sipped a cappuccino and glumly considered her Christmas shopping list:

Tess	Travel Books
Isobel	The Absolute Ultimate Wedding Planner
Jonah	A mat with squishy things that lit up and made noises
Hendro	*Men are From Mars – Women are From Venus*

Ed A set of international plugs and sockets she'd bought in the Great Outdoors, designed to cope with every trans-global electrical emergency – at least that's what it said on the pack.

Kenny and Maeve

A book called: "*Downsizing your Expectations*"

Clementine

An embroidered cushion from Avoca Handweavers with the words: "*There's No Place Like Home*" with the Irish translation beneath.

Lucy A silk evening wrap from Kilkenny Design

She'd never felt less like celebrating the season of good will and she was still trying to work up the energy to draw up a shopping list for her Christmas Day dinner when a headline in the paper caught her eye. *Jobs remain secure as ErinAir falls victim to hostile takeover by American Aviation firm. Paul Brehony sacked as Chief Executive.*

She was forced to push lingering thoughts about Paul out of her mind when Isobel arrived, brimming with happiness, glowing with love.

"Where's Jonah?" Sophie asked.

"Hendro's minding him for the afternoon. There's a match on the telly – so they're all tucked up on the sofa together like two ould fellas – bless them," Isobel smiled contentedly, and Sophie suppressed a twinge of envy.

"So what's on the menu for Christmas Day?" Isobel asked trying to steer the conversation into cheery waters. The last few times they'd met, Sophie had been sad and withdrawn. She'd even begun hinting that she might return to the States, that she hadn't really settled down to life back in Ireland after all.

"Oh, the usual – turkey and ham and all the other stuff," she said disinterestedly now.

"Sounds wonderful. I can't wait. How many of us?"

"Tess and Ed, you and Hendro and Jonah, Jim and Regina, Kenny and Maeve, Clementine, I've asked Lucy and Dennis from college. Cian might just swing by on his way to India and myself . . . all adds up to fourteen, I think." She gave a big sigh and poked at the froth on her cappuccino.

"Are you sure it's what you want to do? No-one expects it, you know."

Sophie nodded resolutely and smiled brightly, forcing herself to be cheerful.

"I couldn't think of a nicer bunch of people to spend Christmas Day with – and we have so much to celebrate this year – Jonah, your engagement, Tess and Ed, even Lucy and Dennis seem to be an item. As for me, I've got the house in Raglan Road restored and I've just spent the last few months swanning about reading books and I think I've got a nice new job lined up in the New Year so really life couldn't be better."

Isobel was delighted to see her looking more cheerful because she had a big favour to ask.

"You remember ages ago, long before Jonah was born, when you were getting the work done on the house, you were talking about some architectural restoration firm in London . . ."

"Vaguely. Why?"

"You must remember – though I wasn't really paying much attention at the time apart from the name – in fact I seem to remember even being a bit rude about it. Anyway – the thing is – Hendro and I have bought an old place of our own in the country. It's not in great condition but it's lovely and we want to restore it in true Edwardian style. So I've phoned them up and made an appointment to see them in London. I have to bring a whole portfolio of photos of the house. What I wanted to ask was, would you come with me?"

Sophie continued to poke at the cappuccino froth.

"I mean, now that you've got over your fear of flying since . . ." Her voice trailed off as Sophie shot her a look. "Well . . .please say yes! You know I don't have a clue about any of that kind of stuff and we want to do a really good job on the house. You treated me to a weekend in Ashford Castle when I really needed it. Now's my chance to pay you back – trip to London and a night in the best hotel. What do you think?"

"OK," said Sophie reluctantly.

"You could have managed this trip to London quite well without me. Why didn't Hendro go?" she said a few days later as they waited to be checked in for their flight.

Isobel was wrapped up in a warm sheepskin jacket, a pair of hip-hugging jeans and a pair of brown suede boots.

"Hendro has a very important match and anyway you have more experience of doing up old houses."

The stewardess called the flight and Sophie and Isobel stepped forward. There were so many flights running between Dublin and London these days that the flight was half empty. Besides – most passengers would be travelling the other way this week, home to Ireland in search of the sort of happy, craic-filled, family-orientated, Christmas that as far as Sophie could see, really only existed in their heads.

Still, Isobel was right about one thing: at least she wasn't afraid of flying any more. Paul Brehony, whose fortunes were now in such sudden decline, had done that much for her. They stepped into the small plane and took two seats near the centre.

After about ten minutes, the stewardess came on the intercom and announced that they would shortly be taking off – just as soon as they were cleared by Air Traffic Control.

"But what about the other passengers?" Sophie asked when she returned from the galley.

"Just you two lassies today."

"You're joking!"

"Not joking! It happens more often than you think. It's more cost effective to let a flight go ahead – rather than cancelling it and risking the possibility of losing the departure slot."

Isobel's mobile flashed with a text message. She checked it and cursed vigorously.

"Oh no. This is awful.!"

"What? What's wrong?"

"It's Jonah.""

"What's happened?"

"I don't know. Mum says it's some tummy thing. I

should go home. I'm really sorry about this, Sophie – but I have to go. I can't leave her to manage alone. It wouldn't be fair. And babies can get very ill very suddenly. I really need to go to him. You'll have to go on ahead and see the architects without me."

"But I don't . . ."

Before she could even finish, Isobel had disappeared through the door and down the gangway. She turned and waved briefly at Sophie before disappearing into the building. Stunned, Sophie gaped after her. Then before she could even think what to do, the stewardess quickly fastened the door and the captain's voice came over the crackly tannoy.

"Ladies and gentlemen. This is your captain speaking."

Sophie, amused and temporarily lifted from her dark mood, by the absolute absurdity of her situation, laughed out loud.

"We will shortly be departing. Please fasten your seatbelts."

"I mean, I don't even want to go to London. I was only going along to do her a favour and now she thinks I can stand in for her just as well. How bizarre is that?" Sophie said to the stewardess who stared at her vaguely and then asked if she would like a cup of coffee.

The plane taxied along the runway, picking up speed, then rising into the sky and bumping through the low-lying winter cloud. Sophie buried herself in *Far From the Madding Crowd* – she was supposed to do an assignment on it for Monday. Fully engrossed in the scene where Bathsheba falls under the spell of the charming Sergeant

Troy, she barely noticed that they were high in the sky now, blue all around, coasting along smoothly. Sergeant Troy went through a swashbuckling display with his sword for Bathsheba. She was enthralled. She was dazzled. She was putty in his hands. Foolish girl, thought Sophie, willing her to have sense and see that Gabriel Oak was a much finer man. She reached the final pages when the captain's voice came over the tannoy once more, crackling and tinny like a bad loudspeaker announcement.

"We will shortly be landing in Luton Airport so may I take the opportunity of thanking you for being such a wonderful set of passengers."

Sophie looked out the window but could see nothing through the dense cloud. She gathered her things and read a few more pages about Bathsheba as the plane completed its descent and landed smoothly on the tarmac. Then it taxied briskly along and stopped suddenly. She looked out at the surrounding countryside once more. That was funny. She hadn't exactly been an A student in Geography but for the life of her she couldn't remember that there were many mountain ranges in Essex and neither did she think that it was quite so close to the English Channel. Still at least she'd landed. Though she hadn't the slightest idea what to do next.

"The captain would like a word," the stewardess told her.

"I wasn't smoking in the toilet – I swear!" said Sophie, flustered. "I've given up months ago."

"No. It's nothing like that. Follow me please."

The captain's back was turned when she walked into the little cockpit. But there was something familiar about it all the same. Her heart leapt, then sank when she realised who it was. A quick glance out the cockpit window at the mountain range in the distance confirmed her suspicions. This wasn't Essex. It was Connemara. And that wasn't the English Channel – it was Galway Bay. And she'd been hijacked. Isobel must have been in on the whole thing.

He turned to face her, and she struggled valiantly to ignore the surge of longing she felt when her eyes met his. He smiled fleetingly, then shoved his hands in his pockets.

Sophie took a deep breath and smiled back at him like a mother would do at a naughty son.

"One last flash gesture, I suppose?" she said.

"Something like that. I couldn't resist it. It's not the sort of thing a guy with real class would do though, is it?"

"Probably not."

There was a pause as they stared at each other.

"So you're in cahoots with Isobel?"

"Yes," he grinned. "She has your best interests at heart."

They sat in silence in the little cockpit for a while.

"I read about the takeover. I'm sorry."

He shrugged.

"Easy come, easy go," he said, clearly trying to put a brave face on things.

"How's Marina taking it?"

He shrugged and grinned crookedly.

"She's gone back to Germany."

"I'm sorry,"

"Don't be. Like I explained to you already, there was never anything between us – the stuff in the papers was Marina's bit of fantasy – marriage to the multi-millionaire. She lives in a bit of a fairytale world. When I said she had me over a barrel it was because she was briefly married to one of my brothers – the black sheep brother. Well, he didn't treat her all that well and to cut a long story short he invested her savings badly and scarpered after six months. She lost everything."

"Where's your black sheep brother now?" she asked, wondering if this was yet another lie.

"The States – he doesn't keep in touch much. Anyway, I hope you have the picture now: Marina was briefly my sister-in-law several years ago and that was the only connection between us. Because of how my brother treated her – I felt some sense of obligation when she turned up on my doorstep eighteen months ago following the break-up of her third marriage. I offered to buy her a small apartment wherever she wanted – but she said that the biggest favour I could do her was to let her spend six months in Fernmount House while she worked on her second novel. Then I couldn't get rid of her without her dragging the whole story of my brother into the press so I just let the situation drift, hoping she'd just get tired and leave in the end. I think she had hopes all along that I would eventually succumb to her charms. She worked bloody hard at it that's for sure, didn't think I suspected for a moment that behind the writer's façade and beyond the way she played on my brother's poor treatment of her, she was just a ruthless gold-digger – plain and simple. When she found out I had no money – she bolted faster than you could say James Joyce."

He shrugged and shoved his hands in his pockets.

"So there you have it – the truth, the whole truth and nothing but . . ."

Sophie should have been glad but somehow it didn't make any difference. The moment had passed and what did any of it matter now anyway? Paul had more important things on his mind than romance. He'd gone from riches to rags in a few short weeks and it would take a man of exceptional courage and fortitude to come through a disaster like that. She wanted to put her arms about him and kiss him and comfort him. But she knew it was too late for any of that.

She gathered up her things and smiled breezily at him.

"Now that you've hijacked me and flown me to Galway, I think I'll hire a car and visit my cousin Kenny. There are one or two family matters I need to sort out with him. I really do hope things work out for you, Paul."

She leaned up and kissed him lightly on the cheek and was gone, tripping down the little flight of steps before he could catch her.

She was cold, sad, the darkness all-enveloping, she was alone. A biting wind snapping at her ears, stinging drops of rain falling on her cheeks. She hurried on quickly up the road, afraid she might cry at any moment.

"Wait! Sophie. Please wait!"

She ran towards the little Portakabin and asked the desk clerk to call a taxi. When she turned around, Paul was standing right behind her.

"You can't just walk away!"

"I can!"

"This is perhaps the greatest chance for happiness you or I will ever have. We should seize it gladly with both hands. Otherwise we may be left with nothing but misery and regret. Do you want that on your conscience?"

"You really are the limit. I've never heard such a load of sentimental crap in all my life!"

"That may be – but it's the truth."

"And, instead of doing flashy flying stunts across the country, don't you think you should tend to your business – in case you haven't noticed it's been robbed from under your feet – just like you robbed it from your friend all those years ago," she couldn't resist the little barb.

She dashed out into the darkness but he caught her by the arm.

"Not that it's any of your business but I never robbed anything from Dermot Stenson. I sold out my share of the company to him years ago."

Sophie laughed, utterly unconvinced.

"Oh please! I'm not some naïve little girl! You're the owner, the man with all the money – the head man, the guy in the papers, the guy on the telly. How come nobody got to see him if he really owned the company?"

"I'm just a regular executive on a salary. I bought Fernmount House with the money from the share sell-out. I advised Dermot to sell out too – but he wouldn't listen so now he's penniless – or relatively penniless in Barbados."

Her head was spinning and she didn't know what to think any more. She'd felt sorry for him and now it seemed there was no reason to feel sorry for him. She'd thought he was staggeringly rich and had suddenly become poor but now he'd told her he'd never been rich to begin with.

"Don't go, Sophie," he said simply.

It was all too much for her.

"I'm sorry," she said and turned on her heel.

She rang the doorbell and at last heard Maeve clip-clopping across the floor of the hall to answer the door.

"Sophie – we weren't expecting you." Maeve welcomed her and led her across the hall which was decked, not with boughs of holly, but with bunches of silver twigs and silver garlands and lots of silver baubles. In the kitchen Maeve quickly rustled up tea and mince pies.

"Direct from Harrods," she declared as she set them down in front of Sophie.

"I'm sorry about the way things worked out with Tess," she said. "I know Kenny upset her. I tried to stop him, but," she lowered her voice, "he's not an easy man to live with, Sophie, and I have a lot to put up with." Her voice trailed away as Kenny appeared through the back door. He didn't seem at all pleased to see Sophie though he made a few half-hearted stabs at small talk as he looked through his post.

"Kenny, we need to talk," she said firmly.

"Talk away," he said reading through a letter.

Sophie smiled apprehensively and took a deep breath.

"You upset Tess terribly and you should apologise. You have no right to bully her. What she does with her house and land is none of your business. How she lives her life is none of your business."

Kenny looked up from his letter and eyed her intently. Maeve shifted about uneasily, looking like she might make a bolt for some country in the southern hemisphere at any moment. Even Sophie began to think about making a quick getaway.

There followed a deadly silence broken only by the quiet sizzle of a ham baking in the oven.

"Point taken," he said quietly.

The two women stared at him in shock. Sophie was speechless.

"I was wrong," he continued. "and I will try to make amends. I started out just wanting to be a good neighbour and then I just got greedy and lost the run of myself. But in my defence, I have done a lot of work for Tess over the years, buying and selling livestock, mending fences and other running repairs and I suppose I felt I should be rewarded in some way for that. Then she made a bit of a fool of me over Robert Franklin too."

He sank down into a chair, his face clouded in confusion and embarrassment and Sophie began to understand and even feel a bit sorry for him.

"Tess is a proud and independent woman and we should all remember that – me included," she said. "But I think she'll be happy to forgive and forget."

Things lightened up quite a bit after that. Maeve insisted she stay the night and Kenny produced a bottle of wine and then a second over the succulent baked ham dinner.

Driving back to Dublin the following day, Sophie felt so pleased at having healed the little family rift that she completely forgot all about Paul Brehony and how he had hijacked her. Well, almost.

Chapter 46

The sitting-room in Raglan Road smelled of cinnamon, mulled wine, and Christmas tree and well-seasoned logs. Jonah sat in his little chair, thrilled to be surrounded by such a magnificent array of sights and sounds. He tracked his mother carefully as she moved about the room filling up people's glasses with champagne. Occasionally he shook his rabbit-shaped rattle in the air just to remind everyone he was still there. Tiger sat curled up at his feet and stared into the flames of the crackling log fire.

Hendro was sitting at the piano singing 'Let it Snow' as Clementine's dainty fingers fluttered lightly across the keys. Lucy and Dennis sat on one of the big green sofas chatting to Jim and Regina, while Kenny and Cian occupied the other. Outside in the kitchen Sophie and Tess prepared to serve up dinner: a warm rich vegetable soup, turkey with sage and onion stuffing and bread sauce, a honey-glazed baked ham, floury potatoes crisply roasted, parsnip wedges dipped in parmesan cheese and also roasted brussels sprouts and Tess's special gravy made with the juices of the turkey, the giblets, a dash of wine and a sprig of fresh herbs.

"Mmm – smells delicious," said Ed, planting a kiss on Tess's cheek.

Maeve put the finishing touches to the big old table, draping her finest Irish linen tablecloth over it, scattering little gold stars and glitter down the middle and then in the centre a magnificent display of deep red roses. She put a cracker in each person's place and even a little wrapped and labelled surprise gift.

At last, Tess called everyone to the table and they took their places as she offered a prayer of thanks before the meal. Soon the room filled up with laughter and talk and Jonah gurgling and the clinking of glasses and crackers being pulled, the warm, cosy buzz of a true Christmas feast. Then when it seemed like no-one could possibly have any more second helpings, not even Cian who was eating like he hadn't seen food for several weeks, when a quiet contented lull fell over everyone, Tess tinkled her spoon on a glass and called them all to order. Then with tears glinting in her eyes, she proposed a toast to absent friends.

"Absent friends," everyone said and clinked their glasses.

"And I propose another toast." She held up her glass and looked around at all the other guests.

"To Sophie, it's wonderful to have you back," she said and looked proudly across the table at her granddaughter.

"To Sophie –it's wonderful to have you back," they all shouted boozily and Sophie felt a horrible lump form in her throat as she fought back the tears.

"Yeah – you do a bloody good turkey dinner for a Sheila," said Hendro and she smiled at him gratefully as everyone laughed and they turned their thoughts to plum pudding.

The house was quiet now. Everyone had gone home and Sophie lay in bed half-heartedly reading a thriller, hoping it would put her to sleep. She was happy about the day, and that she had spent it with people she loved. A warm wave of sleep enveloped her but before she could really sink into it she thought she heard the doorbell, a short ring then silence. She sat up, listened for a moment, then realised it was her imagination. She drifted off once more but then she heard the bell again, this time longer and it seemed louder and this time accompanied by a determined knock. She pulled on her threadbare slippers, threw a dressing-gown across her shoulders and shuffled across the hall. It was probably just Isobel calling back to collect some little toy of Jonah's that had been left behind. Outside a million stars sparkled in a blue-black sky and a frosty mist hung in the air.

She stood on the doorstep and shivered. At first she thought no-one was there but then she saw the outline of a huddled figure disappearing down her front path towards the road.

"Paul?" she called out hesitantly, hoping but not sure if it was him..

He turned and walked slowly back towards her, taking each granite step up to the door with careful deliberation. At last when he stood on the threshold beside her he spoke, his breath a cloud of fog in the freezing night air.

"I've come to apologise."

"Why? What have you done now?" she said, her teeth chattering wildly.

"Kidnapping you in a plane like that – you see that's just the sort of flash thing a guy with real class wouldn't do."

"It was kind of tacky. . ." she said, her teeth banging violently off one another..

"And the timing was bad. There was so much other stuff happening with the business going wallop."

"I definitely wouldn't try it on anyone else. You might get arrested."

"Point taken and I'm really sorry for trying a scam like that with a classy bird like you."

"That's OK," she was floundering a bit now, struggling for something to say, and very cold and tired. She couldn't put together one sensible thought in her head. Then he handed her an envelope.

"Merry Christmas," he said and kissed her lightly on the cheek.

"Thanks, but I didn't get you anything," she said, quite embarrassed now. Though she was unable to resist opening the envelope.

She got quite a shock and gasped when she saw the contents.

"Sorry," he shrugged. "Couldn't think of anything else

– and I know how much you wanted your garden sorted out. Isobel told me."

It was quite a large voucher for Kinvara Budd's landscape gardening service.

"Thanks so very much but I can't take it. I really can't."

"Suit yourself – but she's already booked, can't very well cancel now."

Sophie was lost for words.

"Well, thanks," she said after a brief shivering silence. "You really shouldn't have. And thanks for calling round. Goodnight so. Merry Christmas."

"Goodnight," he said, shoved his hands back in his pockets and was soon crunching across the gravelled driveway once more. She watched him go and wondered what had really brought him to her door on Christmas night.

"Paul?"

He turned, something lovely in his face, something warm and full of possibilities.

"Do you want to come in for a little while? Watch an old movie? Sorry – that was a silly idea. You probably have an early start tomorrow and people to see, things to do . . ."

"Yes – I'd like that. I thought you'd never ask to be honest."

He was across the gravel and bounding up the steps before he'd even finished the sentence.

She was wide awake now. In the sitting-room she stoked up the fire and plumped up the cushions, lit candles and shook the potpourri, turned on the telly and zapped frantically throught the channels for a movie, bustled in and out of the kitchen wondering if she should open wine or offer tea. Decided that it was too late for either and began tugging at a box of Belgian chocolates instead.

"Stop, stop," he said at last and took her firmly by the hand. "What are you doing? Are you always going to fuss like this when I bring an interesting man to the house?"

"What do you mean?" she said briefly wondering if she'd blown it yet again.

"I mean I'm relying on you to bring a bit of class to this relationship – you know – cool Dublin 4 etiquette and restrained elegance."

He pulled her closer to him, his warm breath on her face, his lips brushing against her hair.

"And what do you plan to bring?" she said quietly.

"Me – I thought that you might have guessed that," he murmured huskily, pulling her gently onto the sofa. "I'll be your bit of rough."

The End

ACKNOWLEDGEMENTS

Dear Reader

I hope once again that you enjoy this book, that it entertains you and makes you smile.

Thanks to very many people for friendship, research, support, fun, jokes, yarns and laughter over the past year. If I've left anyone out I hope you'll forgive me: Mary Hanlon, Mary O'Donnell, Mary Ryan, Catherine O'Flaherty, Aisling O'Grady, Jacinta Davenport, Brigid O'Sullivan, Helen Lowe, Peter and Kate McGonigal, Clare McNicholas, Bairbre Ní Chiardha, Toni Uí Chiardha, Florence Hamilton. I would also like to thank my colleagues who have been very supportive and encouraging. In particular the following: Máirín Ní Chonchobhair for *Flora Chorca Dhuibhne*, her wonderful reference book on plants; John Moriarty for practical and perceptive advice regarding plots and pacing; Deirdre O Dwyer for Pythagoras and matters mathematical; Declan Collinge for reminding me what it was like in 1993; Pat Cassidy for 'a lighthouse in the bog'; Michael Flatley, Andrea Muckian, Margaret Brosnan, Isobel Maguire, Noreen Lannon, Vera Whelan, Mary Farrell, Ellen Forde and Paul Barnes.

Máire Geoghegan-Quinn and John Quinn for their hospitality, Eoghan and Catherine Ó Neachtain for friendship, support and racing tips.

To the Ó Ciardha family, for being the most fantastic bunch of in-laws a girl could wish for. To my nieces (the surrogate daughters) – Caoimhe, Róisin and Sorcha, for advising me on matters of fashion and taste.

To the extended group of people that I am lucky to count as family: Susie Bush and Anne Marie Minhall, Anne and Rob Matthews, Maureen and George Redfern, The Minhalls, Tom and Kathy Mellett, Kevin Dever and Catherine, Anne and Harry Canning, Mary Clare and Jean Marc Bourguignon, Angela and Pádraig Ryan, and most especially a wonderful aunt and godmother Auntie Delia.

Fiction, they say, takes flight in the imagination but begins in real life so I am particularly indebted to a number of people who gave generously of their time, knowledge, insight and specialist expertise:
Sian Horan, General Manager of David Lloyd Riverview, on the management and administration of an exclusive leisure centre.
Dr Clare McNicholas, GP
Beverley Turner, Solicitor
David Blaney, Leinster Senior Rugby Squad, on the day-to-day life of professional rugby players.
Tom Mellett, on being a pilot with International Flight Rules ratings
Pádraig Ó Céidigh, Chief Executive Aer Arann on running a domestic airline
Terry Prone, Carr Communications

Jill O'Connor, Ray Di Mascio and Kieran O'Connor, National Flight Centre, Weston Airport
The 'unusual' scheduled flight incident towards the end of the book does actually happen occasionally and thanks to the three separate individuals who confirmed the experience to me.

To my agent, Ger Nicholl, for on-going support and encouragement and for being efficient and effective and kind.

To editor, Gaye Shortland, who once again has blasted away the mists of cloudy matter and shone the torch of clarity – with wit, tact and wisdom.
A very big thank you to Paula Campbell and all at Poolbeg for their hard work and continued support.

To the Irish girls, women, lassies and chicks who write novels, for welcoming me into their midst and making me feel instantly at home, and for encouragement and advice. Particular thanks to Sarah Webb for all her hard work.

A special thank-you to the many people who were kind enough to buy and read *The Men In Her Life* and say nice things and recommend it to their friends. I hope that *Learning to Fly* brings you as much enjoyment.

To my sons:
To Macdara, who keeps my computer skills up to date

and who gave me graphic descriptions of what it's like to be in the front row of a rugby team.
To Sean, who advised me on cars – Ferraris and Chevrolets. I'm only sorry this book isn't called *Learning To Score a Try* or *Learning To Drive a Ferrari*.
And to both for being interested and understanding, and wonderful and for mowing the lawn and putting out the rubbish.

To the man who must endure the most, good counsellor, dear companion, provider of jokes (mostly funny), intrepid navigator, fair and honest critic, bringer of the breakfast and best friend, Pádhraic.

Lastly I learnt about old buildings, history, nature and so much more from my Dad, whose warm and dynamic interest in life and nature and people never faltered during his ninety-four years, not even in his final days. My sincere thanks to those who helped him in the last months: the doctors and nurses, Peggy and Bernice and his many friends and neighbours in Ballinrobe, Co Mayo. In particular I owe a very special debt of gratitude to Fr Pat O'Brien, a gentle priest and a dear friend.

Mostly Dad taught me about life, and how to steer a steady course through its triumphs and disasters – which, in a way, is what *Learning To Fly* is about. So I dedicate this story about Sophie and Isobel and their disasters and triumphs to him.

Also by Poolbeg

The Men in Her Life

MARY HOSTY

"Cool and professional – she could subdue a room full of men in Italian suits with the merest arch of an eyebrow"

Lit Doran, successful businesswoman, sets out to work in her sleek red BMW. As she weaves through the early morning traffic, she applies a sweep of frosted pink to her lips and a hint of shadow to her eyes . . . she's about to meet one of the richest and most influential men in the city . . .

Across town, billionaire property developer Conrad Budd eases his lightly tanned body onto deep luxurious pillows in the bedroom of his vast dockland penthouse. He is dangerously charming, irresistible to women and has an intriguing secret . . . But Lit is too clever and far too busy to succumb to Conrad's charms. Besides, she's already had her heart broken – and that isn't going to happen again.

But soon cracks begin to show in her perfectly constructed world. Her elderly father disapproves of her shallow lifestyle. Her neglected teenage son is starting to rebel and loyal friend Bonnie is just about running out of patience . . .

ISBN 1-84223-125-1